ANN BRIDGE
Emergency in the Pyrenees

Books by Ann Bridge

ANN BRIDGE
Emergency
in the
Pyrenees

McGraw-Hill Book Company

New York Toronto London

ANN BRIDGE
Emergency
in the
Pyrenees

Chapter 1

"A baby? Oh my dearest child, I *am* so glad" Mrs. Hathaway said; she rose from her chair and went across and gave Julia a warm kiss. "Now I shall have a *great*-godchild!" she said happily. "When is it due?"

"Early November" Julia Jamieson replied.

"Oh well, winter babies in London always do well" said the old lady, cheerfully. "So extraordinary—they seem positively to thrive on fog and smoke! Where shall you have it? In a hospital?"

"No—here, I thought" Julia said, in her slow calm tones. "I never feel sure that with what they call 'hospitalised births', you get your own baby back! Anyhow, a baby ought to be born under its own Father's roof, among people who care—not tended by anonymous nurses, with gauze masks over their faces!"

"Have you got room here?" Mrs. Hathaway asked. This conversation was taking place in the Jamiesons' flat in Gray's Inn.

"Oh yes, heaps. Philip did manage to get his old Uncle's set of chambers just below this, and we had a lift put in; I've had lovely day and night nurseries arranged, with their own bathroom, complete with washing-machine!—it ought all to be perfectly easy. The nannie can bring the baby up in the lift to be nursed."

"Oh, I am glad that you mean to nurse it yourself. Young women today don't realise what they miss by not doing that" the old lady said. "There is a completely different relationship between a mother and child with breast-fed babies, compared to those that are bottled from the start."

"Is there really?"

"Oh yes—psychologically, breast-feeding has some profound effect. And *not* a bad one!" Mrs. Hathaway said energetically. "All this modern nonsense that it is injurious for children to love their mothers! How can there be too much affection in the world?" But soon the old lady began doing sums on her fingers.

"November—and here we are in June. Where shall you be during the summer? London can be rather hot and tiring then."

"Well that's rather the question" Julia said. "Philip has got one of these tiresome assignments abroad for July and August, and perhaps longer. So I had thought of going up to Glentoran to stay with Edina and *her* Philip, while mine has to be away."

"An excellent plan. You shouldn't be here alone, in the heat."

"But *my* Philip has another plan" Julia went on.

"What is that?"

"Well his other Uncle had a little house up in the Pyrenees —just an old farm-house, which he converted and made quite comfortable; Philip used to spend a lot of his holidays there, and adored it. The old boy left it to him when he died, and Philip let it to some friends, the Stansteds—and they have offered to lend it to us this summer, for me to stay. Philip thinks it a perfect idea—he says living in the Pyrenees will have a good pre-natal effect on the baby" Julia said, with an amused burbling laugh.

Mrs. Hathaway was not amused.

"What is this place called?" she asked.

"Larège."

The old lady got up and pulled *The Times Atlas* out of the shelf where Philip Jamieson kept his innumerable maps; she opened it, and studied it.

"But my dear child, Larège is miles up in the mountains! —a long way off the main road to that pass"—she opened her bag, took out a tortoiseshell-mounted magnifying glass, and studied the map afresh. "The Grandpont Pass" she pronounced. "I don't think you ought to go there unless you have someone with you" she said firmly. "And can one get servants?"

"Oh, Philip says all that is quite easy" Julia responded cheerfully. At that point Philip Jamieson himself walked in. He kissed Mrs. Hathaway and his wife, called to Buchan to bring drinks, and presently asked—"What have you two been gossiping about?"

"Julia's baby." Mrs. Hathaway chose to reply herself. "First, dear Philip, all possible congratulations; I am so glad."

"Nice, isn't it?" Colonel Jamieson said. "I'm longing for children—I should like to have a whole string of them! We reckon Julia has time for about six, reasonably spaced."

"And does Julia want six?" Mrs. Hathaway asked, rather crisply.

"If Philip will provide a *large* house in the country, with ample staff and endless ponies, I shouldn't mind having six a bit" Julia said. "I don't think children ought to be brought up in a city after about two years old—however healthy you may say London is, Mrs. H.! But I don't suppose actually *having* them is anything to worry about; and I don't."

Mrs. Hathaway had her own views on this, and presently reverted to her earlier questions about Julia's summer plans.

"If Julia is to stay at this house in the Pyrenees, while you are quite out of reach in the Middle East or somewhere, will she be able to get servants locally?—what I believe is now called 'help'?"

"Oh, I imagine so. The last time I stayed with the Stansteds, a couple of years ago, everything seemed to run perfectly smoothly."

In fact Philip Jamieson, manlike, had never enquired as to how this smooth running had been achieved; he and Arthur Stansted spent most of their days out walking and climbing, and he did not in the least realise that all the work of the house had in fact been done by Mrs. Stansted herself and a very willing and domestically skilled step-daughter. "The Stansteds thought Julia might like to go and stay with them for a couple of days before they leave, to be shown the ropes" he said comfortably—"And of course it's no distance from Pau."

"That is a good idea" Mrs. Hathaway said. But the name Pau struck a chord in her mind—a slightly reassuring one.

"The Heriots live just outside Pau" she said. "They might come in handy."

"Who are the Heriots?" Philip asked, without any real interest; he was confident that his romantic, and really rather foolish plan was completely sound.

"Oh, Lord and Lady Heriot. They are one of those old Anglo-French Pau families, who started the fox-hounds and the golf-course and all that. Such an interesting little bit of colonisation in Europe" the old lady replied.

"The fox-hounds were pretty good, I always heard" Philip said; "but I hadn't realised that they were started by the British."

"My dear Philip, can you see the *French* starting a pack of fox-hounds in the Pyrenees?" Mrs. Hathaway asked. "Well, I shall write to Lady Heriot—I haven't seen her for years, but I believe they have grown-up children, who might come in useful to Julia."

"Mrs. H., why are you fussing? It is a charming house, and a heavenly place. And anyhow Colin will be about."

Julia pricked up her ears at this mention of her cousin.

"Colin? Why should he be about out there?"

Philip became cautious.

"Oh well, various things to keep an eye on."

"In the Pyrenees?" Julia sounded incredulous.

"Well there and thereabouts."

"Oh Philip, don't be tiresome! There's only me and Mrs. H. here. *What?*"

"Well I suppose even you have heard of Lacq, the great gas-field just north of the Pyrenees; it supplies something like one-third of France's gas, and no sabotage is wanted there."

"Who'd want to sabotage Lacq? No, never mind" Julia corrected herself hastily. "Where else?"

"Well most saboteurs, whether Communist or O.A.S., come in to France from Spain across the frontier; so it, and Jaca and Pamplona are places to watch too. And of course Bordeaux is both a sea-port and an air-port, so anyone might try to get in there. But none of this concerns *you* in the least" Philip padded breezily—"except that it means that Colin will probably want to take a bed off you at Larège most week-ends."

"Oh, do *saboteurs* always take the week-end off?" Mrs. Hathaway enquired with false innocence. Philip beamed on the keen-witted old lady.

"You precious Mrs. H.! If you were even *five* years younger I should try to recruit you into Intelligence at once!" (It was typical of Philip Jamieson's "sweet blood", as George Meredith called it, that he should be so totally unresentful of having his bluff called.) "No—*saboteurs* work round the clock! But Colin will have colleagues—anyhow he will never be far away."

"And will Julia have addresses and telephone numbers for him?" Mrs. Hathaway pursued, relentlessly—quite rightly, as it proved, she distrusted her godson-in-law about practical matters, his profession apart.

"Oh, Colin will see to all that" Philip replied, still breezy. "And there are the Monniers, who have a house there, and go every summer—the nicest people. He was in the Resistance— I knew him rather well at one time. But it is such a heavenly place—I'm sure Julia will adore it."

Mrs. Hathaway remained doubtful; ex-Resistance French neighbours did not reassure her very much. What she wanted for her precious Julia during her first pregnancy—at thirty-two—was the presence of some reliable person in the house, and a reasonable amount of domestic help. "Well, I shall write to Lady Heriot" she said.

She did so—and the affectionate reply from her long-neglected friend was not reassuring. The Heriots' only off-spring were twin sons, one at Oxford, the other at Cambridge. "That's no use whatever" Mrs. Hathaway said to Julia, when she took the letter from Pau round to Gray's Inn. "Now if they'd had a daughter, she might have been." Lady Heriot further stated that she did not think it at all easy to get any sort of maid-servant at Larège in the summer—"It is getting nearly as bad as in England; the girls all go to the hotels at Oloron and so on, in the towns; and anyhow the Larègeois are wild, wicked people, half-Moors."

"Why on earth should they be half-Moors?" Julia asked. "Does she say?"

"No. But my dear child, do think carefully about this. There is the child to consider."

Julia did consider the child, particularly under the impact of all this discouraging information. For herself, she always adored adventure and new places, and Larège beckoned strongly; Philip loved it, he wanted her to go there; she was deeply in love, and wished to do what *he* wished. But she had a strong respect for Mrs. Hathaway's judgment; and pregnancy and motherhood were things of which she had no experience. Perhaps she ought to have a companion in the house. She bethought her of an existing daughter, the Duke of Ericeira's; her former pupil, who had so recently come over from Portugal to be the only bridesmaid at her wedding.

"I think I'll write to Luzia" she said.

"Do," said Mrs. Hathaway—"if you are really set on going." The old lady had encountered Luzia during her brief stay in England, and had formed a good opinion of her, in spite of her remarkable beauty—great beauty, Mrs. Hathaway had decided from lifelong experience, was more apt to be a liability than an asset. But in this case—"I think she is trustworthy" she said. "Do try to get her. Write tonight."

Julia's renewal of her acquaintance with Luzia Ericeira had been happier than is always the case in such circumstances. The girl whom she had left at little more than sixteen, already with a strong promise of beauty, had reappeared after three years with that promise fulfilled in a restrained, but complete, splendour—white skin, dark hair, Celtic-grey eyes, and a now faultlessly-modelled structure to a noble face; there was nothing chocolate-boxy about such beauty, it was classical and pure. But what had pleased Julia most was that her ex-pupil, always intelligent and gay, was now more gay and more intelligent than ever, and she had pursued her studies; she had forced her reluctant Father to let her take a two-years' course at the Sorbonne in Paris.

"Why the Sorbonne?" Julia had asked.

"Oh well, Papa thought it might be rather embarrassing to

have me as a student at Coimbra—and anyhow the Sorbonne is tops for theology."

"You shouldn't say 'tops', Luzia" Julia said, the ex-governess in her coming out in spite of herself.

"No? I thought one said it, now."

They both laughed, then—the past brought back so close, and its absurdity in the present. Julia asked why Luzia had wanted to read theology, and the girl explained.

"All this questioning, today, about the truth of Christianity —even your Bishops doubting! So I thought I would learn the answers before I went into society, and was pestered with questions. Truly, Miss Probyn, I do not believe that these little modern men know more, or are better Christians, than St. Thomas Aquinas. *He* was a scholar; these, to me, do not write as scholars!"

Julia agreed, though she was less concerned with Christian truths than Luzia; but they had renewed their early friend-ship, now on adult and equal terms, with increased warmth. She had no hesitation in writing to ask Luzia if she would come and stay with her at Larège for six or seven weeks, in August and September—"No idea how comfortable it will be."

Mrs. Hathaway was delighted to have Luzia's acceptance read out to her in Gray's Inn. "What fun to see the Pyrenees! And is it not so very far from Lourdes? I have always so much wanted to go to Lourdes. Shall you have a car?"

Julia had in fact wanted to take her car, but Philip, who had the oddest ideas about pregnancies—based on complete ignorance—opposed the plan. "You won't need a car—you can always hire the taxi from Labielle if you want it. But you hardly ever will; Larège isn't a car sort of place"—and Julia, in her love-lorn folly, again gave way. Luzia, on learning this, thought of bringing her own car; now it was the Duque who objected. Continentals are much more allergic to *carnets* and *triptyques* than the ever-travelling English—"And where would the chauffeur stay?" Luzia also gave way; in spite of the Sorbonne, she had not yet quite reached the stage of thinking it normal to drive about Europe without a chauffeur. But about one thing she was firm—mistakenly, as it proved.

"*No*, Papa, I will *not* take my maid. I shall not need her—and I think the house is not large. For six weeks I can wash my own clothes, and do my own hair. This is a village in the Pyrenees, not a resort of fashion."

Since Julia was to stay with the Stansteds to be "shown the ropes" at Larège, it was settled that Luzia should only join her a few days later. Mrs. Jamieson flew to Bordeaux, and went on to Pau by train—a train so crammed with pilgrims bound for Lourdes that movement through the corridors was impossible; the restaurant-car might as well not have existed. Also it was intensely hot. Julia, tired, thirsty, and regretting her improvidence in not having bought mineral-water at Bordeaux, sat resignedly in a corner of the carriage, looking out of the window. Presently her attention was attracted by a curious sight—an enormous range of mostly rather low buildings, studded here and there with large balloon-like shapes of aluminium, gleaming silvery in the sun, and towering over all four immensely lofty chimneys, from which plumes of red flame and dark smoke streamed out into the sky.

"Good gracious!" Julia exclaimed, and sat upright to study this phenomenon. A small nattily-dressed Frenchman, aroused by her exclamation, got up and went over to the windows.

"Ah, *voilà* Lacq!" he said. "Madame, it is from here that France gets, now, almost half her supply of gas—from below the earth!"

Julia asked what the aluminium balloons were for? Her new acquaintance couldn't tell her that, but he knew the use of the tall chimneys. "In the gas, in its natural state, there are impurities; these, by some complicated process, are separated, leaving the gas pure to be carried by pipe-lines all over France—but there is a certain surplus of pressure which passes into these chimneys to burn itself away in the upper air."

Julia listened with interest; she wished that her informant could have told her more about the complicated processes. But as the chimneys, with their black-and-red plumes of smoke and flame receded, she felt that it was not surprising that no sabotage was wanted here, and that Colin, her dear Colin, should have been laid on to help to guard the source of this strange product from the bowels of the earth from evil-doers.

At last they reached Pau. Mrs. Hathaway, concerned at the whole idea of this journey, had arranged with Lady Heriot that Julia should be met, spend the night with them, and be driven up to Larège the following day. This was just as well, for Pau is unusually ill-provided with porters, even for a French provincial station, and Julia had a certain amount of luggage. She had managed to battle her way through the pilgrims thronging the corridor to the door of the coach, and stood there as the train drew in, looking for a porter, and seeing none. But Mrs. Hathaway had also taken the precaution of describing her god-daughter—"She's quite unmistakeable: tall, and very beautiful, with a golden skin and *deep* gold hair and big grey eyes." This, evidently, had registered with her hosts; as the train slowed down two tall fair young men, precisely alike, ran along beside it, and jumped onto the step below Julia's tall figure even before the engine came to a halt.

"Mrs. Jamieson? Good. Where's your stuff? Any in the van?"

"No, all in my carriage; third along, and all labelled—*red* labels."

"Fine. Dick, you go in and hand it out to me. Let me help you down, Mrs. Jamieson—these steps are so infernally high."

They were indeed—Julia was thankful for a hand to get her down them. Once safely on the platform she was greeted by a grey-haired gentleman, as short as his sons were tall.

"Mrs. Jamieson? Heriot is my name. Clever of you to get to the door. These wretched pilgrims are a perfect nuisance, God help them—they clog the trains just like that new water-weed is beginning to choke the Nile! Now let's come along to where Nick is, and check what Dick hands out, to make sure that you get all your gear."

Dick made rapid progress through the pilgrims; by the time they reached the spot where Nick was standing below the third carriage, he was already pushing Julia's red-labelled suitcases out through the upper part of the window to his brother, and abusing, in fluent and idiomatic French, passengers who obstructed him because they wished to look out. *"Voyons, Madame, on a des bagages à décharger!"*

"Seven—that the lot?" he called down.

"Yes—thank you so much. Oh, but hurry!" Julia exclaimed, nervously, as that peculiar hoot common to French trains indicated that this one was starting again. Dick disappeared—the train was well under way when he succeeded in emerging from the horde of pilgrims, and leapt clear down onto the platform, where he rejoined the others. Julia thanked him warmly—"I could never have managed alone."

"Nobody except Rugby footballers can manage their luggage alone on these pilgrim trains" the young man said cheerfully, as he and his brother picked up Julia's cases and carried them out to the station entrance, where they were stowed in the boot and the back of a large seven-seater car.

"Time I did some introducing" Lord Heriot said before they got in. "This is Dick and this is Nick"—the identical twins shook hands in turn. "Dick is at Oxford and Nick is at Cambridge" he further explained, as they drove off. "I wasn't going to have them both at the same University!—had quite enough trouble over their pranks when they were at Winchester, and nothing could ever be pinned on either of them. The only difference between them is that Dick is an optimist, and Nick is a pessimist."

"And unfortunately that doesn't *show*, at least not immediately" Nick observed gloomily from the back.

This absurd set-up amused Julia; it began to revive her. She asked what they were reading at their carefully separated Universities?

"Physics and Chemistry" the twins said in chorus—*"the* coming thing. If we get good enough degrees we might get jobs at Lacq, and live at home in comfort" said one voice—the optimistic Dick, Julia inferred.

"You'll have to be very good to get jobs at Lacq" their Father said, rather repressively.

"Oh, but we shall! You'll have to cough up for post-

graduate courses, Daddy, naturally—Nick at the Cavendish,
me at the Clarendon."

"I doubt if Lacq would take *you*—the Clarendon hasn't
the same standing as the Cavendish" a gloomy voice said
from behind—Julia laughed; this must be Nick.

"Oh tripe! The Clarendon is tops now; Harwell recruit no
end of people from there" his twin responded blithely.

Julia was not surprised that the twins should wish to live at,
and work from, their home, when at last she reached it. The
huge rambling family mansion, in a park full of exotic trees
on the outskirts of Pau, had been skilfully converted by the
Heriots into three flats, each with large elegant rooms, but
also the utmost modernisation in the matter of bathrooms
and fitted basins—an immense lift bore all four of them, plus
Julia's luggage, up to the first floor, where she was greeted by
her hostess. Lady Heriot was as tall as her husband was short
—that was where the twins got their height, Julia surmised.
She was shown into a charming bedroom, very large, out of
which a bathroom had been carved—"Quite self-contained,
you see" her hostess said. "Now which case do you want unpacked for tonight? Jeanne will see to it all for you—she is
very good, been with me for years." A smiling elderly maid
appeared, and began to deal very competently with the overnight suit-case indicated by Julia. "Dinner not till 7.45—
would you like to lie down? Jeanne will call you. I do hope
you aren't very tired?"

Julia was in fact tired to a degree which surprised and exasperated her; but after a rest and a bath, she thoroughly enjoyed her evening with the Heriots. It was fascinating to sit
among a family with Scottish traits so strongly developed,
here in France, at the very foot of the Pyrenees. After dinner
Lady Heriot talked with affection of Mrs. Hathaway, and
asked after her—Julia said that the beloved Mrs. H. was
beginning to show signs of age at last.

"Ah well, we all have to come to it" Lady Heriot said. In
fact she had obviously not come to it yet—she was brisk,
lively, energetic, and full of interest in Julia and her concerns.
"When is the baby due?" she asked, as she took her guest to
bed. Three months hence, Julia told her. "Oh—and who will

be with you when the Stansteds go?" Julia told her about Luzia—"She comes on Tuesday."

"Do you know the time of her train? I'm a little vague about the Spanish connections."

Julia said that Luzia had promised to write that; she expected to find the letter at Larège.

"Oh, then send me a wire, and the boys shall meet her, and drive her up. What a pity you didn't bring a car! What does she look like? Will she be as recognisable as you?"

"Well not my colouring, but she will be the most beautiful thing they have ever seen" Julia pronounced. "Dark, grey eyes, very white skin—rather what people think of as Irish colouring. But I'll telephone when I get her letter."

"My dear, you can't; the Stansteds haven't got a telephone. You can only do that by stumbling down over those appalling cobble-stones to the Post Office—and once you're there you might as well send a telegram; you won't have to wait so long. In *French*" Lady Heriot said with emphasis. "They aren't much good at telegrams in English."

Julia's heart sank a little. No car; no telephone. Was Philip's idea really such a good one, compared with the familiar safety of Glentoran? She fell asleep slightly disheartened.

She was encouraged, when she awoke next morning, by the astonishing glory of sunrise over the Pyrenees—the great range of peaks, some snow-capped, all lit by the eastern sun, standing up on the further side of the Gave de Pau. And this encouragement was enhanced when she arrived, driven by the twins, at what was really Philip's house. In fact the car could not drive to the house itself, the small cobbled track was too narrow, but there was a car-turn barely 100 yards away—thence the Heriot boys carried her suit-cases along the stony path.

"You're lucky; the road was only widened, and the car-turn put in, about a couple of years ago" Dick said. "Before that one had to park in the square outside the inn, and hump everything from there—more than a quarter of a mile."

"Heavens!" said Julia, wondering—a little unhappily—if

her Philip was aware of the new car-turn when he suggested
this stay at Larège. If not, how did he suppose she would have
managed?—without the Heriots, whom he didn't know. She
owed their help entirely to Mrs. Hathaway.

Many newly-married women are assailed by such doubts as
to the quality of their husbands' grey matter when they presently encounter such lapses from what, to the female of the
species, is the most normal common-sense. But when Julia
actually reached the house, she felt that there was a strong
excuse for Philip having wished her to come there. The strag-
gling village of Larège is strung out along a shelf of the Pyrenees facing south-east, above the valley leading to the Grandpont Pass into Spain; above and below it spread pastures and
meadows, with silvery ridges and peaks behind. The
house was almost the last one on the northern end of this
shelf, surrounded by sloping green fields; one looked across
these at the big church and the central huddle of houses. It
was an old Pyrenean farm-house. What had once been the
stable for the beasts was now a single, enormous, ground floor
room, the entrance reached by stone steps from the path
above; it had been floored with cement, and at the further
end were a sink, a range of cupboards for stores and crockery,
a refrigerator, and not less than three cooking-stoves—one
electric, a wood-burning range for cooking large joints, and a
small gas-stove fired by "Buta-gaz", the French equivalent of
Calor-gas. In the center, under a wide window, a sofa and
several arm-chairs were ranged; on the opposite side stood an
enormous walnut table of local make, with rows of bottles of
wine upright below it, and behind piles of cut wood for the
Briffault stove. Near the entrance, again quite a distance from
the central portion, stood a table laid ready for lunch; this end
of the vast apartment was served, as regards light, by the open
upper half of the old farm door, made as usual in two
sections.

Julia, seated on the sofa drinking Vermouth, looked about
her and listened to Mrs. Stansted's explanations with immense pleasure. She loved the *roominess* of this vast ex-stable,
the light; and simple practicality of sitting, eating and

cooking all in one place. "But what is that?" she asked, pointing to a small walled excrescence in the corner to the left of
the big doorway. Mrs. Stansted laughed.

"Oh, that's the down-stairs bathroom. It used to be *la maison des cochons,* the pig-sty; but it just fitted for a bathroom,
so old Mr. Jamieson put the bath and shower in there, and
the immersion-heater. Come and look, if you're not too
tired."

Julia went and looked. The immersion-heater was vast.
"Doesn't the hot water cost the earth?" she asked.

"Costs nothing!" said Mr. Stansted, also laughing.

"What can you mean?"

"Oh, it's a nice story. Further down the valley the French
Government started to instal a hydro-electric scheme, which
would tap the water from the upper valleys. The Larègeois
didn't care for having their water used, so as fast as buildings
and pipe-lines were installed, they bombed them by toppling
rocks down off the hills above, and busting them. In the end
the Government gave way, and signed a formal agreement
with the Commune of Larège: if they would leave the pipe-
lines alone, they should have *free* electricity for a certain
number of years, for every house marked on a large-scale
map."

"And this is one, of course?" Julia asked, fascinated by this
demonstration of independence in the state-regimented modern world.

"Indeed yes. And that's why the carpenter has electric saws,
and the inn and the grocer vast friges; and why the peasants
leave their lights burning all day. The whole of Larège *hums*
with electricity!—I wonder you didn't hear it as you came
through. But the sands are running out—only a year or two
more, and our hot water will begin to cost money. Come and
eat" he said, rising; while he was recounting the agreable story
of Larège free electricity Mrs. Stansted had walked over to
the business end of this multi-purpose room, and helped by
the Heriot twins set bowls of *garbure,* the simple French vegetable soup, on the table; while she cut slices from a crusty
loaf, Mr. Stansted poured out red wine into large, thick, comfortable tumblers, rather squat.

Julia was hungry: she enjoyed the fresh bread and the *garbure,* and the cold veal with salad which followed it—succeeded by cheese and butter. This was the way to eat here, obviously—no sauces, no puddings, no fussy "made dishes"; and she liked the rather rough, but potent, country wine.

"No, we don't get it here—too high for vines" Mr. Stansted replied to her question. "But we're leaving you some, and Dick knows where to get it if you run short. You go down and fetch a small cask, and then bottle it. The corking machine is over there"—he pointed to the huge walnut table.

"Let's have coffee by the spring" Mrs. Stansted said when they had finished their meal. "Dick, you take out the tray; Nick and I will stack, and join you."

Dick Heriot carried the coffee-tray out through the old stable door, which his host opened for him, and across a tiny gravelled terrace, with stone and wooden seats, immediately outside it—then round the corner of the house and along a narrow path close under its massive stonework to a small lawn, at the further end of which a table and some garden chairs stood under a group of smallish trees with pale silver trunks. At first Julia didn't see the spring, though she could hear a very gentle noise of dropping water—as she looked round, puzzled, Mr. Stansted showed her a tiny grotto behind them, where water dripped from mossy rocks into a minute pool. "But we don't drink that" he said, "we get our drinking-water from the spout in the washing-shed up there" —he pointed behind him, where across the cobbled path, which continued on its way above the lawn, a small open-fronted stone edifice could just be seen.

"You can't drink the tap-water?" Julia asked.

"Better not. Lovely water from the spout, and it's no distance—Angela will show you the jar we bring it down in."

So one had to go and fetch one's drinking-water from a spout, Julia thought. However the little shed was not far away. And any thought of domestic chores was soon banished by the splendour of the view in front of her, when she sat back and looked at it. Like the path above, the lawn was supported on a dry-stone wall, from which the fields beneath it fell away; nothing impeded the view across the valley and round to its head—a huge circle of limestone peaks, gleaming silver in the midday sun like the teeth of a giant saw, with one huge, whiter, block standing up among them.

"Goodness, how beautiful!" she said. "What is the big mountain?"

"The Pic d'Eyzies. Splendid rock—there's some very good climbing on it."

"And where is the frontier with Spain? Can one see it?"

"Come across to the edge of the lawn." Julia did so. "Now you can look right up the valley. All the head of it, and most of the ridge round to the right, *is* the frontier."

Julia looked with deep interest at the silver saw of mountain teeth curving round Larège. This was the frontier that Colin would have to watch; might indeed already be watching, from the farther side, over in Spain. And it certainly was a most beautiful place. Perhaps Philip had been right, after all.

Chapter 2

The twins drove off after drinking their coffee, and Mrs. Stansted presently led Julia up a broad modern wooden staircase into a big low sitting-room on the first floor, with several doors opening off it. "We've put you in here" she said, throwing open the door of a fairly large simply-furnished bedroom with an immense double bed, where the twins had already installed Julia's luggage—"We moved up; we thought you wouldn't want too many stairs. But alas the other bathroom—well it's only a shower and a loo and a basin, really—is up on the next floor. Now can I help you to unpack? Then I expect you ought to rest, oughtn't you?"

Julia said she could manage her own unpacking, and did so —cleverly-arranged built-in cupboards, shelves, and drawers made the bestowal of her belongings easy, but aroused her curiosity: had Philip done this, or his old Uncle? There had been no modern contrivances in the other Uncle's "set" in Gray's Inn, below Philip's rooms, when they took it over. Having unpacked, she was quite glad to lie down on the huge bed; in fact she fell asleep, lulled by the soft dropping sound of water from the spring, and a distant tinkle of cow-bells from the upper slopes, which she could see from her window.

After tea Mrs. Stansted showed her the more immediate arrangements which life at Larège involved. Taking a large glazed earthen-ware jug in one hand, and the rubbish-bucket in the other, she led her guest up the steps onto the cobbled path, and a little way along it to the open-fronted shed where the spout which produced drinking-water flowed steadily into a stone trough, overflowed, and trickled away. "We'll fill the jug as we come back," she said, dumping it; "I want to show you where to empty *la poubelle*."

"The *what?*" Julia asked.

"This—the trash-bucket; they call it 'la poubelle' here."
They walked another hundred yards up the path to a spot
where from a projecting spur above a steep slope, it was evident that many *poubelles* had had their contents shot down
the hillside—Mrs. Stansted added her contribution, hitting
the enamel bucket with the side of her hand to make sure
that everything fell out. Back at the shed they filled the jug at
the spout.

Julia absorbed these details with interest, and with a certain
degree of pleasure; she liked the simplicities of life when she
was equal to them, and no doubt Luzia would empty the
poubelle and fill the drinking-water jug. Over tea she asked
about edibles—"I didn't seem to see any shops."

"No—they don't go in for shops here. The meat van comes
on Tuesdays and the vegetable van on Thursdays."

"Comes here?" Julia interjected.

"No no—to the square outside Barraterre's—that's the inn.
And you get bread from there—they always have bread."

Julia vaguely remembered passing through a square with an
inn; it had seemed to her quite a long way from the car-turn.
"And who carries the stuff up here?" she asked.

"Oh, one has to do that one's self. No one in Larège will
ever go out to work, or even do small jobs for pay," Mrs.
Stansted said.

"Why ever not?"

"Oh, they're most strange people; rather savage, and completely anti-social."

Mr. Stansted here put his oar in.

"Historically and ethnographically, the reason is rather interesting" he said. "When Charles Martel threw the Moors
out of France and back into Spain across the Pyrenees, small
pockets got left in isolated places like this. Of course they
intermarried with the local people, but the Moorish strain is a
very strong thing, and quite untameable."

"And is it certain that they settled here?" Julia asked,
interested.

"Oh yes. Tomorrow I'll show you one of the very old,
massively-built houses which the people still call '*Les maisons
des Sarrazins.*'"

Julia was half-appalled, half-fascinated by these highly original features of Larège. But with her usual practicality she presently pursued her enquiries into the matter of supplies. "Where do you get your groceries—flour and sugar and so on?"

"At Labielle, down in the valley. I usually walk down and take the train, and then have a taxi back. But it's quite a walk from the station up into Labielle."

"Is there a taxi here?" Julia asked.

"No, but there is at Labielle. One telephones for it from the Post Office!"

Wishing more than ever that she had brought her car, Julia decided that she must at least learn her way to the Post Office, and next morning she walked down there with the Stansteds; on the way they showed her one of the *maisons des Sarrazins,* built with enormous, almost megalithic blocks of stone in the lower storey. Besides finding her way, Julia wanted to telephone to Lady Heriot—she had received a telegram from Luzia giving the time of her train's arrival at Pau two days later. She put in the call, and then waited for the connection, sitting on a bench outside the little building in the sun. Below it a long narrow strip of garden stretched down to the next row of houses; the lower part of this was full of potato-plants, but the upper half only contained bare stems —not dug, the soil was undisturbed. Curious as always, Julia got up and went to examine this odd phenomenon.

"Oh, it's just the Colorado beetles" Mr. Stansted said—his wife was still in the *Bureau de Poste* buying stamps. "Listen —can you hear them?" he said, following her down the little path. "You can if your ears are good."

Julia's ears were good; when she reached the point where the living potato-plants still stood she saw that they were covered with black-and-yellow insects, rather like out-size lady birds; and from the two or three infected rows came a very faint, but quite audible, rustling sound.

"Goodness! Is that them munching?" she asked, horrified, watching the creatures swarming on every leaf and small stem.

"Yes."

"How methodical they are! Why don't they eat everywhere at once?" The lower rows of potatoes were untouched, she noticed.

"Oh, they always eat like that: work straight across a patch, from one side to the other—finish a row or two, and move on to the next."

"But can't people spray them, or use a flame-thrower or something?" Julia, familiar with Connaught, where potatoes are still the staple diet, was appalled by the sight of this destruction.

"They haven't got round to that yet, here" Mr. Stansted replied. "It is quite frightful, of course."

"Well, I don't wonder the Irish make such a fuss about importing plants, even from England" Julia said, walking back and re-seating herself on the sunny bench. "This really *is* something to be afraid of." Just then she got her call to Lady Heriot, and gave the time of Luzia's train. "It's most good of you to have her met—I do hope it won't be inconvenient."

"My dear, if she's as beautiful as you say the boys will be thrilled" Lady Heriot said cheerfully. "How do you find Larége?"

"Entrancing" Julia said, and rang off.

The following day the Stansteds asked the Monniers in for drinks. "They're nice neighbours, and your husband knows them—him, anyhow" Mrs. Stansted explained. Julia was interested to meet any friend of Philip's, and particularly a member of the French Resistance—in all her rather varied experience she had never encountered this particular product of World War II. The Monniers proved to be complete charmers, in quite different ways. She was fair, *petite,* and mostly rather quiet—when she did throw a remark into the conversation it was sharply astute, even *cassant;* Monnier however was a terrific talker, and also a highly intelligent one —Julia learned more about the French political set-up from an hour with him than from scores of articles by "Special Correspondents" in the English press. He had the peculiar French gift of acute appreciation of facts, combined with brief and lucid expression—Julia enjoyed him. There was a lot about the O.A.S., and the inner reasons for their antipathy to

General de Gaulle; Julia held her hand over this—she would like, sometime, to get Monnier alone, and go into it more thoroughly, but she was taking no risks with the Stansteds, whom after all she barely knew.

Little Mme. Monnier was more practical. After taking an appraising look at Julia's figure, she found occasion to lead her out onto the gravelled terrace, and like Lady Heriot asked when the baby was due?

"In three months' time."

"*Tiens!* I should have said sooner. Is it *jumelles?*"

"I've no idea," Julia said, startled by the idea of twins.

"You had no radio-photograph taken?"

"No. Can one?"

"Of course—but here, not nearer than at Bordeaux. You have a car?"

"No, no car," Julia replied—she was beginning to feel, a little gloomily, that she and Philip between them were rather falling down on this business of maternity. Good Madame Monnier was obviously troubled too.

"Do you think you will be able to *vous tirer d'affaire?* One can get no help, here in Larège; you will not be alone, I hope?"

Julia said No—she had a friend coming on Tuesday, who would stay with her till she returned to England; in reply to the sensible little French-woman's rather persistent enquiries, she was obliged to say who the friend was.

"Ah! *Espérons.* Now *les Stansted* leave early on Monday, I know; I shall come down the moment after breakfast to give you a little help. On no account go up to empty *la poubelle*, or to fetch water—I do this for you."

But on their way home Mme. Monnier broke out to her husband with vigour. "I always knew the English are mad, but *really*, for this Jimmison, your so dear friend, to send his wife up to Larège!—with twins impending, and no car! This is completely crazy."

Monnier, with masculine calm, asked if she knew definitely that it was to be twins?

"Not certainly—they have not even had an X-ray! But you saw her shape!—I am positive that it will be twins. And who is to be her companion, and help her?—the daughter of a Portuguese Duke! Of what use will *she* be, I ask you?"

In fact Luzia was of a great deal of use, after the Heriot twins had driven her up on the Tuesday, in the late afternoon; they all had coffee out by the spring, a laughing group of youth, which somehow filled Julia with delight—all so good to look at, so happy, so well-mannered, so enjoying one another. But when the twins, with obvious reluctance to part from Luzia, had gone the girl carried the coffee-tray back to the house, asking on the way—"Who brought this out?"

"I did."

"Well, so you do not do again. Carrying trays!—this is *uma loucura*" (an idiocy). "While I am with you, I do this for you." Luzia washed up the coffee-things, and insisted on being shown the store-cupboards, and the working of the three stoves; she was immensely amused by the low-doored bathroom in the former pig-sty. "How one *sees* this as it was when a farm; the cattle stalled, and munching—where now we sit, and cook, and eat. But it is *quite* charming—my Father would like it."

She then hunted Julia upstairs, to lie down and rest—her own room was next to Julia's, also opening off the sitting-room on the first floor; the twins had taken her luggage to it.

"Now rest—I prepare supper."

Julia was once again quite glad to rest, but wondered what on earth they would get to eat under Luzia's preparation? She was agreeably surprised. There was a superb *soupe à l'oignon,* complete with cheese and toast thrown into it, followed by a delicious omelette, salad, and some magnificent peaches. "I brought these from home" the girl said—"with Papa's love."

"Luzia, I had no idea that you could cook" Julia said, as they sat drinking their coffee on the sofa under the big window, in the fading light.

"Oh, I love doing it!—I made the chef teach me. Since I am older I can do more what I like—much more than when you directed me!"

Julia laughed.

"Yes; but now, also, I have more control over Tía Francisca" the girl explained airily. Julia understood. She had often tried to stand between her pupil and the eccentricities of the widowed Duke's spinster sister, who had kept house for him, in her rather dotty and rambling fashion, after his wife's death—she was glad to think of Luzia at last "controlling" her tedious Aunt.

A few evenings later they were drinking sherry out on the tiny terrace with the Monniers when they heard a car pull up, reverse, and switch off at the car-turn.

"*Tiens! Vous avez des visites*" said Madame Monnier—and a few moments later Colin Monro, carrying a knapsack, stumbled down the steep steps and almost fell into the little company.

"I happened to be near here, so I thought I would look you up. Can you give me a bed?" he asked.

"Darling, of course. How lovely to see you" Julia said, rising to give her cousin a kiss—then she made the introductions.

"Could I have a wash?" Colin asked the moment these were over.

"Yes. Luzia, would you show my cousin the top bathroom?—and he will be in the room over mine, so he can take up his things now. Take up the Belling, dear, and put it in the bed, will you?"

"What is this, the Belling?" Mme. Monnier asked, when Luzia had taken Colin indoors.

"Oh, the most invaluable gadget! It's an electric bedwarmer, a sort of round metal thing; you put it *in* the bed, standing upright, and plug in and switch on; and it airs not only the mattresses but the bed-clothes—no propping mattresses against radiators! I brought one out with me."

"I should very much like to see this" Mme. Monnier said. "When one comes to a house in the mountains, especially in winter, to get the beds dry is the problem of problems!"

"You shall, sometime. Do have another sherry, Madame."

When Colin presently rejoined them Julia noticed that Monnier looked rather hard at him; after some general conversation—"You have business at Lacq?" he asked the young Englishman.

"Good God, no! Just cruising around." He turned rather

abruptly to Julia and asked if she knew that lovely Baroque Church in Bordeaux, with the altar standing free, and its great supporting candlesticks, like bunches of gilded flowers? Julia didn't; the Monniers did, and they peacefully discussed ecclesiastical architecture in Bordeaux till they took their leave.

"Why was he so nosey about me and Lacq?" Colin asked, when they had gone—Luzia had stated that she had made Colin's bed, and was now going to see to the supper.

"No idea. He's a friend of Philip's—*my* Philip's; he was in the Resistance."

Colin grunted.

"*Have* you business at Lacq?" Julia asked.

"No. It's just one of a number of places to keep an eye on—sabotage there could be a frightful thing."

"Don't the French keep an eye themselves, so?"

"After their fashion. It's always as well for someone to keep an eye on the French, and their eye-keeping" Colin said, with his still-youthful grin.

They had another lovely supper. But after it Luzia began making some very practical house-keeperly demands of her hostess: they must have a joint of meat, a chicken, more eggs, and vegetables, especially salad—"but onions too. How can one cook without onions?"

"Oh dear, the veg-van came yesterday, and the meat-van won't come till Tuesday—I quite forgot to get any more" Julia said. "How stupid of me."

"Is there no place to which one can drive, and buy food?— since Monsieur Monro has a car?" Luzia asked. "Pau, perhaps?"

"No—one can get everything in the market at Ste.-Marie des Pèlerins" Colin replied at once. "We'll go down there tomorrow and stock up."

They did this. St. Mary of the Pilgrims owes its charming name to the fact that it was one of the staging-posts on the long route across France from Germany and Italy to Santiago da Compostella in Spain, St. James's famous shrine. And the town is as charming as its name. Tall old houses overhang the Gave, the clear green river; there are shaded cafés to sit and drink in, and a crowded, gay, noisy market, its stalls bordering

the sunny streets—in summer these are very hot, as Julia
found when she and Luzia went to buy their meat, and bargain for their chicken, and the salads and *courgettes*. Besides a
joint of veal Luzia wanted steaks, and was extremely fussy
about getting these cut exactly right—the right way of the
grain, the right thickness. "I want to make you a dish!" The
butcher was impressed by her firmness, as the French always
are by any real expertise; he ended by doing exactly as she
asked, and charging less than he had originally demanded.
Colin, tagging along, carried the parcels. But Luzia, their
main marketing done, wanted to buy some of the local *espa-
drilles*—red, with white embroidery on the toes—and some of
the pretty peasant head-scarves of the district; as Julia was
feeling the heat they took her to the inn recommended by the
Stansteds, parked her and their purchases there, and went off
to shop again till lunch—this Colin ordered in advance; he
was familiar with French country inns.

Julia was glad to sit in the cool darkened room, its shutters
drawn against the sun—oh, how tiresome this baby-weakness
was! Sipping a *fine à l'eau* (brandy and water) she looked
through her shopping-list again. Oh dear, they had forgotten
the rice and the onions—but it was too hot to toil out again
and get them; she sat and read *Le Sud-Ouest*, the local news-
paper, which was agreably full of murders, *crimes passionels*,
and dramatic accidents. When the others returned she mentioned this omission—"We'll get them on the way home"
Colin said.

They ate a huge, delicious lunch of French provincial food;
it was hotter in the *salle-à-manger*, close to the kitchen; Julia
fanned herself with the *Sud-Ouest*. "You are tired" Luzia
said, concerned.

"No, only hot. You'd be hot if you had a huge sort of *muff*
attached to your front" Julia replied. "I think babies must
have some sort of central heating in their systems."

Next day Colin's car came in handy again. Julia, having
examined overnight the supply of wine left by the Stansteds
under the big walnut table, decided that they had better get
some more sherry—"Mrs. S. said one could get it in a place
called Jaca. Where is Jaca?"

"Jaca is just across the Pass" her cousin told her. "We'd better take a couple of *bombonnes;* it comes cheaper out of the cask. I expect they've got some—" he delved about behind the vast walnut table, which so oddly served as a sort of wine-cellar. "Yes, here we are" he said, emerging with two enormous balloon-like glass containers, thinly covered with wickerwork. "These each hold twelve litres—twenty-four litres should last you for a week or two!"

"We can't *pour* out of those huge things" Julia objected.

"No—I'll bottle it when we bring it back. Scores of empties! —and I see they've got a corking machine. Sensible people, your tenants."

"Have you got all the papers for going into Spain with the car?" Julia asked. "Luzia and I have got Spanish visas—Philip said we'd better."

"Lord yes!—I was in Pamplona last week."

"Oh. What were you keeping an eye on there?"

"You mind your own business!" her cousin growled—and then laughed.

They drove down the hairpin bends to the main road, and up it to the Grandpont Pass; crossed the frontier smoothly—though with the usual Franco-Spanish delays—and ran down into Jaca. There they first filled the two *bombonnes* at a wine-merchant's, for a fantastically low price—Julia insisted on tasting sherry from several casks before she decided on one—and then went and ate a Spanish provincial lunch at the local inn; this was more impregnated with both oil and garlic than their meal at Ste.-Marie des Pèlerins the previous day, but it was good, and they all ate with relish. Julia prudently insisted on calling back at the wine-merchant's to get a supply of new corks—"No more use bottling new wine with old corks than putting new wine into old bottles" she observed as they drove home.

On their return Luzia was busy rinsing out bottles and setting them to drain on the terrace in the sun, Colin trying to master the intricacies of the corking-machine, and Julia slicing cabbage, onions, and some raw smoked ham to make a *garbure,* when they heard a horn sounding loudly at the car-turn. Julia threw her vegetables into a saucepan of water and set it on the Buta-gaz stove; she was still washing her hands when the Heriot twins walked in—not in the least to her surprise. She introduced them to Colin—"One is Nick and one is Dick, but it doesn't matter which is which, because you'll never be able to tell them apart." They all went out and had sherry by the spring, from one of the newly-corked bottles.

"I say, where did you get this? It is much better than the Stansted's stuff" one twin observed.

"We fetched it from Jaca today—my cousin chose it" Colin said, with a certain pride. "She cares about her wine."

But while checking on the supply of sherry the previous evening, Julia had noticed that the *vin de table* was not very abundant—she seized the opportunity of the twin's presence to consult them.

"Nick—or Dick—do you know the name of that farm, or vineyard, that sells wine? Someone told us you would."

Oh yes, the twins replied; they knew a farmer who sold very decent *vin ordinaire.* "And what is more, I fancy he still has some of last year's left, because we went over the other day and got a supply for His Lordship," one twin said—Julia was in time to become familiar with this odd way of referring to their parents, habitual to the young Heriots. "It was rather extra good. Tell you what—if you care to come and get some tomorrow or the day after, we could meet in Ste.-Marie and take you on; the place is a bit tricky to find, and the old man talks frightfully thick *Béarnais.*"

Julia gratefully accepted this offer. "But the day after better, I think; that will give us more time to wash the bottles."

"And for you to *rest*" Luzia put in. "Two days you are always on the road."

"We can wash bottles now" the twins said in chorus—and wash them they did, with Luzia; the sounds of their laughter, and her objurgations of their carelessness, came out through the open window over the sink.

"What fun the young are" Julia said smiling, relaxed in her garden chair.

"If you ask me, this expedition is entirely in aid of their seeing a bit more of Luzia" Colin said.

"Oh, I don't doubt it! That's what brought them up today,

for sure—but we do need more wine, and you and I are being saved the bother of bottle-washing."

When the twins came out to say Goodbye Julia asked if they should take *bombonnes* to the farm?

"No, the old fellow sells it in small barrels, which one returns later" one twin said. "But we can do that for you. We'll come up and help to bottle too, if you like."

When they had left Colin asked if he could have sandwiches got ready that evening—he wanted to walk next day, and make an early start. Luzia did this for him, grumbling a little at the crusty bread—"*Proper* sandwiches one cannot make; but here is buttered bread, and cold chicken, and cheese. Will this suffice?"

He was out the whole day, having left at 6 A.M.—the two young women did some washing and ironing. "How well you iron, Luzia" Julia said, watching the girl's deft dealings with the collars of Colin's shirts.

"Yes—don't you remember how Nannie made me learn to iron?" They laughed over old times. Then Luzia made her promised "dish," with the steaks she had bought in Ste.-Marie two days before—Julia, sitting and smoking, watched with interest. First the girl rubbed the meat all over with garlic, then dusted it with salt and freshly-ground black pepper, and brushed it with olive oil; she had taken a metal oven-tray out of the Briffault stove, and set it to heat on the electric rings; when it was nearly red-hot she laid the pieces of meat on it—they sizzled and sputtered. "This is *plancia* steak" she announced, as she brought the dish to the table—Colin, who had come in earlier, fell upon it eagerly. "It's jolly good" he pronounced. "Julia, learn how she does it—then you can teach Aglaia." (Aglaia was Colin's enormously rich Greek wife.)

Colin, over salad and fruit, told them how he had climbed the Pic d'Eyzies, the great blunt spear-head which closed the end of the valley. Then he expressed a wish to walk again tomorrow. "Julia, you can drive my car, can't you?"

"What is it?"

"A Rover 90. Goodness, haven't you noticed that?"

"No, but I can drive Rovers—drive any make, in fact! But turn it for me tonight—I hate pulling the wheel round."

"I did turn it—so it's all ready for your wine-foray tomorrow. Luzia, can you get me another lunch?"

"Only hard-boiled eggs—you finished the chicken today."

"That'll do—and some cheese."

The "wine-foray" next day amused Julia, like all the other curious methods of house-keeping at Larège. The two girls had breakfast on the terrace, in the bright early mountain sunshine; then Luzia carried two empty Buta-gaz containers up the steps and along the path to Colin's car. They drove down into the valley and up a side-road to Labielle, where they dropped the empty cylinders and picked up two full ones—then on down the pleasant road to Ste.-Marie. The young Heriots were waiting at a café by the bridge over the Gave, as planned; the two young women were glad of some coffee too, after their early breakfast. The Heriots led them on then, down into the plain to the farmer with the vineyard, a vigorous, oldish man with a grey beard, who first insisted on talking politics with the twins, whom he knew well. "Ah Monsieur Nicolas, why cannot *notre Général* do something for we others, the farmers?"—there followed a long recital of complaints.

"Write to Monsieur Poujade" one twin, rather bored, suggested.

"Ah, *ce Poujade!—il est foutu!*" Anyhow he only concerned himself with the well-being of the trades-people in the towns, the old man grumbled. Luzia, bored too, and irritated that Julia should be kept standing in the sun, at length intervened, in faultless French.

"*Voyons,* Monsieur, is it possible to sit? Madame is come with the intention of purchasing some wine, but she feels the heat. If one could leave *la politique* for a few instants, perhaps?"

The twins and the farmer were almost equally startled by this brusque firmness. Both Heriots glanced at the Portuguese girl with amused admiration; the farmer, muttering apologies, led the party to a table under a trellis of vines, where they sat in welcome shade—glasses were brought out, and at last they got down to the business of wine. The old fellow made them sample two sorts, at different prices; Julia preferred the more expensive one, and indicated this by a nod to the twin who appeared to be doing most of the talking—the optimistic Dick, she supposed.

"How much do you want?" he asked, in English. "The usual size is a 24-litre barrel."

"How many bottles are there in that?"

"About thirty-six."

"Then we'd better have three—it's hot weather, and we're going to be up there for *weeks*."

"Golly—corking 108 bottles! We'd certainly better come up and help with that" said the other twin. "A fearful job." Meanwhile Dick conducted the *marchander*-ing with the farmer: Madame preferred the better wine; if the price was right she would take three "*huitièmes*"—the local name for the 24-litre casks. The old man half-stifled a gasp of satisfaction, and after more efforts on Dick's part—prolonged as bargaining only is in France and Ireland, in the western world—Julia's wine was bought at a quite reasonable price. They had some trouble in stowing the three barrels in the Rover, owing to the presence of the Buta-gaz cylinders, but managed it at length.

They all had lunch in Ste.-Marie; the twins insisted on going home with them to unload their cargo, but the party split up—Dick firmly took Luzia in the Heriot car, while Nick drove with Julia. He soon asked about Luzia, and her family— Julia told him:.

"H'm. Well I think Dick's had it. She doesn't look in the least Iberian, and of course a Duke's all right, but I suppose she's an R.C.?"

"Yes."

"His Lordship won't like that," Nick said gloomily.

"Aren't you going ahead rather fast?" Julia said.

"Nothing like as fast as Dick, once he gets started!" Julia brushed this off with a laugh.

There was no sign of the Heriot car at the car-turn, nor of the other two. Nick turned the Rover for Julia, and then

humped the two gas-cylinders along the path and down into
the house, where he expertly connected one to the stove, and
tried it out. "That's O.K.—we'll leave the wine till that lazy
hound returns from his pleasures," he said, with a slight
drawl. (Julia began to hope that this relative slowness of
speech might enable her to keep the twins apart.) She made
tea, which they drank on the sofa under the big window; it
had been hot all day, and the deep-walled house was pleasantly cool. Presently they heard another car, and in walked
Dick and Luzia. Dick did the explaining—"I took her up to
the dam, to show her where she can have a swim." Julia
smiled; so far as she knew Luzia could not swim—it is not a
very common form of recreation among the Portuguese aris-
tocracy—but she merely asked the pair whether they wanted
tea or sherry? Nick soon hunted his brother out to carry the
three *huitièmes* down from the car—"Her Ladyship won't
like it if we're late for dinner." They propped the three little
barrels up, very neatly and skilfully, on short thick blocks of
wood behind the big bottling-table, so that the taps could be
inverted and the wine flow. "And when shall we come up and
bottle for you?" Dick asked. "Tomorrow?"

"*Ai Jésoosh!* Give us a little time for repose!" Luzia exclaimed. Nick, after a meaning glance at Julia, was stooping
down to count the empties under the great table—Dick asked
"*What* did she say?" Luzia looked apologetically at Julia.

"Miss Probyn, I still forget sometimes."

Julia, laughing, explained. "*Ai Jésus* is a rather low-class
Portuguese expression; it means 'Oh Jesus!' "

"But why does she call you Miss Probyn?" Dick was full of
curiosity about anything that concerned Luzia—Julia explained again.

"You don't look in the least my idea of a governess!" the
young man said, gazing at his tall beautiful hostess. "Was she
any good, Luzia?"

Oh, so it's Luzia now, is it? Julia thought to herself—the
Portuguese girl blushed very faintly, and looked annoyed.

"Madame was everything that is good—teaching, and all
—to a rather ignorant pupil" she replied, coldly.

Nick, straightening up from under the table, said that they were twelve bottles short—"But we'll bring those when we come. Day after tomorrow?"

"No, the day after that" Julia said firmly. "And thank you very much." This was a dismissal, and the twins left. Luzia looked at her watch, and lit up the big stove with chopped wood from behind the table. "There is time to roast the veal —and if your cousin is going to want *des sandvitchs* every day, we had better have some cooked meat. You go and rest"— which Julia did, again lulled by the sound of cow-bells and and falling water. A sweet place, truly.

Colin came in late, when Luzia was saying that they must eat the roast soon, or the meat would be dried up.

"No, no sherry—I had a drink at Barraterre's. I'll just wash."

In fact Luzia had been right—Colin did want sandwiches on both the following days, so the cold veal came in very usefully; each evening he returned late, saying that he had had a drink at Barraterre's. This rather surprised Julia; Colin was not usually a frequenter of inns, he normally preferred to drink quietly at home. Could he be on to something? But she asked no questions.

On the second day Luzia was invited to tea at the Monniers; she decided to take a walk up the slopes first, so Julia was left to a long afternoon alone in the house—she lay and took her snooze on the sofa in the big room, to be at hand if anyone should come to the door. Someone did.

After supper, when they were having coffee out by the spring, the silver saw of the mountains now dark against a rose-flushed sky, Colin asked, with rather elaborate casualness— "Did you ever hear of a type up here called Bonnecourt?"

"I never *heard* of him, but he came to the house this afternoon."

"Why?" Colin looked startled.

"To ask if we wanted a leg of *isard?* Of course I said Yes."

Colin looked a little annoyed. "What on earth is *isard?*"

"The local chamois, or ibex, or something—anyhow Mrs. Stansted told me to get hold of some if I possibly could; it's delicious, according to her."

Before Colin could speak again Luzia broke in.

"Oh, how I *wish* I had not missed him! He is a murderer! —and one so seldom actually meets them."

Colin turned to her. "Why do you say he's a murderer?" he asked rather sharply.

"Oh, because he *is*—and such a clever one! He is not from the village, by origin; he lived further to the west, and also partly in Paris."

"That doesn't make him a murderer" Colin began—Julia shut him up. "Do let her go on, Colin. Yes, Luzia?"

"He used to come here to stay, at the inn, with a lady; then one year he came without the lady, and paid court to an heiress in the village, who had a good house and a rich *terre*, and married her, and settled down. He is a splendid *alpiniste*, and he persuaded her to learn to climb too, and to please him she did; but he managed to drop her off the Pic d'Eyzies!"

"How?" Colin asked.

"Oh, apparently it all sounded quite correct at the enquiry: the sharp rock, the broken rope. But after a proper interval of *deep* mourning" Luzia said, looking amused, "he went away and married the original lady; and now they live in the heiress's house, and she lies in one of those huge stone tombs, like chicken-houses, in the church-yard—I saw her name on Sunday when I went to Mass."

"*Really*, Luzia! Where on earth did you pick up such a story?" Julia asked, rather scandalised.

"Oh, from this one and that." Luzia, doing all the errands, was beginning to find herself quite at home in Larège. "Only today, when I was fetching the bread, Mme. Barraterre was telling me what a wonderful *isard*-hunter this Bonnecourt is. He knows every mountain, and pass, and path, and shoots more of these animals than anyone else."

"When did he say he was going to bring you this leg?" Colin asked Julia.

"He *didn't* say. If he's shot it, I suppose tomorrow—if not, when he has shot it. I think he expected to see Mrs. Stansted, and was rather surprised to find a stranger; but anyhow he promised to bring it to *me*."

Chapter 3

Colin stayed at home all the next day, but there was no sign of Bonnecourt. By the evening he was obviously fussing—obviously at least to Julia, who had known him all his life. Over sherry, out by the spring, while Luzia was preparing supper, she put a blunt question—"Colin, what exactly are you trying to find out, here? What are all these walks in aid of, and this drinking at the pub?"

Even with Julia, Colin could not easily break his ingrained habit of being cagey.

"Oh, the usual sort of thing—routine collecting of information."

"I think you're being very silly to stall like this" his cousin said coolly. "It's obvious that Luzia and I, sitting here all the time, might be able to help you quite a bit—especially Luzia. But we can't unless we know what you're after."

"Why especially Luzia?" the young man asked.

"Oh, because she gets around, as I can't just now—doing the shopping, and fetching the milk from that farm; she talks to everyone, and everyone talks to her—you heard her last night."

Colin sat silent, frowning a little.

"Anyhow your job is no news to her" Julia pursued.

"What *do* you mean? She's a foreigner."

"Yes, but it was she who went into her Father's kitchen at Gralheira and spotted the chief Communist agent, who was after that Hungarian priest Hugh Torrens was getting out, and produced quite a lot of other information; she was only a child then, of course, but Hugh thought the world of her. She's very intelligent. You'd do much better to come clean, Colin."

Colin though impressed by the mention of Major Torrens

42

—who like Philip Jamieson was one of his superiors—could only bring himself to come partially clean, and in a very generalised fashion. There were known, he said, to be Communist groups at Tarbes, a garrison town beyond Pau, and also at Toulouse; their main organisation was almost certainly in Spain, and it was suspected that there was a fairly constant coming and going across the Pyrenees by the small and little-known smugglers' paths. He was trying to check on these and to find out which, if any, of the local people acted as guides.

"Oh, I see. Hence your interest in Bonnecourt; of course he'd make the perfect guide. I wonder why he hasn't turned up? Well, I'll talk to Luzia."

"I wonder if you'd better" Colin said doubtfully.

"Of course I'd better. Ring up Hugh if you want to check on her—though I doubt if you'll be able to hear London through the noise the Colorado beetles make at the Post Office!"

When Julia passed on the gist of Colin's remarks to Luzia, while they were laying the table for supper, the young girl said—"This is not altogether clear to me. I will talk to Colin myself. Of course I should like to help him, but I do not fully understand." She held up one of the squat tumblers to the light, and polished it with a clean linen cloth. "Poor Torrens!" she said, setting the glass on the table. "He was not very clever, but he was more clear than your cousin—perhaps less nervous." Julia smiled, amused that Luzia should so soon have noticed Colin's besetting weakness.

After supper, drinking coffee, the girl tackled Colin, and showed herself one too many for him from the start.

"Of what do you suspect the *isard*-hunter?" she began.

"I didn't say I suspected him of anything."

"No, but you asked Julia about him, and today you stay at home all day, hoping to see him. So you must have ideas in this connection. What are your ideas?"

"Well"—Colin paused, and then spoke rather reluctantly. "It's possible that he might be someone who serves as a guide to—er—people crossing the mountains."

"*To* Spain, or from Spain?"

"Both" Colin said, looking upset.

"I understand. To cause *dégats* at Lacq, and then to escape again."

"I never said that!" Colin growled.

"It was not necessary to say it—it sees itself! And you wish to know, definitely, if Bonnecourt does this?"

Colin looked thoroughly disturbed.

"Luzia, you'd better lay off the whole thing. You can't go round asking those sort of questions." The girl gave him a cool smile.

"One can learn much without asking any questions, if one knows what one desires to know! It shall have attention" Luzia said firmly. "But how I wish *ce monsieur* would bring the *gigôt d'isard!*—Mme. Monnier says it is absolutely delicious!"

Colin hung about for a second day, hoping to see Bonnecourt, who however again failed to appear. The young man had fuller reasons than he had vouchsafed to either Julia or Luzia for wishing to meet the *isard*-hunter and take his measure. He had been given hints, even at home, that the danger of sabotage at Lacq came less from the Communists than from the O.A.S., the *Organisation de l'Armée Secrète,* who had taken a considerable part in the war in Algeria; the Société des Pétroles d'Acquitaine, which operated Lacq, also had interests in oilfields in the Sahara, now become Algerian territory—hence the bitter enmity of the O.A.S. against Lacq and its owners. But the Communists were certainly going to and fro across the frontier too; and it was extremely important for him, Colin, to know which lot—if either—Bonnecourt was assisting. He had gathered for himself that the man was a fine mountaineer, and also that he occasionally went in for smuggling, so he would know all the smugglers' minute paths and by-ways, and be an ideal guide to either party. It was this knowledge which had prompted his original question about him to Julia.

When on the third day the Heriot boys came up as promised to help with bottling the old farmer's wine, Colin was still hanging about. Julia lamented aloud—"I'd hoped to give you *isard* for lunch; a man called Bonnecourt came three days ago, and promised to bring me a leg, but he never has."

"The old wretch!" said Dick. "Usually he keeps his promises."

"Why, do you know him?"

"Goodness yes—we often go out shooting with him." Colin pricked up his ears at this. "He's a splendid type" Dick pursued—"the prettiest rock-climber you ever saw." It emerged from the twins, in their usual strophe and anti-strophe, that they knew that Bonnecourt sometimes went in for smuggling—"Just for the hell of it, really." Julia mentioned Luzia's murder story; the Heriots showed real anger. "That's a typical bit of Larègeois spite and malice! His first wife was a perfect fool—she insisted on climbing with him, because she was jealous of his going out without her; but she couldn't climb for toffee! She jolly nearly killed him as well when she fell—all her own fault—on the Pic."

After lunch—Luzia again gave them *plancia* steaks, this time off the meat-van—Dick Heriot reverted to the subject of Bonnecourt, over coffee; he was plainly troubled by the bad impression local gossip might have created about a man he liked. "He helped a lot of English to escape into Spain during the war" he said.

"Airmen?" Julia asked—she had seen "The River Line."

"Yes, but not only airmen. English civilians living in France too, who missed the bus at all the French ports as they fell to the Germans, one after another; a lot of them came trickling down to Pau, hoping to be safe—but then of course when the Germans occupied the whole of France they were sunk, and had to get out, or try to. Nick, you can remember the story of that funny old English couple that B. rescued, can't you? I seem to recall that it was rather dramatic."

"It was" Nick said. "The man had been in business in Paris for years; when the Germans came he and his wife drove to port after port, but always too late. At last they fetched up at St. Jean de Luz, where a British destroyer was lying off-shore; one of her officers was standing on a *sand-castle* on the beach, bellowing through a megaphone that the ship would take any-one with a British passport to England—but with one suit-case only. The wretched Smiths, or whatever their name was, couldn't face that; they had a carful of all their most treasured possessions. So they drove on to Tardets, and took rooms, and settled down there, hoping for better times."

"Where is Tardets?" Julia asked.

"Oh, a good way west of here."

"Go on."

"Well of course food was terribly short, and everyone collected whatever they could, to keep alive; this old pair were up in the woods one afternoon gathering beech-nuts—full of oil, most nourishing—when they heard a lorry on the road below. They peered out, and it was full of German soldiers in *Pickel-Hauben.*"

"Good Heavens!" Julia exclaimed.

"Yes. If you want drama, that was it. The poor old things had never bothered to get visas for Spain, and the only place for them was Pau; old Smith came bumbling over, but when he saw the queues, and the faces of the people coming out empty-handed, he passed it up, and decided to try to drag his old wife across the frontier. He'd got quite a lot of French money, so he could afford to hire a guide; but apparently he hit on a bad type."

"What do you mean by that, exactly?" Julia asked, frowning over this story.

"Oh—well; he'd lived in France long enough only to pay the man half till they were actually on the path leading into Spain, but that Tardets devil was too smart for him. They had to go at night, of course, and it was pitch dark, and teeming with rain; old Smith was holding his brolly up over his wife when the guide stopped and said—"*Alors,* now go 200 metres up this slope in front of you, and you come to the path; then turn left. Now my money, or I shoot!" What is more he grabbed the umbrella, for good measure."

"But this is hideous!" Luzia exclaimed.

"Oh, well, yes—some of the French *are* hideous, where money is concerned—let's face it. Anyhow the old pair struggled up the slope, alone, and sure enough at the top there was a tiny path, and they went along it, to the left; but they were dead beat, and presently they decided to sit down and have some coffee—old Smith had a Thermos in his knapsack. So down they sat, right *on* the path; nowhere else to sit—

cliff above, a steep slope below—anyhow it was running with water, so they weren't too comfortable."

"How ghastly!" Julia interjected, thinking of the miserable and exhausted old couple sitting in puddles on a mountain-side, in the middle of the night.

"Oh yes, not all nice!—but there was worse to come. For safety Smith had stowed some £300 worth of English fivers in the Thermos, between the glass flask and the outer metal cover; most of the touchable capital he'd got left, of what he'd been able to raise and bring from Paris. Well they each had a cup; but their torch was giving out, and somehow or other, in the dark and that cramped space, between them they managed to knock the Thermos over the edge of the path, and heard it clattering away down the slope below."

"Good God!" Colin ejaculated.

"Yes. Not exactly a cheerful situation" Nick said. "And it was there, sitting in the wet, waiting for daylight in the hope of retrieving the flask and their money, that Bonnecourt came on them on his way back from seeing a couple of British airmen across the frontier into Spain."

"What did he do?" Luzia asked, her fine dark brows knitted over this horrifying story.

"Everything he could. He was carrying a powerful torch with spare batteries, and first of all he went down the slope and found the Thermos. The extraordinary thing was that the glass hadn't broken, so the notes weren't drowned with coffee! Then he gave the soaking old Smiths brandy, and aspirins, and chocolate; and as soon as day began to break he led them down into Spain."

"He shall also have been soaked, in the rain all night" Luzia put in.

"Oh obviously—but he wasn't *old*. He did his best for them with the Spanish authorities, but there wasn't much he could do; they spent weeks in that camp at Vitoria, till at last our Embassy in Madrid got them out and sent them home to England."

"What a story!" Julia said. "Who did you hear it from? M. Bonnecourt?"

"Not originally—we were hardly born then! Her Ladyship

ran into the old pair somewhere in England, a bit later on, and they told her about it; and when we got to know Bonnecourt, Nick had the curiosity to get his version. Nick is the one with the good memory" Dick said cheerfully. "But let's finish this bottling job, and then we'll go down and rustle the old thing up, and make him take us out to get you some *isard*, Mrs. Jamieson."

The bottling finished—the twins were much better at using the machine than Colin—this plan was carried out; but it was Luzia who suggested, in the most natural way in the world, that Colin should go with them to meet this so interesting and merciful person—the young man gave her a grateful glance.

Bonnecourt's house was on the outskirts of the village on the farther side, above the dam. He was in, and as usual Dick did most of the talking.

"This gentleman, Monsieur Monro, is the brother of the lady who stays at present in the Stansteds' house. She is so *dèçue* that you never brought her the *gigôt d'isard* that you promised her the other day."

While Bonnecourt was regretting, and excusing himself, Colin studied him with interest. Medium height, rather slender, with noticeably long arms—he must have a magnificent reach on rocks; a dark, keen face; probably in the late forties or early fifties, Colin concluded; an educated accent, a certain crispness of speech.

"Well, we must not keep this so exceptionally beautiful lady"—a sketch of a bow to Colin—"waiting a moment longer than we can help, after my unfortunate miss the other day. If you two sluggards can be up here tomorrow morning, at six hours precisely, with your rifles, we will see what we can do." He opened the window and leaned out. "Yes, the wind should be right." He turned to Colin. "And Monsieur? I know that you make ascensions."

"I'd very much like to come, but I'm afraid that I'm no shot with a rifle" Colin said. "Could I just be a spectator?"

"You can be a porter, and help to carry down the meat!" Bonnecourt said, with a rather pleasant grin. "*À demain*, then —and please convey my apologies to Madame *votre soeur*."

They all mustered at six the next morning at the *isard*-hunter's house, and set off. Their route lay first up open slopes overlooking the dam and the pool behind it; then they entered thick woods, passing a small inn; the valley now narrowed to a wooded gorge, beyond which it broadened out again and stretched ahead of them, wide and open, full of grazing merino sheep, with their pearl-coloured fleeces. This valley led them close in under the silver saw-teeth of the ridge, and a pull up a steep slope brought them to a group of shepherds' *cabanes,* low wooden structures with rather flat roofs—a bearskin, freshly killed, was pegged out to dry on the door of one of them, to Colin's amazement. There was no one about, but as they examined the skin a couple of the appallingly savage Pyrenean sheepdogs appeared, looking like cream-coloured wolves—and every bit as savage as wolves; Bonnecourt stooped as if to pick up a stone and yelled *"Couchez!"*—the creatures retreated, snarling. Colin had in fact been warned never to go out without a stick, because of the dogs—but so far he had not encountered any.

They pushed on towards a *col* on their right, some 200 feet above the *cabanes;* just before they reached it Bonnecourt said *"À plat ventre!"*—they lay on their stomachs and wormed their way up, the hunter slightly ahead. He had got out a pair of powerful field-glasses, and from behind a small rock he examined the valley beyond. Yes, there were some *isard* there, he told his companions, but they would have to manoeuvre a little, to approach them against the wind; sliding down off the skyline he gave his instructions with great precision. Dick and Mr. Monnro, keeping well below the *col* on this side, were to make their way up to the summit ridge on their left—"to prevent these creatures from escaping into Spain"; when they were in position on the ridge, up by that big rock tower, he and Nick would start to stalk the animals. "You may shoot only when we have shot" he said firmly to Dick, "if they should pass close to you."

Colin and Dick, obediently, kept just below the *col,* and found a gully up which, by a stiffish scramble, they reached the frontier ridge; they crawled cautiously along this, keeping as far as possible to the Spanish side, till they reached the rock tower. There they lay on the sun-warmed rocks and looked out over France into a valley running westwards, roughly parallel with the Larège shelf, but separated from it by a lower intervening ridge. As soon as their heads appeared Nick and Bonnecourt crossed the *col*, also crawling; they made a wide détour, and presently disappeared from view. The two young men lit cigarettes, and waited for some time.

"By the way, Julia—Mrs. Jamieson—is my cousin, not my sister" Colin said. "You might explain that sometime."

"Oh, sorry! Still if you're staying with her like this, it might be just as well to be her brother, especially in Larège!" Dick Heriot said, with a very amiable grin.

At that moment they heard the crack of a rifle, almost simultaneously followed by a second shot—then came two sharp blasts on a whistle.

"That's his signal—we can go down now" Dick said; he got up and began to climb carefully down the rather loose limestone of the ridge, Colin following. The rock presently gave way to extremely steep grass slopes, and on these Colin admired Dick's technique: heels in, knees wide apart, and so bent that he was almost squatting on the ground behind him —the only way to negotiate steep grass fast without the risk of breaking an ankle, or pitching forward headlong. As they reached the foot of the ridge Nick suddenly appeared, some 300 yards away; they walked over to him.

"Yes, *two*" he said. "Old B. let me have the first shot; he can kill them on the wing!—and he got his as well. Did you see the rest of them? There were five."

"No, they didn't come our way," Dick replied. "I wish they had—I'd have liked Monro to see them."

Monro would have liked to see running *isard* too, but he was interested to see a dead one. When they came up to Bonnecourt he had just finished lacing the fine slender legs of the first ibex, with their small pointed feet, together; he slung the animal over the barrel of Dick's rifle.

"There—you and Monsieur Monnro can carry that one" he said, and walked off.

"Why doesn't he gralloch it? It would weigh much less" Colin said.

"They never do, here. You see on steep ground one has to tie them round one's neck to carry them, and they're cleaner whole, for that."

"This isn't steep ground" Colin objected.

"Well, they just don't" Nick said, with finality.

They came up with Bonnecourt some fifty yards further on, again lacing the delicate legs of the second creature together; when he had finished he walked over to a minute stream, washed his hands, and returned to the others. "Now, let us eat something" he said.

By now it was 11.30, and some food was very welcome. Bonnecourt praised Nick's shot, Nick praised his—"Yours was *moving!*" But soon they were interrupted by two Spanish frontier-guards; drawn by the sound of the shots, they had come down to investigate—they greeted Bonnecourt with friendly warmth.

"Ah, Señor Coronel! You have had good sport, evidently. But who are these?"

"Surely you know the Señores Heriot?" The Spaniards now nodded agreement. "And this is a Señor Ingles, who makes a holiday in Larège." The guards, delighted with this break in the monotony of their lonely patrol, sat down; Bonnecourt and the Heriots offered them some of their sandwiches, and Colin followed suit—the guards in return proffered their wine-skins, which they carried slung at their backs. Both Bonnecourt and the Heriot boys knew the trick of drinking from a wine-skin: to hold it a little away from the face, and pour the wine from the spout straight into one's open mouth. Colin had never mastered this art—it is an art—and rather apologetically brought out a collapsible aluminium mug, and drank from that; this greatly amused the Spaniards. But they were intrigued by the mug, and when it was empty they examined it closely, expanding it and pushing it together again. "Very intelligent—very convenient" one said. "Can one buy such in France?"

"This came from England" Colin told him.

"Ah, the Señor speaks Spanish. Does he know Spain?"

"Morocco better" Colin said prudently.

"Morocco! Do the Moriscos speak Spanish, then?"

"Many of them."

"Ah. Well, tell them that we shall not give up Ceuta!"

"You might tell the Caudillo that we shall not give up Gibraltar either" Dick said laughing.

"Ah, my Señor, this is another matter" the older guard said earnestly. "Gibraltar is *Spanish* territory."

"And Ceuta is *Moroccan* territory" Dick replied. "The Señor can't have it both ways."

Bonnecourt intervened. "*Assez!*" he said curtly to Dick; he took out a packet of Gauloise cigarettes, and offered it first to the Spaniards, then to the others. Colin, who loathed Gauloises, refused with a polite apology, and pulled out a packet of Players; to his amusement the senior guard leaned across to him, holding out his hand.

"The Señor Coronel will excuse, but when I have the opportunity to smoke a Playaire, I take it" he said, and suited the action to the word; his companion did likewise, but both tucked the less acceptable Gauloises into their breast pockets. Bonnecourt smiled.

"And how did the Señor bring in these cigarettes?" the younger guard asked—though quite amiably.

"I bought them on the plane to Bordeaux. For travellers, it is permitted to bring in a certain quantity."

"You see that you have no chance of impounding the Señor's cigarettes!" Bonnecourt said mockingly. "Tell me, are you catching many smugglers just now?"

But the Spaniards could take a hand at mockery too.

"Ah, Señor Coronel, when you are occupied with hunting *isard,* who is to do the smuggling?" one asked. The twins shouted with laughter, in which Bonnecourt joined.

Colin was immensely puzzled and interested by all this: that the guards should know Bonnecourt so well, and be on such easy terms with him, although they definitely regarded him as a smuggler. And why did they address him as Colonel? His mind went back to a morning in the office, sitting at a desk with a very senior grey-haired clerk, drinking the usual

horrible office tea, and examining rather fragmentary notes
from the card-index on various Pyrenean characters. Wasn't
there someone who had been in the French Army?—who was.
it? And was he for or against the *régime?* Could this be the
same man? Oh, what a nuisance that one always had to de-
stroy one's notes!—and that his own memory was so fallible.
He wondered if he would get anything out of a talk alone
with Bonnecourt; he decided to try it on.

When the frontier-guards had gone off, climbing up towards the ridge, the others started homewards, Dick and
Colin carrying one *isard* slung from a rifle, Nick and Bonnecourt the other. They did not return via the *cabanes,* but took
an easy lower *col* which led over onto the slopes above Larège,
below the woods where the inn stood. Further down on these
slopes, near the village, were patches of potatoes, many of
them being steadily and audibly destroyed by Colorado beetles; Colin was as appalled as Julia had been in the Post Office
garden.

Back at his house, Bonnecourt turned to active and deft
butchering—a hind-quarter of *isard* was soon handed to the
twins—"*pour Madame votre mère.* Your chef can skin this."
Another haunch he skinned himself, rapidly and skilfully. "At
last, here is the promised *gigôt* for *Madame votre soeur*" he
said to Colin—"I know *she* has no chef!" While Dick and
Nick were carrying their piece of meat out to the car, Colin
took the opportunity of asking Bonnecourt if he would not
come up and have a drink with him at Barraterre's?

"Monsieur Monnro, let us dispose of *les jumeaux,* and then
have a little glass quietly together, here; then we can talk
peaceably. *Un petit moment*—Lady 'Eriott will want the liver
and the kidneys." He quickly produced these from the insides
of one animal, and stowed them in a polyethylene bag, which
he handed to the twins when they returned to say Goodbye
—"I know that Milord likes kidneys."

"*And* how!" Dick said. They also thanked their host, and
took themselves off.

Bonnecourt, again apologising for the delay, hung up
both carcases inside a neat wire-meshed game-larder,
standing in a shaded space on the north side of the

house, and stowed the offals in it on dishes; then he washed his hands at an outside tap, above which a towel hung from a nail, and ushered his guest into the sitting-room, where he produced Vermouth and glasses. Over their drinks Colin opened, rather tentatively, by saying that he had learned from the Heriots how much Bonnecourt had done for English refugees and escapees during the last War—his host agreed, though deprecatingly and very nicely. "Did the boys also tell you that I smuggle?" he asked, cheerfully.

"No—but those jolly Spanish guards seemed to think that you do."

"Ah, they like their joke!" Bonnecourt said.

"Why did they call you Colonel?" Colin asked, still thinking of his session with the grey-haired clerk and the card-index in the office in London.

"I used to be in the Army—I was in Indo-China." He praised de Lattre de Tassigny warmly, and then on a long sigh—"So much courage, and so much blood, poured out in vain!"

Colin expressed suitable sympathy. "I expect many French officers feel that about Algeria too," he added. His host looked at him rather keenly.

"Assuredly! Another sell-out! But I was not in Algeria—I was invalided out of Indo-Chine with dysentery after Dien Bien Phu, and had to leave the Army altogether."

Colin wondered privately whether the Heriot boys knew about Indo-China or not—Bonnecourt's attitude would fit in with the rumours of his helping the O.A.S. But he switched from a possibly awkward subject to mention the story of the old Smiths—on this Bonnecourt opened up. "Miraculous, that the glass in this Ther*mos* did not break" he said at the end. "It would have been terrible for the poor old man to lose all his money."

When Colin got home he found Julia sitting out by the spring. "Well, I've brought your *gigôt d'isard*" he said; "I gave it to Luzia."

"She mustn't put it in the frig" Julia said, making to rise from her chair.

"She hasn't. She's pinning it up in some muslin—one of

her petticoats, I imagine!—and she's going to hang it behind the wine-table, against the north wall."

Julia sat back again. "What a splendid creature that is!" she said. "Now, tell me how your day went."

Colin told her in some detail. The points Julia at once fastened on were the guards' addressing Bonnecourt as a "Coronel", and his having been in Indo-China. "Of course that Army background points to his helping the O.A.S." she said thoughtfully.

"Still, it's all pretty vague" her cousin replied.

"All pointers—you can't have too many. What's he like?"

"A terribly *nice* man, I would say."

She reflected. "What's your next move?"

"I think I'd better get back fairly soon to Pamplona, and check up with the lads there on B. and his goings-on. But I want at least one more day here—I ought to look at the smugglers' paths west of this; they're nearer to Lacq. I've covered most of the rest, and made notes. I'd better do that last stretch before I leave."

As usual he demanded sandwiches overnight from Luzia, and well before 6 A.M. next day he set out. He took the path behind the house up past the spot where one emptied *la poubelle*, and followed it on, up and round the shoulder of the hill, where it passed through a beech-wood; beyond, another valley opened out on his left—he walked through it, and struck up to the frontier ridge. A tiny barely discernible path descended from this; Colin followed it till he could look down on the opposite side, where, still barely visible, it led into Spain. He made a note of the path, and then scanned the further slope; there his eye was caught by two figures climbing up on the Spanish side, over steepish rocks, only some 300 yards away—they had no rope, and seemed to be making rather heavy weather of the rocks, especially the second man, who looked older than the leader. Colin watched them till a projecting bluff cut off his view; he climbed along the ridge in their direction—it might be interesting to learn who and what they were. One of the innumerable limestone towers common in that part of the Pyrenees presently blocked his passage along the ridge; he scrambled down on the French side to circumvent it—the rocks were quite steep and rather loose, from a climber's point of view a nasty place.

Just as he regained the ridge the two men reappeared, and paused on the crest; then they began trying to make their way down into France; but they too had those unpleasant rocks to negotiate. Colin looked about for a place from which he could watch them, himself unseen; a boulder on the ridge a few yards ahead seemed to offer a suitable spot, and he moved carefully towards it. But in so doing he dislodged a loose slab, which fell with an immense clatter; he just saved himself from falling, and reached the boulder—but as he did so he heard a loud cry, and more noise of falling stones. Panting a little, he peered out to see what had happened. The older man had fallen, and was lying at the foot of the rocks a hundred feet below; his companion was working his way down to him, calling out in French, "Jean, have you hurt yourself?"

Colin climbed down too—a good deal faster and more skilfully. In fact the older man had hurt himself considerably; he was bleeding profusely from a scalp-wound, and averred that he had broken his leg. Colin, when alone in the mountains, always carried a small First-Aid case, and quickly strapped up the head-wound with plaster—then he asked in French where they were making for?

"*Now*, to the nearest place where we can find a Doctor" the younger man said, vexedly. "*Grand Dieu*, that this should have to happen at this moment! Does Monsieur know this region, and where we can obtain medical assistance?"

Colin, much struck by the fact of two Frenchmen climbing up out of Spain into France, wanted most of all to find out where they were going, and whether indeed they knew where they were? He replied, carefully, that he didn't know the district very well—he was just there *en vacances*. Had Monsieur perhaps a map? The younger man drew out a large-scale map; Colin peered at it over his shoulder. *Yes*— faint pencil-dots indicated the path by which he himself had gone up to the ridge, which they must somehow have missed on the Spanish side; but the dots led down, not to Larège but to a spot on the Grandpont road close to Labielle, where there was a tiny pencilled X. H'm—that was where they were to have met whoever they had come to meet. Could it be Bonnecourt, he wondered? He thought there were figures beside the X, but they were too faint to read. He put his finger on the name Larège.

"Somehow we must get him there—it is the nearest place, and I have a car. Then we can find a Doctor, and drive him down."

"But how is he to get to Larège?" the young man asked wretchedly. "He cannot walk!" He looked at his watch. "*Mon Dieu*, it is so late already."

"Let us see if we cannot get him along between us" Colin suggested. They took the injured man under the elbows, and tried to support him; but he proved limp and inert, and cried out with pain if he set his injured leg to the ground.

"This is no good" Colin exclaimed. "You stay with him, and I'll go down to the village and try to get a stretcher, and some help."

"You could not go to Labielle?"

"Why? It's miles further away."

"We—have friends there" the younger man said, with slight hesitation.

"Well we'll find them later, when we've got him into the car" Colin said briefly, and hurried away.

On his way back to Larège Colin decided that even at the cost of some delay he had better go down to Bonnecourt's, as a check—if the hunter was out he might conceivably be the "friends" the two Frenchmen intended to meet at Labielle. He also speculated as to whom he could rope in to help to carry the Frenchman down?—he was thickset, and heavy. And what in?—he doubted whether Larège boasted such a thing as a stretcher. On reaching the house he ran in to ask Julia to look out a strong blanket; at a pinch one could carry a man in that.

Julia was lying on the sofa in the big room; Colin hurriedly explained the situation. "Find an old one—we shall have to cut holes in the corners to get a grip."

"What a mercy Dick's here" Julia said, getting up.

"*Is* he? Where?"

"He was going to take Luzia down to the dam for a swim."

"Good—I'll go and find him. Get that blanket."

Striding on through the hot cobbled streets of the village Colin thought how well all this fitted in: Dick to help to carry the patient, and a perfect excuse to call at Bonnecourt's house, which was not far from the dam. He went to the house first—a fair plainish woman, not very young, opened the door to him. No, Monsieur was out for the day. With *la voiture?* Colin asked. "*Mais oui.*"

So he wasn't after *isard,* Colin thought—it might well be as he had suspected. He went a little further along the path, till he could see the dam and the pool behind it—there was no one there. He walked back to the square and turned in at Barraterre's to make his enquiries—Mme. Barraterre was all interest. Colin asked first for the nearest Doctor?

"Dr. Fourget, at Labielle. Is it *pour Madame Jimmison?*— *les douleurs commencent?*"

"No!" Colin said irritably. "It is a man who has fallen in the mountains, and injured himself. We need a *brancard* to bring him down."

"But in this case one must *alerter* the *gendarmerie*; they have a Rescue Service—my sons are volunteers in it! Only it is rather expensive—they alert four communes and send sixty men." She looked eagerly towards the telephone in the narrow hall. Colin headed her off, appalled.

"A little moment, Madame! There is no need for sixty men, or for the *gendarmerie!*—all I need is the *brancard,* and to warn the Doctor."

"Ah *oui, oui,* for the injections!—*le tétanus!*" This surprised Colin—he did not realise how intensely aware of the danger of tetanus French country-people are. In France it is not a matter of infection by the odd shaving-brush from China; it is a daily menace. But Mme. Barraterre was equally well-informed about the rules concerning accidents.

"Monsieur must absolutely inform the *gendarmerie*—they have to make *le constat* in the case of any accident."

"Of course I shall do this" Colin said. "But for the moment

the essential is to bring *le blessé* down, and for that I require the stretcher. Where is the *gendarmerie* post?"

"Monsieur, here in Larège we have none. Only at La-bielle." Again she looked at the telephone. Colin thanked her, and left. They would just have to manage with the blanket. But where on earth was Dick Heriot? He had seen his car at the turn. And what a nuisance this *constat* with the police was likely to be—probably messing up his own enquiries. He walked homewards feeling vexed and frustrated.

By now poor Colin was not only hot, but extremely thirsty; and instead of going into the house he went on to the shed, to get an ice-cold drink from the spout, and sluice his face and hands in the trough. But he never did either. On the lawn immediately below him he caught sight, between the silvery trunks of the trees by the spring, of Luzia in a deck-chair, looking cool and beautiful, with a slightly mocking expression; Dick Heriot was kneeling on the grass beside her, holding her hands, and apparently making a declaration. Irritated and disconcerted, still unwashed and still thirsty, he went back and into the house.

"Did you find him?" Julia asked—she was again on the sofa, stitching away at a rough old Army blanket.

"Not exactly—I mean they weren't at the dam. They're out by the spring; Dick seems to be proposing to Luzia."

"Well let him stop proposing" Julia said with the utmost calmness, "and go up with you and get this wretched man down."

"It's a bit embarrassing to interrupt them."

"Oh nonsense, Colin." She hoisted herself off the sofa, put her head out of the open window, and called—"Dick! Come at once! I want you." She handed the blanket to Colin. "I've cut slits in all four corners, and stitched down the edges, folded over. It should hold."

Dick came in through the big doorway, alone.

"Yes, Mrs. Jamieson?" he asked.

"There's been an accident. I think you'd better go up with Colin and help to bring the casualty down. Can you?"

"Yes of course—if someone could ring up Her Ladyship and say I may be a bit late. She worries."

"We can see to that. Where's Luzia?"

"Here" the girl said, also walking in at the door.

"Oh, good. All right—you two breeze off" Julia said to the two men "Want a drink first?"

"Just water" Colin said, filling a tumbler from the earthenware jug, and gulping down a great draught. "And ring that Doctor too." He had been examining the blanket. "I think that *will* hold" he said. "Come on, Dick."

When they had gone Julia took a writing-pad from the table by the sofa, and wrote two messages in French—one to Lady Heriot, whose number she knew, to say that Dick was helping to bring down a climber who had fallen and was injured, and might therefore be delayed. "Send that as a telegram" she said, tearing off the top sheet—"Save time." She wrote again. "Telephone this one—it's to Dr. Fourget, at Labielle. You can look out his number." (The thoughtful Madame Monnier had determinedly given *cette pauvre Mme. Jimmison* the local Doctor's name.) "If you happen to catch him, it would be handy to know how soon he can come up."

Luzia read through the messages.

"I do this" she said, and went out.

Chapter 4

Dick and Colin made fast time round the wooded shoulder and up the valley beyond it, Colin carrying the blanket; when they reached the two Frenchmen the older man was placed on this, and Colin and Dick took a top corner each, leaving the young man to hold the two lower ones—the legs of the human body weigh much less than the head and trunk. Then they started the long plod back to Larège. In spite of Julia's well-sewn slits this was hard on the hands; more than once they had to pause, set their burden down, and rest. "Extraordinary that there should be no *brancard* here" the young Frenchman said at one of these halts, rubbing his sore palms together.

"Oh, Larège isn't very up-to-date" Dick told him cheerfully.

At last they crossed the shoulder, left the rough going, and started down the better path. Soon the car-turn came in sight—a strange car was parked there besides his and Dick's, Colin noticed. "Nearly there now" he encouraged the young man. In a few moments more—"Now, down these steps—carefully" he said; they carried their casualty down and into the big room.

"Put him on the sofa" Julia said, rising from an armchair; as they did so a stout dark man with a beard got up from another. "This is Dr. Fourget, of Labielle" Julia introduced him. "My cousin, Monsieur Monro, Monsieur *le Médecin*—but I do not know the names of these two gentlemen."

The younger man made no response to this invitation to give his name.

"*N'importe, pour le moment*" the Doctor said, going over to the figure on the sofa. "Open your eyes!" he commanded sharply—the injured man, who had seemed almost uncon-

61

scious, did so—the Doctor looked at his face keenly. "H'm" he muttered. He raised the head and felt carefully all round it, then lowered it again. "Where else is he hurt?" he asked.

"I think the right leg is broken—he cannot walk."

"Perhaps *Mesdames* would leave us, while I examine?" Fourget said. Julia guessed that this meant removing trousers, and went out with Luzia onto the little gravelled terrace; they perched on the stone seat.

"Who are they?" Luzia asked.

"I've no idea. Colin just happened to see the old man fall."

"Where?"

"Coming down off the frontier, in that next valley."

"So coming from Spain?"

"I suppose so."

"But they are French—what do they do, climbing up out of Spain? Julia, I am suspicious!"

"Why?"

"The young one would not say their names, when you suggested it. I think they are *activistes* of the O.A.S." Luzia pronounced.

"They may merely be harmless French tourists, who'd taken a walk into Spain, and were coming back."

"I think otherwise" Luzia said firmly.

"Well, I fancy the one who fell won't be able to do much about blowing up Lacq for some time" Julia replied, lighting a cigarette. "I think he's probably fractured his skull. I noticed Dr. Fourget's expression when he made him open his eyes."

"Yes—why did he do this?"

"I'd guess, to see if the poor creature was squinting. People with fractured skulls generally squint—and he *was,* judging by Fourget's face."

"How do you know this, Julia?"

"Because a dear friend of mine died of a fractured skull, not so long ago, and the Doctor told Philip all about it."

Julia's guess proved to be correct. Dr. Fourget presently came out to tell them that *le blessé* must be got into the hospital at Pau immediately—Dick, following the Doctor, volunteered to drive him down. "I can take out one front seat, and if you fill the space with cushions he can lie flat." Julia resisted the idea of cushions, and made Luzia and Colin bring down bolsters, pillows, and a mattress from the unused spare beds, and arrange these in Dick's car. Fourget offered to take the young Frenchman in his car—"I'll call at my house on the way, to alert the hospital, then we follow." The young man objected—he must be with his friend.

"There's not room" Dick said tersely. Colin intervened. He would take the young man in his car, following Dick's closely; the young man, obviously worried and uncertain, finally agreed, and the casualty, still in the old blanket, was carried up and disposed, carefully, in Dick's car. Then the little cortège drove off, Fourget leading, followed by Dick and Colin.

No arrangement could have pleased Colin better. If Bonnecourt was really waiting at the spot marked with a cross on the Frenchman's map, which he had memorised, he would be able to check on what happened there—if it was not Bonnecourt, he might get a sight of the contact, whoever it was. Before leaving he turned back and spoke to Julia— "Just leave some soup on the stove, if I don't come for supper. I might be late."

Luzia followed him out to the steps.

"I think these are *saboteurs*" she whispered in his ear.

"Why?" Colin asked, startled.

"It is just my idea."

"Oh well, I must go" Colin replied impatiently—and unfairly, since in fact it was his idea too. "But do for goodness sake keep *quiet*, Luzia."

Dick's car was much faster than the Doctor's old Peugeot; and though he had been instructed to drive gently, and on no account to jolt the patient, when they were out on the main road below the hairpin bends, he passed Fourget. So did Colin, with a cheerful wave; after he had done so his young French passenger spoke, rather hesitantly.

"Does Monsieur know this little town, Labielle?"

"Yes—it's a few kilometres down the road. Ah, I think you said you had friends there—what is the address?" Colin asked, with thoroughly synthetic helpfulness.

"We were to meet them at an *auberge*" the young man replied, embarrassedly. "But—*Grand Dieu!*—we are now three hours late."

Colin pitied him; but he had his own job to do. "Was the *auberge* up in the town, or on the main road?" he asked, remembering the pencilled X on the map. "You see the town of Labielle is up a side road."

"It was on *la grande route.*"

"Oh good. Well when we get there we'll go gently, and look out for it." He scorched on till they were nearly at the turn to Labielle; then decelerated, and drove more slowly. Less than a kilometre beyond the Labielle turning, sure enough there was a very small road-side inn—Colin scanned the broad road ahead, here fairly straight; some 200 yards further on a car was parked on the verge.

"This looks as though it might be the place" Colin said, pulling in to the side. "Go and see if your friends are still there." He switched off his engine; the young man sprang out, and crossed the road—as he did so Bonnecourt appeared in the doorway of the *auberge.*

"*Alors!* What goes on?" he asked. "You are *very* late."

The young man began to babble out the story of the accident; Bonnecourt, saying gently—"*Doucement, mon pauvre ami,*" led him indoors. Colin lit a cigarette and sat back in the car to wait, tired, relaxed, and well content—he now knew at least a part of what he wanted to know.

Quite soon Bonnecourt and the young Frenchman emerged from the little inn; Colin could hear Bonnecourt asking— "And where is this gentleman who has brought you here? *Ah, dans la voiture.*" He stepped across the road—but when he recognised Colin he stopped short, with a noticeable change of expression. Colin got out.

"Hullo, Bonnecourt! One of your friends has had a rather nasty accident. Thank God I happened to be up there, and was able to help to get him down" he said, with what he hoped was sympathetic casualness.

Bonnecourt had recovered his composure very quickly.

"You seem to have been goodness itself" he replied. "But where is *le blessé?*"

"Gone on to the hospital at Pau."

"Who took him? Fourget?"

"No. Fourget stopped off at his house to alert the hospital. The man's in Dick Heriot's car."

Bonnecourt looked very slightly vexed.

"How did Dick Heriot come into this?"

"By God's mercy he was up at the house; without him we could never have got your pal down—in a blanket!"

"You could have called in the Rescue Service" Bonnecourt said.

"Yes!—and alert four Communes, and pay for sixty men!" Colin exclaimed. "Be your age, Bonnecourt!—that would have taken *hours!*"

Bonnecourt grinned at him. Was there a grateful complicity in the grin? "We put him in Dick's car because it's the biggest" Colin pursued. "He can lie flat in that."

"What are his injuries? My poor young friend is rather distraught."

"Well he's certainly broken a leg, and Mme. Jamieson got the impression that he may have fractured his skull as well."

"How could he do this?" Bonnecourt asked, vexedly. "Their path was not difficult in the least."

"They weren't on the path—they missed it. I went up by it, and saw them crossing further to the west. Bonnecourt, I don't think that young man of yours is much good for this sort of job" Colin said bluntly—he had decided on bluntness, in the circumstances. "He can't even read a map properly, or he wouldn't have missed that path."

"Did he show you his map?" Bonnecourt asked, frowning.

"Well, I asked if he had one, and he got it out. The path had been marked, too—I saw that."

The hunter gave a discomfited laugh.

"Monnro, you are too observant!"

"Well, what are you going to do now?" Colin asked—they had moved across the road and seated themselves on the low stone wall opposite the little inn. "The old fellow is out for some time, I imagine. Is there much point in your taking this foolish youngster down to Pau and letting the police check on him as well? From your point of view I should have thought it would be much better to take him straight home with you, and bring him back into Spain tomorrow. He's no use, anyhow." For the first time in his life Colin had embarked on bluntness of speech; he found it immensely to his taste, almost intoxicating, after his years of timid caution.

The Frenchman stared at him, a long, slow stare. At last— "You speak of his being 'no good at this job' " he said, "and 'my point of view!' May I ask, first, what you conceive the nature of his 'job' to be?"

Colin grinned—bluntness seemed to pay off. "I'll give you three guesses" he said. "The answer is an eight-letter word. But I should like to have a talk with him before he goes back—in fact that is rather a condition."

Bonnecourt considered.

"I wonder how you reached this conclusion" he said at length. Colin, in the strangest way, felt power growing in him.

"Oh nonsense! Two Frenchmen climbing up out of Spain into France, with a marked map, in *this* district! Only one conclusion was probable—O.A.S. *activistes.*"

"And what is the alternative to your 'condition', my friend?"

"That I alert the police, of course. But I don't want to, really."

"Why not?" Bonnecourt asked, coldly.

"Because you gave us such a splendid day last week—and I like you. But I must talk to this silly young man."

"Why? What are you?" Bonnecourt asked, looking at him suspiciously.

"An ordinary Englishman. And as France is our ally— tedious as your General can often be!—I don't want to see half her gas-supply disrupted by some disgruntled ex-militarists. Really, Bonnecourt, the O.A.S. are a set of emotional clowns!—let's face it."

The Frenchman was silent for some moments.

"I had not realised that the 'ordinary Englishman' was so

well-informed" he said at length. "Very well—I accept your condition. But why did you refer to 'my' point of view?"

"I'd heard it—well, spoken of—and here you were, waiting for these types I'd stumbled on at the very spot marked on their map. Pretty good confirmation, I thought."

"This spot was marked? What idiocy! Well, come to my house at any time this evening—or could you come now?"

"No—I've got other things to do first. I'll be along later. *Au revoir.*" He waited, fiddling with nothing under the bonnet of his own machine till he had seen Bonnecourt collect his passenger, go down the road, turn his car, and drive up again towards Larège.

Colin wanted, in fact, to check at the hospital on the old man's condition, and to get hold of Dick and warn him to talk as little as possible. Had he, too, seen Bonnecourt at the *auberge,* or recognised his car parked further on? He went first to the Heriots, and found the whole family having a late, amply Scottish tea, while Dick poured out the story of the rescue—the twins introduced him, and he was given a pleasant welcome. Presently he asked if Dick had heard how the elderly man was?

"Oh, he broke his leg all right, but they weren't sure if he'd fractured his skull, or merely got concussion. I waited till Fourget turned up, and then left him to it."

"I suppose the hospital wanted to know his name?"

"Yes of course, but he was too far gone to give it. They found his passport on him, though—a Paris address, and oddly enough his name is Maupassant" Dick said, grinning. "He made a *mauvais pas* all right, poor old creature."

"What an adventurous day you have had" Lady Heriot said to Colin. "Are you sure you wouldn't rather have some whisky than that tea?"

"Yes please—much rather." Whisky was brought and Colin drank it thankfully; while he ate scones and sandwiches—he was hungry, having never had a moment to eat Luzia's picnic lunch—Lady Heriot talked gently on about the accident. "So many tourists come into the mountains nowadays who are completely ignorant about climbing; they attempt things that are quite beyond their powers." Then she asked after Julia.

"Oh, she's in great form. And her friend Luzia Ericeira does most of the work, and looks after her like a nannie! She's splendid."

"I do want to meet the lovely Luzia" Lady Heriot said. "In fact I thought of giving a little dance for her here—do you think she would enjoy that? Of course she, and you and your cousin, would stay with us for it."

Colin said it would be delightful, and how kind—but he spoke a little abstractedly; time was getting on, and he wanted to go to the hospital, as well as making *le constat* to the police. He rose, and after thanking his hostess said he must be getting back.

"Where's the other Frenchman, the young one?" Lord Heriot asked, also rising. "Dick said you were bringing him down."

Colin, who had displayed such unwonted vigour with Bonnecourt, was rather taken aback by this question.

"In the end I didn't" he said. "He's staying up at Larège tonight—I told him I'd report on his friend." Dick Heriot gave him a glance like a Red Indian's at this statement.

"You've reported to the police, of course?" Lord Heriot pursued. "Have to do that, you know, here."

"Yes, I know. I'm going to do it now." He took his leave— Dick came down to see him out. On the broad gravel sweep in front of the house, as they walked over to the car, Colin said—"Dick, don't talk more than you can help about all this."

"Where *is* the young one?" Dick asked.

"Up at Larège, as I said."

Dick Heriot looked at him steadily.

"I seem to smell some funny-business about all this" he said. "Why didn't he come down? He said he must be with his friend—wanted to come in my car; now he hasn't come. Have you any idea who these types are? Luzia thought they were O.A.S. *saboteurs*."

"Luzia's always guessing!—but if they were, it would be all the more reason for keeping mum" Colin said, getting into his car and starting the engine. Dick put his head in at the window.

"Why?" he asked pertinaciously.

"Oh, because 'careless talk' never helps anything" Colin said impatiently.

"I say, are you in Intelligence too? We know that Mrs. J's husband is" Dick said. "Gosh, what fun!"

"You just keep quiet" Colin said, and drove off.

At the hospital Colin asked for the house-surgeon—when, after some delay, this gentleman appeared, Colin explained that he had come to enquire after the man who had recently been brought in; "a patient of Dr. Fourget's." He was led upstairs; just as they reached the ward Dr. Fourget emerged. "Ah, this is Monsieur Monnro, the gentleman you want to see" he said to the surgeon—"It was he who brought him down."

"How is he?" Colin asked.

"It does not look well. But I must return to my patients— I leave you now with Dr. Poulain." Fourget walked off downstairs, with his firm steady tread.

Poulain pulled out a little note-book, and began to ask questions. Had Monsieur seen the actual fall? How far was it? About thirty-five metres. "Onto rocks?" the Doctor asked. "Well, there were rocks among the grass—he landed below the actual rock-face." Colin explained what he had done on the spot, and how there had been no *brancard* at Larège. "We could have got him down more quickly if one had been available." Dr. Poulain made another note.

"Will he recover?" Colin asked.

"I think it doubtful. And where is his companion, of whom Dr. Fourget spoke?"

"I left him with friends at Labielle."

"Who are these friends?"

"Naturally I have no idea!". Colin said briskly—his new firmness was beginning to return. "They were waiting for him at an *auberge*, and I left him there."

"This is curious! Well, I think the police would like to see you—there is an *agent* waiting by this man's bed, in case he should be able to reply to questions. *Par ici*, Monsieur"—he led Colin into the long, clean ward, bare except for the two rows of beds, and told the *agent* who he was.

The *agent*, methodically, first asked for Colin's name and address; he gave Glentoran for the latter, and added "*Écosse*." Poulain exclaimed at this—the Scotch were a wonderful people, the medical school at Edinburgh *épatant*. In reply to further questions Colin gave the time of the accident, and described the place with rather studied vagueness. "But they were descending from the frontier?" the policeman asked.

"It had that appearance, but I only saw them a few seconds before *ce monsieur* fell." (Colin had a strong feeling that the more the French police were kept out of it, the more he himself would learn, especially from Bonnecourt.)

"And you reported to the police at Larège?" the *agent* pursued.

"*Voyons*, Monsieur, there *are* no police at Larège!" Colin said sharply. "And no *brancard* either! Hence we had to carry this unfortunate down in a *couvert*. This is wrong" Colin said, firmly carrying the war into the enemy's country; like Dr. Poulain, the *agent* made a note. "And will what I have told *Monsieur l'Agent* suffice for a *constat*, for the moment? I see he has made notes of everything."

The man looked doubtful—Poulain was firm with him. "Let it suffice for the present. You know where to find this gentleman."

"*Écosse* is a long way away!" the *agent* grunted—Colin laughed. "Is Monsieur remaining in Larège?—and at what address?"

"*Aux bons soins de* Mme. Stansted," Colin replied—the Stansteds were better known there than Julia. Then he asked a question himself. "I think you have the name and address of this gentleman"—he gestured towards the bed. "I should like to have them."

"Why?" the policeman asked, suspiciously.

"But to inform his relations! Since it was I who witnessed the accident, I can tell them more than anyone else." Rather grudgingly, and again under pressure from Dr. Poulain, the *agent* opened his note-book, and read out "Jean de Maupassant," and an address in Paris, which Colin jotted down.

But the *agent* also was worrying about the second man—Colin repeated that he had left him with friends at the inn at Labielle.

"He comes here presently?"

"But naturally I assume so" Colin said, untruthfully.

At last he got away from the hospital. He decided to ring up the office in London; it would be quicker, and less public, than from either Larège or Pamplona. He drove to the Hotel de France, best of hostelries, and ordered an early supper—in spite of that tea at the Heriots he felt ready for a proper meal. *Potage du jour* and cold chicken would be sufficient, he said; then he went and got the old hall-porter—guide, philosopher and friend to countless English-people—to put his call through to London. In the telephone-box he looked worriedly at his watch—it was pretty late; he wondered if his particular contact on this assignment, a Major Hartley, would still be there. Much better if he could speak to him—save time and explanations.

Surprisingly quickly he got his connection—the French trunk service is very efficient—and gave Hartley's extension number; to his immense relief he heard the voice he wanted saying "Hullo? Who at Pau?"

"Me; Colin."

"Oh. Doing any good?"

"Not sure yet. I've got one name to give you—take it down." He gave the name of Jean de Maupassant, and the address: 15, Rue Calumet, Paris XVIe. "An elderly type."

"What's he up to?"

"At the moment, nothing—he's in hospital with a broken leg and a fractured skull; they don't seem to think he'll recover. I happened to be close by when he fell, and got him down."

"Was he where one would expect?"

"Yes, exactly there."

"Half a mo" Hartley said—Colin waited. After a pause—"Was he alone?" the voice from London asked, "or was a young man called de Lassalle with him?"

"There was a young man with him, but I don't know his name—an incompetent drip, if you ask me."

"Can you get his name?"

"Yes."

"When?"

"Probably tonight."

"Good. Well look, what we really want to know is, (a) who the local contact is, who gets these people across. I'm surprised this should have happened—he's supposed to be so immensely efficient. Have you got anything on him?"

Colin, quite wrongly from the official point of view, hedged. "I'm working on that" he said. "The whole place is crawling with smugglers. But H., you could perhaps help by telling me one thing—are this pair, whose names you seem familiar with, Cs—or members of the fifteenth, first, and nineteenth letters of the alphabet?"

"Oh, the latter."

"I see. And what's your question (b)?"

"Had they anything—well, active—on them?"

"The one who fell can't have, or it would have gone up with him, wouldn't it? Anyhow his knapsack was very light."

"Can you check on the young one's knapsack?—or have you?"

"No—no chance. I'll try."

"You should really do that" Hartley said. "It's quite important to know whether they bring the doings in with them, or pick them up somewhere—well, closer home. What a piece of luck your running into this pair where you did!"

"I'll try" Colin repeated. "That all?"

"No—one other thing. Are the bobbies of our gallant allies in on this?"

"Only to the extent that they have a man sitting by the old boy's bed in case he becomes able to speak—and that they found his passport, with his name and address—that's how I got it."

"Funny, that" Hartley said—"using his own papers. Well, check on that other *rücksack*"—this time he purposely used the German word—"and give me a ring."

Colin paid the ancient porter for this expensive call, and then went and ate his supper; afterwards he drove back, through Ste.-Marie, and up the wide grey road towards the pass; then up the final hair-pin bends, all the while thinking hard and rather uncomfortably. Colin was a Highlander, and sometimes had curious instincts about people which had often, in the past, proved correct; such an instinct he had, very strongly, about Bonnecourt—that somehow he had an important place in his, Colin's, own life, as well as in relation to his job, and that it was exceedingly important to keep on good terms with him. But was this in conflict with his plain duty? It was on a sudden impulse that he had told Bonnecourt, at the little inn, to take the young man back to Larège instead of down to Pau; but by this action he had already committed himself to being less than truthful with the *agent* at the hospital. His later conversation with Hartley on the telephone had brought his obligations to his service back into the forefront of his mind, and he felt a certain disrelish for his coming interview with young de Lassalle.

He drove first to the little car-space, and turned and locked his car—better to go down to the hunter's house on foot. Luzia heard him; she came up the steps and along the path, calling "Colin! Where do you go?"

"I want to meet someone at Barraterre's. Why?"

"There is something I must tell you—it is very peculiar."

"Well hurry up" the young man said impatiently; he wanted to get this worrying interview over, and go to bed.

"Sit" Luzia said, perching on the wall above the path; reluctantly Colin did so.

"This evening before supper I went to the farm to fetch the milk" the girl began; "and as I crossed the *Place* I see this young Frenchman, whom you took down to Pau, driving through with Monsieur Bonnecourt, in *his* car! This I found very odd—why does he not stay in Pau with his injured friend? And why does this Bonnecourt know him?"

"Look, Luzia, I'm late already. Do let's leave all this till afterwards" Colin said, embarrassed.

"No, you must know now—you might meet Bonnecourt. There is more."

"Well go ahead" Colin said resignedly—"only cut it as short as you can."

"This farm where I get the milk is on that path above

Bonnecourt's house; a little beyond, so that from it one looks over the dam and the pool. They were late with the milk, so I waited outside—and what do I see?"

"Well, what *did* you see?" Colin asked boredly, still vexed by the delay.

"This young Frenchman coming out of Monsieur Bonnecourt's house, in bathing-dress!—and carrying a knapsack in his hand. And he went down to the pool, to the upper end, and left the knapsack on the bank, and went in and swam about, as anyone might do. But then he swam back to the bank, and reached up from the water, and started taking things out of the knapsack and putting them in the water— not dropping them, but *placing* them on the bottom—gently, gently, with great precautions."

Now Luzia had Colin's full attention.

"Could you see what sort of things?" he asked.

"Some rather small packages; but there was a sort of canvas case, such as one carries a camera in, and also a roll, I thought, of this yellow electric wire—do you call it flex? From the canvas case he took a metal thing that shone in the sun; it looked like a clock; he put a stone in the case, to keep it under water, then put back the clock also."

"Then what did he do?"

"Got out, and dried himself on his towel, and picked up the knapsack and rolled it in the towel, and put all under his arm, and went back to the house. So the knapsack must have been empty, or nearly! Was this not odd?"

"It looks odd, certainly" Colin said. "Thank you very much, Luzia."

"What did I tell you?" the girl said. "These are *saboteurs*, and since their plans had gone wrong, he was disposing of their explosives, *I* say!"

"Well don't *say* anything about it. It might be important, or it might not. Could you recognise the exact spot, where he put the things into the pool, again?"

"Yes. If I stood outside the farm, where I stood this evening, I could see it, and take you to it."

"Well don't speak of it to anyone else" Colin repeated.

"I have told Julia."

"Oh, Julia doesn't matter—she never talks." He looked at his watch. "I must be off. Thank you, Luzia."

He went down to Bonnecourt's, but now walking slowly, and thoughtfully. It looked as though what Luzia had seen might enable him to answer Hartley's second question, if he could get to the place at daybreak, before Bonnecourt or anyone else removed what had been placed in the pool—if they did remove it. Goodness, that Portuguese girl was a sharp one! But it also gave him another possible hold on Bonnecourt, and much as he liked the man, he wanted to use all the levers in his power to extract from him what he needed to know.

At Bonnecourt's, over cognac, Colin opened with a very mild talk with the young man. Yes, he had been to the hospital, and spoken with the surgeon. "Your poor old friend is very ill; they are not sure that he will survive." The young man looked distressed; Colin expressed sympathy. Then he fired his first shot. "But the police are waiting by his bed, in case he should recover consciousness, and be able to speak."

The young man blanched at this.

"The police? Why? They do not know his name!"

Oh *what* a fool, Colin thought.

"*Voyons, mon ami,* naturally they looked for, and found, his papers—all authorities do this when an injured man is brought into a hospital; the first thing they wish to know is the name. Monsieur de Maupassant's was on his passport, with his Paris address, in full." As he said this Colin shot a glance at Bonnecourt, and caught a fleeting expression of dismayed astonishment. H'm. *Two* incompetents, and Bonnecourt not best pleased at being saddled with such! But now the young man's state demanded their attention; he looked quite distraught, and began to babble confusedly: "But—but . . ." Bonnecourt got up and put a hand on his shoulder.

"If Monsieur Monnro will excuse you, I think you had better go to bed" he said, with a questioning glance at Colin. Colin got up too.

"But of course. Monsieur must be quite *énervé.* I wish I could have brought better news of his friend," he said courteously.

When Bonnecourt returned after taking the young man upstairs, he refilled both their glasses with cognac before sitting down again. "That was kind" he said then, looking rather hard at his guest. "I think you are kind, though I do not know why." He paused. "There is much I do not know that I should wish to know" he added.

Colin could guess some of the things that Bonnecourt wished to know: whether he, Colin, was working for anyone, and if so, whether it was for the English or the French? But he realised that his host was far too good a poker-player to let this appear to begin with.

"Ask away" he said cheerfully. With what he had learned from Hartley, plus Luzia's information, he felt in a fairly strong position. Bonnecourt reflected before he spoke. At last—

"Why did you make it a condition that you should speak with this young man before he returns to Spain, and then ask him no questions, when I hold him here for you? I could have had him across the frontier hours ago, but for this."

"He didn't seem to me to be fit to answer many questions just now, he was so upset; and anyhow I have managed to learn some of the answers already" Colin replied, coolly.

"Kind again!" Bonnecourt said, this time sarcastically. "May I know what questions you wished to put to him, if he had been less upset?"

"Oh, various things," Colin replied casually. "I *had* rather wanted to look at his knapsack."

"It is in his room—I will fetch it" Bonnecourt said, getting up.

"Don't bother—I know now that de Lassalle has emptied it already."

There was no mistaking Bonnecourt's start at this statement.

"How do you come to know his name?" he asked.

"I learned it in Pau, this evening."

"From the police?"

"I'm not telling you how I learned it, at present" Colin said.

"Very well." Bonnecourt paused. "But what makes you think he emptied it, and of what contents? Or are you not telling me that either?"

"Not *how* I learned it. I gather that among the contents were parcels, probably of explosives, a roll of flex, and a time-clock" Colin said airily.

"But this is fantastic!" Bonnecourt exploded. "Do you keep spies here?" he asked angrily.

"*Doucement, mon cher.* Of course not" Colin said pacifically. "But surely you have not lived so long in Larège without knowing that everyone sees everything? It is their great resource, to watch the activities of their neighbours."

Bonnecourt was not pacified. "But these details!" He checked himself. "Not that I admit them" he added—"villagers invent. But—you have had little time to make enquiries! You only drove up from Pau forty minutes ago."

Colin laughed.

"You see! You know to the minute when I came back!" In fact the upper loops of the hair-pin bends were visible from Bonnecourt's house. The hunter laughed too, though a little reluctantly.

"*Touché!* In fact I know the note of your English car's engine." He paused, obviously considering his next move in this game of poker. "Still" he said presently, "all this is very peculiar. What I particularly wish to know—you told me just now to 'ask away'—is why you suggested that I should bring de Lassalle back here, and let him get away into Spain? You have professed to know what he came to do, and stated that your country objected to it. So why let him go, when he was practically in your hands? You must know, 'ordinary Englishman'!"—he shot the two words out with sarcastic emphasis—"how much the French authorities desire to capture all such. So for what reason?"

Colin hardly paused.

"Well, he's no good, anyhow" he said. "I never thought the O.A.S. employed such silly dopes; he'd have been caught in any case. But the real reason"—now he did pause.

"Yes? The real reason?" Bonnecourt asked, urgently.

"You. Once you'd met him at the spot so dottily marked on his map, you were likely to be involved too, especially as he's such a fool."

"And why should you wish to spare me from being involved?"

"Because—as I told you before—I am English, and I've heard what you did for our people in the last War, getting them across into Spain. Not only the old Smiths—lots of others."

"How did you hear this? Ah, I suppose from the old Heriots, Milord and Milady." He looked more relaxed; he got up, filled their glasses again, and lit a Gauloise. "I do not offer you these—I know you dislike them." Colin lit a Player.

"Well, this is a reason of a sort" Bonnecourt went on. "In fact individual citizens of *perfide Albion* are apt to repay their debts rather generously." He blew out smoke. "I am grateful to you, naturally—it would not suit me very well to be *affiché* by the police with the O.A.S. Over them, at present, the officials create far more trouble than over *les Communistes*. I will give this poor inept another hour to recover himself, and then I will get him away."

"Hadn't I better go, and let you also get a little quiet?" Colin said, rising.

"No—I am never tired! Let us talk; unless *you* are tired?"

"I often am, but not tonight" Colin said. "*Très-bien*—let us talk."

Chapter 5

In fact Colin Monro was distinctly tired. He had been on the go since 6 A.M., walking, climbing, carrying a human body for miles in a blanket, driving his car—and perpetually using his wits: asking questions, making rapid decisions about how best to use the last piece of information he had picked up in the next interview; listening to his inner Highland monitor, and weighing that advice against the claims of his professional duty. It had been a strenuous day, mentally and physically; he was quite tired enough to feel the prospect of another long conversation in French, well as he spoke it, a little daunting. But to find Bonnecourt suddenly so ready to talk was a chance too good to be missed—he was still strongly under the impression, that had come to him as he drove up from Pau, that the *isard*-hunter was not only a key figure in connection with his present mission, but of great importance in his own life in some way not yet clear to him. He sat down again, sipped at his brandy, and then put a question to his host—partly out of personal curiosity.

"Bonnecourt, why do you trouble to help the O.A.S., when it's such a risky business for you? After all France is in rather a better position in the world since de Gaulle came to power than she has been for years; and *he* has done it. So why try to assassinate him? Or to blow up Lacq, come to that?—one of your great economic assets. I don't quite get the idea. Don't answer if you don't want to, of course" he added. "But I should like to understand."

"I should very much like you to understand" Bonnecourt said. "I will try to explain, though you may find the story—don't you say 'long-winded' and 'round-about'?"

"How well you must know English!" Colin said. "All right —be as long-winded and round-about as you like."

"Well, I told you that I had been in the Army" Bonnecourt said—Colin nodded. "For a long time I was in Indo-China, where I, like scores of my countrymen, spent much of our time trying to train the local troops, with remarkably little success—they remained a cowardly and undisciplined rabble, whatever we did. When the Viet-minh started to fight us, we found that *they*, the Communists, had produced, out of the very same human material, highly-trained, orderly, and disciplined troops, who fought extremely well. This was a shock, as you can imagine—it struck right at the roots of my instincts as a soldier, and I began to wonder what it was that they had got, which we had not. The *same* people," he repeated, "fighting badly for us, and well for them."

"Yes, that must have been worrying" Colin said. "What conclusion did you reach as to the reason?"

"At first I thought it was perhaps some sickness, or weakness, in our nation; after all, the events of 1940 were not very encouraging to Frenchmen!" Bonnecourt said, with a wry smile. "Then, later, I was taken prisoner by the Viet-minh; partly my own fault; this dysentery was beginning—and make no mistake, *mon ami*, quite as much as of the body, dysentery is a disease of the will!"

"Did they nurse you decently?" Colin asked, much interested.

"According to their resources, and after their ideas. They have great faith in boiled millet as a specific against dysentery" Bonnecourt said, again with that wry smile. "Often there was not much millet, so then they gave me rice— medically, without great success."

"How ghastly!" Colin said. He wished he could envisage the circumstances better, but didn't wish to interrupt Bonnecourt's narrative with too many questions. "Do go on."

"Well, with their usual attention to detail they also subjected me to a fairly thorough indoctrination—day after day, hour after hour. I have told you, *la dysenterie* weakens the will as much as the body, and I was in a poor state to resist this treatment; without my wish, or deliberate acceptance, my outlook towards Communism altered. And there was the extraordinary success that they had had in training the *indigènes*, turning them into decent troops, as we had failed to do—a thing I had seen for myself."

Colin was rather aghast at this.

"Did you become a Communist?" he asked.

"I was too ill to become anything!—except a corpse, which I nearly did! Then after the truce I was exchanged, and came back to France, and was invalided out of the Army. But I was disillusioned."

"But how did this experience—it must have been frightful—lead you to the O.A.S.?" Colin asked.

"Again by a long and round-about road. When *le Général* assumed power again we remembered what he had done—with British help!—during the War, and were full of hope of better things. But then one disillusionment followed another: the war in Algeria was not carried out as it should have been, and *could* have been, given our troops! I think most soldiers felt that this *sacré* settlement was a sort of betrayal, not only of the *colons*—who after all had created such economic prosperity as Algeria possessed—but of the Army, which had fought there for so long."

"But wasn't the Algerian war bleeding France white? I mean, I see that it was wretched for the *colons*, but could you have gone on indefinitely?"

Bonnecourt threw up both his hands in a despairing gesture.

"If this war had been prosecuted with real vigour, *from the top*, who knows? But we sensed a lack of resolution, a hesitation, long before Evian. We felt betrayed" the French officer repeated.

"So then you decided to support the O.A.S.?" Colin asked. "Of course that started in Algeria, didn't it?"

"Certainly. And I felt that this movement deserved support; it might have given the—do you say 'stiffening'?—that was required to win. *Enfin*, my friend, I am a patriot!—I would do anything to save France." He paused; Colin thought he had finished, but he was wrong. "But of course" Bonnecourt pursued—and then stopped.

"Yes?" No reply. "Of course what?" Colin persisted.

"These murders began, in the hospitals!—and elsewhere. That I could not approve; for a long time I held my hand. One should not murder helpless people in their beds."

"I should think not" Colin said, with energy. These mental gymnastics of an O.A.S. supporter he found hard to follow, though he could sympathise over the intractable problem which Algeria had presented to France. He had himself been in Morocco before the French left, and had seen the superb work they had done for that other North African country before it insisted on its independence. Goodness how tiresome, and how ungrateful, these emerging nations were!— biting the hands that fed them, developed them, educated them; that poured out money, skill, and devoted service, only to be ejected with contumely in the end.

"Well, did you turn Communist then?" he asked.

"Very nearly! One turns from one creed to another, seeking the one that will best serve one's country." Bonnecourt paused. "But recently, I came to the decision that the O.A.S. was probably of the most value to our country" he said.

Colin wondered privately how blowing up Lacq would really serve France, but he left that aside.

"Do you help Communists across the frontier now too?" he asked, almost gaily, as Bonnecourt got up and refilled their glasses; after two cognacs he felt rather less tired.

"My friend, for a reasonable sum I help *anyone* across the frontier. After all, one must live. But the English pay best— and for longer."

Colin stared at him.

"May I know what you mean? Did you ask money from all these Royal Air Force"—he used the full French phrase— "men whom you led to safety?"

"But naturally not; I took them as they came. They were in need. But presently I was employed by the British Intelligence Service" he said, looking amusedly at Colin—whose face, at this startling statement, completely gave him away.

"Ah! So the 'ordinary Englishman' is connected with Intelligence! No wonder he is so well-informed" Bonnecourt said merrily. "Doubtless he telephoned to London this afternoon from Pau, and learned much. Certainly it was not old Four-get who told you de Lassalle's name."

Colin took his time. "Are you still on the pay-roll of Intelligence?" he asked at length.

"This I too am not telling *you*, just now! But had we not better be a little more frank with one another? You have helped me; I should wish to help you. After all, in a sense we are colleagues, or have been."

But Colin's ingrained caution had taken the upper hand again; he did not wish to go too far with Bonnecourt until he had had the chance to check with Hartley as to the hunter's present status with Intelligence. However he did not hesitate.

"I always prefer frankness" he said. "What do you want me to be frank with you about?"

"Had you advance information that these two would be coming over from Spain? Were you sent up to look out for them?"

Checking on Pamplona, Colin thought!—but this was plain sailing.

"Definitely *not*" he said. "I was simply taking one of my walks to get an idea of the frontier—and of course keeping an eye open for the paths you and your fellow-smugglers find so useful—probably with *heavy* knapsacks!" He grinned at Bonnecourt, who grinned back at him. "I came up on this side, as I think I told you, by the path they ought to have taken, and saw them on the Spanish slope; I traversed across to get a good look at them, and so I came to see the old man fall. You know the rest."

Bonnecourt was silent for a moment.

"Is he actually dying?" he asked then.

"The surgeon didn't go quite as far as that. But if I were you, Bonnecourt, I should waste no time about getting that idiot de Lassalle away. If Maupassant were to come round enough to be able to speak, and the police come up here and find that silly fool, you'll be in for trouble."

"I take him tonight."

"Good. Then I don't think I'd better delay you" Colin said, getting up.

"No—*un petit moment*—and a little more frankness!" Colin sat down again.

"What am I to be frank about this time?" he asked, smiling.

"I have reflected" Bonnecourt said, rather slowly. "You are right in saying that the villagers here amuse themselves by watching all that goes on; but I have the best reasons for knowing that what they report is seldom at all detailed, or clear."

Colin guessed what was coming.

"I suppose you really mean accurate" he said, a little trenchantly—"though you don't want to use the word." Bonnecourt laughed.

"Monro, you are fully up to standard! Yes, I mean that." "*Alors?*"

"So was it *la belle Portugaise* who described to you the contents of this young simpleton's knapsack? I know that she comes up in the evening to fetch the milk for Madame your sister from the farm above this house, and she is almost the only person you had time to speak with."

Colin thought fast. He realised that he had perhaps been injudicious in saying quite so much, earlier, about de Lassalle's performance at the pool, though it had undoubtedly brought results.

"Look, let's do a deal" he said. "We'd each rather like to help the other, but we both have our job to do. If I undertake not to ring up and alert the police, either on this side, or in Spain, will you guarantee not to have all that stuff fished out of the pool and disposed of elsewhere?"

"Why must it be left?'"

"Because I want to see it."

"And of course report?"

"But naturally. What I don't propose to report, locally anyhow, is who was meeting these two types, and going to drive them on to—well, where they hoped to use what they brought!"

"*Entendu.* Only local reports would inconvenience me— London is far away! So it was *la Portugaise?*"

"Just a second. There's one other thing I'd like to know first." Ever since he heard Luzia's story one part of Colin's mind had been fidgeting about the canvas camera-case which the girl had described—why have something so elaborate merely to carry a time-clock in?—it could easily have been wrapped in a handkerchief. He had a vague, hovering notion that this might have some significance for him.

"Well?"

"What exactly is the purpose of the canvas case that the time-clock was being carried in?"

Bonnecourt grinned broadly.

"*Quelle astuce!* It is a gas-mask container." He grinned more broadly than ever at Colin's expression when he brought out this statement. "I see that this explains itself! Now, when do you wish to conduct your search in the pool?"

"Early tomorrow—'first light', as our Transatlantic allies say. So I really must get to bed now." He got up. "Do remember that I've spent most of today succouring O.A.S. personnel!"

Bonnecourt gave a rather sardonic smile.

"And doing a little long-distance telephoning, and ascertaining some useful facts. Not a wasted day! But was it *la Portugaise* who saw de Lassalle?"

"Yes, it was."

"Ah. You should employ her! Well, tell me when you have seen all you need to see, *cher collègue!*—for I cannot leave all that dangerous stuff in such a public place."

"I'll do that" Colin said. "Thanks for the drinks, Bonnecourt." He left.

On his way home Colin considered what he had heard. Bonnecourt had been right in surmising that the words "a gas-mask container" had rung a bell in his head; his mind went back to that room in the office in London, where the grey-haired clerk had given him some briefing about Lacq, as well as the notes on frontier characters. For many sections of the great plant the workers had to wear gas-masks, carried in canvas cases; the sight of these of course aroused no suspicion, and it had already happened at least once that the nerve-centre at Lacq—the narrow, but immensely long control-room, with instruments registering all the different gas-wells—had been damaged by explosives brought in by *saboteurs* in gas-mask holders. How stupid of him!—he ought to have guessed at once what Luzia's "camera-case" was. But why had Bonnecourt told him this? What an enigma the man was.

When he got in Colin went across the great room to the three stoves, and switched off the Buta-gaz from under the sauce-pan with his soup—most of it had boiled away. Then, very quietly, he stole upstairs; but in the sitting-room Julia was still up, in an armchair by the fire, knitting away at some baby-garment in white wool—the sight of her, so unusually occupied, smote him with almost a wave of love for his cousin. He went over and kissed her.

"You've had a long day" she said. "Whisky? It's there under the window."

Under Julia's régime at Larège whisky, so appallingly expensive in France, was reserved for "long days"—otherwise people had to make do with sherry or Vermouth. In spite of his cognacs with Bonnecourt Colin felt like a whisky, and a talk with Julia in the pleasant warmth of the wood fire, and the soft light of the lamp by which she was knitting—he poured himself out a glass. "Not for you?"

"No—bad for baby! How's that poor old creature?"

"I shouldn't be surprised if he's dead by now—they weren't very hopeful at the hospital."

"Why did the young one come back with Bonnecourt? I thought he was all set on being with his friend."

"Oh, so Luzia's told you she saw him? And about his goings-on at the pool, too?"

"Yes. Colin, I think her guess about them may be right."

"I know that it is—dead right!"

"Oh. Did you get on to London from Pau?"

"Yes. They knew about them." He went on to tell her how Bonnecourt had been waiting for the two Frenchmen at the *auberge,* and of his impulsive decision to get the young man taken back into Spain.

"So *that's* what he does! Has that silly creature gone?"

"I expect they're on their way now. But J., darling, I'm wondering if I did right?"

"What are they? Commies?—or O.A.S., as Luzia thinks?"

"Luzia always seems to be right! They *are* O.A.S. But you see I had a feeling that I didn't want Bonnecourt to get into trouble—which would certainly have happened if the police had contacted that dolt!" It was an immense relief to Colin to spread his problems out in front of Julia and get her views, which in the past had usually proved sound.

"It's a bit early to decide whether you did right or not" she said thoughtfully. "I wish we knew more about Bonnecourt —besides the Heriots liking him so much, and what he did for our people in the War. But sometimes one's hunches are right."

"I do know more. He told me tonight that he's been enrolled, and paid, by Intelligence."

Julia laughed, her long laugh.

"If that's true, it's really funny! And of course it would justify your hunch completely. But you'll have to check with London on that."

"I shall do that tomorrow. Another job first. Is Luzia in bed?"

"Yes—she went some time ago."

"Oh, well I shall have to rout her out early tomorrow— don't pay any attention to us. We'll be back for breakfast. Goodnight—bless you."

Colin went up the further flight to his room, took a shower, and got into bed; he set his immensely powerful alarm-watch for 4.45 A.M., put it on the little bed-table, and switched off the light—almost immediately he fell asleep.

Being roused by the alarm next morning from his heavy and exhausted slumbers felt like having the living heart torn out of his body; but he went downstairs in his pyjamas, and tapped on Luzia's door.

"*Entra*" a sleepy voice muttered—he went in.

"Could you get up and dress, and come down with me to the farm? I want to check on all that stuff before people are about."

"Of course. In ten minutes I am ready." She switched on her bedside lamp—Colin noted with approval that the girl didn't sleep with her face smothered in cream; her beautiful pale skin was its natural self, her long black hair spread out over the pillow.

Day was just breaking as they left the house; the light strengthened as they walked through the sleeping village; by the time they reached the farm one could see fairly clearly.

"You stay here" Colin said, as Luzia stood and stared at the pool. "Tell me where to go—and then you can signal: right arm if I'm to go right, left if left."

"To the far end. Do you see a small clump of rushes? About a metre beyond that is the spot."

Colin walked down to the pool, rolled up his shirt-sleeves to the shoulder, and lying flat on the grass reached down into the water and felt about—he could touch the bottom, but felt nothing but mud. He looked back at Luzia; her right arm was extended like a sign-post. He edged along the turf, his hand still exploring in the water; presently his fingers felt the roll of flex—he pulled this out, looked at it, and put it back. Next he found some small packages; these too he looked at and replaced. What he wanted was the clock, and at last his searching fingers found it; he drew it out, rinsed off the mud, and put it in his pocket. The gas-mask container he couldn't find, but that didn't matter—the Office would know all about those already.

"This is all you bring?" Luzia asked when he rejoined her.

"Yes—I've got the important thing. We know about the rest."

Larège was slowly coming awake as they walked back. Troops of cows were moving deliberately up towards the pastures; men with scythes over their shoulders were setting out to cut the year's second crop of hay in their tiny fields— with the strong Pyrenean sun they would make it and cock it in forty-eight hours. The pair brewed coffee in the big room, and ate the crusty bread with appetite—then Colin went back to bed and had two more hours sleep before, again roused by his alarm-watch, he drove down to Pau.

He went first to the hospital, where he learned from an- other, younger house-surgeon that old Maupassant had died in the night without recovering consciousness. But if this was the *Monsieur Écossais* who had witnessed the accident, the surgeon said, he believed the police wished to interview him. Colin said he would look in on them.

"I think they go up to Larège to see Monsieur."

"Oh well, that is all right—I am returning."

But he did not hurry over his return. Julia and Luzia could be counted on to give nothing away, or be in the least indiscreet—cast-iron witnesses, both of them! He drove to the Hotel de France and ordered, and ate, a second *petit déjeuner;* then he telephoned to London. Hartley was by now in the office—"Well, what about that *rücksack?*" he asked at once.

"Yes, they had some of the doings with them—flex, a clock, and a little of what else you might expect."

"Got this?"

"Got the ticker—I left the rest."

"And what about the type who acts as bear-leader?"

Colin spoke slowly and carefully. "You must be a bit clever about this. Have you got the old list of our helpers in this part of the world in the last war handy?"

"I've got it in my head" Hartley responded briskly. "I'm older than you!"

"Oh, fine. Well, pay attention. Was there a *good short* among them?"—he stressed the two words.

"Say that again."

"Good short."

There was a moment's pause—then a loud laugh came down the line, all the way from London to the Pyrenees "Oh, Bernardin! Yes, of course; the best of the lot! Why—you don't mean to say he's the one?"

Colin realised that Bernardin would be the code name used (as always) by Intelligence for real people.

"Yes. Is he still with us?"

"I'd have to check on that. I rather fancy so, on a small retainer basis." The laugh came down the line again, louder than ever. "Well, I'll be damned! The old bastard!" After a pause—"And what about the young one who came in too?"

"I lost sight of him—I think he must have slipped off" Colin replied, disingenuously. "The old fellow's dead."

"Did he tell the coppers anything?"

"No—he never spoke again."

"Oh well, that's all to the good" the man in London said heartlessly. "Have they been at you?"

"They're coming today, I gather—I ought really to get back to see them."

"All right. When are you going over to the other side? You might drop that time-piece on the boys at P.—they'll get it to us."

"Tomorrow, I thought." Colin understood that "P." meant Pamplona. "That all?" he asked.

"Yes, I think so. Jolly good show! Oh wait—one other item. Anything on Tarbes yet?"

"No, I've had no chance."

"Well have a look round when you get back. Write a report from P.—it'll be brought over." Another pause. "Damn B.!—the old rascal!" Hartley said. "Good enough. 'Bye."

When Colin got back to Larège he found that the police had called, and been dealt with as prudently as he expected. Julia had assured them that Monsieur Monro had made a full *constat* to the *agent* in the hospital the previous day, and asked if they had no record of it? Of course they had; and in her usual convincing fashion Julia had described the bringing down of the injured man: "We placed him on that sofa, where Messieurs are now sitting"—the police shifted uneasily in their seats. And Dr. Fourget had said he must be got into the hospital at once, and the young Monsieur Heriot had taken him in his so large car, where he could lie at full length. (At this point in her narrative Julia made a mental note that someone must ring up Dick and cause him to bring back the mattress and all those pillows and bolsters belonging to the Stansteds.) Oh, certainly—in reply to further questions—she had seen the younger man; he had seemed quite distracted! He too had driven off to Pau, but she could not say in which car—perhaps in the Doctor's, perhaps in that of her cousin.

"She was *mar*vellous" Luzia said to Colin, as Julia recounted all this. "So frank—and so untruthful!"

"What did *you* say?" Colin asked, grinning.

"Nothing—I left it to Julia! I pretended I did not understand French, and showed them my passport; this convinced them that I was just a foolish foreigner."

"Are they coming back?" Colin asked Julia.

"They didn't say so. They would have liked to get more on the young man, but unless they picked something up in the village they've got nothing to pin it onto Bonnecourt—and after all no one but us saw Lassalle, if that's his name, come here, and he drove away in your car. So lucky that this is the last house but one—no village spying." She paused, and glanced at Luzia. What could she say that she had left upstairs, and wanted fetched?

But for Luzia the glance was enough.

"I go to fetch some water" the girl said, and went out with the earthenware jug. Blessing her pupil's quickness—"*Was* B. working for us in the War?" Julia asked.

"Yes—when I said 'Good Short' Hartley knew at once. His code name was Bernardin."

"Then it *is* funny, after all" Julia said.

"So Hartley thought" Colin said. "He couldn't be sure without checking, but he seemed to think he might still be on the pay-roll."

"If he is, that's funnier still" Julia said. "You and he supposed to be working against one another!—and in fact chums, hand in glove—and you and I both protecting him from the lawful authorities of his own country."

"Well don't go *on* about it" Colin said, rather irritably—his official conscience still gnawed at him about the whole Bonnecourt business. He got up. "I'd better go down and try to see him—I promised to let him know when I'd seen all I wanted in that pool, so that he could clear the stuff away—though where one *stows* plastic in a village, I don't know."

"Bury it in the potato-patch under the beetles" Julia said, laughing, as he went out.

Colin found Bonnecourt in his sitting-room, drinking

brandy and soda—he looked hot, and rather tired; evidently he had only just got in.

"I just came to tell you that I've seen all I wanted to see, thank you" the Englishman said; "I'm surprised you're back so soon."

"I couldn't risk taking that neurotic fool over the mountains, with every *douanier* on the alert after the accident" Bonnecourt said. "I just put him in the *malle* of the car and drove him across to Jaca." He paused. "Did you take any of it?"

"Only the clock. You don't catch me going about weighed down with explosives" Colin said.

"You are perfectly right. Well, I thank you—you are very reliable, Monro! It can all stay where it is till tomorrow" Bonnecourt said, puffing at a Gauloise—"for me, I propose to get some rest! Will you have a drink?—excuse me that I do not suggest it before; I am half-asleep!"

"No, thanks. I must get back."

"What about old Maupassant?" Bonnecourt asked suddenly.

"He died in the night. Without speaking" Colin added.

The Frenchman crossed himself—Colin, Presbyterianly brought up, had a moment's cynical wonder whether this gesture was for the repose of the old man's soul, or in gratitude that he had not spoken. "The police came up to question me, but Mme. Jamieson satisfied them" he went on. "I don't think you ought to have any trouble. I was out."

"Ah. Down in Pau, telephoning, no doubt?"

"Exactly."

"And were you satisfied?"

"As to your identity, yes, *Bernardin!* But the rest—" Colin said. The hunter burst out laughing.

"Oh, how much I like the English!"

Colin ignored this. "Well, I'll say Goodbye—I'm off tomorrow."

"To England?"

"Perhaps. I'll be back in about a week." As Bonnecourt rose and wrung his hand he said, on a sudden impulse—"Keep an eye on Madame Jamieson while I'm away. If the season isn't over you might take her some more *isard;* she loves it."

"I do both these things. *Au revoir,* my friend."

Colin didn't hurry his departure the following morning; Pamplona was within a day's drive. So he was still in the house when the *facteur* brought the post—the only thing ever delivered in Larège. It included a letter from Lady Heriot to Julia, inviting all three of them to "a small dance" a week hence. "Of course you will all stay with us." Luzia was as excited as all nineteen-year-olds, however sophisticated, are at the prospect of a dance—"We say Yes, Julia, don't we?"

"Oh course we accept for you—how delightful. But I'm not sure that I want to trail down to Pau and sit up late—I can't dance at the moment, and I've no clothes for a party. You and Colin can go."

"I shan't go either" Colin said.

"But you will be back?" Luzia asked anxiously. "If Julia does not go, of course I will not leave her unless you are here."

"Yes, I'll be back all right, but I shouldn't be much good to Julia if I went off dancing—and anyhow I'm a rotten dancer."

"I daresay Mme. Monnier would come up and stay with me" Julia said. "Do accept if you'd like to, Colin."

But Colin refused firmly—and after he had driven off to Spain a visit to the Monniers produced the information that they, too, had been invited to the Heriot's dance, and had accepted. "A ball in this beautiful house—what a privilege!" Madame Monnier said. "Everything always done so perfectly—such food, such wine!" The Monniers were going to stay with friends in Pau for the event, and Mme. Monnier wished to go a day in advance to get a hair-do; they offered to drive Luzia down with them. Luzia wanted to have a shampoo and set too, and also to buy a frock—"You told me we should be in the wilderness!" she said reproachfully to Julia, who refrained from riposting that it was no fault of hers if Luzia mopped up peers' sons, and had balls given for her! Instead she walked down to the Post Office, and arranged on the telephone with Lady Heriot that the Portuguese girl should go to them a day earlier, to facilitate shopping and hair-dressing.

"My dear, I wish *you* would come" Lady Heriot said. Julia laughed.

"Dear Lady Heriot, I am *just* mobile—but with the mobility of the larger mammals. A cow wouldn't really grace your party!"

"My husband doesn't dance either—he was hoping that you would sit out with him."

"How sweet of him. But really I think better not."

"And your cousin won't come? Won't he be at Larège?"

"Oh yes—he'll be back by then. But he has nobly decided to stay and look after me" Julia said. "I wish he wouldn't; I should be quite all right. But he's not much of a dancing man, anyhow. So sorry. You *are* kind to let Luzia come earlier. Goodbye."

Chapter 6

Colin was only due back in the evening of the day on which Luzia and the Monniers drove down to Pau, an arrangement which slightly troubled Luzia. "Can you not telephone to him, and cause him to return a day sooner?" she had asked Julia a few days before—but in spite of Philip Jamieson's optimism, Colin had never given his cousin a telephone number. "Poste Restante, Pamplona" was all he had vouchsafed—"and don't write from here unless you have to; better not." Telegraphing to a Poste Restante seemed to Julia so silly as to be laughable; she laughed, and did nothing. "I shall be as right as rain, and he'll come" she said. Dick Heriot drove up one day, bringing back the pillows and mattress on which poor old de Maupassant had lain when he was taken down to the hospital to die; the young man was not best pleased to learn that Luzia was being taken to Pau by the Monniers—he had hoped to escort her himself. "Madame helps me to shop" Luzia told him. "Her Ladyship would have done that" Dick said, rather gruffly—he went away discomfited.

In spite of her qualms about leaving Julia alone, even for a day, Luzia thoroughly enjoyed her shopping in Pau. It is in fact an excellent shopping centre; the Portuguese girl was surprised to find such good shops in such *minute* streets— and whenever they felt tired, or in doubt, there were constant pauses for rest and coffee under the clipped trees on the big *Place* outside the Hotel de France. Mme. Monnier, with true French carefulness, would not allow the stranger to buy anything in a hurry; they went to shop after shop. Eventually Luzia settled on a white dress with full filmy skirts, glittering with *diamanté*—but the bodice was too low, she said; it must be pinched in, and layers of tulle added.

"I find it charming as it is" Mme. Monnier said.

"Not for me—and Papa would be horrified!"

They had lunch, and then again wandered through the small streets in pursuit of accessories—sandals, cobwebby stockings, an evening bag and long white kid gloves. Mme. Monnier protested over this last item. "They cost a fortune, and it is no longer *de rigueur* to wear them at balls." "I always wear them" the Duke of Ericeira's daughter said with finality.

Dick had succeeded in arranging that he should at least pick Luzia up at the France at 6.30 and drive her home, and this he did; he eagerly agreed to take her in for her shampoo and set next morning, and to collect the frock after its alterations. And there was most of tomorrow, and tomorrow night too! The young man had really few anxieties as he drove this marvellous being back to meet his parents: her beauty, her rank, her pretty though slightly foreign English—even His Lordship was bound to approve. In fact, over drinks before dinner, Lord Heriot succumbed completely; Luzia's preference for sherry rather than a cocktail sealed his approval. "That's a very nice, well-bred girl" he said to his wife, as they were dressing for dinner. "D'you think she might become a Protestant? That's the only thing against her."

"No, I'm sure she wouldn't" Lady Heriot said, combing out and re-doing her long, greying hair in front of her dressing-table. "R.C.s never do. What's more, if Dick were to marry her I'm positive that she and her Father would insist on all the children being brought up as Catholics."

"Good God! Would they really? Why?"

"Oh, that's one of their rules" Lady Heriot said, pushing silvery combs carefully into place behind various puffs and curls on her head. "You'd better face it, James."

Lord Heriot pondered.

"Don't care about it much" he said. "Romans!" He reflected again. "Still de Gaulle's a Roman Catholic, and he's the best man this country's got. I suppose it might be all right." He came over to his wife. "Put these damned studs in for me, dear, would you? Cursed things!"

Lady Heriot swung round on her dressing-stool, and adjusted the fastenings of her husband's shirt.

"Thank you. What do *you* think of her?" he asked then.

"It's hard to tell, with anyone so beautiful. But on the whole I'm inclined to think she's *good*—and that's all that matters."

While the old Heriots, down in Pau, were comparing their assessments of Luzia, up at Larège Julia was getting supper. She made enough for two, but there was no sign of Colin; rather late, she ate her own, and made and drank coffee. When at ten her cousin had still not turned up she decided to go to bed; unworried, she put the heavy key of the big farm door under a tile below the stone seat on the little terrace, and wrote a note in Spanish, which she stuck into the huge key-hole, to say where it was. Then she went up to bed. She felt heavy with the weight of the child within her, and a little tired after the unwonted exertion of getting supper and doing the washing-up alone, but with her usual composure she read a psalm in bed, said her prayers, lay down and slept well.

Next morning on her way up to the top bathroom to wash she looked into Colin's room—it was empty. Oh well, something must have held him up. Still unworried, she returned to her room, dressed, and went downstairs and put on the coffee. The note was still in the key-hole of the big door; she took it away, and retrieved the key from under the tile. She ate her breakfast indoors—though it was a beautiful morning, somehow she didn't feel inclined even to carry a tray out onto the terrace. After breakfast she washed up, put on a *garbure* for the evening, peeled enough potatoes for two meals—there was cold veal—and washed some salad and put it in a damp cloth in the frig. Then she settled down on the sofa and began to write a letter to her Philip. Goodness, she *was* tired!—how Luzia had spoiled her, doing all the work. Anyhow Colin was bound to return today.

When the letter was three-parts written Julia remembered *la poubelle;* in fact she could smell it faintly, and decided that she must take it up and empty it. There was not a lot in it, Luzia had dealt with it before she left—only the potato-peelings, the outer leaves of the lettuce and the cabbage and onions for the *garbure*, tea-leaves and coffee-grounds. All the same it seemed quite heavy as she carried it up the stony path to the place where rubbish was pitched down the hill-side; the sun was already hot, and the heap of refuse on the slope smelt very disagreable; it made her feel a little sick. She walked back to the house; going down the very steep and uneven steps onto the terrace, bucket in hand, she stumbled and fell. It was not very far, only the last four steps, but the fall shook her. She picked herself up and carried the *poubelle* into the house, where she set it in the sink and turned the tap on to rinse it—there a curious pain overtook her. She turned off the tap and went back to the sofa, and tried to finish her letter to Philip, but somehow she couldn't concentrate. The pain wasn't severe, it was just a dull nagging *malaise;* how silly! It couldn't be the baby; that wasn't due for another two months. Perhaps she had better have a drink—it was after twelve; she got up and fetched a sherry over to the sofa. But when it was there on the table beside her she kept on forgetting to drink it; all her faculties seemed numbed by a sort of vagueness and dimness.

How long she remained there she didn't really know; she was roused by the smell of something beginning to burn. She got up—it was the *garbure;* she poured a jug of hot water into the saucepan, and lowered the gas under it and the potatoes. She looked at her watch—two o'clock. Why *didn't* Colin come? She remembered that she hadn't laid the table, and tried to do that, but she kept on forgetting things—she was in a sort of mental cloud, only consciously listening all the time for the sound of the car. Eventually she gave it up and went back to the sofa, where after one or two sips she again forgot to drink her sherry. She abandoned the idea of lunch too—she didn't feel like eating; with a great effort she managed to put the veal and the salad back into the frig, and turned the gas out, finally, under the saucepans.

The slight but persistent pains went on, and at last Julia suspected that she must be in labour, prematurely—perhaps because of her fall. Oh, *why* hadn't Colin come?—and what was she to do? Philip was so longing for this child; she must let it be born safely. She decided, by a great effort of will overcoming this curious mental numbness, that she must get down to the Post Office and ring up Dr. Fourget at Labielle; he would come and arrange something. She set out, up the steps and along the path—but when she reached the car-turn another slight pain came on, and once again the vagueness overtook her; she sat down on the low wall, almost unable to remember why she had come.

The woman from the next house to the Stansteds' happened to be coming out onto the path, and saw Julia, slumped on the wall; she stopped and asked if she was all right? Julia looked at her vaguely, and for a moment did not answer; this worried her neighbour more than any actual signs of labour. "Has Madame *douleurs?*" she asked, giving Julia's shoulder a little shake.

"Un peu" Julia replied then, still looking vacant.

The sensible peasant, who had borne many children herself, and helped still more into the world, realised that something was seriously amiss here—in normal labour women might cry and howl, but this curious remoteness, vacancy, betokened something different.

"Has Madame telephoned to the Doctor?"

"No. No, I am on my way to do this" Julia said, hesitantly.

"I will do this for Madame—if Madame will write the message, and give me the money, I shall take it to the *Bureau de Poste.* Now Madame should return to the house; I help her." And the good woman led Julia back and down the steps, and replaced her on the sofa. "Where is this foreign friend of Madame, who stays and helps her?" Like all the Larègeois, the neighbour knew all about Luzia.

"She is gone to Pau" Julia said, speaking very slowly—even speaking was an effort. She took up the block on which she had been writing her letter to Philip, tore off the half-finished sheet, and carefully printed out, in block capitals, a message in French for Dr. Fourget: "I am ill—I shall be grateful if you will come as soon as you can." Mercifully she had her purse beside her; she gave the neighbour the note and the money, and then relapsed again into that clouded consciousness.

In fact her well-meaning neighbour didn't take the message to the Post Office herself, she gave it to one of her older children; but the child met friends on the way, and went off on some frolic—it was only three hours later that she came home, and reported that the Postmistress had left the message at Dr. Fourget's house, as he was out. Julia spent most of those three hours in a sort of dulled drowsiness, only aware of the slight, but somehow *heavy* pain. She wished her aspirins were not upstairs, but she couldn't face the climb to get them; instead she made some coffee, and drank that—this roused her a little, and she looked at her watch. Goodness, it was nearly seven!—why on earth didn't Fourget come? And what *could* have happened to Colin?

Now she began to get frightened. She lit a cigarette, and told herself to take it easy; she was just considering whether she should make another attempt to get at least as far as the inn and telephone from there when a figure appeared, silhouetted against the sunset sky, in the big doorway.

"Madame Jimmison?" a voice called.

"Who is that?"

"*C'est moi*—Bonnecourt."

"Oh, thank God!" Julia exclaimed. "*Entrez.*"

The hunter walked into the big room. "I bring Madame some *isard*" he began—but stopped short as he approached the sofa, and saw Julia's face, blanched and drawn. "Madame is ill?" he asked.

"I'm afraid so. I fell, and I think perhaps the child is coming prematurely" Julia said. "Do have some sherry—it is on the big table" she added; but then she began to feel vague again.

"Madame has sent for the Doctor?"

"Yes—at least Madame from next door said she would telephone for me. But he hasn't come."

"I see to this. I will get my car, and fetch Fourget, if he doesn't reply to the telephone." He went over, felt the coffee percolator, now cool, and peered inside; there was plenty in it, he plugged it in again, and rinsed out Julia's cup in the sink—then he brought her a fresh, hot cup. "Let Madame drink that—I fetch my car. I return very soon." He went out.

It was some time before he returned. Having fetched his car he first telephoned to Fourget, who was out; he bullied the Doctor's house-keeper into giving him various possible numbers, and tried them all, in vain—he rang back to the Doctor's house and left an urgent message that he was to come to Larège at once when he got in: *"La maison de Stansted."* In his absence Julia drank her coffee; she felt enormously comforted by Bonnecourt's arrival—now at last there was *someone* who would do something. Actually Bonnecourt did quite a lot when he came back. He asked when she had last eaten?

"At breakfast—I haven't felt hungry since. But there are things on the stove and in the frig" Julia said—she couldn't remember what they were. "Do have something," she added. Bonnecourt looked into the saucepans on the stove, glanced into the frig, and took some eggs and milk out of it. "Madame has some cognac?"

"I think so—it should be on the big table."

Bonnecourt found the brandy—deftly he broke three eggs into a bowl, and set a pan of milk on the gas; while it warmed he beat up the eggs with a fork, and poured the warmed milk onto them, adding brandy and sugar; he strained the mixture into a jug, found a glass, and gave a tumbler-ful to Julia.

"Now drink this" he said.

Julia obeyed, again immensely comforted. How clever he was!—the egg-flip was something she really could take. "This is delicious" she said. "But do please eat yourself—I am so sorry I can't get it for you."

"Ne vous inquietez pas, Madame—I will eat, with *remerciments."* He got out the veal and salad (prepared in vain for Colin's lunch) from the frig, and ate them at the partly-laid table; he found the bread and wine without being told where to look for them, from time to time refilling Julia's tumbler—"You should finish this, Madame." Julia did finish it; she still felt the dull pains, and the curious clouded dimness of everything, but with Bonnecourt there she was

no longer so frightened or anxious. The hunter however was anxious; while he rinsed out the percolator and prepared fresh coffee he glanced at his watch. This woman was in a grave condition; *ce maudit* Fourget!—why didn't he come?

In fact it was after 9.30 when Fourget turned up; Bonnecourt heard his car, and went out to meet him. The Doctor came in, washed his hands at the sink, took vaseline out of his little bag, and made a cursory examination; after washing his hands again he asked Julia how long the pains had been going on?

"Oh—well for some time; I'm not really sure when they began—it was after I fell."

Fourget asked about the fall, but briefly; then he led Bonnecourt outside.

"It is a labour, but it is a false presentation" he said worriedly. "The child cannot be born naturally; it will mean an operation. She must go to Professor Martin at once; his clinic is at Pau. He is a great expert—but there is no time to lose. Who will take her? And it would be wise to advise the clinic that she comes."

"I take her" Bonnecourt said. "Do you inform the clinic, please."

"I do this—and I will come myself, naturally, after I have telephoned. You know where it is? On the Route de Toulouse—No. 300. Now I will tell Madame."

"I tell her" Bonnecourt said. "You go and telephone." He knew how slow Fourget's car was.

"Why is her friend not here, the beautiful foreign demoiselle? Someone should put Madame's *effets* together for her —she is not fit to do it herself."

"This shall be seen to" Bonnecourt said, and hustled the Doctor off.

He too wondered why *la belle Portugaise* was not there. He had only returned from a climbing trip with some Frenchmen away to the East that afternoon, after an absence of several days—on his way out with them he had killed an *isard*, cached it, and retrieved it on the way home; remembering Colin's parting request to him, at his house he had cut off and skinned a leg to take to Julia. While he was doing this his wife stood by, anxiously informing him that she had been visited in his absence by plain-clothes police—"The *Sûreté;* I am sure of it. They wished to ask you where this young man is, who crossed the frontier with *le vieux* who fell, and whom you took away in the night. I told them I knew nothing." Bonnecourt, busily skinning the *gigôt,* had found this news disconcerting—the last thing he wanted was to have the Special Police, the *Sûreté,* on his track. How had they connected him with de Lassalle? Monro had allowed the young fool to go free, and had told him, Bonnecourt, that old Maupassant had died "without speaking." Could young Monro have given him away after all? He had decided to ask Mme. Jimmison when he called if she, too, had been visited by the *Sûreté*—but finding her in such straits he let it alone.

Now, when Fourget had gone off in his old car, he returned to the big room, and reported to Julia, very cautiously and gently, what Fourget had said. "Professor Martin is excellent—he has an international reputation, and a very pleasant *clinique,* with a good nursing staff. But this cannot be an easy birth; for the sake of the child you must let me take you there at once, where you will have the most expert care."

Julia was slightly aghast at this. But she was beginning to feel so desperate that the idea of "expert care" was infinitely consoling. Even now, however, she was practical.

"It's a bit late—after ten" she said. "Will they take anyone in at this time of night?"

"Dr. Fourget has gone to telephone to warn the Professor of your arrival. Now, if Madame will tell me which her room is, and where I can find a suit-case in which to pack her things, and what she most requires, I will do the *emballage.*"

Fortified by the egg-flip, and still more by this thoughtfulness, Julia managed to tell Bonnecourt where her room was, with her suit-cases under the bed, and what she most needed: several *chemises de nuit,* her dressing-gown, and a light bed-jacket.

"Slippers?" Bonnecourt asked—he was showing himself in his best colours, moved by Julia's courage and common-sense.

"Oh yes, of course; thank you. And my brush and comb and powders and things are all on the dressing-table. But perhaps I had better come up"—she half-rose, and sank back again.

"Leave it to me, *chère* Madame." He went upstairs, and very soon returned with a suit-case which he set on the table beside the sofa, and opened to show her the contents. As he checked them over—"You ought to be a lady's-maid!" Julia said smiling. "You have thought of everything."

"Madame, I am a married man."

While Bonnecourt was taking the case out to the car Julia remembered Colin, and scribbled a note—again in Spanish—to tell him where she had gone, and why; when Bonne-court came back she asked for, and added, the address of the clinic.

"Leave that in the key-hole when we go" she said. "Lock the door and put the key under the tile—I'll show you." She got up, put some packets of "Week-End" cigarettes out of the cupboard into her handbag, and tried to reach down a light coat from some hooks by the door; but raising her arms again seemed to cause that dull pain—Bonnecourt sprang forward, unhooked the coat, and helped her into it. He was even more impressed by her calmness, and practical atten-tion to details like leaving the note for Colin in such a situa-tion, than he had always been by her beauty. As he helped her up the steps and along to the car he asked—"Why is Madame alone? Where is Monsieur her brother?"

"Oh, he had to go over to Spain" Julia said—"I expected him back yesterday, but he must have been held up."

"And the Portuguese *demoiselle?*"

"She's gone to a ball in Pau" Julia said, laughing a little—it suddenly struck her as funny that Luzia should be at a ball while all this was going on.

It was exactly 10.30 when they started down, and a bright moonlight night; the neighbour, whose child had caused the lamentable delay in despatching Julia's telegram to Fourget, had heard and seen the coming and going of cars, the Doctor's and Bonnecourt's, and was on the watch—she came out and spoke to Julia.

"Madame goes to the hospital?"

"No, to a *clinique*—thank you for all your help, Madame" Julia said politely.

"This is well" the woman said; she stood watching as the car, an immensely antique Bugatti, drove off. How came M. Bonnecourt to be taking Madame to Pau? It was all *most* interesting, she told her husband when she went indoors.

Just an hour earlier Colin reached the frontier at the Grandpont Pass. He had had one day's unexpected delay, and then two punctures on his drive from Pamplona; he was worried at being so late, and the meticulous checking of his passport, papers, and car-number at the French frontier-post fretted him. In fact the *Sûreté*, on the hunt for de Lassalle, had called on Julia as well as on Mme. Bonnecourt three days before; they were much less easy to foil than the *Gendarmerie*, and Julia had been driven into giving them her "brother"'s name, and the make and number of his car. Yes, she believed he had gone to Spain.

The French police are very thorough. De Maupassant's name had told them quite a lot, and Colin himself had unwittingly given them a vital clue when he mentioned to the *agent*, at Maupassant's bedside in the hospital, that he had left *ce jeune homme* to meet friends at an inn in Labielle. They wasted twenty-four hours combing the numerous *auberges* in Labielle itself; drawing a blank everywhere, it occurred to some bright spirit to try, next day, the small inn on the main road. There the landlord recollected perfectly the arrival of Bonnecourt, whom he knew by sight, in his familiar old car, and his waiting for over three hours until a *Monsieur* had driven up in a *voiture de sport Anglais*, bringing a young man. (The "G.B." number-plate on English cars on the Continent is a terrible give-away.) The Englishman had gone on alone in the direction of Pau; Monsieur Bonnecourt and the young man had returned up the valley. This sufficed to send the Special Police to interview both Julia and

Mme. Bonnecourt; finding neither of the two men they wanted, they had alerted all the frontier-posts with Colin's car-number; his name had been recorded when he last crossed the Grandpont into Spain. They also deployed extra men on foot to patrol the frontier to keep a look-out for Bonnecourt. The latter they missed, since his climbing expedition had been entirely inside France; but the moment Colin drove off the frontier-post was on the telephone to Pau, to report that *ce* M. Monnro was on his way to Larège; a sergeant on a motor-cycle was despatched from Pau to find him there.

The sergeant missed him too. Driving fast, in the brilliant September moonlight, Colin reached Larège at a quarter to eleven; as always he turned his car before hurrying to the house; he found it dark and empty. There was no answer to his agitated knocking. He put on his torch to look for the key in the familiar hiding-place—by its light he caught sight of the note stuck in the big key-hole; he pulled it out, and sitting on the stone bench outside the door he read it hastily. Oh God!—a miscarriage. *Poor* Julia! He hurried back to the car, and drove off to the clinic in Pau—but not unnoticed by the neighbour, who also observed the G.B. plate. Ah— *Monsieur le frère!* What an eventful evening! Colin, reck- lessly negotiating the hairpin bends down to the main road, was irritated and blinded by the headlight of a motor-cycle coming up towards him—in fact that of the *Sergent de Po- lice;* having at last passed his light he shot on towards Pau.

The sergeant, a few minutes later, also found Julia's house dark and empty; getting no reply to his vigorous knocks he started to enquire on the spot, and banged at the door of the nearest house. Here he struck oil with a vengeance. The neighbour poured out her exciting story: the English Mad- ame appeared to be having a *fasse couche,* and the neigh- bour's own child had taken a telephone message to the *Bu- reau de Poste* for Madame, asking Dr. Fourget to come. He came, and presently drove away again; a little later M. Bonnecourt had driven Madame off to Pau in *his* car. Then Madame's brother had arrived, and had also driven off, pre- sumably to Pau.

The *sergent* pricked up his ears at the mention of Bonnecourt. Where, in Pau, were they going?—to the hospital?

Non, the neighbour said, proud of her knowledge: she asked Madame this, and Madame had said to a *clinique*.

"What address?"

"*Voyons, Monsieur*, when a woman in labour is being taken to the Doctor in the middle of the night, one does not ask her for addresses!" the neighbour retorted vigorously. "I am not the police! I have given Monsieur all the indications I can—let him use them."

The sergeant climbed down; Madame's information had been of great value, he said. He took her name, and turning his machine he also shot off to Pau. The head-quarters of the *gendarmerie* would know all the *cliniques* of *accoucheurs*—with good fortune they would succeed in pouncing on Bonnecourt, and he, the sergeant, would be congratulated. He drove down the bends and along the main road, very satisfied with his evening's work.

Julia and Bonnecourt arrived at Professor Martin's clinic, on the further outskirts of Pau, about half an hour after midnight; there was a gravelled drive in which the hunter parked his car. They were expected; a nurse opened the door at once and took Julia's suit-case; then a senior nurse—in fact the principal *sage-femme*—led Julia into a room where Martin made his examination; Bonnecourt sat in a sort of waiting-room, where he was presently joined by Fourget. "No, he has not yet finished, *Monsieur le médecin*," a nurse told Fourget. They waited—the minutes seemed long. At last the Professor—a tall, lean, grey-haired man, with an impressively intelligent face—appeared, and greeted Fourget, who introduced Bonnecourt; in a few moments Julia was brought in by the matron, and placed in a chair.

"Now, Madame" the specialist began, "it is my duty to put the situation clearly, so that Madame can make her choice. The child is wrongly presented: the legs, not the head, are towards the mouth of the womb, so a natural birth is not possible—it is only the head which can emerge naturally through the cervix. I can do one of two things—either attempt, with instruments, to change the position of the child

in the womb, so that the head can emerge, or deliver it by a
Caesarian section, through the wall of the abdomen."

This was a pleasant problem to be faced with at one
o'clock in the morning, after being in pain and fruitless labour for well over twelve hours—Julia considered it as best
she could. She was taken aback by the idea of a Caesarian
section; she was newly-married, she had a beautiful body,
and did not like the idea of a great scar down the front of it.
But Philip's baby was the all-important thing, and she asked
the Professor—"For the child, which course is the safest?"

His reply horrified not only Julia, but Bonnecourt as well.

"I cannot advise Madame—the decision is hers. She is
adulte et consciente, and must make her own choice."

"But how can I? I am not a specialist, like *Monsieur le
Professeur*" Julia protested. "*Why* can you not advise me?"

"*C'est la loi de France, Madame*" Martin replied, relentlessly.

At this point Colin hurried in—Julia got up, and clung to
him. "Oh Colin, what am I to do?" She began to explain the
position to him in English; Martin interrupted her in furious
French—"Madame, I forbid you to speak in a language that
I cannot understand!"

Julia, wretchedly, put her halting explanation to Colin in
French; Colin in his turn asked Martin which course he
would advise? The Professor repeated his tiresome phrase
about Madame being "adult and conscious."

"But this is monstrous!" Colin exclaimed in French. "Madame is not a specialist in these matters, like *M. le Professeur.*"

"*C'est la loi de France*" Martin repeated inexorably.

Julia, despairingly, turned to old Fourget, and asked for
his opinion? Benignly, sadly, the country Doctor put on a
complete po-face, and said that Madame alone could decide
—it was the law of France.

"But no help, no advice, from those who know, as I do
not?"

"Unhappily no, Madame."

Julia looked questioningly at the Matron, and at the two

or three nurses who stood by—all returned her glance with a blank, expressionless stare. "Bloody *loi de France!*" she exclaimed.

Colin went over and took her hand. "Take your time" he said in English—"just think quietly." He turned to Martin, who again looked angry at the sound of a foreign tongue. "I merely counsel Madame to reflect for a *petit moment*" he said.

Martin still looked angry.

"In any case, the child is dead!" he said irritably. "I cannot hear its heart beating." He stumped out of the room.

Julia was completely stricken by this pronouncement; the tension and anguish of the moment, already over-sufficient, were given a fresh twist. As she turned to Fourget, saying— "*You* didn't tell me that!" the old head *sage-femme,* a small mouse-like creature, came over and took her hand. "Let Madame come to the couch." She led her into the adjoining room, where Martin had made his examination, and laid her on the hard bed. There, saying gently "*Madame le permet?*", she again loosened her clothes, and placed a small wooden stethoscope—shaped like a mushroom, and in fact familiarly called *le champignon*—against the protuberance on Julia's abdomen, and listened. "Ah" she said happily—and added confidentially."*Monsieur le Professeur* does not realise that we notice it, but he has grown *very deaf* this last year. I can hear the baby's heart beating perfectly."

Colin, Bonnecourt, and Dr. Fourget had all come, anxiously, to the door of the examination-room, and stood there looking on, half-horrified, half-hopeful; at the little old *sage-femme's* clear declaration both the Frenchmen, quite unembarrassed, went over and listened to the *champignon* themselves, and stated roundly that they could hear the baby's heart beating like a drum!—Colin, with British hesitation at this strangely public performance, nevertheless followed them, and listened too. Certainly there was a firm rhythmic sound coming through the ear-pieces of the *champignon*.

"Well now you'll have to settle" he said to Julia.

They went back to the other room, and the tiny *sage-femme* summoned the Professor.

Oddly enough at the moment when Colin had taken her hand Julia had suddenly begun to pray, something she had not thought of doing before; she had put up a brief petition for the unborn child, and for wisdom to make a right decision. Short as it was, the prayer had calmed her distress a little. And even with all those blank, unhelpful faces watching her, there had suddenly flashed into her mind the recollection of a lovely pedigree cow at Glentoran, greatly beloved by Philip Reeder, which had had a calf wrongly presented: a first-class vet had come post-haste from Glasgow and tried to turn the calf round, but he failed—the little creature was removed piecemeal, and a week later the cow also died. No!—she didn't want to die, and she urgently wished Philip to have the child on which his heart was set; her decision was clear. When Martin came back—

"Monsieur le Professeur, I desire to undergo the operation" she said in a firm voice.

Those few words produced an extraordinary transformation-scene in that rather bare room. All those faces, hitherto utterly blank, were suddenly wreathed in beaming smiles; there was a chorus of *"Ah, c'est très-bien"* from the *sage-femme* and the nurses, while Martin rubbed his hands, saying—"Madame has made the right choice." He told a nurse to telephone for the anaesthetist at once, and the matron to prepare all in the operating-theatre. Old Dr. Fourget came over and wrung Julia's hand—"Bravo! Madame makes *une belle décision."*

Julia was greatly shocked.

"My God, what a set of bastards they are, not to have told me themselves!" she said to Colin indignantly in English. This time Martin didn't protest; he wanted to make his preparations—but as he started to leave the room Colin caught him by the arm.

"Where is the nearest hotel? I wish to remain close by."

"The Victoire—it is only a hundred metres further down the road; it is simple, but Monsieur will be quite comfortable there."

"But can I get in, at such an hour?" By now it was after 1.15 A.M.

"I have them telephoned to." The Professor spoke to a nurse. "And inform Monsieur of the reply. I must prepare; I wish to lose no more time" he said to Colin, and went out.

The matron and a nurse were leading Julia away—Colin intercepted them. "Darling, I shall be at a pub only a hundred yards away; I'll see you as soon as they let me."

She kissed him. "Precious Colin!"

Bonnecourt profited by Colin's interception, and went over to Julia; he took her hand, and kissed it.

"Madame, I regret our hideous *loi*—I am ashamed of it!" He was full of some emotion, which made him less articulate than Frenchmen normally are. "Madame's great courage makes me feel proud—as the English are apt to do."

Julia was surprised, and rather embarrassed; it was not the ideal moment for dealing with any emotion. But even then she realised that something—she herself, or the English "thing"—had hit the hunter for six. She took her usual way out of any crisis, lightly and graciously.

"Monsieur Bonnecourt, I can't thank you enough. You have been infinitely good to me."

"Madame, I would do the same a thousand times over." The little head *sage-femme* was beginning to tug at Julia's arm, but Bonnecourt persisted, giving the nurse a gentle shove. "*Un petit moment!* I hope Madame will have a son, with some of Madame's great qualities" he said nervously, and again kissed Julia's hand.

Julia had wanted to thank Fourget too; but the old Doctor, after the *belle décision* had been taken, had gone off—he did not care for such late hours. So the matron succeeded in hustling her patient away to go through all the tedious procedures before an abdominal operation: the shaving, the washing, the swabbing with iodine, the enema; the pointless enquiry—in Julia's case—about false teeth, which must be removed before an anaesthetic. Colin and Bonnecourt waited while the nurse telephoned to the Victoire—Colin explained his delay, Bonnecourt related how he had, so luckily, taken a *gigôt d'isard* to Mme. Jimmison, and found that she was in labour . They could hear the nurse, outside in the hall, desperately urging the Exchange to ring the hotel again: "But let them arouse themselves! It is urgent." Colin looked out through the door—it had occurred to him that he ought to put a call through to the Office and make them cable to Philip Jamieson and let him know about Julia; but he would have preferred to do this rather less publicly— nurses were running to and fro, and even as he watched a small man, followed by another carrying a bag, came in; the anaesthetist and his assistant.

"I want to ring London" he said to Bonnecourt; "but not from here. Where's a good place?"

Bonnecourt grinned broadly.

"Why not the Heriots?"

"But they're having this dance tonight" Colin objected.

"*Raison de plus!* We might get some supper, and even champagne" Bonnecourt said. "Anyhow there you can be sure of privacy."

"Yes—yes, I think that's a good notion" Colin said. At that moment the nurse returned to say that the little hotel had reserved a room for Monsieur, and when would Monsieur be arriving?

"Oh, when I can!" Colin exclaimed impatiently. "Say in about half-an-hour, or three-quarters."

"Monsieur remains here? The operation will take more than *une demi-heure*" the nurse said, rather officiously.

"No—I go to the house of *le* Lord Heriot" Colin said. "You can ring me there if I am wanted. Come on" he said to Bonnecourt. "Can you show me the way?"

"Of course" Bonnecourt replied. They drove off, Bonnecourt leading.

Chapter 7

The streets of Pau between one-thirty and two in the morning are empty and silent, but outside the Heriot mansion there was a glare of light from the first-floor windows, and the sound of music and voices; numbers of cars were drawn up along the drive and on the broad gravel sweep—Colin looked round for a place for his own. Bonnecourt however pulled up at the front door, and got out.

"Where is Pierre?" he asked of several chauffeurs who were hanging about, smoking.

"*Chez-lui*—he entertains us, a few at a time" one of the men replied, grinning.

"Fetch him!" Bonnecourt said, curtly—he turned to Colin, who had parked his car. "Just wait a second—I shall put my car away" he said in English, and drove off towards the garage, converted from the former ample coachhouses. Pierre, the old chauffeur, met him; he knew the hunter well, and readily unlocked the door of an empty garage, and re-locked it after Bonnecourt had driven his car in. "Monsieur remains for the night?"

"Probably. Keep the key, Pierre.

"Monsieur has no luggage?" the old man asked, looking doubtfully at Bonnecourt's rather worn climbing-suit and dusty mountaineering boots.

"No—I do not dance! *Merci*, Pierre."

In fact neither Colin nor Bonnecourt were in the least dressed for a ball; both were travel-stained, dusty, and sweaty, and the hired butler, laid on for the evening, looked at them with hostility when he opened the door of the flat.

"Milady has guests" he said, repressively. Colin took over.

"First I wish to speak with the Comtesse d'Ericeira, who is staying in the house—but also with Milady, if she is free."

He stepped into the hall past the man, followed by Bonne-court. "My name is Monro" he said firmly.

As always on such occasions the regular servants were about, including old Jeanne, the housemaid—she overheard Colin's request for Luzia, whispered to the butler, and slipped away; in a moment the Portuguese girl appeared, ravishing in her new dress.

"*Alors!* What goes on?" she asked. "Colin, you look very dirty!"

"I am—and starving too! You know Bonnecourt?" The hunter bowed. "Listen, Luzia—Julia's baby has come pre-maturely; Bonnecourt brought her down tonight to the clinic here—probably saved her life."

"But why were you not there? You said you would be."

"I was held up—never mind about that," Colin said im-patiently.

"The baby is born? Is it a boy or a girl?"

"It isn't born yet—she's having a Caesarian at this moment."

"What is this, Caesarian?" Colin explained.

"*Ai Jézush!*" Luzia exclaimed distressfully. "*Why* did I leave her? Oh, what can I do?"

"Get us each a whisky, and some supper, if there's any going. And take me somewhere where I can telephone—I've got to ring up London."

At that moment the music stopped, and many of the dancers came out into the hall, Lady Heriot among them; she caught sight of her two unexpected guests, looking so strange among the ball-dresses and white ties, and went over to greet them. Luzia spoke hurriedly.

"Julia is being operated on for a baby; it comes too soon" she said. "And they want whisky, and Colin—Monsieur Monro—desires to telephone."

Lady Heriot took everything in turn, calmly. "Is Mrs. Ja-mieson at Professor Martin's clinic? Ah, well then she'll be all right—he's wonderful. Mr. Monro, you'd better come and telephone from my bedroom—there are people everywhere else!" She led him into a room where the bed and all the furniture were covered with bright evening wraps; she pushed some of these aside from the head of the bed. "There's the telephone; I'll get Jeanne to bring you some whisky. I'm afraid that butler-man isn't much good—these people laid on by the day never are. The boys will see to Bonnecourt. Don't worry about your cousin—though it's terribly tiresome for her, and anxious for you. Where's her husband?"

"I don't know, but the Office will; I want them to cable to him. Thank you very much, Lady Heriot."

Colin put through his call to the Office, and noticed with relief that there was an ashtray with a butt in it on the bedtable; he lit a cigarette himself—clearly Her Ladyship didn't mind smoke in her bedroom, and he wanted one badly. When the number answered—"The Duty Officer, please. A call from France" he said. When the night Duty Officer spoke the young man gave his name, and then started to dictate "an urgent cable" to be sent to Colonel Jamieson.

"But he's back" the Duty Officer said.

"Back where?"

"Here in London—at his house, I imagine. He got home this morning."

"Oh, good. That will save time. Well ring him up at once and give him a message, will you? Got a pencil?"

"*Now?* It's after two" the Duty Officer protested.

"Yes, *now*—his wife's ill." Colin dictated the gist of the cable that he had composed in his head as he drove to the Heriots, and gave the address and telephone number of the clinic.

"And where will you be, Sir?"

"Either at the clinic, or the Hotel Victoire—I don't know the number, but it's on the Route de Toulouse too, close by. Look it out and tell the Colonel." (Colin knew that the Office had telephone directories for every town in Europe.) He made the Duty Officer repeat the message and the two addresses over to him, and rang off—then he dialled the Exchange again, and told them to ring back and give the price of the call. At this point old Jeanne came in bearing a small tray with a bottle of whisky, a syphon, and a tumbler; thankfully Colin poured out a drink for himself, and swallowed two or three mouthfuls—they did him good, and glass in hand he went out into the hall.

There he encountered a fresh scene of excitement. Three uniformed *agents de police* were interviewing Bonnecourt, while the guests looked on in fascinated consternation. The sergeant on the motor-cycle, primed by Julia's helpful neighbour up at Larége, had reported on his return to Police Headquarters in Pau that Madame had been taken to a *clinique d'accouchement* by Bonnecourt himself; the well-informed *gendarmerie* forthwith sent a car with three officers to Martin's establishment. (It is in fact the practice of the *Sûreté* to send rather dumb men in uniform to conduct their preliminary enquiries; they prefer to keep themselves in the background.) The police car missed Colin and Bonnecourt at the clinic by a matter of minutes; but an excited nurse, who had overheard Colin talking to Bonnecourt, said that the Monsieur Anglais and his friend had driven off to the house of *le* Lord Heriot—and thither the police followed them.

In fact after his wife had told him of the visit of the *Sûreté* to his house, Bonnecourt realised perfectly well that to go down to Pau was to put his head into the lion's mouth; but when he found Julia so ill, and heard Fourget's report on her state, he never hesitated—he was not a person who did hesitate. He took the precaution of making old Pierre, the chauffeur, lock up his car, but after that he trusted to luck. However, it looked as though his luck was not going to hold; when Colin came out of Lady Heriot's bedroom the three policemen were saying firmly that they wished to take *ce Monsieur* to the Commissariat for interrogation; at once.

Before Colin could think of any useful intervention Luzia, glittering in her white dress and pearls, with diamond stars in her dark hair, stepped forward and put in her oar. Why had *ces Messieurs* of the *Sûreté* called on her friend three days before at Larège, and troubled her? Doubtless this was why Madame had now suffered a *fausse couche*, and was even at this moment undergoing an operation. Old Lord Heriot, emerging from his dressing-room, where he had been restoring himself with a furtive whisky, overheard this, and first questioned Luzia, in English; the girl gave him angry details of the police visit and Julia's distress—"and now Colin—Monsieur Monnro—tells me that she is being operated on to deliver the child."

The old peer, whose family had lived in Pau for three generations, and done much to build up the little town's prosperity as an English tourist resort, knew exactly where he stood with the local authorities; moreover he had liked Julia when she stayed with them, and was shocked by what had occurred. He spoke sharply to the *agents*. What *was* all this? It seemed that innocent British citizens had been frightened, worried, made ill— and now they, the police, come to his own house, and disturb his party. *"C'est peu agréable!"* the old man said. "Surely *Messieurs* know who I am?" He suggested, brusquely, that the police should come into his study and explain this extraordinary intrusion; sheepishly, the police agreed, distinctly embarrassed. They were even more embarrassed on entering Lord Heriot's study, which was full of rather loverly couples sitting-out; Lord Heriot coolly told the young men and women to clear off—"I'm busy. Carry on on the stairs, if you must." Startled by the sight of the police the young people went, eager to find out what was going on. The music had begun again, but not everyone went into the big drawing-room to dance; many stayed in the hall, discussing these exciting goings-on in lowered voices, and looking curiously at Colin and Bonnecourt. Dick didn't like any of this—he took the hunter by the arm, down in the lift, and out by the back door; thence he led him across the garden into the darkness of the trees, beyond the blaze from the lighted windows.

"Where do we go?" Bonnecourt asked.

"Well somewhere out of reach of the bloody *agents*, for the moment!" Dick replied. Luzia had already told him about the *Sûreté*'s men calling on Julia, and their enquiries about de Lassalle; he fully realised in what danger Bonnecourt stood—he had had a very fair idea, for a long time, of his friend's activities, besides smuggling and hunting *isard*. "We've got a very very *old*, stupid gardener, who's been no use for years; tonight he may be!—I'm going to park you in his cottage while we think about the next move. I don't think you'd better go back to Larège just now—do you?"

"Definitely *not*. Thank you, Dick."

Dick Heriot had some trouble in arousing the ancient gardener, who was rather deaf as well as stupid—but at last he opened the door of his cottage, and blinked sleepily at them. "Ah, Monsieur—*comment ça va?*"

"This gentleman stays here tonight" Dick said. "I know you have a second bed, where your daughter slept till she married—how is she, by the way?"

"A third child, Monsieur, last week—a boy!"

"Oh, marvellous! Well now, Lucien, bring the *matelas* off the other bed in here, and put it on the floor by the fire, so that Monsieur can sleep in the warmth." He turned to Bonnecourt, while the old man shuffled off—"Sorry you never had any supper, but I thought I'd better get you out of the way while His Lordship was keeping the police occupied. Smart, isn't he?"

"You are all 'smart'—and kind also" Bonnecourt said. When the old man returned, dragging a mattress and some blankets, Dick shook him by the shoulder and addressed him sternly. "You say nothing to *anyone* that this gentleman is with you—this is understood?"

"It is understood, Monsieur."

"You stay put till I come" Dick said to Bonnecourt, and returned to the house. This was counter-espionage and no mistake, he thought gleefully, as he left the darkling trees and came into the lighted space below the windows; the police-sergeant was still standing near the front door. Just as well he'd taken Bonnecourt out the other way. He went up in the lift, found Nick, and told him what he had done.

"Good enough" Nick said. "His Lordship must soon have finished with those types. Clever old thing, isn't he?"

At that moment the door of the study opened, and Lord Heriot and the three policemen came out into the hall. After listening to their excuses, and their reasons for regarding Bonnecourt as involved in the escape of an O.A.S. *saboteur*, the old gentleman had given them a long lecture on the wonderful work that M. Bonnecourt had done in helping

members of the "Royal Air Force" to escape into Spain during the last war—"After all, we and the English are allies,
n'est-ce pas?" The *agents* agreed politely, but remained firm:
their orders were to take *ce Monsieur* back to the Commissariat for interrogation.

"Oh very well—though I dislike this behaviour in my
house extremely" Lord Heriot said.

But where was Bonnecourt? No sign of him in the hall, or
the room where the dancing was going on, or at the buffet in
the dining-room. Rather apologetically, the police asked
Lord Heriot's permission to question the servants—the but-
ler-for-the-night, pointing to Nick, said that he thought he
had seen *ce jeune Milord* go out with the other gentleman
"not dressed for a ball"—glowering at Colin as he spoke.
Nick protested that he had never left Luzia's side—which he
had not; and as the twins were indistinguishable, and Luzia
supported Nick's statement, the wretched *agents* were flum-
moxed. They said, uncomfortably, that they ought to search
the flat—led, stiffly, by Lord Heriot they walked through the
various bedrooms, but there was no opening of cupboard
doors; and in the servants' quarters the regular staff, headed
by old Jeanne, all averred that they had seen nothing, and
muttered *"Mais par example!"*—looking with detestation at
the intruders.

While this performance was going on Luzia murmured to
Dick that she wanted to go to the clinic, and hear how Julia
was; Colin said he would go too—he had snatched a hasty
supper at the buffet while Lord Heriot was interviewing the
police in his study, and Dick was hiding Bonnecourt in old
Lucien's cottage. "But I'd better wait to see these infernal
police" he said, "and tell them where I am." At that moment
Lord Heriot and the three *agents* re-appeared, and he told
his host where he was going.

"Yes, of course. I do hope everything will be all right"
Lord Heriot said. "Oh, by the way, you had a call to London, didn't you? The *Inter* called up to say that it cost 225
new francs."

"Oh yes—sorry, I didn't hear the ring. I told them to report the call" Colin said. As he handed over the money Nick

uttered a dismal protest—"*Really*, your Lordship!" Colin, amused, thought how Scotch Lord Heriot still was; but then the French were just the same about money; he wouldn't have lost the habit out here.

"Oh well, debts are debts" Lord Heriot said, pocketing Colin's notes. "Thanks, Monro."

Luzia appeared, a white scarf thrown over her shoulders above her white dress.

"Dear Lord Heriot, will you make my excuses to Lady Heriot? I leave your lovely party for a very short time—I do want to go to the clinic and hear how Julia is."

"Oh yes. Is Monro taking you? If not I'd better telephone to the garage for Pierre."

"*I'm* taking her" Dick said. "We shan't be long. Come on, Luzia."

Colin need not have worried about seeing the police. The three *agents*, who had gone down in the lift after their fruitless search of the flat for Bonnecourt, were outside the front door questioning the waiting chauffeurs—thanks to Dick's prudence in using the servants' entrance on his way to the cottage, all were able to vow that they had seen no one except *le jeune Milord*, strolling in the garden and returning to the house. Thwarted again, the most senior policeman installed a subordinate in Colin's car before driving back to the Commissariat; Dick and Luzia were allowed to go alone, and Colin, still unsure of these suburban by-ways of Pau, followed them.

It was well after 2.30 A.M. when they arrived at the clinic, where Luzia in her glittering dress, her head starry with diamonds, created a fresh sensation among the nurses on this night of sensations—the emergency operation on the beautiful English lady, the visit of the police! The Professor had finished operating, and was on his way to bed, but courteously came down to report. Madame was still under the anaesthetic, but perfectly well; so was the baby—a boy, very small, only two-and-a-half kilograms—but "perfect," and quite healthy. Luzia cajoled Martin—who like the nurses was struck by such a dazzling apparition—into letting her take a peep at Julia's baby; the minute creature was swathed all over in cotton-wool, with hot-water bottles round it; its head, the only part visible, was bright red. "Why is it red?" the girl asked. "Will it remain so? It is *very* ugly!" The specialist laughed.

"New-born infants are often red—it will not last. But it is a mercy that *ce Monsieur* brought Madame to me when he did; she was in an exceedingly grave condition. Another two hours—and the good God alone knows what might have happened!"

Colin, standing with Dick Heriot in the doorway of the babies' *crèche*, overheard this, and was smitten with compunction. He had promised both Julia and Luzia to be back at Larège on a given day; but he wasn't back, and hadn't even telegraphed—without Bonnecourt's blessed intervention by now Julia, and her child, might both be dead. When Luzia turned and looked round at him with an accusing stare he went out of the room.

Dick followed him.

"Where *is* Bonnecourt?" Colin asked in the passage, in a low voice. "We must get him away—he's saved Julia's life, besides everything else."

"I stowed him in a place in the garden till we could fix something."

"Well get him away at once—out of this country. *I* can't help—I've got this bloody *agent* tied to me, like a tin can to a dog's tail! But I expect B. knows where to contact our people in Pamplona."

"Why should he know that?" Dick asked.

"Oh, he was on our pay-roll during the last War" Colin said, recklessly.

"No! Goodness, that's funny!" Dick exclaimed, laughing. "All right—we'll see to him. You'd better get to bed, Monro; sleep well with your police chum!" He turned as Luzia came out. "Come on, Mademoiselle la Comtesse—'On with the dance.'"

"You are rather silly, Dick," Luzia pronounced, as on the drive she crammed her flowing skirts into the car. "I am sorry to have left your Mother's ball, but do hurry. I think something should be done immediately about M. Bonnecourt" she added as they drove off. "*Where* is he, actually? I saw you take him away."

"I've hidden him."

"Well, he should be got across the frontier at once. If the *Sûreté* are anything like our Special Police, they will not rest until they find him, now that they have seen him. And they only saw him because he brought Julia down. Will you *act*, Dick?"

"Yes, I'll act" Dick promised. "It's all poor Monro's fault, letting everyone down by failing to turn up on time. But don't be sour with me, sweet." He put a hand on hers.

"Drive! Fast!" Luzia said, removing her hand. "At this moment only one thing is important."

In fact Dick had no need to act—Nick had already done so. His Father had described him to Julia as a pessimist—and one thing pessimists do is to foresee difficulties, and also, in some cases, arrange to avoid them. After his twin had driven Luzia off to the clinic Nick reflected on all he had just heard. If the *Sûreté* had been up at Larège harrying Mrs. Jamieson things must be pretty serious; they certainly wouldn't be satisfied with the rather perfunctory search of the flat carried out under his Father's eye—they would come back and go over the whole place with a small-tooth comb. He must get Bonnecourt away immediately. Money—B. might need that. He himself had almost none; he went to his Mother's room and raided her familiar, idiotic hiding-place, under the handkerchiefs in her dressing-table drawer—yes, nearly 5000 francs! Nick pocketed this, and went out, also by the back door, to the garage, where he told the chauffeur to put on his uniform and get out the family Humber, familiar to the police for miles around. "Take it out by the garage entrance, and wait outside in the road."

"At this hour of the morning, Monsieur?" Pierre protested —he was enjoying his role of host to the local chauffeurs.

"Yes. *Ne discute pas, Pierre! Vas-y-de suite!*"

While the old man, grumbling, went off to change Nick took a roundabout route through the gardens to Lucien's cottage; on his way he looked through the trees towards the front of the house. Yes; sure enough there was a policeman at the door. He had less difficulty than his twin over getting in—at his first knock a voice, Bonnecourt's, said "*Qui est là?*"

"*Moi*—Nick. Open quickly."

The hunter had been sleeping on the mattress in front of the fire; he let Nick in immediately. "What happens?" he asked.

"I'll tell you outside—come along. Don't wake the old boy."

Softly they went out, and closed the door—a mercy Lucien was so deaf, Nick thought. As they walked through the shrubberies—"I think you'd better clear off now, before they start setting up road-blocks and all that" Nick said. "Get into Spain, I should."

"I agree—'like Hell' as I think you say. But—perdition!—I have practically no money with me; I came here unexpectedly."

"I've brought over 4000 francs—will that do you for the moment?"

"Oh, amply. *Merci, mon cher* Nick."

"Have you contacts in Spain?"

"Indeed yes." But as he stowed away Lady Heriot's notes in an inner pocket he stood still and said—"There is my wife."

"We'll see about her. Send us an address in Spain where we can contact you."

"Monro will know this."

"Oh will he? How odd! Well never mind," Nick said, walking on—then he stopped again, among the dark laurels. "Tell me where you want to cross from. I'm coming with you to wherever you want to be dropped."

"You drive?"

"No—I'm taking you in my Mother's car, with the chauffeur. Better security, I thought—all the police know old Pierre by sight."

"*Quelle astuce! Merci, mon cher.*"

"Well where do we go?" Nick asked, walking on.

"Tardets" Bonnecourt replied instantly. "I was born there."

"Good enough. I suppose you'll cross by that path where you met the old Smiths, and retrieved their Thermos?"

"By that—or by no path! I shall get some more sleep in the house of friends, and learn how the situation is before I cross; the frontier patrols may not have been alerted so far to the west. This is very good of you, Nick."

They went out through the big garage gate; no police there yet, Nick noted thankfully—in fact with so many cars and chauffeurs about it could not have been a better night for evading the police unnoticed. The Humber was waiting in the small road outside, far away from the main entrance —"Tardets" Nick said to Pierre as they got in.

"Tardets? At such an hour?" the old man grumbled, nevertheless starting his engine.

"Yes, Tardets!" Nick said.

While they were still in the small quiet roads of the sub-urbs Nick suggested in English to Bonnecourt that he should lie on the floor of the car, "just in case"—Lady Heriot's tartan rug was as usual folded up on the back seat, and the young man spread it over his passenger. This also proved to have been a wise precaution; as they drove through the main streets of Pau, twice police, waving torches, held them up— but recognising the venerable car, Pierre's familiar face, and Nick's grinning countenance, the *gendarmes* waved them on.

"I don't much care about this" Nick said, still in English, to Bonnecourt when they were clear of the town. "I think we'd do better not to go through Ste.-Marie de Pèlerins—we are so well-known there. Can't we by-pass it?"

Yes, one could take a *bi-furcation* towards Orthez, north-wards, and after Ste.-Marie bend south again, and rejoin the main road to St. Jean-Pied-de-Port, Bonnecourt replied from the floor. "But I must sit up to see the turning."

"All right, do." Quietly the hunter rose from the floor and sat on Nick's right.

"Quite soon, now" he said after some time, also speaking in English. "But could we go more slowly?" Pierre, still vexed, was pushing the Humber along at a considerable speed.

"*Ralentissez, Pierre*" Nick said.

"*Pourqoui? Moi, je voudrais me coucher!*" the old man replied.

"Unless you wish Milord to *congédier* you first thing to-morrow, you obey orders!" Nick said firmly. "Drive more slowly."

"If Monsieur Nick intends to be prompt, he means today! In two hours we shall have the dawn" the irrepressible Pierre replied—both the men in the back laughed.

"There is the turning—to the right" Bonnecourt said after a moment.

"*Ici à droite, Pierre,*" Nick transmitted the direction in French.

"This is not the direct route to Tardets, Monsieur" the old man protested. "After all, I know these roads, *moi!*" Nick leaned forward and took him by the shoulder.

"Pierre, either you do what you are told, or *I* drive" he said, very slowly and quietly. Reluctantly, the chauffeur turned to the right, still grumbling—"*Moi,* I do not under-stand what goes on."

"This is not necessary. To obey orders suffices" Nick Her-iot told him.

After a considerable *détour,* still following Bonnecourt's directions the car turned left—that is to say south—again, and well beyond Ste. Marie regained the main road, which here swings up in a big loop towards the Pyrenees; Tardets lies almost at the apex of this loop. But some distance short of the little grey mountain town, and well before the dawn, Bonnecourt, constantly staring out of the window, touched Nick on the shoulder. "Let him stop here."

Nick told Pierre to stop. They were on a quiet stretch of road between beechwoods—quite out in the country.

"Monsieur Nick said he wished to go to Tardets; this is not Tardets" the chauffeur replied. He was one of the few people who knew the twins apart.

"Pierre, one other word, and I will give you the beating of your life, and throw you out on the road" Nick said, still slowly—now it was Pierre who laughed. *"Monsieur Nick est impayable"* he said, pulling up.

Bonnecourt got out, and wrung Nick by the hand. "I cannot thank you enough; I hardly thought we should manage it."

"Send us an address" Nick said—he hadn't much faith in Colin. "Address it to my Father; *his* mail won't be tampered with! We'll keep an eye on Madame, and let you know how she is."

"Thank you—and please also let me know how all goes with Mme. Jimmison and her child. Such a courageous, such a courteous woman—truly noble!"

The big car had to drive on some distance before reaching a place where it could be turned, in the mouth of a small lane leading up to the left; Pierre manoeuvred it round, and started back towards Pau. As he did so, they saw in the headlights Bonnecourt standing at the roadside—he was too prudent to enter the lane while the car was there, but Pierre was not deceived.

"Ah! this is the place. Not in Tardets at all! And now will Monsieur Nick tell me why the police pursue his friend, who must be driven all over the region in the middle of the night to evade them, and hides his car in our garage?"

Nick spoke rather carefully. "Pierre, you know M. Bonnecourt perfectly well; he is our friend. But do you ignore the fact that he saved the lives of countless members of the Royal Air Force"—Nick rolled all those R's in the true French fashion—"during the last War, taking them across the frontier at the risk of his life? Tonight he has again risked his life to bring a friend of ours down to a *clinique* here, because she was having a *fausse couche*."

"Then why do the police seek him?" Pierre pursued obstinately.

"I do not know—and if I did I should not tell you! For you there is only one essential: to keep that garage door locked, and your mouth shut. Is that understood? We owe M. Bonnecourt much."

"C'est entendu" Pierre said. "Now, without *ce Monsieur,* can we return by the direct route, through Ste.-Marie?"

"Yes."

But the return journey showed how wise Nick's pessimistic precaution in making the *détour* had been. There were roadblocks on both sides of Ste.-Marie des Pèlerins, and the police were much more pertinacious than those in Pau. Nick's evening clothes lent colour to his story that he had been at a party with friends near St. Jean Pied-de-Port, and the Humber's papers confirmed his statement that he was a son of *le* Lord Heriot; but it was all rather disturbing, and took a long time—day was breaking as they approached Pau.

"Let Monsieur Nick continue to tell his own lies" old Pierre growled, seeing another road-block ahead. And this time even the Pau police were more difficult; there had been time for them to be more fully briefed, and they wished to know why the young Milord had left the grand ball at his home?—they knew positively that the man they sought, Bonnecourt, had been seen in Milord's house. Nick managed to bluff it out. For him, he had not seen M. Bonnecourt, he had occupied himself with the guests of his parents; but he had slipped away to visit friends who were also having a party that night, as he had long since promised to do—the party of Miladi Heriot had been given *à l'improviste* for a Portuguese young lady, the daughter of the Duc de Ericeira. Doubtless the police would have a record of her entry, some weeks ago. Her *prénom?* Luzia.

He just got by with it, with this flourish of details, but he was devoutly thankful when Pierre had swung the Humber in through the garage gate; the young man got out and closed and bolted it—he thanked Pierre, and once more enjoining him to keep his mouth shut, he walked across to the house.

The party was over. No cars encumbered the drive any more, but a small, rather sleepy *agent* still stood by the front door—Nick saw him from a distance, and went round to the back; here the door was locked. But when people have been brought up in a house as children they know it as rabbits know their secret runs and burrows; Nick Heriot bethought him of two other places, the laundry and the old bakery.

Both the doors were locked, but there was a window in the laundry which could be eased up with a coin and climbed through, because it had a defective catch—he and Dick had used it dozens of times for surreptitious entries. He used it again now, and made his way through a maze of passages to the front hall, where he went up in the lift. The temporary butler, like the cars, had gone, and the lights had been turned off; early daylight was beginning to filter in through the Venetian-shuttered windows—but in the dining-room light, Nick saw, still shone. He went in, and found his twin and Luzia, tucking into the last of the lobster patties, and sipping champagne.

"What have you done with Bonnecourt?" Dick asked at once. "He's gone—I went to Lucien's, and he isn't there."

"No. I thought he'd better clear out, so I took him off."

"Where to?"

"Tardets—that was where he wanted to go."

"Ah, this is good!" Luzia interjected. "You remove him! Excellent, Nick—always you do the right thing."

"Have any trouble?" Dick asked—as he spoke he found a clean tumbler, and poured some wine into it for his brother.

"Not too bad on the way out. I decided to by-pass Ste.-Marie, going, and that was just as well—there were road-blocks all the way as we came back, and they're pretty tough here in the town now," Nick said, drinking champagne from his tumbler, and taking a lobster patty himself. He yawned. "Goodness, I am sleepy! What a night! Where's Colin?"

"Gone to that little pub just beyond the clinic—the Victoire."

"Julia has a baby boy" Luzia pronounced, triumphantly. "Very small, and very *red*—but perfect. And the Professor says that it will not remain red; it will become normal."

"Jolly good" Nick said, yawning again—he emptied his tumbler. "Well I'm going to get some sleep; I'm no good at these late hours. It's broad daylight!"

"I too would sleep" Luzia said. "But it was a lovely party. How kind your Mother is! And I am so happy that Julia has her baby."

Chapter 8

When Colin Monro left the clinic, still accompanied by his policeman, he took his car barely a hundred yards on down the broad main road to where a very modest sign indicated the Hotel Victoire; he turned in and drove up to the front door. The Victoire was as modest as its sign—it was merely a large suburban house which had been converted into an hotel; when Colin rang the bell there was a long pause before a middle-aged man in a dressing-gown opened it, and announced himself as the *patron*. "It is Monsieur Monro, who comes from the *clinique?*" he asked. Colin said "Yes". Then the landlord caught sight of the *agent*, who was standing at the foot of the steps.

"Who is this? Only one room was commanded by the Professor Martin."

"He can stay outside; he doesn't need a room" Colin said coolly.

The *patron* was worried.

"Why does an *agent* accompany Monsieur? Here, we are not accustomed to having the police on the premises! I would wish to understand a little more."

But Colin had had enough. He had been on the go for twenty-one hours, and simply had to get some sleep; the newfound toughness which had helped him at Labielle ten days earlier returned now. He walked in past the landlord, and himself slammed the hotel door in the *agent*'s face, telling him brusquely—"You can wait in the car." (He had not only taken the keys but used the hidden burglar-switch which disconnected the engine before he got out.) Then he turned to the *patron*.

"I too am not accustomed to being followed by the police —I am English, myself! I arrive from Spain a few hours ago, and learn that Madame my sister"—he thought it prudent to stick to the Larège version—"had been taken to Professor Martin's clinic for an immediate operation; naturally I follow her. I went on to the house of Lord Heriot to inform her intimate friend, the daughter of the Duke of Ericeira, who is staying with Lady Heriot, of this critical situation, and there this creature attaches himself to me! How can I know why? I come back to the clinic to learn the result of the operation—*Grâce à Dieu* it has succeeded—and now I wish to sleep!" He took out his passport and slammed it down on the desk in the hall. "Let the *patron* examine this, and allow me to sign the registration, and then, in the Name of God, take me to my room!"

This display of indignation and firmness combined produced its effect. The landlord looked at the passport and saw that all the exit and entry visas were in order, including one showing an entry at the Grandpont barely six hours before. He gave Colin the registration slip to sign, and then led him up to a rather old-fashioned bedroom, with a large brass bed, several arm-chairs, and some massive furniture; a fitted basin was its only concession to modernity. No, no private bath-room; there was one along the corridor—"*et le ouattaire aussi.*" (*Le ouattaire* is the peculiar expression still current in provincial French tourist resorts frequented by the English for the lavatory, deriving from the word water-closet.) He thanked his host—no, he did not wish to be called; he would ring when he desired his *petit déjeuner*. He took out his things, had a quick wash—the water was only tepid—put on his pyjamas and fell thankfully into bed. Before switching off the dim bedside light he glanced at his wrist-watch as he wound it—3.30 A.M. He fell asleep at once.

The young and healthy, like Colin Monro, are very good at catching up on fatigue; given a chance they simply sleep it off. Colin did this, in that antique but excellent bed, for eight hours; he was aroused not by a knocking at the door, which didn't penetrate his slumbers, but by the *valet de chambre*, in his green baize apron, shaking him by the shoul-

der and announcing that an English Monsieur, a Colonel, desired to speak with Monsieur.

Colin sat up, stretched, and rubbed his eyes. "*Who* wishes
to speak with me?" he asked sleepily.

"*I* do" Philip Jamieson replied cheerfully, walking into the
room after the servant; he went over to the windows and
flung back the shutters, letting in a flood of bright Southern
light. "Shall I tell this chap to bring you some coffee?—it
may help you to wake up!"

"Yes, do—have some yourself" Colin said, putting a hand
up to his eyes; he found the sudden brilliance of the light
almost painful. Jamieson gave the order, adding "Prontito!"
he was obviously in tearing spirits.

"They won't understand that here" Colin said, shoving his
pillows up behind him to lean back against them.

"Oh yes they do—*he* did" Philip said. "I've got a son!" he
then announced, triumphantly.

"Oh, you've been to the clinic already? How's Julia?—she
was still 'under' last night" Colin said, now more awake.

"Splendid—a bit doped still. The nurse said she mustn't
talk much, so I came off—they told me I should find you
here. Thanks for getting that message to me" Jamieson said,
sitting down in one of the armchairs, and lighting a cigarette. Colin looked at his watch—it was twenty minutes to
twelve.

"You've made pretty good time" he said. "How did you do
it? Oh, here's the coffee—good. Make that man put it down
somewhere, and give me a cup." Jamieson caused the *valet*
to dump the usual overcrowded and ill-arranged tray on the
big dressing-table, and dealt skilfully with its contents: he
poured Colin out a cup and took it to the bed-table; then he
cleared the tray and arranged it properly with one plate and
knife, butter, and a couple of *croissants,* the delicious pastri-
fied rolls beloved of the French, and set it down on Colin's
knees on the honey-combed dimity bedspread.

"Oh, thanks" his cousin-by-marriage said, drinking the
coffee. "Well go on—tell me how you managed to get here so
soon."

"Oh—well naturally when I heard about Julia, and the baby coming too early, I came out at once. The B.E.A. planes only reach Bordeaux quite late, after two; so I got the Office to lay on a charter-plane, and to fix with the Consulate at Bordeaux about a hire-car. It was all quite easy: Buchan came with me to the airport to drive my car back, and we touched down at Bordeaux soon after eight—a very nice young chap from the Consulate met me with a perfectly good Citroën; he'd even had the sense to bring a Michelin map, so I simply blinded on here, and went straight to the clinic."

Colin was now sufficiently awake to fall to greedily on the *croissants* and butter as he listened to this recital.

"Very nice" he said, with a sarcastic grin. "All this on the British tax-payer, I suppose?" Philip was quite unperturbed.

"I've just saved the British, and various other European tax-payers, several millions of pounds by—well let us say 'successful dealings' in one or two oil-producing countries— so I don't worry about them! I shan't worry if I have to foot the bill myself either—I can afford it."

"Oh, were you heading off that Commie attempt to make trouble in the OPEC oil-fields?" Colin asked, interested.

"More or less." But Philip Jamieson never took much interest in a job he had finished; he cared about the present.

"Why is there a policeman in the hall?" he asked. "That *valet* man said he was here to watch you. What have you been up to?"

Colin buttered another *croissant*. "Didn't you see Hartley yesterday when you got back?" he asked. "He could have put you in the picture."

"No—he happened to be out. Have a go yourself."

"Well give me another of those roll things—I've had nothing to eat since breakfast yesterday but two or three lobster patties, and I'm hungry. Thanks" he said, as Philip put a plate of *croissants* on the bed.

"Well go ahead."

Colin proceeded to relate the whole story of how he had encountered Maupassant and de Lassalle up on the frontier, the old man's fall, and subsequent death in the hospital; he laid stress on the marked map, and his curious instinctive impulse, when he found that it was Bonnecourt who was waiting for the pair at the inn outside Labielle, to let him take de Lassalle away. "Of course I didn't know then that he had worked for us—it was just a hunch."

"How *do* you know that this man worked for us?" Philip asked crisply—it sounded to him as though Colin had behaved irresponsibly.

"He told me, later that night, and I checked next day with Hartley. I'm sure now that I did the right thing," Colin said, again a little on the defensive.

"What do you say his name is?"

"Bonnecourt—but we called him Bernardin."

"Oh, *him!*" Greatly to Colin's pleasure, Philip Jamieson practically repeated Hartley's phrase—"I'm told he was one of the best people we ever had." After a pause—"Well go on" he said. "Did he get this young O.A.S. type away?"

"I imagine so, and I also imagine that that is what all the present fuss is about—though *how* the Sûreté pinned it on to Bonnecourt I don't know; you see I've been in Spain for the last week."

"The Sûreté? Are *they* activating about this?" Jamieson asked, looking slightly disturbed.

"So Luzia told me last night—well really this morning—at the Heriots. But according to that old gynae at the clinic it was really Bonnecourt who saved Julia's life; he found her ill up at Larège, all alone, and brought her down, *just* in time."

"Why was she alone? Where was this Ericeira girl?—Julia wrote that she was going to be with her the whole time."

"Well to tell you the truth, Philip, this whole idea of yours of sending Julia to Larège was a complete nonsense!" Colin said, with some irritation. "It's a hopeless place—not a servant to be had, no telephone in the house, no food ever delivered; you even have to bring the drinking-water down in a crock from a spout 50 yards away! It was crazy, *I* think, to put a pregnant woman out on a limb like that. Sorry—but that's what I feel."

Philip Jamieson was considerably taken aback by this on-slaught—especially coming from Colin, usually so uncertain, not to say timid. But he stuck to his point.

"Why was Julia alone? Where was the Ericeira girl?"

"She'd come down for two nights to the Heriots, here in Pau; Dick Heriot has rather fallen for her, so his Mother put on a dance for them."

"Who are the Heriots? Oh, I remember, friends of Mrs. Hathaway's; lived here for ever. Julia wrote that the boys had been quite useful."

"She'd have been *sunk* without them" Colin retorted. "They've done everything possible for her. And Luzia has worked like a black—cooking, cleaning, doing the washing and the washing-up; fetching the bread and milk every day, and the damned meat and vegetables from the village— *when* they come! How you suppose Julia would have man-aged alone I can't think; after all *you* didn't lay on Luzia! The whole thing was crazy" the young man said, quite an-grily—"so don't you go criticising Luzia for taking a couple of days off."

For the first time Philip Jamieson realised, startled, that his rather romantic notion of Julia's staying at Larège might be open to criticism. But he was still not deflected from his enquiry.

"It all seemed to work quite easily when I stayed there two years ago" he said pacifically—"I'd no idea that it would be so complicated now. But if *you* weren't there, why did Luzia leave Julia alone?"

"Well, that was an accident" Colin said. "I was due back in the afternoon of the day Luzia left, but I got held up. I came away first thing yesterday, but I had *two* burst tyres— it would have to happen like that—and you know what Spain is! By the time I got to Larège Bonnecourt and Julia had started down, but she left a note for me; I was only about fifteen minutes after them at the clinic. Oh the *bloody* French." He described the hateful scene: Julia's agonised appeals for advice, the stony-faced refusal of the two Doc-tors to give it, and the general delight when she opted for a Caesarean. Philip was horrified.

"I can't think why this should have happened" he said presently. "She was so fit, and she always takes everything so calmly. I wonder if anything could have happened to upset her?"

"Luzia said she thought she was worried by the *Sûreté* types calling on her."

"The *Sûreté* called on *Julia?* What on earth for? And when?"

"A day or so before Luzia left, to enquire about Bonnecourt—and me, I gathered. I haven't got it all pieced together yet; everything has been such a shambles: Julia's baby, and then the *gendarmes* turning up at the Heriots in the middle of their ball."

"Did they do that?" Colonel Jamieson's face grew darker at every phase of Colin's recital.

"Oh yes—when I came out after telephoning to the Office from Lady H.'s bedroom there were three of them in the hall, questioning Bonnecourt—and all the guests looking on! They wanted to take him away for interrogation, but then they started to talk to me, and old Lord Heriot was pretty tough with them; he took them into his study to explain their goings-on, and meanwhile one of the twins took Bonnecourt away. Oh, and Luzia said her piece too, in front of everyone!—she told the *agents* that she was sure it was the *Sûreté*'s visit that had brought on Julia's miscarriage. They didn't like that at all" Colin ended, rather more cheerfully.

"Nor do I." But Philip kept his eye on the essential point, as always.

"Where is Bonnecourt now?"

"I don't really know—I think Dick or Nick hid him somewhere on the place. It can't have been *in* the flat, because the police searched that when they found he'd disappeared. But I went back to the clinic to hear how Julia was, and then came straight on here, to get some sleep."

Philip smiled—he remembered Colin's endless desire for sleep on the yachting trip where he first met his Julia.

"Well, he can't stay there, obviously" he said. "In fact he can't stay in France at all, for the moment. Once the *Sûreté* have their claws into anyone they don't easily let go—least of all those who give 'aid and comfort' to the O.A.S.! I think we'd better go round to these Heriots and find out where he is; then we must arrange something. How quickly can you get dressed?"

Colin said that he must shave, and it would take about ten minutes, all told.

"All right—I'll wait in the garden."

The Victoire had a charming garden, gracefully sheltered with acacias. Philip could have done with a drink—it was now past noon; but the Victoire was "dry", he learned from the *patron,* so he made do with a *citron pressé,* fresh lemon-juice and soda. He sipped this in a chair under the thin-leaved trees, alternately rejoicing over the fact that he had got a son, and pondering on how best to rescue "Bernardin", who had done so much for England in the past, and now for him, Philip—it seemed that he owed both his son, and the life of his wife, to this man.

When Colin came downstairs the wretched *agent* was fast asleep on a chair in the hall—the young man went out to the garden.

"What do we do about that poor devil who's tailing me?" he asked Philip.

"Oh, leave him where he is." Philip too had seen the sleeping policeman. "We'll go in my car—no use having too many police about."

But when they arrived at the Heriot mansion there was an *agent* at the door there, too; he asked for their names, and their business. While Philip was showing a visiting-card Colin pushed hard on the bell of the upper flat; before the *agent* had finished his enquiries Dick Heriot opened the door.

"Oh, hullo, Colin! Come on in. These gentlemen desire to speak with Milord" he said firmly to the *agent.* "They are friends of ours"—and he led them indoors. Philip was rather startled by this easy handling of the French police; he had not realised to what extent Lord Heriot was the uncrowned king of Pau. Going up in the lift Colin introduced him— "This is Julia's husband, Colonel Jamieson. He's just flown over."

"Smart work!" Dick said. "How is Madame?"

"Very well, thank you. A bit sleepy still."

"So are we all. In fact His Lordship hasn't surfaced yet—won't till tea-time, I don't suppose! Nor has Her Ladyship; but do come in"—as he opened the door of the lift—"and have a drink. I think Nick's awake."

The flat was full of maids clearing up after a major party: brushing carpets, emptying ash-trays, and plumping cushions. "Jeanne, where can we sit in peace?" Dick asked the old servant.

"In the boudoir of Milady—we have terminated there, Monsieur Dick."

"Her Ladyship *hates* this room being called the boudoir" Dick said, "but Jeanne can't learn the word 'morning-room.' What will you drink, Sir? Gin?—or sherry, or some of last night's champagne?"

"I think gin; thank you very much." As Dick went out—"What a nice boy that is" Philip was saying, when the door opened again, and to his embarrassment apparently the same young man re-appeared; however this one repeated "Oh hullo, Colin!"—and then asked—"Who's this? Mr. Julia?"

"Yes, this is Colonel Jamieson. How did you guess, though?"

"Oh, the *gendarmerie* are creating like mad on the telephone! *Monsieur le Colonel* checked in at the *clinique,* and then at the Victoire, and now he has vanished—and you too, Colin! I expect your wretched tin-can follower will be hanged, drawn, and quartered by tonight" the young man said in slow tones, with a dry relish.

"Philip, this is Nick Heriot; he and Dick are twins—identical, as you see."

The Colonel did see, since at that moment an exact replica of the young man who was shaking his hand came in, bearing a tray of drinks and glasses.

"Best I can do" Dick said. "Jeanne wanted to polish up the glasses, but I didn't think you'd care to wait for that." He poured out for his guests—"Only soda for me this morning" he said. "Why have balls?" He turned to Jamieson. "Now,

Sir, I don't imagine this is purely a social call—unless you want to see Luzia?"

"I don't in the least want to see Luzia" Jamieson said, rather haughtily.

"Oh well, some people always want to see Luzia" Nick put in. His brother cuffed him lightly. "Put a sock in it, Nick!" He turned back to Jamieson, slightly thrilled to meet some-one so high up in Intelligence. "How—if at all—can we be of use to you, Sir?"

"I gather that you have a man called Bonnecourt stowed on your premises here" Philip said, rather slowly and pon-derously. "I want to get him away—he can't stay in France now. He has been—well, very useful—to us in the past, and I must arrange to get him to safety at once."

"Oh, that's all been seen to" Nick said cheerfully. "I took him over to Tardets this morning, before daylight."

"Where is Tardets?"

"Away towards St. Jean Pied-de-Port—it's his home town, and full of his friends. It was from there that he operated during the War."

"Did he say what he was going to do?" Jamieson was a little concerned at this airy way of dealing with one of his Office's most valued former agents.

"Yes. He said he should lie up and get some sleep, and find out what the situation was on the frontier, and then cross to Pamplona. Colin, he said you'd have an address for him there—have you?"

"Of course." It was Jamieson who replied—Nick looked at the older man with interest. Aha and oho!—Pamplona must have an Intelligence branch of some sort.

"Did you see any signs of police activity near the fron-tier?" the Colonel asked; methodically—albeit rather igno-rantly—pursuing his enquiries.

"We never went near the frontier, so I wouldn't know about that—it's miles away, though Tardets is the nearest town to it, actually. But there was plenty of fuss on the main road—on the way back there were road-blocks on both sides of Ste.-Marie des Pèlerins, and again here."

Jamieson frowned.

"None on your way out?"

"Not here at Pau; we by-passed Ste.-Marie on the way to Tardets, just in case; because the police had stopped us once or twice in the town here, and I didn't like it all that much."

"Did the police who stopped you see Bonnecourt?" Jamieson asked, still frowning.

"Oh Lord no! I put him on the floor, with a rug over him" Nick replied, grinning. "You see I dug out our old chauffeur, whom all the local police know by sight, and Her Ladyship's tumbril of a Humber—which is equally familiar! I thought that might be good camouflage."

"You seem to have acted very wisely" Jamieson said. "All the same—" he paused. "Colin, I think you'd better drive over to Pamplona and find out if Bonnecourt has turned up there."

"Now?" Colin asked dismally. "I haven't had any lunch."

"You've only just finished your breakfast!" the Colonel retorted. "Get some lunch on the way."

"Am I to telephone, or to telegraph?" the young man asked.

"Telegraph—better to *Madame* J., at the *clinique*. Simply say *'arrivé'* or *'non-arrivé'*; then I shall know what goes on" Jamieson told him.

"Well, could I take *your* car? If I go back to the Victoire and get mine I shall have that bloody *agent* with me again, and that will make endless delays at the frontier."

"That's a sound idea" Nick put in. He had glanced out of the window during this interchange, and saw the hired Citroën on the drive. "If that's your Cit., Sir, it has no G.B. plate—a help in itself."

"If you are Nick, I think I must recruit you!" Colonel Jamieson said, at last smiling. "All right—off you go, Colin." He turned to the two young Heriots. "Perhaps one of you will take me back to the Victoire? I'll use your room till you get back, Colin, and your car."

As Colin went out Luzia Ericeira walked in. "Oh, how is Julia, Colin?" she asked him in the doorway.

"Find out from her husband!" Colin said irritably. "I'm being sent back to Spain." He went out, slamming the door behind him.

Luzia stood still, looking at the three men, for a moment; then she went over to Jamieson, who like his young hosts had risen at her entrance. "May I now call you Philip" she asked, holding out her hand.

"Yes, Condesa."

"And how is Julia? You have seen her already?"

"Just for a moment. She's quite well, but a little doped still."

"Naturally. Have you seen the baby? Is it still red?"

"No, not in the least—just the ordinary colour of babies" the Colonel said, startled by this peculiar enquiry. "Why should he be red?"

"Last night, just born, he was" Luzia said—"*Very* red. But the Professor said that it would pass. I am glad it has; the colour was terribly ugly."

The twins and the Colonel all laughed. But her next announcement was no laughing matter.

"Dick, do you know that the Special Police are going all through the house?—those *en civils?*" (She meant plain-clothes.) "They come to my room just now, and look in the cupboards, and under the bed. I think they seek for the hunter of *isard,* your friend."

Nick went straight to the window; he was just in time to see Colin swinging Philip's hired Citroën round the curve and out of the drive; but he also saw several men in plain clothes heading off through the gardens.

"That's the *Sûreté* all right" he said. "I'd better go and make sure that they don't harry old Lucien, and that Pierre doesn't make a clot of himself about last night." He went out. Dick however was angry.

"They came into your *room?*" he asked Luzia. "Oh, we can't have this—what a nerve! I'd better go and see that they don't wake my parents. Excuse me, Colonel." He too hurried out of the room.

"These are not very pleasant people" Luzia said, going over and pouring herself out a glass of sherry from the tray

Dick had brought in. "Naturally in Portugal we have our Special Police also—it is necessary, with the Communists seeking to infiltrate everywhere. But I think our PIDE behave with more courtesy."

This was something that Philip Jamieson particularly wished to hear about—not the PIDE's courtesy, but the behaviour of the *Sûreté* in regard to Julia.

"Were you there when they went up to Larège and called on my wife?" he asked.

"Of course."

"How did they behave? It is important to me to know this."

"Very unpleasantly. They accused her of lying when she told them that Colin had gone away; they went all through the house, throwing our dresses out of the *armoires* onto the floor, instead of looking behind them, as they could easily have done—and when they returned to Julia, downstairs, they made threats as to what would happen, to her and to Colin, if this foolish young Frenchman who escaped was not found."

"How did my wife take all this?" Jamieson asked, again frowning.

"Calmly—Julia is always calm. But she was disturbed. It was extremely unpleasant" the Portuguese girl repeated.

Philip was shocked by this report.

"How long ago was this?" he asked.

"One day—no, perhaps two, before I came down to Pau— I do not remember exactly. She seemed to have recovered herself completely, or I should not have left her. But it could have been this disturbance which brought on the *fausse couche*. Oh, how I wish I had not come away!—that there had not been this ball! But—*enfin*—she and the little one are both all right, and that is the essential."

Philip Jamieson had spent a great part of his official life in assessing people's characters, and particularly their reliability as reporters of events; even in this short interview he took Luzia's measure, and gave her full marks. (At the wedding, when she had put in an appearance as Julia's solitary bridesmaid, and at the luncheon afterwards, he had spoken to her very little—though even then he had registered the deliberate way in which she had worn the simplest of dresses, and played down her own great beauty in order to give the bride pride of place.) He took this opportunity of consulting her further.

"Condesa, have you any idea *why* the *Sûreté* should have connected M. Bonnecourt with this young de Lassalle's escape?—and my wife also?"

"I cannot be sure; I only make a guess" Luzia said, measuredly. "Colin took an impetuous decision to let the young man go, when he found that it was Bonnecourt, whom he likes so much, who was waiting for him and his friend at the *auberge;* but he went on to Pau and made his *constat* about the accident to the police who waited at the old man's bedside in the hospital—the one who fell, I mean. I think it possible that he said more than was necessary, and so gave the police a clue."

Jamieson knew Colin well—he thought it more than possible.

"Did Colin speak to you of this?" he asked.

"A little—when I told him that I had seen this young Lassalle emptying a knapsack of curious objects into a pool. He took me there next morning—*very* early, before people were awake; I showed him the spot, and he found these things; but he only took away a clock."

"A clock?"

"Yes. It was in a camera-case, I think—but the case he left."

"What sort of case?" Jamieson was thinking furiously, regretting that he had not checked further with the Office before he left London, nor questioned Colin more fully before he sent him back to Spain.

"Of canvas—such as one carries a camera in."

Jamieson at once got a very fair idea of what the camera-case really was—he changed his line of questioning.

"Did anyone in Larège suggest to you that these two men belonged to the O.A.S.?"

"No. But I told Colin at once that I was sure they were O.A.S., and *saboteurs,* wishing to cause *dégâts* at Lacq; this was merely my idea, but I think it is that of the *Sûreté* also!" Luzia said, looking amused. "Why, otherwise, do two Frenchmen *climb* over the frontier, instead of crossing by car? Only to avoid the control posts, is it not?"

"I agree with you" Philip was saying, with approval, when one of those two confusing twins came in.

"Well, I just beat them to it at old Lucien's" he said; "they were still hunting through the bushes. I took away the mattress from in front of the fire—that *would* have been a giveaway!—and rubbed it into the old boy to say that he'd been asleep all night, and seen no one. But they were ahead of me at the garage—they're all over the place! However Pierre was still in bed, and so sleepy that they hadn't got any sense out of him—I asked them what they wanted to know, and they poured out the police report of the Humber having been reported passing through Ste.-Marie des Pèlerins in the small hours. So I repeated my patter about Pierre having driven me to a party near St. Jean Pied-de-Port, which of course squared with their records. Very important always to tell the same story!" he said to Philip, with a grin.

"I think you must be Nick" Philip was beginning, when again the duplicate of the young man he was speaking to entered.

"Well, I've chased those bastards out of the house" he announced with satisfaction. "I told them I should ring up the *Préfêt* if they didn't clear off. Going into the bedrooms of our guests!—*quelle idée!* Which is my glass? Righteous indignation makes one so thirsty. Anyhow I don't think they disturbed the parents."

As he spoke the door opened, and old Lady Heriot walked in.

"*Who* didn't disturb your parents, Dick?" Lady Heriot always knew her sons apart. "Good morning, Luzia." She paused in midroom. "I see you have a guest—please introduce him."

"This is Colonel Jamieson" the twins said in chorus. "My Mother, Lady Heriot."

"Oh, how do you do? How excellent that you were able to come. How is your wife?—and the child?"

Philip repeated that they were both well.

"I am *so* glad. We all took a great fancy to Mrs. Jamieson when she was with us. Where are you staying?"

Philip said that he was at the Victoire.

"Ah yes—most convenient. But the *cuisine* there is only rather moderate. I hope you will lunch with us?"

Philip accepted; it was now after one o'clock, and from what he knew of small French hotels he realised that the *repas du midi* at the Victoire would begin sharp at 12.30, and end at 1.15.

"Is His Lordship awake?" one of the twins asked.

"No, dear. He was tired, and when he is tired he is apt to sleep badly—so I gave him an immensely potent pill! I believe they call it Tuinal" she said to Jamieson, with a sly smile which reminded him of the grins of her indistinguishable sons. "Such a mercy, in this exhausting modern world, that these pills which knock you out completely, and yet do no harm, should have been invented."

"You oughtn't to use expressions like 'knock you out', Your Ladyship" one of the twins expostulated.

"Dearest, why not?"

"I don't think it's in character with you, nor with your age bracket."

"If Lady Heriot will allow me to say so, I think the phrase is completely in character—and that she is independent of any age brackets!" Philip was impelled to say.

"Oh, how kind you are! Darling, tell them one extra to lunch." As a twin went out—"Darling, am I not to be allowed any sherry?" she said to the other.

Philip was enchanted by this. How seldom in the exhausting modern world one met a Mother who refused to pour out a drink for herself when an able-bodied son was there to do it for her—most women nowadays, silly fools, mixed and handed drinks to young men lounging in arm-chairs. He resolved there and then to see to it that his Julia should be as firm later on with the minute object, now in the *crèche* in the Rue de Toulouse, as Lady Heriot was with her strapping offspring. Probably Julia would be, anyhow, if they had *enough;* she was very sensible. He must have a talk with that Professor man presently, and find out whether she could ever have normal births—he had a vague idea that three Caesarians was about the limit; but the Professor had still been in bed when he went to the clinic.

The luncheon was pleasant, the food admirable; and Philip was increasingly attracted by his elderly hostess—her natural sympathy, and her shrewdness. At one point—"Have you telegraphed to Mrs. Hathaway about the baby?" she asked him.

"No. I'm afraid I never thought to."

"Oh, but you *must*. Mary's only child died; Julia is her god-daughter, and the nearest thing she has to a child of her own. She ought to know at once. Nick dear, bring the block and pad off my desk in the morning-room; then Colonel Jamieson can write his message, and you can telephone it."

"Mayn't I eat my *Baba au Rhum?* She's done it rather well today."

"Oh, you greedy child! All right—'finish your dinner', as Nannie used to say!" She turned again to Jamieson. "I am sure you know Mary Hathaway?"

"Yes, of course. A most splendid person. We met last— before our wedding—in rather distressing circumstances." He mentioned old Professor Burbage's sudden death in the Scillies, the funeral, and how gallantly the old lady had in-sisted in going through with the meal afterwards in the hotel—"She *would* eat the 'funeral baked meats' with the people who had been kind to him in the Islands."

"Yes, of course. Mary is gallant; really *valiant*. Thank you for telling me this, Colonel Jamieson; of course she didn't, only reported that silly old fool's death. Why she was so attached to him I can't think." Lady Heriot paused. "Do you believe he was a traitor? *I* do."

"No. I think he was just one of these learned fools, who are wholly without common-sense. He slipped up once, and the Russians kept the heat turned on him for a very long time. That does break people's morale."

"Oh well, you are very charitable, I see—or perhaps

merely very discreet!" She rose. "Let us go and have coffee. Nick, will you now graciously consent to bring that pad and pencil off my desk?"

In the drawing-room, constantly advised by Lady Heriot, Philip wrote out his telegram to Mrs. Hathaway. "*Don't* say a Caesarean" the old lady told him—"that will worry her. Just say 'safely', or something. And give the address and the telephone number of the clinic—I expect Mary will want to ring up. She's a great telephoner."

All this good counsel would have exasperated Philip from anyone else, but he had so succumbed to his hostess that he meekly followed her suggestions, and submitted his telegram for her approval.

"Yes—very nice. I think you were wise not to mention the weight; five pounds *is* rather small. Dick dear, please telephone that from your Father's study."

When Jamieson left Nick drove him back to the clinic in one of the Heriot cars, which an *agent,* still stationed at the gate, allowed to pass unquestioned. "Busy, aren't they?" the young man said. "Your brother-in-law, or whatever he is, seems to have stirred up a regular hornet's-nest."

"Cousin-by-marriage. Yes, it looks like that; they seem very persistent."

"Well let us know when you hear if Bonnecourt has got clear. He's a splendid person, and what he did for the English in the last War was nobody's business." As he swung into the drive at the clinic, "Just ring us if there's anything we can do" Nick said, and drove off again.

The nurse on duty was rather reluctant to let the Colonel see Julia—patients reposed themselves in the afternoon, she pronounced. However Philip persisted, and it proved that Madame was awake—much more awake than she had been in the morning, in fact; the effect of the anaesthetic had now entirely worn off. Philip offered her a cigarette.

"Oh no, mustn't smoke. The taste of the tobacco gets into the milk in twenty minutes, and it may put the child off— anyhow it's not good for them. Mustn't eat chocolates either, for the same reason—so I've stopped at once."

"Dearest, how horrid for you. Do you mind *my* smoking?"

"No, not a bit—puff it at me!" she said, smiling and re-laxed. But when her husband got down to business and told her that a telegram might come addressed to *her*, and that she must have it taken round at once to the Hotel Victoire, she became very alert.

"Who from?"

"Colin—to let me know about Bonnecourt. We want to be sure that he's got away; but as the *Sûreté* are so active I thought it best to have the telegram sent to *you*, here."

"Quite right. Where has precious Bonnecourt gone?"

"To Pamplona, we hope. I've sent Colin over to find out if he's turned up. As things are, he can't possibly stay in France at present."

"How was he to get to Pamplona?"

Philip recounted Nick Heriot's neat move in carting Bonne-court over to Tardets in the small hours. Julia laughed and reflected.

"Well if B. can't stay in France pro tem, he'd much better go to Glentoran" she said at length. "They're terribly short of gillies just now, Edina said in her last letter—and there can't be all that difference between stalking *isard* and stalking red deer! They've let both the shooting-lodges, and they're starved for good stalkers—I know there's at least *one* cottage empty since MacKerrow left."

"Quite a possible idea" Philip said. "Bernardin", with his tremendous local reputation, might be rather an embarrass-ment to Philip's own people in Pamplona if he stayed there for long. "Actually I expect we could employ him ourselves; but a base in Scotland could be useful between jobs" he said reflectively. Then he enquired after his tiny son.

"Oh, he's terrifically tough! The old head *sage-femme* had him brought in before lunch and put to the breast; of course there won't be any milk for twenty-four hours, or more, with a prem baby; but if they suck it's supposed to stimulate it, and bring it along quicker. And he sucked like absolute mad! He was *furious* when nothing came."

"What *is* he getting?" Philip asked, laughing.

"Oh glucose, or Cow-and-Gate or something, from the bottle" Julia said easily. "They really do know all the answers here—and the old *sage-femme* says he's as greedy as a pig!"

Philip Jamieson laughed again. All his eager, and ignorant, anticipations concerning paternity were being fulfilled to the most delightful degree in this modest little place outside Pau: his wife so determined to breast-feed the child, his son himself already possessing sufficient vigour to be both greedy, and furious. But then the tiny old *sage-femme* came in and said that now Madame really needed repose; Philip bent over the bed and kissed Julia.

"Bless you. Just have Colin's telegram sent across when it comes. I'm going to get some sleep—I had precisely two hours-and-a-half last night!" He went away.

Chapter 9

Colin's telegram only reached Philip after a certain delay. It came in time to be delivered at the clinic soon after 8 P.M., but Professor Martin was then paying his evening visit to Julia, so it was only after he had left her that the old head *sage-femme* took it in. Julia read it with interest. The office of origin was given as Jaca, and the message, in French, read: "Not arrived but time probably still insufficient stop propose remain for present if you agree stop R.S.V.P. Colin."

Julia was puzzled at first as to why Colin should be telegraphing from Jaca; then she realised that he could not have got to Pamplona by the time he wired—he would have rung up from Jaca on his way through, made his enquiries, and telegraphed from there. She asked for her despatch-case; she wanted to write a note to Philip, but the little old *sage-femme*, whose firmness was in inverse ratio to her size, said "Not at present!" It was time that the child should be put to the breast again, and Madame must not exert herself, or it would be bad for the milk. So once more the swaddled infant was presented with the still milkless breast, sucked and tugged in vain, and wailing with rage and frustration was borne off to get his bottle. Only then did Julia address an envelope for the telegram, scribble a note explaining where Jaca was, and add some words of love. She rang her bell, and asked to have the note taken round to the Colonel Jamieson at the Victoire—"It is to be given to *Monsieur le Colonel* personally" she insisted. "To no one else."

Philip had finished his unexhilarating dinner in the equally unexhilarating *salle-à-manger,* and was sitting smoking under the acacias in the garden of the Victoire in the warm September night, when under the arc-lights he saw a nurse come trotting up the drive—he went over to her.

149

"I am Colonel Jamieson," he said. "Do you bring a letter from Madame my wife at the *clinique?*"

The nurse was nervous and flustered.

"You are *surely le Colonel Jimmison?* Madame said I was to give the letter to him personally."

"Certainly. How else should I know that Madame is at the *clinique?* How is *le petit?* Has the milk come yet?"

That did it. With the *agent* hanging watchfully about Philip did not particularly want to take the young nurse into the hotel and get the *patron* to identify him; he was relieved when she replied, smiling, that they expected the milk in yet some hours; Madame's breasts were swelling. Then she handed over the letter, and pattered off again down the drive. Philip returned to his chair; the light over the front door just enabled him to read the telegram and Julia's covering note.

He sat for some time and digested these tidings. It would have been a relief to know that Bonnecourt was safely at Pamplona, but Colin knew the district and the distances, with which he himself was unfamiliar—it might be all right, but one couldn't be sure. And Bonnecourt had *got* to be got out, and to some place of safety. After some reflection Colonel Jamieson decided that he had better go up to Paris himself, put the situation to his colleagues there, and get the *Sûreté* to lay off Bonnecourt—and Colin, come to that! He went into the hotel and asked for a railway time-table; as he did so the *agent* got out of Colin's car, and watched him. Philip refused the *patron's* help; he thumbed through the railway guide, and saw that there was a train to Paris at 10.50 P.M. It was now ten minutes past nine; heaps of time, but he would do well to ring the Office in Paris and arrange to be met—Philip knew about the shortage of taxis in Paris —and also get a telegram off to Colin, who had certainly better stay at Pamplona in case an emergency dash was needed in some direction or other. But he didn't want to do any of this from the hotel; better from the Heriots. He would have liked to pack his small case and take it with him, but that would mean more delay; and if he tried to use Colin's car, he would have the *agent* on his tail—really on his back!

He handed the time-table to the *patron,* said he was going out, and set off on foot.

Jamieson had taken note of the way from the Heriot mansion to the Route de Toulouse when Nick drove him back to the clinic, and retraced it; he found the great house without much trouble. Lights were still burning in the first-floor windows, but there was another *agent* at the door, who asked him his business as he pressed the bell.

"To see Milord Heriot," Philip said curtly.

As before, it was a twin who opened the door.

"Oh hullo—come in. We're answering the bell ourselves, so that the *agents* shan't try to pump the staff—anyhow they're asleep now, poor old things. What can we do?" he asked, as they shot up in the lift. "And how is Mrs. J?"

"Doing very well, thank you—and the baby too. I'm afraid I really want to use your telephone—I hope that won't be too much of a nuisance. The police are rather nosey at my hotel."

"Not a bit. His lordship has gone to bed. Has Bonnecourt got out all right?"

"Well no—at least he hasn't got to Pamplona yet."

"Oh, so Colin's wired, has he?" the young man asked, as he spoke leading the Colonel into his Father's study, and closing the door. "I'm Nick—may I know what he says?"

Philip remembered that Nick was the twin who had so intelligently removed Bonnecourt the night before; he handed him Colin's telegram.

"Well, he would have had to move pretty fast to get to Pamplona by the time Colin rang up from Jaca" the young man said, handing back the telegram; "unless he managed to slip across the frontier and get onto one of the timber-lorries from Roncal." Unlike Jamieson, he had the whole Pyrenean countryside in his head, and knew all the means of transport. "So I shouldn't think we need to worry yet. Now, what do you want to do next?"

"Send a telegram to Colin, to tell him to wait at Pamplona for the moment."

"Can't do that till tomorrow morning—telegraphs pack up at eight."

"Oh." Philip, accustomed to the all-night telegraph service in England, was rather irritated. "I'd like to put a call through to Paris, too, if I may" he said. "I want to get our people there to cope with the French."

"The *Sûreté?*" Nick asked.

"Actually, no—we usually work through the *Deuxième Bureau*. But they can pass anything on to the *Sûreté*."

Nick was interested. "Why not deal direct with the people concerned?"

"Why have M.I.5 and M.I.6?" Jamieson replied, with a dry smile. "The same idea—division of function, internal and external."

Though Nick had been born and brought up in France, these *nuances* about its Intelligence Service had never come his way—as the differing functions of M.I.5 and M.I.6 do not normally come the way of ordinary British citizens. But he refrained from asking any more of the questions which sprang into his mind. "Well, telephone away—there's the machine" he said.

Philip used the telephone on Lord Heriot's big desk— neatly piled, he noticed as he waited for his connection, with papers concerning property, the Anglican Church, the Golf Club, and local charities. When he got the Office in Paris he said that he was coming up on the 10.50 train that night and that he was to be met the next morning. "Tell the Major—I shall want to see him, and I may stay the night." After ringing off he got the *Inter* again and asked to be given the price of his call while he held on; but he was cut off.

Nick overheard Jamieson's talk to Paris.

"Where's your luggage?" he asked.

"At the Victoire—I didn't want to waste time packing, *or* to use Colin's car, with that *agent* in it; I walked round."

"Oh. Well hadn't I better put you up a razor and tooth-brush and things? Plenty of spares here—people leave them behind, and Her Ladyship refuses to send them on; she has them disinfected, and keeps them for cases of emergency, like you!"

"Well, thank you—that would be very convenient" the Colonel was saying, when Dick walked in.

"Oh, good evening, Sir. I hope Mother and child are both doing well?"

"Very well, thank you." Jamieson found the Heriot twins, with their absurd resemblance and their cheerful good manners, extremely engaging.

"Colonel Jamieson's going up to Paris on the 10.50" Nick said. "Oh, have you got a sleeper, Sir?"

"No—but that doesn't matter; I'll take a chance on it."

"If you tip the Wagon-Lits attendant heavily enough he'll probably put you into one" Dick observed. "Anything else we can do?"

"Well yes. When it is possible to send telegrams again, tomorrow morning, I should like one to be sent to Colin at Pamplona."

"Oh yes. By the way, has Bonnecourt fetched up there all right?"

"No—but there has hardly been time, your brother says." Philip glanced at his watch; it was ten minutes to ten—he had just an hour before his train. "If I could have a block, I will jot it down" he said.

"Put it in French" Dick said, handing his guest a block and a pencil; "even so, it will get a bit garbled."

The Colonel, wishing he knew the French for "stay put", wrote carefully—"Remain where you are for present stop. Julia and child well stop telegraph any news to her P." He handed the block to Dick, who looked the telegram over.

"They won't take a wire with only an initial" he said. "Better put 'Phillips, care Heriot.' Colin will understand." He was greatly enjoying being able actually to lend a hand to a high-up member of the Secret Service. Jamieson made the alteration—at that instant the telephone rang loudly—it was the *Inter*, to give the price of the Paris call. A few moments later Lady Heriot appeared in a flowing flannel dressing-gown, a net over her grey hair.

"Who was that ringing up?" she asked her son. "Oh, good evening, Colonel Jamieson. How is your wife? Nothing wrong, I hope?"

"No, Madame is fine." It was Dick who replied, briskly; as

he spoke he shut the door, which Lady Heriot had left open. "Security!" he said. "I never feel sure these days that a *Sûreté* man hasn't sneaked up in the lift to just below floor level to eavesdrop! Did His Lordship wake up?"

"No, dear. I wasn't asleep, so I heard. But what *was* the call?"

"Only the *Inter* letting Colonel Julia know the price of a call to Paris" Dick said. "He's going up on the night train."

"Oh, the 10.50." She glanced at a pretty mahogany clock on the wall. "Just time for a drink before he goes. Fetch some whisky, dear."

Jamieson was longing for a drink; he loved Lady Heriot more than ever. She had sat down in one of the heavy leather arm-chairs in her husband's study; seated there, so serene, in her old-fashioned dressing-gown and hairnet, giving thoughtful hospitality to a stranger in the middle of the night, he thought her almost perfect.

"I suppose you are going to Paris to try to arrange about M. Bonnecourt?" she said. "But what shall you do about the house at Larège? You realise that the baby can't be moved for another two months, till it is *à terme*, the full nine months; and if your wife is going to nurse it herself, as I gathered from Luzia that she intends to do—I am very glad; that is so *right*—of course it is a matter of feeds every two hours. So Mrs. Jamieson won't be able to leave Pau for the next eight weeks either. Oughtn't something to be arranged about shutting up the Larège house, till the Stansteds come back? And if your wife and Luzia have left any belongings there, they should be fetched down; the Larègeois are apt to be rather light-fingered."

Philip was rather aghast at all this. He had of course not had the faintest idea that premature babies could not be moved, still less that they must be fed every two hours; he had another urgent job abroad impending very soon, too.

"I think this will have to be worked out when I get back from Paris" he said. "Possibly tomorrow night; if not, the following day. Could the Police be asked to keep an eye on the house till then?"

Dick, coming in with a tray of decanters and glasses, over-heard the Colonel's last words—he laughed.

"*All* the local police seem to be occupied watching this house and the Victoire, or manning road-blocks, or patrol-ling the frontier for our dear B." he said. "*Maman,* a tiny whisk, with all these excitements?" He arranged a minute glass for his Mother. "Please help yourself, Sir" he said to Jamieson, who poured out a comforting tumbler.

Nick re-appeared, and handed a plastic wallet with several compartments to the Colonel. "Razor, shaving-stick, soap, wash-rag, a collar and some clean hankies" he said. "That do?"

"Splendidly. Thank you very much."

"Your Ladyship, what are you doing, up and drinking at this hour?" Nick asked his Mother.

"Talking with Colonel Jamieson. The telephone rang, so I came out; I didn't want to disturb your Father by talking in the bedroom. He's asleep. But it was only the wretched Ex-change."

This reminded Philip that he had not paid for his telegram to Colin or his call to Paris; he pulled out some notes. Lady Heriot made no movement to take the money.

"I don't really like your paying for calls which are only made to help dear M. Bonnecourt" she said.

"You'd far better let him. His Lordship will create when the bill comes in, if there are calls unaccounted for," Dick said, taking the notes. "You'll hardly credit it, Sir, but my dear Father keeps a book in which *all* calls have to be writ-ten down, and a box to put the money in; and checks both with his telephone account."

"I will credit it; my own Father used to do exactly the same" the Colonel said, with an embarrassed glance at his hostess.

"The Scots are such *thorough* people" Lady Heriot said tolerantly. "Dick, write up the call, and put the money in the box. Then I think one of you ought to bring the car round, if Colonel Jamieson is to catch his train."

"I will" said Nick, and went off.

It now occurred to Philip that he ought to send a message to Julia to say that he was going to Paris—he mentioned this to the old lady. "Perhaps Luzia could let her know to-morrow?"

"Yes, of course—or one of the boys can take a note round. Do write one—paper in the top right-hand drawer."

The drawer of Lord Heriot's desk was as methodical as the top of it: neat wooden partitions held three different sizes of writing-paper, with appropriate envelopes. Jamieson scrawled a note, ending "Probably back day after tomorrow. Dearest love. P."—and put it in an envelope.

"We will get that round early tomorrow" Dick said. "Come on down, Sir." Philip thanked his hostess, and was taken down; Nick's Dauphine was just drawing up as they went out of the front door.

"*Agents* to the right of them, *agents* to the left of them, volleyed and thundered" Nick misquoted irritably as the Colonel got into the car, and he drove off. "I hope you'll be able to do something to quell them in Paris, Sir. They're getting on Pierre's nerves, hanging about the garage all the time."

"I'll try" Philip said. But he was still a little anxious about Bonnecourt. "You're Nick, aren't you?" he asked of the young man who was driving him through the lamplit streets —"The one who took Bonnecourt away?"

"Yes, that's me."

"Well, if it weren't inconvenient, it might be a good thing if you went over to this place that ends in "ETS" tomorrow and tried to find out what's become of our friend. If we can contact him, we can get him out; if we can't, we can't."

"How would you get him out?" Nick asked, curious.

"By air, probably—but that can be arranged later. The essential thing is to know where he is."

"We might try" Nick said, rather gloomily. "These people are frightfully cagey when anything's going on."

"Well *do* try" the Colonel said. "Everything *may* be all right; but if he could have got down to Pamplona by these timber-lorries that one of you mentioned, I'm rather sur-prised that he hasn't."

When Nick got back after putting Jamieson onto his train he let himself in with his latch-key; in the flat he found Dick still up, and reported what the Colonel had said about Bonnecourt. "He was a bit bothered, I could see that; though he didn't actually say so."

Dick reflected. He liked the idea of sleuthing to help British Intelligence very much; but he also turned his mind onto his knowledge of Bonnecourt's character, and methods.

"Well?" Nick asked, as his twin remained silent.

"I was thinking. Of course B. could cross the frontier anywhere, however much of it's being patrolled. But he's a lazy old hound, and if his scouts have told him that there's a lot of activity going on, he may have gone to ground somewhere in Tardets—after all, it's his home town."

"So what?" Nick asked.

"So tomorrow morning you take Her Ladyship over, and let *her* do the enquiring. She has a terrific memory, and I'd expect she still remembers the names and addresses of troops of his relations."

"Probably all dead by now" Nick said, glumly. "Still, I agree she's the best bet. All right—we'll go over to Tardets tomorrow."

Philip Jamieson did secure a sleeper, had a wash, aided by the contents of Nick's plastic wallet, took off everything but his shirt, and settled down in the cool clean berth. But it was some time before he could get to sleep. As the train jolted along past Lacq—whose glaring flood-lighting and red plumes of flame, so conspicuous at night, he didn't see because the shutters were drawn—on past Orthez and Dax, he lay thinking about Julia, so amazingly snatched from death by Bonnecourt, whom he had never met; about his minute son and *his* health, and all the unforeseen complications which Lady Heriot had outlined to him. Julia stuck for two more months in Pau—and he had got to go abroad again in three weeks! The gamp in London, prudently engaged by Julia for November, would have to be cancelled too; and the house at Larège dealt with, and Luzia sent home. For the first time Philip began to realise what marriage involved, and to wonder, disturbedly, whether it was really compatible with his job. It was maddening to have to leave Julia and the child just now; but Bonnecourt *must* be got out—that was an inescapable obligation, apart from what he had just done for them. Philip Jamieson felt almost inclined to curse his job; he wondered when, if ever, he and Julia would be able to have some real leisure together, and what sort of life he could give her? Coming home at intervals to beget another of the six children she had said she wanted, and then leaving her to face the risks of pregnancy and child-birth alone, while he went off to outwit "the enemy" in unreachable places—would she accept that? He worried at the problem almost till the train reached Bordeaux; he had just got to sleep when the jerk to a stop, the clamour and shouting outside in the big station, re-awakened him. But after that he grew calmer; he would be back within two days, and they were both all right—there would be nothing to worry her. He fell asleep, and slept, at last, soundly.

An office car met him at the station. "Major Monteith said you was to come to his flat for breakfast, Sir" the chauffeur said; there, after excellent coffee they repaired to the Major's study, where Philip posed his problem. Major Monteith remembered "Bernardin's" War record, but he knew little about his recent activities, except for this new blow-up over the disappearance of young de Lassalle.

"The French are a bit upset about that" he said—"in fact quite nasty. They seem to have got the idea from the Police at Pau that young Monro was in some way involved, as well as this man Bonnecourt. Was he?"

"Up to a point. Colin was actually on the frontier and saw that old man fall, and helped to carry him down to Larège, to my house. He telephoned for the Doctor, and the old boy was taken to the hospital in Pau."

Monteith was flipping through a file. When he had received the telephoned message to say that Colonel Jamieson was coming up from Pau to Paris on the night train he had jumped to the correct conclusion as to the reason for this sudden journey, and caused a clerk to bring the relevant papers round to his flat.

"Oh yes—old Maupassant. And young Monro, quite properly, made a report of the accident to the police, since he had witnessed it. But you see both these types were definitely O.A.S., which the French don't care about at all; and according to the *Sûreté* investigators, de Lassalle was dropped by Monro at some pub—his car's a Rover, isn't it? —so conspicuous in France!—and taken away by Bonnecourt afterwards. *His* car is pretty recognisable too—a vintage Bugatti! And young de Lassalle has never been seen since. The *Sûreté* are convinced that Bonnecourt slipped him back the same night over the frontier, into Spain; B. is known to be a climber's guide, and a hunter of the local chamois, or whatever it is; he knows those mountains like the inside of his pocket! So you can understand what their attitude is."

Philip reflected on this.

"Yes, I do see" he said at length. "But that's the *Sûreté*'s attitude. You're in touch with the *Deuxième Bureau;* they must know perfectly well what Bernardin did in getting Allied airmen across the frontier in the last War—surely even the French keep records! Can't you get someone in the *D.B.,* on an 'old-boy' basis, to tell the *Sûreté* to lay off Bonnecourt for a bit? *We* owe him a lot in the past—and at the moment *I* owe him my wife's life, and that of my son."

The Major looked embarrassed.

"My dear fellow, I'm terribly sorry, but just now all the 'old-boy' business is out" he said. "The French are as sour as vinegar with us at present, because of our special relationship with the U.S., and the Common Market, and this and that. They simply won't play—it would be no good my trying. Least of all" he added, "when one of *our* people is under suspicion of having connived at the escape of an O.A.S. *activiste*. Most unfortunate, that. Do you know what *did* happen?"

Philip knew a certain amount, but as things were he decided not to pass it on to Major Monteith.

"I was barely twenty-four hours in Pau" he said, "and most of that time I spent in seeing my wife, and getting some sleep. Thank you for making the position so clear,

Monteith. Could you get the Office to book me a sleeper back to Pau tonight?"

"Of course. You'll lunch here, I hope?"

"May I let you know? I have some friends I want to look up. What I *should* like is a bath and a shave—but don't let me delay you."

Armed with Nick's wallet, Philip shaved and had a bath, while his host departed to the Office; then he sat and considered. How tiresome the elected politicians were, rotting up really *serious*, professional, international business with their rivalries and quarrels! His own job was of course mainly political, but its discipline ruled out quarrels or personal egotism. In spite of Monteith's discouragement, he presently rang up a very old friend in the *Deuxième Bureau*, and was warmly pressed to come round and see him— "*Quelle chance de te voir, mon cher Philippe.*" With Colonel de Monceau, at least, the "old-boy" basis still existed. Philip explained his presence in France by the birth of his son— Frenchly, his old colleague was delighted; he got up and embraced Philip. Then Jamieson went on to try to smooth things over for both Bonnecourt and Colin. Jean de Monceau was of an age to remember "Bernardin" 's war-time record himself—"*un type magnifique*" he said. He was shocked to learn that his old friend Jamieson had had to leave his hotel in Pau on foot because an *agent* was sitting in Colin's car. "But they do not derange Madame?"

"I think they may, at any moment—that is partly why I want you to help, Jean. They are pestering the Heriots, too; hanging about the house night and day, and worrying their old chauffeur to death."

"But why do the *Sûreté* occupy themselves with this wonderful old *Milord Écossais?* For three generations his family have lived there, really *creating* Pau as a tourist centre."

Philip was carefully vague.

"I wasn't there, so I am not perfectly clear as to what happened. But after Bonnecourt drove my wife down from Larège to Professor Martin's *clinique*—which saved her life, *and* the boy's!—Colin followed them; and it seems the police were on his track, because they suspected him of complicity in the escape of this young O.A.S. man, de Lassalle."

Colonel de Monceau became very alert—he rang a bell on his desk; when a clerk entered he told him to bring the de Lassalle file—"or of de Maupassant." Then he turned to Philip.

"*Was* this young Monro implicated?"

"Very little, I think; he happened to be up on the frontier when old Maupassant fell, and naturally helped to get him down and to the hospital—and then made the *constat* to the police. But that was enough for them to record his name and his car, and track him round from the *clinique* to Lord Heriot's house—where he went to ring up the Office in London, to let me know that the child was coming prematurely. Actually they drove there in Bonnecourt's car, and the *agents* came and interviewed Bonnecourt in the middle of a ball the Heriots were giving. It was rather disagreable."

"Most unfortunate—a great lack of tact," de Monceau said. At that moment the clerk brought in a file—excusing himself, the Frenchman studied it with accomplished speed.

"It seems that 'Bernardin' disappeared while Lord Heriot was speaking with the police, and has not been seen since—nor his car. Do you know where he is now?"

"In Pamplona, I *hope*" Jamieson said, with a frank grin.

"How did he get away?"

"Well, strictly between ourselves, Jean, one of the Heriot twins hid him in the garden, and later the other drove him off on the floor of the car, under a rug, to a place near the frontier—*still* while the ball was going on!"

"Ah, *ces jumeaux*! I met them two years ago, when I was *en vacances* in Pau; so intelligent, so gay—and Madame their Mother is a lady in a thousand!" He turned to the file again. "But young Monro—where is he?"

"I sent him to Pamplona in my car, to find out if Bonnecourt had turned up, and told him to stay there to—keep on reporting" Philip said prudently. "But look, Jean, can't you get the *Sûreté* to lay off all this nonsense? You know that we're on your side about Lacq—that's what we sent Monro over here for. It's too silly to have an *agent* sitting in his car all the time, and troops of others hanging about the Heriot's house." He went on to repeat, indignantly, Luzia's report of the visit of the *Sûreté* to Julia at Larège—"The young Comtesse is convinced that their behaviour had something to do with bringing on the *fausse couche* of my wife."

"This shall have immediate attention" Monceau said. "I am distressed; I call Pau at once. *Mon ami,* will you lunch with me? We meet too seldom! Twelve-thirty, at the *Bouteille d'Or* on the *Rive Gauche?* I do not ask you to the house—my wife is away, and our present cook is very indifferent. Yes? *Perfect!*"

But while Philip was dealing with the *Deuxième Bureau* in Paris—very successfully, as it proved—all sorts of things were going on in Pau. The twins got hold of their Mother early, and explained that she must go over to Tardets, "to find out what Bonnecourt's up to", Dick said. "Nick will take you in the Dauphine—we don't want the Humber barging through those road-blocks again. I'll stay here, in case anything happens."

"Take Luzia round to the *clinique,* perhaps" Nick observed ironically. "There's that note from Colonel Julia to be dropped, anyhow."

"Oh, what fun," Lady Heriot said. "Yes, of course—Bonnecourt's old Aunt runs that rather dreary little hotel, and then there's his charming sister, Madame Pontarlet, who keeps the *épicerie.* I'd love to see them again. But how long will it take? If I'm not back, you must give your Father his lunch, Dick." Lord Heriot, like many old men, had managed to create the tradition that he could not really be nourished without the presence of some member of his family when he ate his meals.

"I'll see to feeding His Lordship. You get dressed and breeze off to Tardets, *maman*" Dick replied.

But long before Dick and Luzia set out for the clinic Julia, quiet in her bed, was suddenly confronted with a quite unexpected problem. The old Professor came in to see her, pronounced her condition excellent, and then said—"But today Madame must register the birth of the child, with its names."

"Oh. Where does one do that?"

"At the *Mairie*."

"But I can't go to the *Mairie*" Julia protested.

"No—let the husband of Madame go and make the registration."

"Oh, fine. He's at the Victoire; be an angel, Professor, and get someone to ring him up and ask him to come round."

But when telephoned to, the Victoire stated firmly that *M. le Colonel* was not there; he had not slept there; he had gone out for a walk after the dinner, and had never returned —he had asked to see the railway time-table, but had not said where he was going.

Julia was quite aghast when the Professor passed this information on to her.

"But he wouldn't go back to London without telling me! Did he take his luggage?"

"They did not say—I will ascertain." He opened the door, called for a nurse, and told her to enquire about the Colonel's luggage; then he came back to the bed-side. "Meanwhile, let Madame address herself to the matter of registering the birth of the child, since her husband is absent. What names?"

"I don't *know!*" Julia exclaimed wretchedly, "We hadn't settled anything—it's come so early; and we couldn't know if it would be a boy or a girl?"

"Well, Madame must now decide on the names."

"Why must it be done today?" Julia asked, impatiently.

"A child must be registered within three clear days of the birth. Your son was delivered yesterday, in the early hours; but today is Saturday, and the *Mairie* closes at noon. So the registration must be made today."

"Bloody old *loi de France* again!" Julia muttered to herself.

"*Plait-il?*" the Professor asked—fortunately he was too deaf to hear her words.

"Nothing. Professor, do please ring up the Heriot's house;

they may know where my husband is. This is all *too* frightful."

"Calm yourself, Madame! If you get *sur-excitée,* it will be bad for the milk, which is all-important for the child."

But the call to the Heriots was not any more helpful than that to the Victoire. No, the Colonel Jamieson was not there. But the Comtesse de Ericeira was coming round at once to see Madame, bringing a note from *M. le Colonel.* And in barely five minutes Luzia walked in, cool and beautiful, bringing Philip's note, which Julia read with the greedy eagerness of a young wife in love.

"Oh, he's gone to Paris!" She looked at the letter again. "But he doesn't give the telephone number, so we can't ring him up. Oh dear!"

"Why do you want to ring him up?"

"The baby's names must be registered today, and we hadn't settled on anything."

"Then you must decide yourself. Philip will agree to whatever you say" the young girl affirmed. "Just reflect quietly!"

Julia did reflect. One of the names must be Philip; but she wanted also to commemorate Bonnecourt, to whom her and Philip's son owed his life. And there flashed into her mind a recollection of something the hunter had said on that nightmare drive down from Larège barely thirty-six hours before. To keep her from worrying—she recognised his thoughtfulness and tact with gratitude, now—he had made conversation, and at one point mentioned that he had worked in the past for British Intelligence; Colin had already told her this, and rather clumsily, in her distracted state, she said so.

"Ah, but did he tell you the name I worked under?"

"No; do say—" Julia, belatedly remembering her manners, had asked.

"Bernardin. Down here, we all had names from the *Chanson de Roland*—it is so close to Roncesvalles." And then he had startled her by quoting—

> "And Roland brave, and Olivier,
> And many a paladin and peer
> On Roncesvalles died."

Even at that difficult and anxious moment, she found it remarkable to hear Marmion quoted by a Pyrenean mountaineer—now in this fresh anxiety, she found the name she needed. "I want him to be called Philip Bernard," she said.

"I tell Dick. Do you think he might come in?"

"Ask the old *sage-femme.*"

Dick was allowed in. Julia explained the position—"And it must be done before noon, Professor Martin says."

Dick looked at his watch; it was 11.30.

"Not much time to spare—and they're madly tough about closing dead on time at the *Mairie*. I think I'll try to lay His Lordship on; he can usually quell them." He went and telephoned. "He's coming round at once" he reported. "Better get the names written down, and the hour of birth—and of course your home address in England; then it will be all ready."

Luzia, unasked, gave Julia her despatch case; the young woman took out a sheet of her Gray's Inn writing-paper, and wrote on it her and Philip's names, and the date and hour of the child's birth—she added in French: "It is our desire that the child be called Philip Bernard," and signed it. "Will that do?" she asked Dick, handing the piece of paper to him.

"They'll want to know your husband's occupation" he said.

"I think 'Colonel' is enough for them" Julia said firmly. "They should be able to guess from that that he's a soldier by profession." The young man grinned.

A few moments later the old *sage-femme* ushered in Lord Heriot. "There are too many persons in Madame's room" she said brusquely, and brushed Dick and Luzia out.

"You look very well" Lord Heriot said. "Now, this registration—have you got the names written down?"

"Yes." She gave him the sheet of paper; he put on his glasses and studied it.

"Yes, that's clear enough. Is Bernard a family name?" he asked.

"No" Julia said flatly. He looked her straight in the eye; then he smiled. "Oh, I see. Very nice—very graceful. Well, I'd better be off and get this job done; very tiresome, these *petits fonctionnaires.*"

"You *are* kind!" Julia said, as he went out.

Lord Heriot arrived at the *Mairie* at five minutes to twelve; he was told that the registrar had already left. The old man was calm, but extremely firm. "Registrations take place until noon, to which it lacks five minutes. Let him be fetched, or let someone else act for him. Otherwise I telephone to the *Prèfêt*." In fact the registrar was still in the building, having a wash-and-brush-up before going out to lunch; after some agitated toings-and-froings he appeared—Lord Heriot gave him Julia's paper, and said that he wished to register the birth of this child.

"Milord comes rather late" the official said, glancing at the clock.

"Monsieur causes me to wait several minutes" Lord Heriot replied with asperity. Eventually big books were got out and opened, entries made, and a thin, rather scruffy sheet of paper handed to Lord Heriot, confirming the fact that the birth of Philip Bernard Jamieson, a British subject, had duly been registered at Pau, Basses Pyrénées. Lord Heriot thanked the registrar rather stiffly and drove back to the clinic, where he handed the sordid document to Julia.

"That job's done" he said. "Now, you young people, what about coming home and getting some lunch? Let us know if there's anything else you want" he said to Julia. "Always there, you know, and delighted to be of use."

Chapter 10

While all this was going on at Pau, Nick Heriot and his Mother were pursuing their enquiries for Bonnecourt in Tardets. Once again Nick by-passed the road-blocks near Ste.-Marie des Pèlerins; after they regained the main road he pointed out the lane up which he thought Bonnecourt had gone. "Should we try there?" he asked.

"No—I know no one up there" Lady Heriot replied. "Let's go straight to the *épicerie;* Mme. Pontarlet is much brighter in the head than the old Aunt at the inn. Though of course I shall have to see her too; she'd be hurt if I didn't, and she'll be bound to hear that I've been in the town."

The *Épicerie Pontarlet* was crowded with customers—naturally enough on a Saturday—when the Dauphine drew up; Lady Heriot remained in the car.

"Go in and tell Mme. Pontarlet that I should so much like to see her" she told her son. Pretty Mme. Pontarlet came out at once, leaned in through the door, and warmly embraced his parent. "Miladi! How it is good to see you!"

"Come and sit with me for a moment, Pauline" the older woman said. "Nick, go and get a *fromage de brebis* and a kilo of *jambon de Bayonne*" (raw smoked ham)—these were two of the most expensive items in the shop's repertory. "Here's my purse."

"Unless you filled up yesterday there's nothing in it" Nick said, ruefully. "I rifled it to give Madame's brother some cash, night before last."

"Never mind—Madame will trust me. Bring the bill, in that case" Lady Heriot said.

Pauline Pontarlet's brown eyes opened wide at this interchange; she understood some English.

"It was Monsieur Nicolas who brought my brother away from the police?" she asked.

"Yes. But now, Pauline—" the old lady got down to business; rather unsuccessfully, as it turned out. Mme. Pontarlet was not only bright in the head, but cautious as well. When Nick re-appeared with his purchases she left the car, again embracing Lady Heriot, and ran back into her busy shop.

"Where now?" Nick asked.

"Let's drive about a little; I must think. Turn up one of those side streets—just keep going."

"Doesn't she know where he is?" Nick asked, as he obeyed these curious instructions.

"Yes, she does, but she won't tell even *me* where. Don't get into a blind alley!" Lady Heriot said urgently.

"*Maman,* what on *earth* goes on?" Nick asked, surprised that his Mother, of all people, should insist on these manoeuvres. Tardets is anyhow a rather sinister little town, with the dark grey stone of its high houses, the narrow streets, the general sense of compression—and it usually seems to be raining there; rain was beginning to fall now— Nick suddenly felt uncomfortable and nervous.

"It's a little bothering. The place is full of *Sûreté* men— they've been to Pauline, and to everyone connected with him, and she was too frightened to say a word."

"How did the *Sûreté* trace him here? Oh, I suppose the *D.B.* have that on their files, and passed it on." Nick recalled his illuminating conversation with Colonel Jamieson the night before.

"I have no idea *how* they knew, but anyhow they're here, upsetting everyone" Lady Heriot said. "Anyhow let us go to the inn—we *must* find him, and old Mme. Dutour is so silly that if she knows anything, I'm sure I can get it out of her."

The inn was another grey house, in another grey street.

"Leave the car outside and come in" Lady Heriot said. "We'll order an *apéritif*—if the worst comes to the worst we can have lunch, though it won't be good."

The inn at Tardets is a chilly and unwelcoming place. In some strange way the greyness of the streets outside seems to have seeped into its rooms; in the gaunt, sparsely-furnished parlour such warmth as there was was furnished not by any fire in the empty grate, filled with elaborately folded paper covered with dust, but by old Mme. Dutour's welcome.

"Miladi! What a pleasure! How goes it with Milord? And this is a son?" She shook Nick by the hand.

"Have you someone now who attends to the bar, Madame? My son would like a little refreshment."

"But yes; my great-nephew, Marceline's son, makes his apprenticeship here as bar-man. *Permettez*"—she made for the door.

"My son will find his own way," Lady Heriot said firmly. "Sit down, Madame, and let us talk a little. It is long since we met."

"Ah yes—*le bon vieux temps!* During the War we constantly saw Miladi here, helping the escape of those of the Royal Air Force, and of others, into Spain."

Old Mme. Dutour had herself, immediately, led the conversation into the desired channel; only a little skilful pressure on Lady Heriot's part was necessary to learn what she wished to know. But silly as she might be, at first even Mme. Dutour was hesitant—"The *Sûreté* have been here; he is in danger" she said.

"I know this—and I have come, precisely, to learn where he is, and to see him. Then the Royal Air Force will secure his escape." Unscrupulously, Lady Heriot said what she knew to be most convincing; *how* British Intelligence would get Bonnecourt away she had no idea, except that one of the twins had said something about his being flown out—but "The Royal Air Force" was still a name to conjure with, in France.

"Who is so good as Miladi? She helps everyone!" the old woman exclaimed. But it was sometime, even then, before Mme. Dutour could be brought to the point; at last "He is with Marceline" she hissed in Lady Heriot's ear. "But this place is watched—do not go there direct, I implore you, Miladi! These creatures watch every face, every car."

Lady Heriot promised to take all precautions, and kissed the old landlady Goodbye. Back in the car—"Drive out along the road towards St. Jean Pied-de-Port" she told Nick.

"Oh, is he out that side?"

"No, he's with Mme. Bertrand, his other sister. But we won't go straight there; presently let's wait in a wood or somewhere, out of sight, till we see whether we are being followed. Old Madame says the inn is watched the whole time."

They couldn't be absolutely sure, after Nick had slung the car up a wood-cutters' track among the beech-trees, whose leaves were already taking on a coppery tinge, whether they were being followed or not. A bus and several large touring-cars shot by at speed; but presently two small cars, travelling much more slowly, came past, both full of little men peering intently out of the window.

"Those could be them" Nick said, ungrammatically but lucidly. He had chosen his spot with care—just beyond the track where they had hidden themselves the road made a sharp bend to the right—the moment the two little cars were out of sight round this he shot down the track onto the main road, and drove back towards Tardets at top speed. "Any sign of them?" he asked his Mother.

"No, nothing in sight" Lady Heriot said, slewing round to look out of the rear window. "That was perfect, dearest."

Mme. Bertrand, whose husband was a lawyer in quite a good way of business, lived in a neat little villa on the outskirts of Tardets on the western side, so they were able to reach it without returning through the town itself—once more Nick admired his Mother's astuteness in causing him to drive out along the road towards St. Jean. The villa had a small drive with a gate, which was shut. "Open the gate, and drive in" Lady Heriot said.

Even before they rang the bell the door was opened by Mme. Bertrand herself.

"Lady Heriot! It is too long since we see you!" She spoke in English. "But who is this?" she asked, with a glance at Nick.

"Have you forgotten my son Nicholas? May we come in, Marceline?"

"Of course—I am enchanted." All the same there was here an evident guardedness, a hesitation. "If you would wait just one moment, Lady Heriot, I will go in and prepare to receive you."

Lady Heriot knew the lay-out of the villa perfectly: besides the kitchen there was only one sitting-room, and probably Bonnecourt was in it.

"Do not trouble, Marceline. If you are thinking of causing your brother to climb out of the window, please let it be! I have come expressly to see him."

"My brother! But—but why should Miladi imagine that he is here?" Mme. Bertrand stammered.

"I don't imagine—I *know* he is" Lady Heriot said brusquely. "Don't be silly, Marceline; of course he is in danger, but I have come to arrange matters. Please to let us come in—I am a little tired, and I should prefer not to remain standing." As Mme. Bertrand stood aside, Lady Heriot walked past her and straight into the sitting-room; there, at a little table, sat Bonnecourt, playing Patience with two packs of small cards, as cool as a cucumber. But some of his calm left him when she came in.

"Miladi! What brings you here?"

"*You!* Why aren't you in Spain?" She sat down in one of the small, uncomfortable French versions of an arm-chair. "Why are you lingering here? You have been most good to Madame Jamieson, and to our people in the past—but now you are really being troublesome."

Nick, who had followed his Mother into the room, had never till that moment seen the hunter look in the least embarrassed; now he obviously was.

"Miladi, I ask your pardon—I am ashamed to have put you to so much trouble. But perhaps we had better discuss this matter alone. Marceline, can you not go and prepare some luncheon? And Nick, you can perhaps amuse yourself in the garden—*behind* the house! What car are you in?" he added sharply.

"My little Dauphine."

"Where did you leave it?"

"*In* the drive—on Her Ladyship's instructions!"

"*C'est très-bien.*"

"Marceline, don't bother about lunch; we must get back" Lady Heriot said. "Just a cup of coffee, perhaps." When both Nick and the young woman had gone out she turned a stiff gaze on Bonnecourt.

"Now perhaps you will explain to me why you are here? Even if the whole frontier has been alerted, as I imagine, that can hardly trouble *you*, or prevent you from crossing."

"Miladi is, as always, perfectly right. The frontier is my *manoir*—I come and go as I please, patrols or no patrols" the man said, with a certain contained pride.

"Then why haven't you gone, you tiresome creature? Here is poor Mr. Monro gone driving off into Spain to look for you, and Colonel Jamieson leaving his wife to dash up to Paris on your behalf—to say nothing of our poor old Pierre turning out in the middle of the night to get you away. And here you sit playing Patience! Really, Bonnecourt, I am exasperated! *Why* haven't you gone?"

The brusque, motherly familiarity of this rebuke made the hunter laugh.

"There are two reasons. But first, please, how is Madame Jamieson? Was the child delivered safely?"

"Yes, thank you very much."

"A boy or a girl?"

"A boy—and they are both getting on quite well. Now, may I have your famous reasons?"

Bonnecourt laughed again.

"Yes. First, there is my wife. I wished to arrange that my family should bring her over to stay with them, when I leave."

"Well I should have thought you could have settled that with Pauline in five minutes" Lady Heriot said crisply. "No need to hang about here for over twenty-four hours! What was the other reason?"

"*Ma voiture!*"

Lady Heriot just managed not to laugh. She had known Bonnecourt for over twenty years, and for many of them had recognised his fantastic attachment to his old Bugatti, which only his constant attention and mechanical skill kept on the road at all. But for a man to risk his neck, even for such a vintage rattle-trap, struck her as both funny and crazy.

"The boys said that it had been put in our garage" she said, "after you brought Madame Jamieson down to the *clinique*."

"Yes—I ventured to take this liberty. But with these *éléments* of the *Sûreté* everywhere I was anxious! I did not wish to leave France without ensuring its safety."

Again Lady Heriot only refrained from laughing with some effort. Which was Bonnecourt most anxious about, his wife or his car? Her guess was the *voiture*—he had had it longer! But arbitrary as she was, she could always adjust her tone to the immediate need, and switch from asperity to gentleness.

"My dear friend, I perfectly comprehend both these anxieties of yours" she said, pleasantly. "As regards your car, I doubt whether even the *Sûreté* would attempt to touch it on our premises; and we will gladly keep it for you as long as you wish. But surely for Madame your wife, the essential thing is *your* safety; and this is what I have come over here to arrange—since you have failed to take the trouble to do that yourself!" she added, with a return to her earlier brusqueness.

"And how does Miladi propose to ensure my safety?" Bonnecourt asked smiling—Lady Heriot always amused him when she got tough.

"Oh, I leave the arrangements to the experts, like poor Colonel Jamieson! What I now ask of you, Bonnecourt, is to remain in this house until you hear from him, or from me. It is essential that he can see you. Have I your promise?"

"Miladi, yes—unless the *Sûreté* should come, and I am obliged to leave."

"Will you then go to Pamplona?"

"Yes, I will."

"If you do have to leave, you must arrange to send a message." Lady Heriot considered. She had no knowledge whatever of Secret Service procedure; but she had plenty of common-sense, and an intimate acquaintance with all Bonnecourt's family. "Let *Pauline* telephone to me" she said—Pauline, in her opinion, was more reliable than Marceline.

"Telephone calls may be tapped" Bonnecourt interjected.

"Of course"—the old lady spoke impatiently. "Give me a moment, and I will think what she is to say." She paused. "Yes:—'The foreign order has been executed.' Will that do? —just what a shop might say, I think."

"It is perfect. Miladi ought to be in Intelligence!"

Marceline came in with a tray of coffee.

"Oh, how good of you, my child." Lady Heriot poured herself out a half-cup. "Call Nick" she said to Bonnecourt— "We really must get home."

The hunter went through and summoned Nick, who was smoking in an arbour in the well-stocked kitchen-garden, with a low whistle—when the young man came in Bonnecourt asked him whether he had any idea of Colonel Jamieson's plans on his behalf? "Madame your Mother seemed to think he desired to see me."

"Yes, he does. That's important, I gather."

"But if I must remain here to meet him, how long is it before he returns?"

"No notion. As long as it takes him to fix with the *D.B.* to make the *Sûreté* lay off you, I imagine" Nick said airily— "which you probably know more about than I do."

"That could take all eternity!"

"Not with him, I think. I got the impression that he is a fast worker."

"And if he fails?"

"Then I'm sure you'll be told, provided you stay put."

"What sort of a man is he?" Bonnecourt asked, with sudden interest.

"I've hardly seen enough of him to know. Good-looking; very able, I should say—or he wouldn't be where he is; rather *débrouillard*—and the tiniest bit stuffy" Nick added.

"Stuffy? What does this mean?"

"Oh well, rather formal. He's Scotch, like my Father."

The hunter laughed, and changed the subject. Or didn't he, Nick wondered, when Bonnecourt said—

"I am so glad that Madame Jamieson has got a son, and that she is well. Pray give her my best congratulations."

"Right—I will."

"This is a most wonderful person" Bonnecourt said slowly; he spoke as though the words were being drawn out of him by some force beyond his control. "Courage; generosity and consideration for others, even when in distress herself. I wish I saw more of the English now, as in the past I did!" he broke out.

Nick, embarrassed, said foolishly—"You see *us*."

"Yes; and always with pleasure. But you are not as Madame Jamieson—except for Miladi! They are made somewhat of the same clay." He made an impatient movement, as if to jerk himself out of this mood. "*Allons!* I know that *Madame votre mère* is anxious to get home. But"—he paused in the passage, and held his friend's arm. "If you should hear when this Jamieson is returning, do me a favour, *mon cher Nick*, and give a *coup de fil* to my sister Pauline, at the *Épicerie* Pontarlet—she will pass on the message."

"How shall I word it?" Nick asked—after going through all those road-blocks forty-eight hours earlier he was even more alert than Lady Heriot to the *Sûreté's* activities. "I can't just say 'The Colonel has arrived', can I?"

"Naturally not. If you hear *before* he comes, say to Pauline—'The formalities will be completed at such an hour.'" Bonnecourt grinned as he said "The formalities." "If you only hear after he has arrived, say 'Formalities completed here.' But if I knew in advance, I might be able to facilitate matters for the Colonel; perhaps save him a journey."

"Don't go doing anything silly, Bonnecourt!" Nick said, a little anxiously.

"Of course not. But do keep an eye on my car, will you?"

On the way home Nick drove straight through Ste.-Marie des Pèlerins, to save time—to his surprise the road-blocks were being removed, and the car was waved forward.

"That Jamieson man seems to be quite an effective type" he said—and he repeated the remark as they passed through Pau with no police checks. "It's something to make the *Sûreté* lay off like this, and so fast." There was still an *agent* at the front door, but he stood aside and saluted politely. "Fresh instructions, definitely" Nick observed.

They were only fifteen minutes late for lunch—long enough to cause Lord Heriot to grumble, but not to spoil the food. While they were having coffee the telephone rang—Nick answered it. "Yes—yes—good; yes, of course. Yes, one of us will meet you. Yes, we went this morning—that's all fixed. Oh yes, definitely better already, thank you. Good-bye."

"What was all that?" Lord Heriot asked, rather irritably—he always preferred to take telephone calls himself, to know what was going on; but he could no longer get out of a chair as quickly as his sons.

"Mr. Julia. He's coming down on the night train, and he wanted Mrs. Julia to be told."

"But you said we'd meet him. That infernal train gets in now at a quarter to six!—I can't have Pierre turned out at that hour."

"I said *one of us* would meet him" Nick repeated, patiently. "That means me or Dick, not Pierre."

"And what's this about something being 'fixed'? I suppose you mean arranged—can't think why you can't talk English!"

"Dearest, he said that to muddle the French, in case they were listening-in" Lady Heriot intervened.

"Yes, but what *has* been arranged, or fixed?" the old gentleman asked crossly. "I hate this being kept in the dark! *You* haven't told me why you went to Tardets this morning, Eleanor. Were you 'fixing' something?—and if so, what?"

The twins, simultaneously, burst into uncontrollable laughter; but Nick gave a questioning glance at his Mother—she nodded, almost imperceptibly.

"Dearest, if I tell you, you must promise to be very discreet" she said gently. "You see this is all to do with the Secret Service, so one has to be very careful."

"Can't imagine what *you* can do for the Secret Service" her husband replied, sourly.

"She did what no one else could have done, this very morning" Nick snapped.

"*Dar*ling! Do leave it to me" his Mother said reprovingly. She turned to her old husband, and laid her hand on his arm.

"Dearest, Colonel Jamieson simply *must* see our nice Bonne-court; he had disappeared, so I went to Tardets to find out where he was. That's all."

"Oh. Did you find him?"

"Yes—but I shan't tell even you where!"

"Did you see Pauline? Pretty girl, that."

"Yes. She wanted to be remembered to you—I'm sure she'd have sent her love, if she'd dared!"

Somewhat pacified, Lord Heriot presently went off to play golf, and Nick immediately rang up Mme. Pontarlet. Planning his call, as he waited to be connected, it suddenly struck him how odd it was that he had no idea of the hunter's Christian name—to them he had always simply been Bonnecourt. But he didn't wish to say "Your brother" on the telephone; that might not be wise. When at last he got Pauline herself he said—"Here Nicolas. I speak for Lady Heriot; I have a message for the person about whom she made enquiries of you this morning. Will you write it down?" Mme. Pontarlet was audibly flustered, but eventually pronounced that she had a pencil and paper— *"Mais soyez prudent!"* she added anxiously.

"I am. Write this: 'The formalities will be completed tomorrow at 6.30 hours.' Repeat it, will you?"

Poor Pauline repeated the words. "But will *he* understand this?"

"Yes. Write it down, and then read it over to me." After a pause, Mme. Pontarlet read out the message, adding—"It sounds most strange."

"Never mind. How soon can you get it to him?"

"I send a boy at once—on a bicycle, with a parcel; he will have it within half-an-hour."

"Fine; thank you." Certainly there were no flies on Pauline!—an admirable idea to send a parcel of groceries as cover for the message.

Luzia was waiting in the hall when he came out of the study after telephoning.

"I think I go to see Julia, and tell her that Philip returns tomorrow."

"Good idea. Is Dick taking you?"

"No—he took his Father to *le golf*. But I can walk."

"I'll take you" Nick said. "I rather want to see what the *agent* situation is at the Victoire, anyhow."

"Do not wait for me" the Portuguese girl said when Nick set her down at the clinic. "They may not let me see her at once, if she is resting. I can walk back."

"We'll see" Nick replied. While he definitely regarded Luzia as "booked" to his brother, he very much enjoyed her company himself.

In fact what with Lady Heriot's late return to luncheon from Tardets, and then Nick's telephoning, it was nearly a quarter to four when Luzia walked into the clinic, and the "period of repose" was well over—she was shown into Julia's room at once.

"The milk's come!" that young woman pronounced triumphantly. "He's had two terrific feeds—one at half-past one, and another just now. The Professor says the natural milk is far the best thing for him, and I seem to have gallons! But he can't be moved for two months, not even as far as Larège —so as soon as I can move I must shift to the Victoire; there's always a terrific demand for beds here."

"Shall you take the baby to the Victoire?" Luzia asked, sitting down.

"No—while he's so tiny he'll stay here; I can walk round and feed him. They'll bottle him at night, so that I can get some sleep. But I wondered, as Philip's in Paris, if you could go and book me a room? And what about you, darling? Won't your Father be wanting you back, now that there's no more cooking and housework to be done? What an angel you've been!"

"Yes, I think I should soon return to Papa. But Lady Heriot—what a sensible, *good* person this is!—has already planned that I should go up to Larège and pack all your things, and mine, and bring them down, and shut up the house. Philip comes back tomorrow; there was a call from Paris. So now we can get his consent." (Portuguese women have an almost Mohammedan attitude towards their menfolk, perhaps because of the long Moorish occupation of their country.)

"Philip comes back *tomorrow?*" Julia exclaimed.

"Yes; at some terrible time, just before six in the morning! I came to tell you this, but then we spoke of other things."

"Well I hope he'll like the baby's name! However, it's done now" Julia said cheerfully, "so let's go on talking of other things. Where's Bonnecourt? Did he get to Pamplona all right?"

"No." On the way to the clinic Nick had primed Luzia about his Mother's activities that morning. "He simply stayed in Tardets, too lazy to move himself!" the girl said indignantly; "and also worrying about his *terrible* old motor-car."

"Well when *is* he going to clear off?" Julia asked, rather anxiously.

"Since he did not go, now he waits to see Philip, who has plans for him; Lady Heriot made him promise this. She is formidable, this lady!" Luzia said admiringly. "Her husband, her sons, her friends—for all she arranges everything, and all love her in spite of it. Generally, people *hate* those who seek to arrange things for them."

"Yes" Julia said, thoughtfully and slowly, staring at a place above the door where the plaster was peeling off the wall. Marriage was hitting her too, as it had hit Philip in the train the night before; probably it would be several years before her extremely small son started hating her because she "arranged things" for him, but in time he would—meanwhile she had a husband who was wholly accustomed to arranging things for himself. Dashing off to Paris without a word to her! And more than half his time spent in remote places overseas. Still staring at the peeling plaster, her mind turned to her former pupil and dear friend; she would have her marriage problems too, especially if she took a young Heriot for her husband, with their Low-Church Scottish outlook.

"Yes—Lady Heriot has made a splendid job of her marriage" she said. "Not always an easy thing to do. Luzia, don't answer if you don't want to, but what goes on between you and Dick?"

Luzia was quite untroubled.

"He goes on proposing, and I go on saying that I have not made up my mind," she said blithely.

"Do you like him? Could you marry him?"

"I think so, in time; but not till I am sure. I will not be hurried! I should wish Papa to meet him and like him, also; it would be rather cruel to marry against Papa's wishes, since I am his only child."

This sage, considerate continental view of marriage—as a family concern, not just a matter of one's individual preferences or passions, struck Julia forcibly. There would be fewer divorces and "broken homes" in England and America, she reflected, if it prevailed in those countries too. She had thought a good deal about Dick and Luzia, and about the old Duque, to whom she was much attached; after all, she was responsible for bringing the two together, however involuntarily. Now—

"Would your Father mind your marrying a Protestant very much?" she asked.

"Oh no—why should he? I am a Catholic, so my children will be brought up as Catholics, whoever I marry" Luzia said. There was a joyful certainty, a serene assumption of something unbreakable in the girl's voice, as well as her words, which again struck Julia with great force.

"Do you think the Heriots would mind their grandchildren being Catholics?"

Again Luzia was perfectly calm and clear.

"*She*, no; she is without such prejudices. The old Lord—probably yes; but in the end he agrees to what she wishes, and she will wish what her sons wish."

"Have you talked to her about it?" Julia asked, surprised by this certainty.

"Merciful God no! But I stay there now some days, and I have come to know them."

Julia's real preoccupation was still with her dear pupil's happiness, and whether Dick Heriot, amiable and well-bred as he was, would be an adequate partner for someone of Luzia's intelligence and subtlety. But that could not be approached directly.

"Where should you live?" she asked.

"If Dick should get this appointment that he so much

wants at Lacq, I suppose partly here; but if he and Papa got on well, and he came to like Portugal, I think later we should have to live there. Someone must look after Gralheira; it is a big estate, and the peasants must be watched over, and their interests safeguarded. I could learn to do this, of course, but it would involve being there a great deal of the time. And one cannot have a *good* marriage if the husband works in one country, and the wife in another!"

You're telling me! Julia thought; but all she said was—"No; it is rather complicated." Again the girl's sense of duty and responsibility impressed her. This was the old Europe, where property-owners expected to make personal sacrifices to "safeguard the interests" of their tenants—a very far cry from the world of slum-landlords and take-over bids.

Luzia had been reflecting too.

"Yes. It *is* complicated. I do not see it clearly yet, Miss Probyn." (Julia was touched by the old familiar form of address, reflecting such a basic part of their relationship.) "Nor am I sure in my mind. If I become sure, Dick must come and meet Papa, and see Gralheira, and all there is to do there."

The old *sage-femme* came in at this point to say that Madame ought to rest; the baby must shortly be fed again. As they kissed one another Goodbye Julia said—"Bless you, dear child. Take your time! And you'll go and book me a room at the Victoire, a week from tomorrow, won't you? I'm sorry you should have the bother of packing my things and shutting-up Larège, but that will be a great help, too. There are no bills except at the farm for milk, and at Barraterre's for the bread. You'll have to get the money from Philip— how lovely that he'll be back tomorrow."

"I do all this. I like to do something for you, who have done so much for me, and been so patient when I was a silly child."

When Luzia left the clinic she found Nick and the Dauphine outside. "I said you should not wait" she remarked, as she got into it.

"Well, I did wait. The *agent* has cleared off from the Victoire—Colin's car is empty. Full marks to Jamieson" Nick said approvingly, starting his engine.

"Oh, but now we go to the Victoire" Luzia said, as the young man set off in the opposite direction.

"Why?" He pulled up, and turned carefully in the stream of traffic on the Route de Toulouse.

"I must book a room for Mme. Jamieson—in a week she leaves the *clinique,* and stays there to feed the baby, till it can be taken home."

The room booked, Nick drove Luzia back; his parents were having a rather late tea.

"Mrs. J. all right?" Lord Heriot asked.

"Yes—the milk has come, and now she nourishes the child" Luzia said, with continental frankness. "Lady Heriot, I am so sorry that we are late, but I went to take a room for her at this little hotel."

"Why doesn't she come and stay here?" Lord Heriot grunted—he liked Julia, and could never have too much company.

"I think it would be rather far—the infant remains in the *clinique,* and must be fed every two hours; from the Victoire she can walk round in eactly one minute."

"Good God!" This astonishing arrangement silenced Lord Heriot. "Every *two* hours!" they heard him mutter, as he stumped off to his study.

Later Luzia succeeded in getting her hostess to herself, and explained that Julia agreed to her going up to Larège to pack, close up the house, and pay the remaining bills. "It may take more than one day, but I could stay at Barra-terre's."

"Certainly not. If you stay anywhere it must be with the Monniers. But I see no need for you to stay at all; Dick can drive you up and down—he has nothing in the world to do, and I expect he would like to." Like Julia, Lady Heriot rather wanted to know how things stood between her Dick and the Portuguese heiress, but she did not attempt a direct approach. "And he's quite useful about things like switching off the water and the electricity" she added. "Of course you'll have to do that when you've finished in the house.

Who is the key to be left with? Oh, we can ask Colonel Jamieson when he gets back. All right—you and Dick had better go up first thing tomorrow. It's Sunday, but you can get on with the packing—Dick can go to Evensong when you come home. I will have some sandwiches got ready."

"How kind you are!" Luzia said. "But dear Lady Heriot, there is one other point. As soon as I can, I should return to Papa; only I would rather see Julia safely into the hotel before I go, and do her unpacking and all this for her. But she only leaves the *clinique* after another week—would it be inconvenient if I stay so long? Please be frank."

"My dear child, the longer you stay the better I, and my husband, and most of the members of my family will be pleased!" Lady Heriot said briskly. She realised, with a certain approval, that she would get nothing out of Luzia about Dick; the girl was keeping her own counsel. If she spoke to anyone it would be, quite rightly, to Mrs. Jamieson, the friend of her childhood.

Luzia and Dick set off for Larège soon after eight. Colonel Jamieson had been collected off the night train at that unearthly hour by Nick; Dick went to his room and ascertained that the key of the house, if they finished in one day, should be left with Madame Barraterre. Luzia had decided to go to 10.30 Mass up at Larège; they unlocked the house, and she directed Dick to clean out the frig while she was at Church —"Throw away *all*, and empty the *poubelle;* switch off first, and then wash out the dishes of food, and the ice-trays, and wipe down the inside with warm water." She hurried off to Mass, passing the tomb of the first Mrs. Bonnecourt in the Churchyard.

To Luzia the packing-up and clearing away was all rather sad. She had loved Larège, and been happy there with her dear Julia—as they ate their sandwiches by the spring she looked with genuine regret across and up the valley at the silver saw of peaks enclosing it. They were drinking some of the country wine which the twins had helped them to buy down in the plain only a few weeks before, and this brought her back to a practical matter— Luzia was never far from the practical.

"All this wine, which you and Nick bottled for us! Now what do we do with it?"

"Leave it here. I'm sure the Stansteds will take it off Philip; it's much better than anything they ever buy."

"No—let us take some down for Julia. She enjoys a little wine."

They finished all the packing, and Dick carried the suit-cases and several bottles along the path to the car; but when he came back, and made to turn off the water and electricity, she stopped him.

"No! The house is not clean; one cannot leave it so. The floors must be washed, and the stairs also—for this one must have hot water. Oh, how strange that no one in this place will work!"

"Well we can't get it done now," Dick said.

"No. We come back, and *I* do it. But let us go and settle these accounts—that will leave us free tomorrow."

Dick was slightly appalled at the idea of Luzia scrubbing floors, and resolved mentally to bring up a maid from Pau next day; but he was also impressed. It would be something to have a wife who knew about houses being clean—it had never struck him that this one was not.

Luzia had borrowed some money from Lady Heriot, who had replenished her purse since Nick emptied it. After paying Madame Barraterre—who was full of eager enquiries for Madame Jimmison, and rejoiced at the birth of a son—they left the car in the *Place*, and went on to settle the milk bill at the farm above Bonnecourt's house. There was rather a long pause here, while the good woman did sums with a stub of a pencil; Dick and Luzia perched on the stone wall outside the farm, looking down onto the dam, and the pool where de Lassalle had sunk his explosives and his time-clock. While she was showing Dick the very clump of rushes by which she had identified the spot for Colin, the door of Bonnecourt's house opened; the blonde woman came out and walked rather hesitantly up the field towards them.

"Ah, it *is* La Comtesse!" she began—but just then the farmer's wife came and said that she was owed 16 francs; Luzia paid her and thanked her—yes, they were leaving, and would require no more milk. When the farmer's wife had gone back into the house she turned to Mme. Bonnecourt. Between Nick and Dick, Luzia had been slightly informed as to the hunter's movements, and expected an anxious enquiry about them; she was greatly surprised when Mme. Bonnecourt addressed herself to Dick, opened her purse, and handed him 4000 francs in notes.

"*C'est bien, Monsieur Nick?* You made this loan to my husband—he wished it to be repaid, when the occasion offered."

Dick was flabbergasted.

"Have you seen him?" he asked—after all, only yesterday his Mother had been scolding Bonnecourt in Tardets, miles away.

"No. He sent word, and the money, and said I should seek occasion to repay you—and this morning I have seen the Countess at Mass, so I imagined that she has returned. I was coming tomorrow, but now I see you here, and come at once."

Luzia had rather taken to Mme. Bonnecourt when she met her before, and guessed that she did not have too easy a life; she would have liked, now, to say something reassuring, but before she could think of any innocuous sentence the rather faded little blonde said—"A thousand congratulations to Madame Jimmison on the birth of her son! I am sorry that you do not return to Larège." And before either of them could reply she hurried away downhill, across the fields, to the hunter's house.

Chapter 11

Much earlier that morning, when Nick Heriot went to fetch Colonel Jamieson off the night train, he had been agreeably surprised to find, at last, no *agent* at the front door; he had left the Dauphine in the drive overnight. On their way back from the station he mentioned this—"And no wretched *agent* at the Victoire either, yesterday evening, so Monro's car is usable again. Fast work, Sir, if I may say so."

"Oh, old Jean did do his stuff, did he? Good." The Colonel kept silent on his private opinion of Major Monteith and his advice. Then he asked whether Bonnecourt had got to Pamplona? Nick, giggling a little, reported his Mother's raid on Tardets the previous day, and its outcome; Jamieson was irritated. "Well really, what a bastard the man is!"

"Actually, you know, he isn't really; he's more of a card, in Bennett's sense. Anyhow he promised Her Ladyship to stay put till you came, and I sent a message—he and I fixed a code—by his sister Pauline at the *épicerie* to say that you would be here first thing this morning."

"Oh, thank you. Well I don't think I'll go over immediately—this afternoon will be plenty of time." Major Monteith had failed to secure him a sleeper, and after sitting up all night among more pilgrims to Lourdes—the richer ones invade even the first-class carriages—Philip decided to sleep in, in the bedroom offered by Nick. This twin arranged for him to be called in time for lunch, and promised to drive him round afterwards to collect Colin's car at the Victoire—then, Philip thought, he would be able to look in on his wife before driving over to see this unknown, tiresome, but apparently so valuable Bonnecourt. He had spoken to London from Paris, and been given a free hand to get the hunter out by whatever means seemed best to him. "When he does turn up at P., probably simplest to drive him down to Gib, and have him flown back from there" Major Hartley said. "Especially since you think you can lay on this cover-job for him in the Highlands. Ghillie-ing should be right up his street!"

But the day didn't work out quite as he planned. First Dick came in to ask about the key of the Larège house, just as he was getting off to sleep; after that he slept, and heard nothing of Nick's setting out with his parents to the English Church. But rather later old Jeanne, intensely embarrassed, roused him to say that a very ancient Professor had called, and desired most urgently to see him immediately. "He will take no denial—I told him that M. le Colonel could not be, disturbed, but it was no use."

"What's his name?" Philip asked, sleepily and irritably.

"I think, of some Saint—Professor Bernard, could it have been?" poor Jeanne said. "I am agitated; I cannot recall! But Milord and Miladi are out, and Monsieur Nick also. If *Monsieur le Colonel could* come to see him?"

Very reluctantly, M. le Colonel got up, pulled on his clothes, and went out to the hall, where Jeanne ushered him into the *salon,* announcing—"*Le Colonel Jimmison.*"

A very old man in a shabby black suit, with grey hair, a grey beard, and thick pebble glasses, got up slowly and carefully, as the old do, out of a chair. As Jeanne retired shutting the door, he asked—as the nurse had done at the Victoire two nights before—"*C'est bien le Colonel Jimmison?*"

"Yes!" Philip said sharply. "But may I ask who you are, and what the devil you want?" He was intensely irritated at having been awakened from much-needed sleep to see this doddering old creature.

To his astonishment, the old man burst out into loud laughter. "*Ah, c'est bien le Colonel Anglais!*" As he spoke he pulled off the pebble-spectacles, the grey wig and beard, revealing a young-middle-aged face, full of intelligence and gaiety. He went forward with his hand held out. "Bonnecourt" he said. "I thought to save Monsieur the Colonel a drive to Tardets—my sister Pauline brought me over. But I left a message with my sister Marceline, Mme. Bertrand, to say that I had come here, *en cas que.* Lady Heriot said that you wished to see me."

Vexed as he was by this sudden change of the agreed plan, Jamieson's first reaction was one of admiration for Bonnecourt as an actor: that slow effort to get up out of his chair, the shambling old man's steps across the room. This man could do anything in the way of impersonation.

"Yes, I do wish to see you" he said. "I was coming over, as you arranged with Lady Heriot—a little later." Jamieson spoke repressively; he was still rather annoyed. "But since you are here, we may as well discuss matters at once. Of course you can't stay in France for the present—de Lasalle's disappearance has made that impossible." Bonnecourt nodded. He expected some questioning from the Englishman about this episode, but none came; the Colonel passed it over as an accomplished fact, earning Bonnecourt's respect.

"Now I have a proposition to put to you" Jamieson went on. "As you cannot remain here, I assume that you will want some occupation. If you would still care to play the old game with us, as you did in the past—with what success!—there is always work for someone with your qualifications; will you come and join us again?"

He studied the hunter's face as he waited for his reply: it showed first emotion, then eagerness.

"But *yes*. This could be marvellous! Where should I go?"

"Your assignments would be settled presently by the Office, of course. Immediately you would go to a place in Scotland belonging to cousins of my wife—they need a stalker at once."

"A ghillie!" Bonnecourt interjected—"and to stalk the red deer! Splendid."

"Yes, that would be your apparent work, between jobs abroad. But you would have a house, regular occupation, and a small but certain income—and very pleasant quarters for Madame."

"She could come too?"

"Not *with* you; we must get you out as fast as we can. But certainly she can join you there later, and Madame Reeder —she is the sister of Mr. Monro—would do everything to make things easy for her in new surroundings."

"This forest belongs to Mr. Monnro's sister?" the hunter

asked, startling Jamieson by his knowledge of Scottish terms—although usually composed mainly of naked hills, the Scots speak of a "deer forest" as they do, more accurately, of a "grouse moor."

"No—actually it belongs to Monro himself" Jamieson replied, amused. "But while he is working, his sister and her husband live there, and look after the place."

"*Tiens!* This young Monnro a *propriétaire?* One would never suspect it—he is so"—the man hesitated for a word —"modest."

"Well never mind about Monro" Philip said, rather impatiently—his own word for Colin was not modest, but wet. "Listen, Bonnecourt—if you take on our job, and you and Madame Bonnecourt go to Glentoran, you will have to make her understand that there will be times when for reasons that you cannot explain to her you will just have to disappear, at short notice, for weeks at a time, when we need you. Can you guarantee this? Are you prepared to make it a bargain?" Philip was worrying, not unnaturally, at the prospect of some wretched Frenchwoman, stranded in Argyll and suddenly deserted by her husband, going to the local police, or "creating" in some way.

Bonnecourt's answer, which came without the slightest hesitation, surprised Jamieson as much as it reassured him.

"*Monsieur le Colonel,* I see that you do not realise—how should you?—that my poor wife has had long experience of sudden, and unexplained, disappearances on my part! She will be *enchantée* to know, when we are in Scotland, that they are *for*, and *with*, your people—not those others! She has always loved the English—and *hated* the Communists!" he added, in a burst of frankness.

"Good" Philip said briefly.

"But—excuse the question—what about my employers in Scotland? Will they accept my sudden disappearances, if they should happen at an inconvenient time? And would my wife receive my salary when I was absent?"

"Look, Bonnecourt, I've told you that Mrs. Reeder is Colin Monro's sister" Philip said, this time patiently. Concerned as he was at the moment with trying to combine marriage and the Secret Service himself, he could sympathise with the Frenchman's anxieties. "She knows all about Intelligence, and will understand why you are being sent there, and under what conditions. I must try to arrange with the Office that you are not sent away during the stalking season!" he added, smiling. "And of course your salary will be paid all the year round; it is really an Office responsibility, but the Reeders are very well off, Office or no."

"Have the Reeders agreed to this plan?" Bonnecourt asked.

"Not yet; they haven't even been told—no time. It is my wife's idea—she knows they are short of stalkers at Glentoran, and suggested this as a cover-job for you, at once; in fact they need an extra ghillie now."

The hunter's face glowed, suddenly.

"It is Madame who thought of this solution for us? After all she has been through! She is wonderful."

Philip was startled by this tribute to Julia, and a little disconcerted.

"She's very practical" he said temperately—"and she does know the situation at Glentoran backwards; she was partly brought up there—that's why this plan occurred to her." But now Philip himself reverted to the practical aspect.

"I think I would prefer to have you flown out to Spain" he said. "I gather you rather come and go as you choose across the frontier, but we don't want any slip-up this time, and the whole place is alerted."

"Their alerts will not disturb me!" Bonnecourt said.

"I dare say not. But if you agree to work with British Intelligence again"—the hunter nodded—"at present you are under *my* orders." He spoke firmly. "Can you get back to your sister's house in Tardets, in that dotty disguise of yours? Where is the car that drove you over? Here?"

"My sister Pauline waits in a small *Place* close by. But where do I meet the plane?"

"I haven't settled that yet. I only returned from Paris this morning at a quarter to six, and in fact I was getting some sleep when you came" Philip said, in a rather chilly tone. He felt that Bonnecourt, valuable as he could be to the Service, was enough of a "card" to require rather repressive measures; it would be no good giving him any rope at all, or he would get completely out of control. "I had intended to come over and see you this afternoon" he said, with intention, "at the address where Lady Heriot understood that you were to be found."

Bonnecourt took the point instantly.

"I regret. I apologise. I had hoped to save you a journey." He paused. "Would the Colonel allow me to make a suggestion, in spite of my *gaffe* in coming here, after my promise to remain at Tardets?"

"What about?" Philip asked cautiously.

"This affair of being flown out. Doubtless the Colonel knows that there is a flying-club at Pau; the members fly small private planes: Éméraudes, Jodels, Piper Cubs and Vagabonds Piper. Nick and Dick have several friends who fly such planes: small two-seaters, with a range of 500 kilometres."

Philip didn't know any of this, and was interested; it could be quite useful. A private plane, on a private flight, would be much less conspicuous than a helicopter.

"Would 500 kilometers get to Spain and back?" he asked.

"Easily. This is what I wished to suggest. And there is a place at no great distance from Tardets—but remote, *remote*, right up in the mountains—where one could land and take off, for which such planes require so little space: the Plateau de Permounat."

"I'll make a note of that" Philip was saying, when a crunch of tyres on the gravel of the drive outside indicated the arrival of a car—he went to the open window and looked out.

"That's the family, coming back from Church" he said, turning into the room again. To his amusement Bonnecourt was hurriedly adjusting his wig and beard in front of a Venetian mirror—he was having trouble with the beard.

"Come to my room—you'll never get that done in time" Philip said, and led the hunter to his bed-room; as he closed the door after him he heard the click of the lift as it stopped in the hall. "Or perhaps you would like to see them?" he asked.

"*Mon Dieu, no.* Miladi would kill me if she knew that I had done this, breaking my promise. Colonel, for the love of God, do not tell her!" All this time Bonnecourt was arranging his wig and refractory beard in front of the shaving-glass—Jamieson laughed at his dismay.

"All right. I suppose I can talk to the boys about the flying-club, and this place you mentioned?—what was the name, by the way?" He drew out his tiny note-book, and wrote down "Le Plateau de Permounat."

"There are other places too" Bonnecourt said, putting on his pebble-glasses; he was satisfied with his beard at last. "The Plateau de Barthaz, or the Cirque de Crauste. They are all small 'valleys of elevation', as I believe the scientists call them, with a smooth grass surface, level, affording sufficient space for one of these little planes to land and take off again. But Permounat is especially convenient in the matter of distance, because it is so near both to Tardets and to Berdun."

"What is Berdun?" Jamieson asked. But he never heard the answer, because at that moment there was a knock on the door, and Nick's voice outside asking—"Colonel! Have you surfaced yet?"

Bonnecourt shot into the bathroom like a scalded cat.

"Surfacing—half-dressed" Jamieson called back. "I'll be with you in about ten minutes. That do?"

"Perfectly—no hurry." Nick's steps were audible retreating down the passage; Philip opened the bathroom door.

"He's gone. How shall you get out?" he asked Bonnecourt.

"I descend by the *escalier de service*, and tell Jeanne that I could not make the lift function" the hunter said, with a grin; as he spoke he resumed his old man's attitude, bent his shoulders, and shuffled slowly towards the door. "Then I rejoin Pauline."

"And you really *will* stay put this time?" Jamieson asked. "It's essential, you know; we might even fix this fly-out for tomorrow. The sooner you're out of this country, the better."

"I remain where I told Miladi." Suddenly he laid a hand on Jamieson's arm. "But one thing I forget—*ma voiture!*

What is to become of it? At present it is in one of the garages here, but unless it is run from time to time, it will be ruined."

Philip considered. He summoned back into his mind what Colin had told him, and what he had heard in Paris, from Monteith and de Monceau, about de Lassalle's escape.

"But surely that's the car you picked that young O.A.S. man up in, after the accident?" he said, "And drove him off towards Larège? Both the *Sûreté* and the *D.B.* are firm on that—a Bugatti, isn't it? Listen, Bonnecourt—that car is completely compromised anyhow; even if we arrange for you to come back eventually, you could never use it again in France."

"Could you get it to Scotland for me?"

"No" Philip pronounced emphatically. But he was touched, as well as irritated, by the expression on the hunter's face when he said that. "How old is it?" he asked.

"Nineteen years!"

"Yes—that's an old friend. Well if you work for us for a bit we'll *give* you another car; I can't promise a Bugatti, don't know if they're still being made, but how about a Bentley?"

"Ah, a Bentley would be marvellous! But what becomes of the old one?"

"Let's leave that to the twins—they will think of a suitable burial for it."

"They could drive it into the Gave—in a deep place. But I do not want it broken up, or sold to some brute who will murder the engine."

Philip looked at his watch.

"I'm sure you can trust them" he said. "Now, hadn't you better get off to meet your sister? At what time will you reach home?"

"Let us say 15.30 hours."

"Right." He watched with admiring satisfaction as Bonnecourt, with his old man's shuffle, moved to the door and along the corridor to the back stairs.

In the salon he thanked Lady Heriot for putting him up. "However now I can return to the Victoire—all my stuff is there, and it is close to the *clinique*."

"How d'you mean you 'can' return?" Lord Heriot asked. "I thought you were there before you went to Paris."

"Yes, but then it was all over *agents*, tailing him; now it's been de-loused, just like this place" Nick said.

"Ah, yes—a comfort, that. Pierre is in much better form today" Lord Heriot said. "Did *you* arrange that in Paris?" he asked Jamieson.

"Friends of mine saw to it" Philip said.

"And how is your wife? Did you manage to see her this morning?" Lady Heriot enquired.

"I'm ashamed to say I didn't; I overslept. I must go round the moment after lunch." In fact Philip was longing to see Julia, and was planning the afternoon in his head; recalling his doubts in the train up to Paris, he had been speculating which to do first—see Julia, or tackle Nick about getting Bonnecourt flown out.

He took Nick first. After luncheon—during which Lady Heriot informed him that Dick and Luzia were at that moment at Larège, closing up the house—he asked Nick if he could drive him round to the *clinique?* But downstairs Jamieson made no move to enter the Dauphine.

"I want to talk to you for a moment" he said, as he spoke instinctively moving away from the house across the gravelled sweep, and out onto the wide lawn.

"Yes?" Nick asked, following him.

"Do you or your brother belong to this flying-club here?"

"You mean Les Ailes Basques? No, we don't."

"But you have friends who do?"

"Yes." Nick was beginning to scent something interesting. "Any of them English?"

"Yes, three are."

"That would be best. It's this business of getting our friend out to Spain. Would any of them know a place called"—he had pulled out his note-book, and looked in it—"Le Plateau de Permounat?"

"Well they could check it on the maps; I know it's fairly close to Tardets."

"And do any of their planes have petrol-range enough to

fly on into Spain to a place with a name like Verdun, and back?"

"Oh, you mean Berdun, that old abandoned airfield. Half-a-minute." Nick went over to his car, pulled a map out of the pocket, spread it on the bonnet, and studied it. "Yes, here we are—no distance from the Jaca–Pamplona road. That would be well within their range." He looked at Jamieson with interest. "Goodness, Sir, you *are* up in this district!"

"*I'm* not—this is all Bonnecourt's idea."

"Bonnecourt's? But you haven't seen him!"

"Yes, he came over this morning." Philip enjoyed Nick Heriot's face at this announcement.

"The man must be mad! Did the servants see him too?"

"They only saw an old Professor, with white hair and beard, stumbling along; but it was Bonnecourt all right. He's agreed to come back to work with us again, and to live in Scotland as a stalker between assignments; the one condition he made was that you or your brother should drive his car into the river, so that it shouldn't be broken up" Jamieson said, smiling. "I promised him that you would."

"He's nuts about that car. In fact he's nuts altogether!" Nick exclaimed impatiently. "He *promised* to stay at Tardets." He put away the map, and got in.

"He's a very good impersonator" Jamieson said, as they drove off. "Well, will you get on to one of your flying friends at once, and try to lay him on for tomorrow or next day?"

"I'll *try*" Nick said. "But most of them are usually in the air on Sundays." He pulled up, suddenly, half-way down the drive. "We'd better think this out a bit first. I'd rather get Acland—he's much the best pilot, and you have to be pretty nippy for these tiny landings and take-offs. Let's have another look at the map"—he took it out again and spread it across the steering-wheel and Jamieson's knees. "Plateau de Permounat; here we are. Yes—good; the main axis runs roughly East-West; well nearly North-East South-West. That's all right; those are our prevailing winds. You see on these minute air-strips the planes can only land and take off against the wind—but of course you know that."

"What about the other place, Berdun?"

"Oh, that's all right in any wind—it used to be a proper airfield. The last time I was there, last year, there were still the red-and-white markers along the main runway, and even a ragged old air-sock; quite a lot of bushes beginning to grow up, and the odd goat browsing, but Tim Acland managed all right." He started to fold up the map.

"Just a moment" Philip said. "How long will it take Bonnecourt to get to this pick-up plateau from Tardets?" He and Nick both bent over the map.

"On foot, at least six hours" Nick said.

"All right—minimum of seven hours notice. That means letting him know in good time. Very well—let's go on."

"Just one thing, Sir. How much can I tell Acland?"

Philip considered. "Does he know Bonnecourt by sight?"

"I'm not sure—he used to do a bit of climbing before he started flying, so he easily might."

"Then I think you'll have to tell him about B., and his past record, and that he's being got out with official approval. Don't say why he has to leave, if you can help it. I take it he's a trustworthy person?"

"Oh Lord yes. All Aclands are madly pious" Nick replied cheerfully, starting his engine.

Philip asked to be dropped first at the Victoire—there he got out Colin's keys, and checked on the Rover; it had not been tampered with, as he half-feared, and started with no trouble. He went in and said he would be wanting his room that night; the *patron* was having his siesta, but the all-purposes, round-the-clock *valet* took the message. "Since yesterday we no longer have an *agent* here" he announced cheerfully. "This is well, *n'est-ce-pas?*"

Philip drove even the short distance to the clinic, to put a little life into the Rover's battery. After all these minor delays once again the "period of repose" was over; the old head *sage-femme* took him straight in to see Julia. His wife lay in bed, calm and beautiful; he was struck, suddenly, by the sense of *abundance* that she gave: of beauty, calmness, and strength. Beautiful she had always been, and decided, and nonchalante when she chose; but this was something different. Could it be due to this new fulfilment, he wondered?

She asked first about his journey to Paris—presently,

when all that had been dealt with—"I had to give the baby names, and register them" she pronounced. "I hope you'll like them."

"Why did you have to do that while I was away?"

Julia told him about the limit of *trois jours francs* for registering a birth, and the *mairie* closing at noon on Saturdays. "Kind old Lord Heriot did it for me, just before they packed up."

"What *have* you called him?"

"Philip Bernard." She watched his face.

"Bernard isn't a family name—my Father and Grandfather were both called Robert Philip," he said, doubtfully.

"Yes. But neither of them did much about seeing that this child came into the world at all" Julia replied, in her slow tones, smiling a little mockingly at her husband. He laughed, at last seizing the point.

"Yes—I see. Quite right; well done."

"I'm so glad you're pleased. It was torture suddenly having to decide, with you away. How *murderously* tiresome the *loi de France* is" Julia said; but still calmly, passing a considered judgment. Then she asked if Bonnecourt had gone to Pamplona?

"No! He came over to see me this morning."

"Gracious! To the Heriots?"

"Yes; in disguise!"

"Oh, what fun. Isn't he nice?"

"He may be nice, but he's going to be a bit of a problem unless he can learn to be more disciplined" Philip said. He told Julia that the hunter had agreed to go as a stalker to Glentoran, as a cover-job—"So now you'd better write to Edina, hadn't you? He may get there quite soon."

"How soon?"

"Well I hope to get him flown out to Pamplona, the day after tomorrow probably—and Colin will drive him straight down to Gib, and have him flown home from there. You'd better write that letter at once, to catch tonight's post. I shall have to ring Colin too, and tell him; I'd better go back to the Heriots to do that—the telephones here and at the pub are so infernally public."

"Well give me my despatch-case" Julia said. "Oh, what about Madame B? Is she going too?"

"Yes. Not immediately. We can see about her later on."

"Well I'd better know when she is going, so that I can warn Edina. The French may be bloody-minded, but they are *clean*" Julia stated firmly. "Goodbye, dearest—come back and collect my letter, won't you?"

But no sooner had she started writing than the old *sage-femme* brought in the infant Philip Bernard to be nursed. "Madame writes—this is wrong" the old woman said, as Julia drew down her nightdress; she swabbed one nipple with a mild disinfectant, wiped it with a piece of gauze, and put the child in position; he began to suck at once, while the old woman looked on.

"This is well. For a premature, he is a strong infant" the *sage-femme* said, swabbing Julia's other breast. "If he will take more, let him, today."

When she had gone out Julia lay in that strange, unique tranquillity induced by nursing a child. This is perhaps the most calming occupation in the world: so everyday, so normal, and yet so evidently necessary that even the stupidest woman can hardly escape a passive satisfaction in it. Julia—less stupid than people sometimes supposed, misled by her expressionless beauty—surrendered completely to this satisfaction. When the swaddled baby, disgruntled, abandoned the emptied left breast—practically spitting it out, with a small angry wail—she turned the creature round, and gave it the other one, carefully inserting the nipple into the small helpless mouth. Goodness, how *silly* babies were, she thought; the infant let the nipple escape, and made two or three boss-shots before he finally fastened on this second source of food, and sucked away contentedly. Julia was delighted; hitherto one breast had sufficed her tiny son. She wanted him to be strong, and well-nourished. She relaxed again into that blissful tranquillity.

The old *sage-femme* too was pleased to find that the baby had tackled the second breast—"Ah, *voila!* Now Madame can finish her letter." She dumped the baby casually down on the bed, and gave Julia back her despatch-case. But before Julia had finished writing to Edina Reeder at

Glentoran announcing Bonnecourt's arrival as an extra stalker, to be followed later by his wife—"and as she is *French,* Mrs. Cameron really must make the cottage at Ach-an-Draine *perfectly* clean"—a little nurse opened the door and ushered in Dick, weighed down with suit-cases; he dropped them, and went out to fetch the rest. Then Luzia came in with Julia's Burberry and water-proof hat, explaining that she had only noticed these on the hooks by the door when the cases were already in the car.

"Put them in the cupboard," Julia said, as Dick came in with two more cases. "How kind of you both."

"Do not forget the *vinho*" Luzia adjured Dick; grinning, he went out, and returned with his arms full of bottles— several of the sherry they had purchased at Jaca, more of the *vin du pays* that the twins had bought and bottled for Julia.

"Luzia says you're going to the Victoire next week—that miserable place is *bone* dry, so I thought we'd better bring you down a little sustenance" the young man said.

"Thank you. Put them in the cupboard" Julia repeated. "No, wait—leave one bottle of sherry out. Luzia, give me my handbag" she took a cork-screw out of it. "Now would you go and find another glass somewhere. There are two on the washstand—wash them out, Dick, like a dear. I feel like some sherry, after all this child-bearing!"

"Well, this is a regular tooth-glass party" Dick said presently, when they were all drinking sherry. "Often they're the best kind."

Julia made some practical enquiries about what they had done. "You left the key at Barraterre's?"

"No, because we return tomorrow to make the house clean. But Mme. Barraterre is paid—she sent her felicitations on the birth of the son."

"I shouldn't think the Stansteds would notice whether the house was clean or not" Julia said, with calm uncharitableness—"except perhaps the frig."

"*I* cleaned out the frig while Luzia was at Mass" Dick said proudly—"I made a wonderful job of it, I assure you."

"Also we paid for the milk" Luzia continued. "And while we wait for this good soul to make her reckoning, which takes *long*, there arrives Madame Bonnecourt—who gives

Dick *thousands* of francs, which she says Nick lent to her husband."

"Goodness, has Bonnecourt been back to Larège?" Julia asked—she just managed to suppress the word "too."

"No; she said that he sent it. This is a strange being!—it seems that he does as he pleases" Luzia said, looking amused. While she was speaking Colonel Jamieson came in, ushered by the little nurse—he caught the last words.

"Who does as he pleases, Condesa?" he asked. "Hullo, Heriot! You must be Dick—just left your brother."

"This guide-person at Larège," Luzia said—the nurse had not quite closed the door; Jamieson did so himself. "We were there today" Luzia went on, "packing."

"Did you see *him?*" Jamieson asked; after the morning's performance he felt that Bonnecourt was capable of anything.

"No, only Madame. But she had heard from him, and he had sent money; for Nick."

"For Her Ladyship, you mean really" Dick said—Jamieson brushed the observation aside.

"What is she like?" he asked Luzia with interest.

"Not young; once pretty, now faded; and I think a *nice* person" the girl said. "One sees that she is devoted to her husband, and often in anxiety about him. But she keeps her dairy beautifully" she added—"this I saw one day."

Jamieson glanced at his wife, whose despatch-case was on her knees. His one desire now was to get rid of Dick and Luzia, collect Julia's letter to Glentoran, and post it.

"How good of you to go up there and pack" he said courteously to Luzia. "Well, I shall be seeing you at dinner— Lady Heriot has been kind enough to invite me. Dick, I believe your Mother hopes you are at Evensong."

"Oh Lord, I forgot all about it! Well, it's too late now." But they both took the hint; Luzia kissed Julia, and the pair went off. Philip at last kissed his wife. "Is that letter done?" he asked.

"Not quite. First I had to feed the child, and then they came."

"Well you'd better tell Edina that Mrs. B. is a good dairy-hand" he said, as Julia opened her case—while she started to write again he rinsed Luzia's glass out in the basin and helped himself to sherry. He lit a cigarette, and sat quietly, while his wife scribbled away.

"Do you know yet when he goes?" Julia asked.

"No. Not tomorrow; Nick says his good pilot won't be free till the day after."

"Tuesday. How long will it take Colin to drive to Gib?"

"Well, better allow two days—it *could* be done in one, I think, but safer to say two."

"That brings us to Thursday. Fly home, one day—could B. be sure of getting a flight on the Friday?"

"Not by any means. Better reckon London on Saturday."

"Well we all know about the lack of trains and buses in Scotland on the Sabbath!" Julia said, sardonically. "Even if the Office flew him to Renfrew, he couldn't get on. I'd better say Monday or Tuesday week, at earliest, for him to reach Glentoran." She wrote away—then looked up at her husband.

"You know, much the most sensible thing would be to have Colin fly home with him, and take him up" she said. "Then they could go on the bus from Glasgow, like anyone else; Colin would know where to get off, and no need for exciting helicopters landing in the Dairy Park, or strange cars dashing up from Machrahanish. If you want Bonnecourt to get to Glentoran unobtrusively, that's the way to do it."

"I think you're right" Jamieson said. "Of course I've only been there once; and arrived, and left, by sea. But this seems a sound plan. I was going to drive over to Pamplona anyhow tomorrow to see Colin and tell him about picking B. up—telephoning from France to Spain is hopeless! But now we can switch cars at the same time. No point in my Bordeaux hire-car being left at Gibraltar indefinitely—I can take it back when I have to go home."

"When *do* you go home?" Julia asked, putting down her pen.

"Look, dearest, do get that letter finished—then we'll discuss plans" her husband said firmly; obediently, Julia completed her missive to Edina, and licked down the envelope.

"There" she said, tossing it across the bed. "Now—may I ask some questions?"

"Yes." He went over and kissed her. "Bless you!" He was thinking that if marriage and Intelligence could be made compatible at all, Julia was one of the few women to make them so. "Ask away" he said, sitting on the bed and taking her hand.

"Well first, when do you have to get back?"

"In about a fortnight. What a mercy they sent for me to come home and report just at the appropriate moment! But I shall have to return to my Sheiks and finish the job—well really as soon as I conveniently can."

"Taking about how long?"

"No idea."

"I see." Julia considered. "*Not* conveniently, on any date" she said. "However! I gave Buchan and Mrs. What's-it weekly cheques up to the end of September, but now I shan't get back till the middle of November; I'll write out some more, and you can hand them over when you get home."

"Right. What about the gamp?"

"I was coming to her. You'll have to ring up her organisation—I think it's called 'Monthly Nurses Ltd.', but you'll find it in the big address book on my desk—and find out how much we ought to pay for the cancellation. Then you can send them a cheque, and explain."

"I will. What about Nannie Mackenzie? You'll want her a month sooner, won't you?"

"Goodness, so I shall. How clever you are! I hope to God she'll be free. You'd better ring up Edina and find out about that. Oh yes, and cancel the wretched *accoucheur* too—*he* won't be wanted. How complicated babies can make things, when they're born out of due time! Dear one, I'm sorry to give you so much bother."

"Nothing matters, so long as you and he are all right." He looked at his watch. "I must go now, or I shall be late for dinner. See you late on Tuesday, or some time Wednesday." He bent over the bed and gave her a long embrace. "Bless you, my darling."

Chapter 12

Philip Jamieson felt that "Operation Bernardin," as it came to be called, owed a great deal to the young Heriots, and their local knowledge. When Dick was told of the plan after dinner—they were sitting in the boys' own room, which housed shelves-ful of books, their wireless and record-player, and a welter of scientific papers—he said at once: "There's a *cabane* up at Permounat. Hadn't we better make sure that the shepherds have gone down? They ought to have by now, of course. Or do you not mind the odd peasant seeing B. being picked up and flown off, Sir?"

In fact this is the sort of thing Intelligence does mind very much; one can seldom be absolutely sure that the peasant is really a peasant.

"Is there any means of finding out?" the Colonel enquired.

"Yes, I can ask when I'm up at Larège tomorrow—they all take their flocks down roughly at the same time, and one valley usually knows what the other valleys are doing. I'll see to that."

Philip turned to Nick.

"If we only hear tomorrow evening whether there are still shepherds up there, either we must find another place, or stand it all off till they do go. So Wednesday will probably be the earliest day in any case."

"I'll keep in touch with Acland. He's all on, and loves the idea" Nick replied—"and I'll go over when the day is fixed and tell Bonnecourt accordingly." It had already been decided by Jamieson not to risk a telephone message, even via Pauline Pontarlet, but that Nick should drive to Tardets and instruct the hunter when to go up to the plateau. "Anyhow, Sir, I've been thinking" Nick went on. "If you're going to

203

drive over to Pamplona tomorrow and change cars with young Monro, it would be much better to make it Wednesday; you'd hardly get back here before first light on Tuesday, and you said you wanted to be on hand for the pickup."

"Yes, I do." If there is one thing Intelligence feels strongly about it is not letting an agent be collected by anyone who does not know him by sight; all too easy for "them" to put a counter-agent on board a train or a plane. "Does young Acland know Bonnecourt?" he asked now.

"Oddly enough, no; he's always climbed with the other guide."

"Then either you or I will have to be up at this plateau."

"If you don't mind riding pillion on a motor-bike over rather rough going, I could get you up to within an hour's walk of it."

"Excellent" the Colonel said. Dick looked surprised.

"What mo-bike?" he asked his brother.

"Dr. Fourget's. You know he's forever chugging up the most ghastly tracks on it, where his car can't get, to reach cases." He turned to Jamieson with a grin. "You wouldn't believe, Sir, how often the peasants here impale themselves on their dung-forks, in the highest spots—or gash off their thumbs with hatchets! I rang the old boy up and he says I can borrow his machine."

Philip laughed at the idea of the self-impaled peasants, but he was relieved that he could be taken to check Bonnecourt's actual departure.

"Very well—settle with young Acland for Wednesday, if your brother reports all clear by then."

"I'll go and collect the bike tomorrow in any case, to have it ready" Nick said. "Dick and Luzia can drop me off at Labielle on their way."

This reminded Dick of the matter of scrubbing the floors; he went off to see his Mother, and laid on a sturdy young housemaid for the purpose.

"No, of course Luzia mustn't do that" Lady Heriot said. "Emma can go—she'll enjoy the outing."

"Whoever suggested that the Countess should do such a thing?" Lord Heriot enquired.

"Luzia did!" (The Portuguese girl had absented herself earlier to write some letters.) "I gather she's been doing quite a lot of scrubbing for Mrs. Jamieson."

"All nonsense, from beginning to end!" the old man said. "Where's that fellow Jamieson? I meant to tell him off about it."

But Jamieson, leaving his excuses with Nick, had gone back to the Victoire. Next morning he started at six, blinded up over the Grandpont Pass and down the further side. After leaving the mountains he turned West, crossing low foothills and outlying ridges—the Spanish slope of the Pyrenees is much more gradual than the abrupt approach on the northern side—till presently he was down in the Aragon valley, the vast rolling tawny plain of Northern Spain, where small towns perch on steep little hills. One of these, a sign-post informed him, was Berdun, and he slowed down to look at it—fantastically crowning its hill-top the white and blue-washed houses, jammed together on the summit, glittered like silver in the sun. Berdun, Verdun? Probably the same name originally; B and V were practically interchangeable in Spanish, the man thought—anyhow a *dun*, a fort; indubitably a Celtic place-name. He must tell Julia; it would please her, as it did him. He drove on more slowly, looking for the abandoned airfield. Yes, there it was—the forlorn, deserted little control-tower of mud-coloured brick, the ragged windsock, also mud-coloured with age, flying from a pole close by. Well he must bring Colin out and check all details with him on the spot. He drove on, fast, to Pamplona—there was a lot to arrange, in a short time.

Colin was staying at the Hotel Bristol—so much Jamieson had managed to learn in their abortive telephone conversation the evening before; it was now getting on for two, and they had lunch. Philip explained the arrangements for getting Bonnecourt to Glentoran, and that Colin was to take him the whole way.

"Oh, good—I shall see Aglaia; Edina's asked her up for a

bit." (Aglaia was Colin's wife.) "But has B. got a Spanish visa? He'll want it at Gib."

"I shouldn't think so for a moment—he seems to me too casual for words."

"Oh, have you met him?"

"Yes—I'll tell you about that presently. I shall have to ring up Gibraltar after lunch and get all that fixed. I expect I'd better do it from your local H.Q.—who is this Sẽnor Mo-reño?"

"The local *garagiste!*" Colin said grinning.

"Oh well, very often it's the barber" Jamieson said, re-signedly; the peculiar methods of his Service held no sur-prises for him. "Box at all sound-proof?"

"No, no box—an extension in his bedroom. He mounts guard outside; or I do, in this case. Who shall you speak to?"

"Well, as it's all rather a rush, I think I'll ring the Convent. I know Bramwell, the A.D.C. But as we're not sure of the day yet, you'll have to let him know when to meet you at La Linea, once you're well under way."

From Sẽnor Moreño's bedside telephone Jamieson put through his call to the Governor's oddly-named house in Gibraltar. No, Major Bramwell was out—"the Duty Officer speaking."

Philip embarked on one of those complicated telephoned explanations which are supposed to convey their meaning without, if possible, giving too much away to unwanted lis-teners. Fortunately the Duty Officer was very quick at the uptake.

"Yes, I see. Two flights home, and a Spanish visa needed for the—er—newcomer. Well, I or Bramwell had better go up to La Linea to see to all that, when we know the day and time. *What's* the name of this man of yours who's bringing him? Oh, Monro. Not Colin, by any chance? It is?—oh, it will be nice to see him again; we were at prep-school to-gether. My name? Satterthwaite. Right—when we hear, we'll be there."

Philip passed all this on to Colin; then they drove out,

Colin now in his own Rover, Philip in the hire-car, to inspect the derelict airfield.

The track to it from the road was rather bumpy from long disuse, but they got their cars along and parked close under, and behind, the shabby little control tower; Philip got out and walked back to the main road. When he returned—"Go two yards farther on, and you'll barely be visible" he said. "You may have to wait here some time, and you don't want to arouse curiosity. See if you can pull in closer under the tower." Colin did this, and Jamieson again went out onto the road.

"All right" he said when he came back. "Completely un-sighted." Then he walked out to examine the airfield itself. A hoopoe flew up in front of him from between the tufts of yellowish grass; it alighted again, raising and lowering its delicate crest, and moved away with quick light steps. Philip walked on. As Nick had said, red-and-white markers, their colours dimmed by the prevailing tawny dust, still outlined the main run-way; the whole place was becoming overgrown with grass, withered to a pale gold at summer's end, and here and there sagey bushes had begun to spring up. But he saw no goats, and there was nothing else to prevent a safe landing. Satisfied, he went back to the cars.

"Well unless you hear to the contrary, be here, ready, from 10.45 onwards on Wednesday" he told Colin. "Full up with air, oil, and gas. Have you got plenty of money?"

"I think so—but I can always get more from Moreño."

"Well don't run short. It's only for food and an hotel on the way, and possible breakdowns! Bramwell will see to everything at Gibraltar." He said Goodbye to his wife's cousin, and drove, hard, back to Pau.

The Plateau de Permounat is a most peculiar place, aston-ishing to anyone unfamiliar with the western Pyrenees. It lies high, among rough wild surroundings; set between the grey ridges and rocky slopes is an oval of fine grass over 200 yards long, as smooth as a lawn or a cricket-pitch, and abso-lutely level save for four enormous boulders, as big as cottages, standing at one side of it. Here Colonel Jamieson came on that Wednesday morning, after jolting uncomfortably on the pillion of Dr. Fourget's motor-cycle up some exceedingly uncouth tracks, till Nick parked the machine at a farm; then they walked uphill for another hour. Dick, on his return with Luzia and the sturdy Emma from their house-cleaning at Larège, had reported positively that all the flocks and shepherds had already come down from the high pastures, including Permounat; Nick had driven over to Tardets next day and given Bonnecourt word to be at the Plateau by 10.30 on the Wednesday; then he had told the obliging Master Acland to be there by 10.20—and Philip had sent a brief telegram to Colin: "Wednesday as arranged."

"What an extraordinary place!" Jamieson exclaimed, as he and Nick reached the top of a shallow *col*, and looked down onto the green little plateau. "I never saw anything like it in my life—not in the Alps, nor the Caucasus; nowhere."

"There are several of them about here" Nick said, starting down. "Let's wait in the *cabane*, out of the wind."

In spite of Dick's reassurances, the mere mention of the possible presence of shepherds at Permounat had caused Philip Jamieson to take certain simple precautions; he had taken a haversack with an out-size flask of cognac, and three or four small glasses, along with his sandwiches—knock-out tablets he always carried in his pocket as a matter of course. These measures proved to have been wise—when Nick pushed open the door of the *cabane* and walked in, a sleepy peasant roused up from one of the bunks on which the cheese-making shepherds slept when their flocks were grazing the high pastures. Nick asked him, rather brusquely, what he was doing there?

"I miss one sheep—all yesterday I seek it, and do not find it" the man said, rubbing his eyes. "So then I sleep—today I seek it again."

"Gently" Philip said to Nick. "Let me talk to him." He commiserated with the man over the loss of such a valuable animal as a sheep, and offered him a glass of cognac before he renewed his search—as he spoke setting his glasses out on the rough wooden table, and opening his flask.

The peasant was delighted. He drank, wiped his unshaven lips, drank again, and asked where *ces messieurs* came from?

"From Pau; we make a small ascension" Philip said. While they talked he looked at his watch; it was ten minutes past ten. None too much time—please God young Acland didn't arrive too soon. He told Nick, in English, to ask the man the best way up a small peak at the further end of the plateau; while they went to the door and looked out he re-filled the shepherd's glass, and crumbled a couple of tablets from his small phial into it. When the pair returned, Nick reporting the route—a sharp boy, Nick, Jamieson decided, always able to act on a hint without any dotting of i's or crossing of t.'s—he handed the drugged glass to the man. "Another *petit verre*, Monsieur, before you renew your search."

The peasant was already a little dopey; he had had one good glass of brandy on an empty stomach. Gratefully, wishing the strangers good health and good fortune, he drank away at the second, while Philip kept his eye on his watch, and listened for the sound of Acland's plane.

"Go out and look if there's any sign of B." he said to Nick. "I'd rather he didn't see this man." Nick went off.

In fact the timing was perfect. Three minutes before the very light, faint hum of the plane became audible the peasant slumped over sideways on the rough bench beside the table; Philip went to the door of the *cabane* and summoned Nick—"Come and help me to lay him on one of the bunks."

"What's happened to him?" Nick asked, surprised.

"I put him out—had to. Take his feet." Together they lifted the man onto the bunk; Philip laid a blanket over him—"Chilly, up here" he said. "But he'll be all right in a couple of hours." They heard the sound of the plane, went out, and watched Tim Acland's neat and precise banking and turning, till he landed on the minute lawn-smooth space, and came to a halt.

"Well, that was all right" the young pilot said, leaning out of his machine. "Wind absolutely perfect! How do you do, Sir" he said politely to Jamieson. "Where's my passenger?"

"Due in eight minutes" the Colonel said, looking at his watch.

"Then I'll turn her." With considerable skill he manoeuvred his machine round, taxied back to the far end of the plateau, and helped by Nick turned again, till he was facing into the wind. He had just completed this performance when a figure appeared, coming over another of the small *cols* between the rocky peaks which surrounded the strange little spot, and walked rapidly down towards them; with immense relief Jamieson saw that it was really Bonnecourt—he was beginning to fear that this end of the Pyrenees might be alive with unwanted peasants.

"Morning" he said to the hunter. "Here's your pilot, and your plane. Now you know the drill—Monro is waiting for you down on the far side; he will drive you to Gibraltar, fly with you to England, and take you right up to this place in Scotland. He'll take you to the Office on the way, and introduce you—but you're well remembered there!" he said pleasantly. "After that you will get your orders from London."

"Admirable" Bonnecourt said. "I am infinitely grateful!" He turned to Nick. "Have you put *ma pauvre voiture* into the Gave?"

"Not yet" Nick said, laughing—"There hasn't been time. But I will, I promise you. One can't do everything at once—and there has been quite a lot to do."

"Thank you—I know that I can rely on you." Then the hunter turned to Jamieson. "And how soon may I expect Madame my wife to join me in Scotland?"

Philip was amused at the order in which Bonnecourt placed his enquiries—*voiture* first, wife second. But his reply was gentle and considerate.

"I thought you would wish to see the house, and the general situation, and write to Madame about it all, before she comes. For *her*, there is no hurry—in fact it will be more prudent that she does not follow you too soon; and she will wish, presumably, to make arrangements for the care of the property at Larège during your absence—which may well be of some duration. But my wife has written already to her cousin, Mrs. Reeder, asking her to ensure that all is made easy and pleasant for Madame Bonnecourt."

"Madame Jamieson *se charge de cela*? In that case, all will certainly be well," Bonnecourt said. "Please give her my thanks." He paused, and looked a little hesitantly at Jamieson. "This lady in Scotland is like Madame?" he asked.

"Not to look at; she's more like Monro black and white."

"But she has the same character?"

Jamieson was surprised afresh by Bonnecourt's preoccupation with Julia and her character.

"Well, she's very competent, and very kind" he said. "I'm sure your wife will get on with her, and be taken good care of." He looked at his watch—he was anxious to get the plane and its passenger away before anything else inconvenient occurred—the unexpected shepherd had been nuisance enough. But the hunter took his arm.

"Just one moment, Colonel. Would it be possible for my wife to come down and speak with Madame Jamieson, who knows this place in Scotland so well?" he asked, almost wistfully. "It—it would reassure her." He turned to Nick. "*Mon cher* Nick, I am sure you would not mind bringing Madame down."

"Look, Bonnecourt, if it's safe, we'll certainly arrange that" the Colonel said, firmly. "But if it means a risk for her, or for all our operations here, it may not be possible. Leave it to me. Now you'd better hop in and get off. Goodbye—*bon voyage*, and au revoir in London."

Bonnecourt, shaking hands with him and with Nick, climbed into the little plane. But just as Tim Acland started up his engine a sheep, baa-ing loudly, came down off the further slopes and started across the small run-way, heading towards the *cabane*.

"Oh God! Chase the damned thing away!" Jamieson said to Nick. "It's probably looking for its master." Nick, laughing, tried to chivvy the animal back up the slopes down which it had come; but sheep are not easily driven by anything but sheep-dogs, and the creature continued to cavort about on the grass, vainly pursued by Nick.

"Get off the moment you can" Jamieson said to young

Acland; then he hurried across to the *cabane*, went in, and
shut the door, to keep the sheep's voice from its owner's ears.
Probably he had given the man a strong enough dose, but
peasants were very close to the animal world, and the links
between them incredibly strong—he was taking no chances.
In fact the shepherd was stirring faintly under the blanket;
but when, to Philip's great relief, the sound of the plane's
engine taking off drowned the baa-ing, the man lay still
again. Through the small cloudy window Jamieson saw the
little machine rise, clear a low *col* at the western end of the
plateau, bank, and head away South; he went out to see it
better. Nick, fairly howling with laughter, was dancing
about between the sheep and the door; Philip shut this after
him, and stood watching till the plane disappeared.

"Well that's all right" he said, as the hum of the engine
died away in the distance. "I'll just stow the glasses, and
then we'll go. What a brute! Keep it out." He kicked at the
persistent sheep, slid into the hut, and shut the door behind
him; stuffing the glasses, rolled in a handkerchief, into his
haversack, he rejoined Nick.

"There you are—go in and find your master, you silly old
thing" Nick addressed the sheep, propping the door ajar
with a stone; they could see the animal sniffing in the entrance as they climbed up to the small *col* from which they
had come down. "Probably eat half a blanket, and die of it"
Nick said—"I ought not to have left the door open." He
made as if to turn back.

"Oh, bother the sheep!" Jamieson exclaimed unsympa-
thetically. "It's given us enough trouble already. Come on."

They paused for a sandwich at the farm where they had
left the Doctor's motor-cycle, and then had a jolting journey
back to Pau. Philip picked up his car, drove to the clinic, and
hurried in to speak to Julia; he had returned from Pamplona
too late the night before to see her, and left too early that
morning. She was just starting her mid-day meal; after a
hasty kiss he went to eat at the little hotel—"I'll come in
again just before four" he said. "That all right?"

"Perfectly. Did it all go according to plan?"

"Yes—and dead on time. See you presently."

During the "period of repose," when Julia must not be disturbed, Philip drove round to the Heriots, where he found Tim Acland being given a belated lunch by the twins in the deserted dining-room.

"Oh yes, everything O. K." the young man reported cheerfully—"except that Berdun was absolutely covered with goats! I flew low, and circled, but they wouldn't move, so I shut off the engine and simply *yelled* to your cousin to chase them away; I don't know if he heard, but he picked up the idea, and hunted them to the side of the field. So then I landed and dropped your man, and they both got into the Rover and drove off."

"Did you see any other cars, or police, about?" Jamieson asked.

"Not a soul except the goats—if goats have souls! Then I flew back. The petrol just held out nicely; I was a little nervous after that extra circling, which I hadn't allowed for, because it's a close-run thing anyhow, to Berdun and back—let alone the détour to that plateau. But all went well."

"And all they know at the Ailes Basques is that Tim had a lovely solo fly out Westwards" Nick said gleefully. "So I don't see how even those nosey-parkers of the *Sûreté* or the *D.B.* can suspect anything, let alone fasten on something."

Philip Jamieson thanked young Acland warmly. "We are most grateful to you" he said. "I should like to offer to pay for your petrol, at least—but I'm afraid you wouldn't accept it."

"Not on your life!" Tim Acland replied fervently. "It isn't everyone who gets the chance to fly a secret agent; I shall *hug* this (to my own bosom, of course) all my life. 'Our Man in Larège'—I flew him out." Jamieson could only laugh.

When he went round to see Julia later he found something else nice too—the quite novel experience of having a person to whom to recount his adventures in perfect security, and who took an intense interest in them. This was altogether different from reporting to Major Hartley or anyone else at the Office—attentive and friendly as they always were. Julia was concerned about his discomfort on the pillion of Dr. Fourget's motor-cycle, horrified at the discovery of the peasant in the *cabane* up on the Plateau de Permounat, and laughed wildly over the sudden appearance of the sheep, which had threatened the take-off.

"Oh darling, *how* ridiculous!" she said. Philip, happy to be amusing her, recounted young Acland's trouble with the goats at Berdun.

"Really, animals are the last thing one would expect 'the opposition' to lay on as a Secret Weapon" Julia said— "though I see that they could be quite a useful one." Philip was rather disconcerted by this.

"I don't really see how they can have been laid on this time, at either place" he said. "The shepherd up at the Plateau seemed just an ordinary dumb peasant; and how could any Spaniards have got the idea of smothering Berdun with goats, precisely this morning?"

"Darling, I didn't mean that they had—I'm sure it was all completely fortuitous today. It just struck me as a possible bright idea. Couldn't you use it yourself?—have droves of camels in reserve to blanket airfields if some anti-you Sheiks try to fly in to obstruct your operations?"

Philip Jamieson only half-laughed. "I think you may have got something there. Camels could be moved much more quickly, and less noticeably, than oil-drums. Thank you, dearest." Then he passed on Bonnecourt's request that she would see his wife, and tell her about Glentoran. "He seems to have immense faith in you—he was rather touching about it. I said you would, if it was safe for her."

"Of course I will. I know the very cottage they'll be in, and its nice little garden; so lay that on at any time. I'm sure I can encourage her—it's all a fearful uprooting for the poor little woman. Luzia likes her" Julia said, inconsequently.

The *sage-femme* now came in with Philip Bernard in her arms to prepare for the next feed; this time she dumped the creature, still swathed in cotton-wool, in his Father's arms. "*Voilà!*—let *Monsieur le Colonel* hold his son", she said.

Philip gazed in a sort of bewilderment at the tiny creased face, now so close to his own.

"He's not in the least like anyone" he said. But at that moment the baby began to howl angrily, disliking the strange arms, and wanting his food. "Yes he is—he's *exactly* like you when you disapprove of anything" he said to Julia. "Good!"

Philip would have liked to watch his child being fed, but in spite of his promises to sit perfectly quiet the old *sage-femme* was adamant—no, the infant was premature, and the Mother must not on any account be distracted. To his own surprise, as much as to Julia's, Philip deposited a light kiss on the little pink forehead before the old woman took the creature from him.

"Well I must ring up the Office anyhow" he said to his wife "and report. I'll do that from the Heriots, and come back later."

"What a bill you must be running up at the Heriots for telephone calls!" Julia said, holding out her arms for the baby.

"Not a bit of it—spot cash every time! Lord H. is very tough about all that," Philip said.

"*Voyons, Monsieur le Colonel!* You must absolutely leave Madame in peace now" the old *sage-femme* said, exasperated—Philip blew his wife a kiss, and went away.

He found Lady Heriot having tea alone. The twins were out, and her husband, she said, was at a meeting of the Cemetery Committee. "So many people come here, and then go and die, that we are running short of space—and land is getting terribly expensive. I expect it will end in our having to give up a piece of the garden, but it will be most inconvenient; so far from the old cemetery, and from the Church. I wish fewer people wanted to die in Pau!"

"I expect they like living here, and then Death overtakes them" Jamieson said. "I should quite like to die in Pau—or even better up at Larège." He refused the cup of tea she offered him, saying that, as so often, he wanted to telephone. "I'm afraid I am a terrible nuisance, but I may just catch the man I want at the Office if I do it at once. Oh please don't get up!—I know my way to the study."

He was in time to catch Major Hartley.

"Yes, safely over, and on his way to Gib" he said, in reply to the Major's enquiry. "No, flown out.... Private enterprise, laid on locally.... No, no hitches, except for a few goats.... I said *goats*—smelly animals, with horns! Yes, this A.M. You'd better ring Gib—the A.D.C. was out when I tried.... No, two passages; I've told young C. to go with him right up to his destination—sorry to take C. off your job, but it can be done more unobtrusively that way ... Argyll —my wife has got him a job as a ghillie.... Oh yes, free at any time; it's on C's sister's place.... Yes, they'll look in on you on their way through, and C. will put you in the picture.... Lord no!—they'll take the bus; that's what I meant by unobtrusive. You don't *listen!* ... By the way, tell MacPherson to lay on camels, fifty or a hundred.... To block the airfield, of course—no plane can land on a strip covered with camels."

Loud laughter came down the long line from London to Pau.

"How brilliant!" Major Hartley said. "Why didn't you think that one up sooner?"

"*I* didn't think it up—it was my wife's idea."

"Congratulations to your wife" Hartley said. "All right— I'll see to everything. Expect you in about a fortnight."

"Let me know when you hear from Gib—it's impossible to telephone across this ghastly frontier. Tell Paris; they can ring me" Philip said urgently. "And some time take time out to slap down Monteith; he's an ass!"

"Oh—why?"

"Tell you when I see you."

While he was actually at the Heriots' telephone, so conveniently private, Philip took the opportunity to ring up Colonel Monceau in Paris, and thank him for his good offices. "It is all much more convenient and agreable now" he said carefully—"and the action was taken so promptly. I am most grateful."

"And our old friend—he is gone?"

"Yes, but only today. This is a monster—utterly regardless of instructions" Philip said. Now there was laughter over the wires from Paris.

"Ah, my friend, you and your colleagues will find that you have your hands full enough with that one! It is an individualist! But he can be of great value. Well, *bonne chance!* How is Madame?—and the son?"

"Both splendid, thank you." Then he asked if he could bring Madame B. down to see his wife without creating difficulties? "She well knows the place to which they go; she would like to encourage Madame."

"By all means; she is no longer under observation."

"Excellent—a thousand thanks. See you again soon, Jean, I hope." He rang off.

As usual, it took a considerable time before the *Inter* could be persuaded to give the price of the calls: Philip wrote the date and time of both in Lord Heriot's book: "London; Paris," and his own name—but not the two highly secret numbers; he added the cost when he learned it, and went back to the drawing-room. There he found the twins returned and drinking tea, with Luzia.

"*More* telephoning?" Dick asked, as Jamieson put several notes down on the tea-tray.

"Yes indeed—I should be lost without the blessed privacy of this house." He thanked Lady Heriot once again.

"Well now, if you got the person you wanted, have a cup of tea—this is a fresh pot" his hostess said. This time Philip accepted gratefully, and ate some buttered brioches as well. Presently Nick observed, thoughtfully—

"I think we ought to carry out poor old B.'s last wishes."

"Which were?" his twin enquired.

"First, to drive that poor crazy old car of his into the Gave, to save it from the knackers."

"What is this, 'knackers'?" Luzia asked, curiously—she was always interested in unfamiliar English expressions.

"Well literally, people who kill very old horses, and sell the meat to feed dogs—but nowadays it goes for anyone who breaks up cars and uses some of the bits," Nick replied.

"I think you ought to do that" Lady Heriot said. "But won't it look the least bit dramatic if you do it in broad daylight?" Now Luzia gazed at her hostess with intense interest—really, the English! "And it will have to be quite a *deep* place" she added.

"I know, *Maman*. But there's a spot, a good bit downstream, where that little tributary comes in; it has scoured out a pretty deep pool—I went and threw stones into it this afternoon. It would hide any car, and there are no houses near by; the bank is very steep, practically vertical, and there's quite a firm grass field right to the edge."

Jamieson listened to all this with as much interest as Luzia—he had committed himself to Bonnecourt over the disposal of the ancient Bugatti, but he was fascinated by Lady Heriot's concern with this unusual undertaking. She continued with her questions.

"How should you do it?"

"I drive it down, and to the lip of the river-bank; Dick follows on in his Jag and gives it a good push from behind when I've got out. Or I might put it in gear, switch on the engine through the door, and jump aside. But it all means a certain degree of accuracy—it would be much easier by daylight."

"Yes, I see." Lady Heriot pondered. "But during evening daylight most of the peasants are roving about, going to drink at the *buvettes*, or to call on their lady-loves. I think it would be far wiser to go at daybreak, when all but the very *old* men will be sleeping off their various forms of pleasure."

Jamieson was awestruck by his hostess's perspicacity, and still more by her frankness.

"O.K.—we'll go tomorrow, first thing" Dick said. "You always know all the answers, *Maman*".

"Oh, could I not go too? I should love to see a car driven into a river!" Luzia exclaimed.

"Yes—I'll have you called" Lady Heriot said. Philip asked when this demolition squad would be setting out?—he too wanted to see one part of his promise to Bonnecourt fulfilled.

"Well, say a quarter to five—it will still be practically dark then, but by the time we get to the place it will be light enough to see what we're doing; if not we can wait till it is."

"Right—I'll be round here at 4.45" Phillip said.

The following morning was overcast, and it was almost in pitch darkness that Jamieson drove round from his hotel to

the Heriots; there the old Bugatti and Dick's Jaguar were
marshalled on the drive, and with their headlights on they
drove in convoy through Pau, still a sleeping town, and out
westwards into the open country beyond, Nick in the Bugatti leading. He did not take the main route by Lacq and
Orthez, but crossed the river in the town itself, and then
followed the much smaller road which hugs the southern, or
true left bank of the Gave de Pau. Presently he signalled
with his hand to the cars behind him to slow down, and
switched off his headlights; then he drove on, slowly—the
others following. Presently they came to a small village in
which an ancient stone-built bridge spanned a fair-sized
stream; some 400 yards further on Nick slung the Bugatti to
the right into a broad grassy meadow, crossed it, and pulled
up on the very lip of the bank overhanging the river.

By now day was breaking, in spite of the clouded sky;
when Dick pulled up behind Bonnecourt's old car, and
walked across to the river's brink, there was light enough for
him to see the whole lay-out. There was an almost vertical
drop of over 20 feet into the Gave, which here, thanks to the
erosive efforts of the tributary coming down from the Pyrenees, had expanded into a wide pool, in which the grey-
green waters swirled and eddied—there had been rain in the
mountains, and the river was running bank-high.

"Perfect" Dick said. "At the moment" he added cautiously.
"Any idea how much this pool dries out in the summer?"

"No—but we shan't have summer again for another eight
months; and by then we'll have had lots of time to put a
plastic bomb under the poor old thing, if the pool shows
signs of shrinking," Nick replied.

"I agree. All right—on we go. Will you start the engine, or
shall I give her a shove?"

Luzia and Colonel Jamieson had also got out, and had
peered over the edge of the bank; they listened to the twins.

"Push it with your car; do not let Nick start the engine—
he might get caught in the door, and be carried away" Luzia
said urgently. Dick looked at her, surprised and rather disconcerted by this concern for his brother.

"I agree" Jamieson put in. "Either let us push it over the

edge by hand, or Dick give it some propulsion from behind with his car. We can see what we're doing now." He looked carefully at the meadow. "I think there's just enough slope to get a run on it by hand. Back away a bit, Dick." The young man did so. "Now, Nick, reverse her a little—That's enough" he said, when Nick had backed the Bugatti about 30 feet. "Now let's push her." Nick released the hand-brake, and together the three men propelled Bonnecourt's beloved old car over the edge of the bank—it fell with a colossal splash into the pool.

"Well that's all right—not a sign of it showing" Colonel Jamieson said, leaning over to inspect the water after the splash had subsided. "Safe till next summer, anyhow. Good." He walked back to his own car, while Dick turned the Jaguar.

"Yes, the sooner we clear off the better" Nick said—as he spoke he bent down and began to brush up the grass with his hand where the wheels of the two cars had crushed it. "Peasants notice everything" he observed. "I wish we'd brought a rake. Dick, go and kick off the rim of the bank where the wheel-marks show; that's a frightful give-away."

Dick made no move to do as his brother asked. "Oh, come on—I want some breakfast!" he said; he felt vaguely disgruntled. But Luzia went straight to the steep edge and began to kick at the turf, rather incompetently, with her small white sandals.

"I say, look out—you might pitch over" Dick said anxiously. "Don't do that, Luzia."

"If you will not do it, *I* will" the girl said. "Someone must —here security is involved." Jamieson joined her; with his large Scottish feet and strong shoes he was much more effectual, shoving great chunks of grass and soil over the lip of the bank into the river, till at the actual edge there was soon no sign that a car had gone over. Nick continued to scrape away at the grass, in silence; he felt uncomfortable. Something new and disturbing was going on; he was not yet certain what, and was a little afraid of finding out.

All the others now helped to scratch up the crushed grass and remove the wheel-marks.

"Well, that's the best we can do," the Colonel said. "Now let's get away. Do we have to go back through that village?" he asked Nick.

"No. If we go on to Lacq there's a bridge over the Gave, and we can take the main road back to Pau. I thought that would be better—they may have heard us coming through."

"Quite right." He turned politely to Luzia. "Condesa, will you come with me?"

"Thank you—but I drive with Dick" the girl replied. "But you will take Nick, of course."

Nick was rather relieved—somehow he didn't very much want a tête-à-tête drive with his brother just then, and got thankfully into Jamieson's car. Dick was relieved too. Luzia had been a bit sharp with him, and he had wondered what was going on in her mind about Nick; but this looked as though everything was all right. (Dick, as his Father had once told Julia, was an optimist.)

As the two cars, Jamieson's leading, turned out from the field into the road an old man came hobbling by with a scythe over his shoulder—he signalled to them to stop.

"You do the talking" the Colonel said to Nick, pulling up. "Better satisfy him if you can."

What the old man said he wanted was a lift some 3 kilometres down the road, to a farm where he was being employed to cut the second crop of hay, the aftermath. But when he was installed in the back seat, the blade of his scythe projecting dangerously out of the window, he began to ask questions. *Ces Messieurs* had wished to fish in the Gave? But here the current was too strong, and also it was too early in the day. Nick was very ready.

"No, we do not fish; we are geologists" he said.

"*Géologistes?* What is this? I never heard the word."

"We study the structure of the rocks and the soil; it is an important science" Nick said firmly. "*À la longue* it is helpful to agriculture. And one of the best and easiest places for this study is the banks of rivers, where the face of the soil is exposed; hence we go to look at the Gave."

The old man was impressed—"Ah, *les Messieurs* are scientists! *Tiens!*" But he was not altogether satisfied. "And why do *ces Messieurs* go to examine the banks of the Gave at such an hour?"

"Because we have to cover several hundred kilometres of the Gave today—so like Monsieur, we start early for the day's work!"

Now the old man laughed, at last contented. When he got out he wrung Nick's hand warmly with his own gnarled, brown, and wrinkled one.

"*Bonne chance*, Monsieur, with your enquiries. If you discover something of use to agriculture, please pass it on to *Le Général!*—we others, we feel that he ignores us."

"You handled that very nicely" the Colonel said to Nick, as they drove on. "I am in luck here, to get such good help on the spot—yours, and your Mother's. Oh!"—as the road bent right and crossed a bridge—"Is that Lacq?"

In the bright early light that astonishing place, Lacq, lay spread out before them—the acres of low white buildings, the silvery aluminium globes, and towering over all the four great chimnies, their black and red plumes of smoke and flame streaming out on the morning breeze.

"Yes, that's Lacq. I hope to get a job there sometime; I think it's one of the most worthwhile places in the world" Nick said, with a fervour which surprised his companion.

Chapter 13

Luzia was rather silent on the drive back to Pau. She had
been upset by Dick's behaviour on the bank of the Gave, and
wondered whether she had perhaps provoked it by her impulsive protest against the idea that Nick should start the
Bugatti's engine and jump clear. She knew quite well how
Dick felt about her—had she been indiscreet? (Discretion is
really Rule I for Portuguese young ladies.) But she had also
been impressed by Nick: his choice of the spot, and by his
practicalness over ruffling up the crushed grass, and getting
the wheel-marks removed from the lip of the bank, about
which Dick had been so uncooperative. She had never consciously compared the twins before; Dick was her declared
suitor, Nick simply a friendly and amusing figure in the
background—now she found herself driven to make a comparison, and it was not in Dick's favour.

Over breakfast, for which Colonel Jamieson stayed, a
small interchange took place which reinforced the girl's
good impression of Nick. Lady Heriot, again in her hair net
and flowing dressing-gown—it was still only a quarter to
seven—presided over the meal; she apologised for the absence of rolls. "The baker doesn't get here as early as this;
you will have to put up with toast." In response to her interested enquiries she was given a full account of the drowning
of the Bugatti. Presently Nick asked Colonel Jamieson when
it would be convenient for him to bring Madame Bonnecourt down to be told about Glentoran?

"Oh, any time now; my wife seems very fit. Bring her
today, if you like."

"No, I don't think that would do; it would fuss her. She
will want some notice. But I can go up today and let her

know—for tomorrow? And would the morning or the afternoon be best for Mrs. Jamieson?"

Lady Heriot intervened.

"I should bring her in the morning, Nick; poor Mrs. Jamieson has this awful *repos* in the afternoon. Then she can come and have luncheon here, and do some shopping before you take her back."

"I don't think having lunch here is a good idea, *Maman*" Nick said. "It would un-nerve her."

"Oh, why? We know him so well, after all; I should like to meet her."

Luzia was impelled to speak.

"Lady Heriot, in this Nick is right; she would be intimidated by coming here. I think that tomorrow, when she has seen Mrs. Jamieson, it would be better if I took her to *déjeuner* in some small, quiet place. Please forgive me for suggesting this, when you are so kind; but I am sure that for this little woman it will be easier, done so. She must meet one stranger tomorrow in any case, and hear much that will be strange to her; after all, her whole life is about to be turned upside down."

Nick glanced gratefully at Luzia; his Mother regarded her benignly. Considerate herself, she liked consideration for others in the young.

"My dear child, do whatever you think best; you know her, and I don't." She paused. "If you are not too tired, mightn't it be a good plan for you to go up with Nick, and arrange it all with her?"

"Yes, I do this—I think it a very good idea," Luzia said. For Mme. Bonnecourt it certainly was, but in her new hyperconscious state of mind about the twins the girl was troubled by the sense of pleasure that came over her at the idea of driving up to Larège, for the first time, with Nick.

Dick broke in. "*Really*, Your Ladyship, why on earth should Luzia have to do this extra chore? Nick can perfectly well tell Mme. B. to be ready to come down tomorrow; he and I have both known her for years. Luzia's been up for *hours* already."

Lady Heriot glanced at the rather surly face of her son,

then at that of her young guest. With great wisdom she decided to leave this to Luzia to handle.

"Dick, do not be foolish; I am not at all tired" the girl said lightly. "I think Madame Bonnecourt might like it if *I* make this plan with her—about the shopping, and lunch, and so on. *Entre femmes!* This is different from a message from a man." She turned to her hostess.

"I know Madame Bonnecourt only a little" she went on, "but I have seen that she is not an adventurous character; not at all like her husband!"

The emphasis in her tone rather startled Colonel Jamieson.

"Don't you like Bonnecourt?" he asked.

"I do not know him enough to like or dislike him; I know only what I am told. But would you not agree that he is adventurous? That is all I said."

"Yes" he replied, amused; very soon afterwards he left, after promising Nick that he would arrange with his wife to receive Madame Bonnecourt the following morning. He went back to the Victoire, had a bath and a shave, and then walked round to the clinic. To his amazement Julia met him at the door of her room, up, and dressed in a close-fitting house-coat.

"Goodness, are you allowed to walk about?" he asked anxiously.

"Oh yes—it's a week today, and a Caesarean is even less bother than a normal labour—actually after those people get up nowadays in no time; none of that three weeks in bed any more. What a bore it must have been! Well, how did it go?" As she spoke she lay down again on the neatly-made bed, and leaned back against the pillows.

He told her how it had gone. "That boy Nick is very bright; he'd chosen a perfect spot, and there aren't many—I had a good look at the river as we drove down it, both before and after." After a pause, he mentioned the slight breeze that there had been between Luzia and Dick—Julia's interest was at once aroused on behalf of her precious pupil.

"Did they quarrel?"

"No, you couldn't call it that, but she slapped him down

pretty hard. I think she's probably got engaged to the wrong twin."

"*Is* she engaged to him? She wasn't three days ago."

"Oh, how would I know? But Nick is a really first-class boy, and I get the impression that Dick is rather—" he hesitated.

"Rather what?" Julia asked, intently.

"I think insensitive is the word I want. No, even that is too strong. He's just not very quick at the moral uptake, whereas Nick recognises all the implications of any situation at once."

Julia was troubled, remembering her talk with Luzia about marrying Dick such a short time before; she had shown no doubts then about Dick's character, only concerning her own feelings, and whether "Papa" would like him.

"Oh dear, I hope she hasn't committed herself. Luzia would never go back on her word" she said unhappily. "I wish I could see her. What's she doing today?"

"Going up to Larège with Nick to tell Mme. Bonnecourt that you'll see her tomorrow morning, and give her all the low-down about Glentoran. I hope that's all right?" His wife nodded. "That was typical" Jamieson went on; he proceeded to recount Lady Heriot's suggestion about luncheon, and how Luzia had backed up Nick's veto of the idea immediately. "They see things in exactly the same way—whereas poor old Dick sat like a stuck pig, and never said a word."

"I don't suppose he felt like talking much, if he'd been slapped down in front of everyone" Julia commented.

"P'raps not. I wonder if *she* knows them apart? I don't, unless they tell me," Jamieson said. "It would be frightful if they both proposed and she accepted the wrong one, not knowing which was which!"

"It's rather frightful anyhow" Julia said. "Dick has been making all the running, and Nick accepted that; he told me about it himself, quite early on, and didn't seem to mind in the least—in fact he was rather funny about it. But of course he's seen a lot more of her since." She paused, leaving the implication unexpressed.

"So that even if he had fallen for her himself by now, he would be too high-minded to cut in, you mean?"

"Probably. Oh dear! Darling, do try to get her to come round and see me as soon as ever you can—I might learn something."

"It's always rather risky to interfere, isn't it?"

"Oh dearest, don't be obvious! Of course it is, but other risks are worse. And *I* brought her here, and got her mixed up with these infernal identicals!" Julia's colour was rising, as it did when she was wrought up; Philip went over and took her hand.

"My darling, I will get her here as soon as I can" he said. "Now do relax—I'm sure you oughtn't to get upset. Won't that be bad for the creature?"

Julia lay back obediently. Yes, it would be bad for the baby if she allowed herself to get into "a state"; the old *sage-femme* had been dinning it into her now for a week that any emotional disturbance could alter the character of the milk —hence her disapproval even of letter-writing before a feed. She clung suddenly to Philip's hand, and held it to her mouth. So quick and grave a danger as had ushered in the child's birth had made a more deeply-fired and unbreakable bond between them than anything she had dreamed of; the future held both more and fewer weapons against them now. Fewer, because of this new bond; more, because any risks touching them also, henceforth, touched the small Philip Bernard as well.

Philip stood silent by the bedside. He realized that some strong emotion was stirring in Julia, and guessed at its nature; but he asked no questions. Presently her hold on his hand relaxed; with a last kiss she let it go.

"Yes—I will keep quiet" she said. "I'm sorry. Give me a cigarette. Oh no, I mustn't. Have one yourself."

He drew up a chair, sat close to the bed, and smoked.

"What was all that?" he asked presently, very gently.

"Oh, just realising about us, and *him*. 'For 'im, and 'er, and It, And two and one makes three'—Kipling understood so well, didn't he?"

Philip was pleased by the quotation, which he was familiar with; it gave him a very fair idea of the thoughts that had moved her to such an unwonted demonstration as holding his hand and kissing it. But he mistrusted his own powers of expression, and was ready to leave it to Kipling.

"Yes, he did; and I do. My darling, do please take all possible care of yourself; now, and when I go away. And I will do the same, I promise you." He bent over the bed and gave her a long kiss; he was still doing this when as usual the door opened and the old *sage-femme* came in, carrying the baby.

"Ah—here is Fortune's hostage!" Philip said, smiling as he straightened up. "*Bonjour*, Madame—I'm just leaving." He went and put a finger under the minute pink chin. "Well, Master Philip Bernard, how goes it?"

"It goes well; he gains weight" the *sage-femme* said proudly. "Madame is a good mother." Philip Bernard's only response was a hungry howl; his Father laughed.

"That's right, my boy; you look out for Number One! At your age, it's your first duty." He turned to his wife. "I'll find out what Luzia is doing later, and bring her round."

In fact he was not able to do this till fairly late in the afternoon. On Lady Heriot's advice Nick and Luzia drove up to Larège soon after breakfast—"Then it will be done, and Luzia can have a nice little shut-eye after lunch; she got up so early, but one really can't take a siesta in the morning" the old lady said.

"How *nice* your Mother is" Luzia remarked to Nick, when the Dauphine was clear of the town, and he no longer had to concentrate on the traffic.

"She is; but why do you say so now, especially?"

"Because she is much older, and long in a position of authority; and yet when she has one idea and you and I another, and we reject hers, she is not *contrariée*, but accepts it—although we are so young."

"Her Ladyship liked your idea, when you explained it" Nick said. "She saw at once that you were right."

"You were right first."

"I said it first; but you were right too, all along. How old *are* you?" he asked unexpectedly.

"Nineteen. And you?"

"Twenty-one—same as Dick, of course."

Luzia frowned a little, pondering; he had expected her to laugh at this glimpse of the obvious, but she sat silent beside him. Nick's heart began to beat rather fast. Her appreciation of his Mother, her use of the word "we" about their plans for Mme. Bonnecourt, and what she had said both to him and to Dick when they were drowning the hunter's old car, brought the thoughts and feelings, which he had pushed away and refused to recognize then, flooding back into the forefront of his consciousness. Of course she was wonderful; there could be no one like her, ever. But by the time he had realised this Dick was so obviously pursuing her that he had tried to "leave well alone", as the pessimist in him put it. Now, since this morning, it all looked rather different; but did these small episodes add up to anything? Of course the only thing that mattered was that *she* should be happy, and would she be happy with Dick? There were things Dick simply didn't *see*.

Twiddling through the narrow streets of Ste.-Marie des Pèlerins Nick again had to concentrate on the traffic; once through the pretty, sunny little town, and out again on the broad blue-grey road, to check his troubling thoughts and break the long silence he started asking Luzia about her home. (He thought he was changing the conversation.)

"Tell me about Gralheira" he said. "It's a huge place, isn't it? I looked it out on the map, and the estate seemed to run right up into the Serra."

"Yes, it does—a long way."

"Aren't there pine-forests there? Do you get a lot of resin?"

"Yes—I believe something like 6000 barrels a year."

"Six *thousand!* But that's worth a fortune; resin is in terrific demand today, for plastics, and all sorts of things. What does your Father do with it?"

Luzia was driven to a fresh comparison between the twins. Dick had never looked Gralheira out on the map, so far as she knew; certainly he had never said so, let alone asked about the resin.

"I know it is sold; I suppose this helps to make us rich" she said. "But I am not sure that Papa disposes of it to the best advantage; he does not know much about these modern sci-entific matters, though he is always anxious to find more money, to build extra hospitals for the villages, and to em-ploy more doctors and nurses. Plastics!" she said, with the little frown which usually accompanied concentration in her. "This is these *very* disagreable vessels in light colours, which it is impossible to keep really clean?"

Nick laughed.

"Yes; those, and a lot of other things too."

Luzia's little frown persisted; she was still thinking.

"Are plastics difficult to make? Do they require a *huge* factory?"

"I don't think so. People with the requisite know-how can make them in quite small units, I fancy; it's a regular light industry."

At that the girl fairly beamed.

"Light industry! That is what Dr. Salazar is always want-ing for Portugal. How wonderful if we could have a factory or two on the estate, to make these horrible 'plastics', and use our own resin. Then not so many of the young men would seek work in Oporto, or go to the Overseas Terri-tories; they could live and work at home, and their mothers would be glad."

Nick was kindled by this sensible eagerness.

"How near is the railway?" he asked. "You'd have to be able to get your products out, as well as the other raw ma-terials in."

"Sâo Pedro do Sul is only about 25 kilometres away, but the railway runs across our land; we could always have a station built. Oh, this could mean much!" Suddenly she sighed. "Poor Papa! If only he could find someone to help him over all this. He is not young any more, and I know so little."

"I don't suppose it would be too difficult to find a manager in England to run a plastics factory, only I suppose he'd have to speak Portuguese. Is it difficult to learn?"

"Those who know Italian declare that it is impossible!" the

girl said, laughing. "They say it is just a *patois!* But Miss Probyn spoke it quite well, and I think learned it without much trouble."

Again Nick's thoughts were brought back towards the point from which he had meant to deflect them by talking about Gralheira. To help an aging land-owner, whose desire for more money was wholly based on his anxiety to improve the medical services on his property, and to start up light industries—what a worthwhile job! As good as Lacq, or better. And if it were combined with seeing a lot of the exquisite creature now sitting beside him, who obviously also cared about social welfare, in the simplest possible way: Mothers not losing their sons!

Nick cut his thoughts off sharply at that point, as he had tried to do before. They had almost reached the turn to Larège; he swung up the hair-pin bends and parked the car in the square; then they walked down to Bonnecourt's house.

The interview with Madame Bonnecourt did not help much to stifle Nick's dawning love for Luzia. The young girl proposed tomorrow's expedition with the utmost delicacy and skill to the hunter's wife; taking her time, and giving the rather timid little woman ample opportunity to ask her own questions.

"Yes, he left yesterday" she replied to the first of these. "Monsieur Nicolas will tell you; he saw him go."

Nick said his piece about the fly-out.

"And how does he reach this place in *Écosse?*"

Nick explained that his friend Monro was driving her husband to Gibraltar; from there they would fly to London, and M. Monro would later take him all the way to Scotland, to the *propiété* of his sister—"where he will be the hunter of the red deer instead of the *isard.*"

"This he would like, I think" Mme. Bonnecourt said, looking more reassured. At a nod from Nick, Luzia took over.

"Madame, we have a proposition to make to you—by your husband's express desire. Madame Jamieson is a cousin of M. Monro, and spent much of her childhood at Glentoran; she knows the place like the inside of her pocket!—even to the very house where he and you will live. Monsieur Bonnecourt wished that you should meet Madame, and let her tell you about it. Would it be convenient to you to come, perhaps as soon as tomorrow? M. Nicolas and I could come and fetch you, in the morning, and bring you back in the evening, so that you could do some shopping as well."

Both Luzia and Nick were rather touched by Mme. Bonnecourt's reaction to this idea.

"Ah, Madame Jamieson! My husband thinks her a marvel. But is she able to see people? Surely she has just had this child, by an operation?"

"Yes indeed—and owes everything, child and all, to the promptness of Monsieur Bonnecourt!" Luzia said warmly. "But she is now very well, and would greatly like to see you, and tell you everything, and answer all your questions. There is so much you must wish to know!"

Madame Bonnecourt was clearly pleased by this plan. "This is very kind. But—tomorrow; at what hour should we have to leave?"

"Would a quarter-past nine be too early?" Luzia asked, doing a rapid sum in her head. "As you know the drive takes nearly two hours, and at 12.30 Madame Jamieson has her mid-day meal; after that there is the period of repose. I should like you to have plenty of time with her. Could you perhaps do your milking a little earlier, just for once, to give you time to arrange all in the dairy, and dress?"

Now the faded little woman almost glowed. "The Countess might be a farmer's wife herself!" she exclaimed to Nick; "she understands everything."

"And when you have seen Madame Jamieson, I thought that you and I could take our *déjeuner* in some nice quiet restaurant, and then go shopping together" Luzia added, "till Monsieur Nicolas brings you back in time for the evening milking."

The hesitant little person suddenly became enthusiastic. "In Pau there is an *excellent* coiffeur" she said. "I might be able to get a proper *shampouin* and *mise-en-plis*, for a change!—I so seldom get to Pau. I will ask my neighbour to milk the cows for me in the evening; certainly she will do this. Oh, must you go? Not an apéritif?" Luzia had risen, and excused herself; they would be late for luncheon if they did not leave at once.

"*Alors,* nine hours and a quarter tomorrow. You are so good." She came with them up the field, obviously to arrange with the *voisine* about the evening milking next day; they left her in towering spirits.

"You did that beautifully" Nick said, as they walked back towards the *Place*. "I've never seen the little creature so lively before."

"It cannot be altogether easy to be the wife of this Bonnecourt" Luzia replied crisply.

"Why do you say that? You seem rather anti-Bonnecourt" the young man said.

"Only from a woman's point of view. Probably he is a wonderful agent, and you and Dick assured me, some time ago, that he did not really murder his first wife! But I think he is selfish and careless about this one. Why can he not drive her down to Pau sometimes, to have her hair arranged? Till now, he had his car. When he married her she must have been pretty" the girl said, getting into the Dauphine—"Now she irons his shirts, and milks the cows!"

Nick had never given much thought to Mme. Bonnecourt; she was just a dim figure in the hunter's background, who occasionally brought in the glasses for drinks. He was struck by Luzia's swift recognition of what her life was like. What an understander this girl was!

"Perhaps you're right" he said. "I've never seen much of her." As he spoke he thought of his mental criticism of Dick, that he didn't *see* things. Did he, Nick, not see them either? —or not quickly enough? If so, would he be of any more use to Luzia?

That young woman, however, was now concentrating on Mme. Bonnecourt.

"I am sure I am right" she said, as they wound down the hair-pin bends. "I am so glad that they go to Mrs. Reeder. She will have no romantic illusions about this Bonnecourt; she sees people as they are, as Miss Probyn does—Intelligence or no Intelligence! She will keep him in his place, and ensure that he treats his wife with proper consideration."

Luzia had seen a certain amount of Edina Reeder during Julia's various wedding celebrations in London, and had made a favourable assessment of her, with her usual speed.

"I can't see Bonnecourt coming much under the thumb of any woman" Nick replied, doubtfully.

"No? You idealise him, I think. In any case you do not know Mrs. Reeder."

"Isn't she Monro's sister?" Nick asked, still doubtful.

"Yes. But it is she who wears the trousers!" Luzia replied, startling him by her acquaintance with this idiom. "It is not impolite in me to say this?" she asked, noticing his surprise.

"Not a bit—but where did you pick it up?"

"I have heard Dick say it of Madame Monnier. Only some things are suitable for men to say, and not for us."

"No, I think that's all right for you."

"I ask Miss Probyn. I want to see her today, and the baby."

In fact on their return Lady Heriot greeted the girl with a message from Colonel Jamieson that he would call at 4.45 to take her round to see his wife. "He said four, but I told him that you really must get a lie-down this afternoon. I'll have tea sent to you in your room at four" said her hostess, who had sensible middle-aged ideas of what constituted comfort.

Julia had been a little anxious about this interview with Luzia; she was worried by Philip's comments on the twins, and wondered how to tackle the subject. But it all went unexpectedly easily. After the girl had reported how eagerly Mme. Bonnecourt had accepted the idea of coming down to see her, and still more of getting a shampoo and set in Pau, Julia asked if they had had a nice drive? "You've never been out with Nick before, have you?"

"No. Yes, it was nice. Nick is very nice—he thinks."

Julia waited. This sounded promising. After a pause—"Miss Probyn, I should like to speak with you about this" the girl said.

"Do, by all means." She took a plunge. "Is Nick in love with you now, too?"

Luzia half-laughed.

"He has not said so; but I think he is, perhaps. At least he takes an interest in my circumstances" she added, rather sharply. "Imagine!—he has looked out Gralheira on a map, and has seen that we have forests on the Serra, and asked me what Papa did with the resin from the pines? He says that resin is now very valuable, one can make plastics from it; we could have one or two small factories on the estate, and give employment to our younger people. I am sure Papa has no idea of these modern possibilities—Nick could help him greatly."

Julia, remembering the eight telephones on the Duke of Ericeira's desk at Gralheira, could not feel that he was particularly old-fashioned; but perhaps the manufacture of plastics was a little outside his range of ideas.

"Still, you can't go and marry someone merely because he could be a help to your Father" she said.

"I will not marry anyone who cannot! When Papa dies, I must look after Gralheira; it will be mine, and the well-being of all those people will be for me to care for" Luzia said energetically. "Listen, dear Miss Probyn: I do not marry Dick! Seven times he has asked me, and seven times I say No. But not once has he spoken of the modern uses for resin!" She paused. "He thinks more of himself" she concluded.

"Could you love Nick?" Julia asked, a little hesitantly.

"I think that probably I could. It is just that till today we have barely spoken together—it was always Dick who came after me, and took me about. This makes all a little complicated; everyone assumes that it is Dick who is my suitor—Nick also" Luzia added rather distressfully.

Julia pondered.

"Yes—of course Nick wouldn't want to cut his brother out" she said. "And *you* can't very well propose to Nick."

"Miss Probyn, *quelle idée!*"

"Quite so, dearest." She went on considering. Should she quote Philip? Probably wiser not to, yet.

"I think your best plan" she said at last, "is to get hold of Dick and tell him, once and for all, that you will never marry him—in a way that he can't fail to understand. You told me yourself, before, that you hadn't made up your mind, so I daresay your seven refusals weren't very convincing."

Again Luzia gave a reluctant half-laugh.

"Oh Miss Probyn, you are always right! And I see that I have been wrong—uncertain. I like them *all* so much!" the girl said.

"Who, the Heriots?"

"Yes. they are *good* people: responsible. Even old Lord Heriot, who can be most terribly boring, does so much for Pau—committees, cemeteries! But now I do what you say— I give this poor Dick his *congé.*"

"Tell Nick when you have" Julia said.

"This is not easy."

"No, but you've got to be fair to Nick too."

"I suppose so. Oh, it is complex! And so soon I must return to Papa. Tell me, when do you go to the Victoire?"

"The day after tomorrow."

"*Bien,* I come and pack for you, and instal you." She gave her former governess a kiss, and went away.

Philip was waiting for her, and drove her back; naturally he came in for a drink, and when he left it was time to dress for dinner, so Luzia had no chance for her talk with Dick. Over coffee afterwards Nick reminded his Mother that he and Luzia would again want an early breakfast, in order to leave at 7.15 to go up and collect Mme. Bonnecourt.

"Why on earth must Luzia make *another* first-light start?" Dick asked. "Can't you fetch Mrs. B. by yourself?"

"I have said that I go" Luzia put in, mildly but firmly. "This little person requires reassurance; I try to give it to her."

"Quite right" Lord Heriot observed unexpectedly. "Terrible upheaval for her. Scotland isn't at all like Larège. I'm glad you're helping her all you can, Condesa."

Luzia looked at him gratefully. This unlooked-for support nerved her to arrange her interview with Dick that night, and get it over; she thought fast, but spoke calmly.

"I am very glad that you approve, Lord Heriot. Do you use your study just now, or could I telephone?"

"Telephone by all means," the old gentleman said, benignly.

"Oh, thank you. Dick, could you come and get the connection for me?"

In the study Dick asked who she wanted to ring up?

"No one. I wish to speak with you; the telephone was an excuse."

"Well, speak away" Dick said. He lit a cigarette with hands that trembled a little. "What is it?"

"How many times have you asked me to marry you?" Luzia tackled her problem as best she could—not very well, she felt.

"Six or seven, and you've always said No."

"Did you believe me?"

"No, not altogether. I thought if you really disliked me you wouldn't have gone on coming out with me for drives, and so on. But what *is* all this? I'm sorry I was sour down by the Gave this morning, if that's what's eating you."

"No. What is 'eating me' is that I did not make you believe me, and did go on driving with you. Of course I could not leave Mrs. Jamieson, but I could have been more—definite" the girl said carefully. "Here I was in fault, and I ask your pardon. But now—" she paused.

"Well, what now?"

"I *am* definite. Dick, I cannot marry you—never in this world! You must believe this."

The link between identical twins is mysteriously close; it led Dick more rapidly, and nearer, towards the truth than the events of the day alone could have done. Hurt and angry, he nevertheless behaved, at last, very well.

"Do you think Nick is in love with you?" he asked.

"He has not said so. Till today we have hardly spoken with one another."

"I expect he is; who wouldn't be?" Suddenly he caught her hand. "Luzia!—dearest, lovely one—are you *sure* you can't marry me? Oh, I do love you so much!"

"No, I am sure. I cannot, ever."

"Why are you so sure just today, all of a sudden? Have

you found out that you're in love with Nick?" the boy asked, bitterness surging up in him at last. Luzia made a desperate attempt at honesty.

"I have learned more of Nick—but not that I love him. One cannot go so fast!" the girl exclaimed, desperately. "Love is one thing; marrying is another. Love is often unwise; marriage should be wise—one cannot marry only for oneself!"

"What on earth else would you marry for?—I mean, what's the point of getting married, except loving a person?" Dick had all the normal British ideas of romantic infatuation as the only basis for marriage; often a very shaky foundation.

"One's duties—one's responsibilities!"

"Oh, what rubbish! I never thought you were a prig" he exclaimed impatiently. "Do you mean you would make some *mariage de convenance* for money, or something?"

"Not for money. We do not need it" the girl said, with a sudden haughty expression.

"Oh, I'm sorry. I take that back." Dick rubbed his hands over his face and hair, pitiably distressed. "I don't know what I'm saying."

"I think it is better that we say no more" Luzia said, sadly. "I have no more to say; for you and me, this is *finis*. We shall only hurt one another if we go on talking." She got up. "Goodnight, Dick. Oh, I am sorry!"

"Hold on a moment" the young man said—even in his distress his Father's rigidity about the telephone held him.

"You haven't had a call. We must make one, and put some money in the box, or he'll notice. Who'd you like to call?—the *clinique?*"

"No, it is too late. Call the Victoire, and as soon as you get the number, disconnect" Luzia said; troubled as she was, she could not help smiling at this particular form of English absurdity. Dick telephoned, instantly rang off, wrote the Victoire's number in the book, and put some coins in the box.

"Now I say Goodnight to your Mother, and go to bed" Luzia said, and escaped to the drawing-room, whence her kind hostess took her away to her room. "Between us all, I think we work you rather too hard" Lady Heriot said. "Largely Colonel Jamieson, of course—these soldiers have no mercy! But *all* men are merciless. Sleep well, my dear." For the first time she kissed her young guest Goodnight. When she had left the room Luzia cried. What had she meant? And how kind she was!

Lord Heriot was still sitting in the drawing-room when his wife returned. Dick had not reappeared; Nick had gone off some time before.

"Well, I like that girl" the old man said, putting a fresh match to his cigar, and puffing away. "But I think it's time she made up her mind which of them it's to be, if she's prepared to marry either. First it seemed to be all Dick; now she goes out with Nick as well."

"Should you like her to marry one of them?" Lady Heriot asked, surprised.

"Yes. She can't help being an R.C., though that's a pity. But I think she'd do better to marry Nick than Dick—she's too smart for Dick. Are they both after her, do you suppose?"

Lady Heriot stared at him. In all their years of marriage her husband had never before come out with such a definite opinion on their sons' characters; in fact she had not thought him capable of it. Mothers who are in the least observant get to have a sort of sixth sense about what is going on inside their children: Dick's face at breakfast, Nick's face at luncheon, had made her guess that something had gone wrong between Dick and Luzia, and that there was at least a possibility of things going right between her and Nick, which would be a much better arrangement; her husband was quite right.

"I wish I knew" she said, thoughtfully. "Nick would suit her much better, I agree; and I think she could be an enormous help to him—she's very perceptive."

"Jolly him along when he gets low, you mean?"

Lady Heriot smiled at her husband's use of words; that was exactly what she meant, though she would have expressed it rather differently.

"Yes. Only up till today Dick has been making all the

running, and I'm so afraid of Nick not liking to make any move now, because he's so fond of his brother."

"That's all nonsense! If he finds he cares about her enough, he'll make a move all right! The trouble is that really it's all up to her—and she can't possibly make any move. I think you'd better sound both the boys about it, and try to find out how things stand."

"I'll see" his wife said cautiously. Lord Heriot threw the end of his cigar into the fire, and went off to bed.

Nick had been upset by Dick's outburst over another early start for Luzia, skilfully as the girl had smoothed it over; when she asked Dick to help her to telephone he wondered what *that* betokened, and too nervous to sustain the usual calm dullness of family after-dinner conversation, he went out to stroll in the garden, and thought, long and wretchedly, about Luzia, Dick, and himself—always coming back to Luzia. It was clear to him that she oughtn't to marry Dick; clearer now even than it had been that morning as they drove up to Larège. But how did she feel about it? Where did she stand with regard to Dick? And would he, Nick, really do her all that much better? Yes, a bit better, honesty forced him to admit—because he *saw* more. And now at last the young man gave free admittance to the thoughts he had twice tried to extinguish in the car that morning. He loved her as he had never loved anyone before, and could never hope to love anyone again.

Lord Heriot may have been right in telling his wife (even while his son was pondering and worrying in the darkened garden below the windows) that if Nick found that he cared for the Portuguese girl enough, he would make a move; but Nick being the self-deprecating person that he was, this was by no means certain. However he received the necessary impulse from another source. When the oblongs of light on the lawn, coming from the drawing-room windows, disappeared, he realised that the family had gone to bed, and went in, but not straight to his bedroom. He had left a book in his and Dick's sitting-room, and went to fetch it—he must try to read himself to sleep. (Nick was a poor sleeper at the best of times.) The light was on; Dick was there, fiddling with the record-player.

"Hullo" he said—"I thought you'd gone to bed, like all the rest."

"I'm just going—I've come to get my book." He hunted about among the litter of papers and magazines. "Ah, here we are." He made to leave the room.

"Half a minute" Dick said.

"Yes?" Nick was seldom impatient, but he did not feel equal to any encounter just then; he stood with his hand on the door.

"No, come back" his brother said; and now something in his voice arrested Nick's full attention; he came back and stood by the untidy table.

"Luzia's given me the bird. She says she won't ever marry me."

"When was this?" Nick asked.

"Just now, in the study, when we went to telephone. That was only an excuse. I thought you might as well know." He went out, shutting the door behind him.

Chapter 14

Luzia's second drive up to Larège with Nick the following morning was not nearly as pleasurable as the first one; in fact it was rather gloomy. She was burdened by Julia's injunction to tell Nick that she had dismissed his brother, but could not quite bring herself to do so, lacking some excuse; the young man, immensely relieved as he had been by Dick's brusque statement, felt that it was impossible to cash in, as it were, immediately on his twin's generosity. There had been generosity behind it, but Dick's words were prompted by an emotional impulse: the need to tell someone, and most of all the person closest to him in the world. Oh, this terrible twinness!—suddenly it struck Nick as frightening. The pair were very silent till they reached Larége and picked up their passenger, who was waiting for them in the *Place*.

As good luck would have it, Edina Reeder's letter to Julia, saying how glad she and her Philip would be to employ Bonnecourt as a stalker, and do all they could to make his wife's life easy and pleasant at Glentoran, arrived just over an hour before Mme. Bonnecourt got to Pau. Philip Jamieson had in fact taken rather a chance on this, driven by circumstances: Bonnecourt had simply got to be removed from France at once, Julia had suggested it, and she knew the set-up completely; moreover he had spent several days sailing with the Reeders himself, and formed his own opinion of them. "They're sensible people" he said, when at one point his wife had expressed belated qualms about his launching the hunter off to Scotland with Colin before getting any reply from her cousin. "They won't throw him out; it will do for the time being, anyhow I expect they'll find him jolly useful." All the same he was definitely relieved to see Edina's letter, when he went in to pay his usual morning visit to his wife. "That's all right" he said. "Now all you have to do is to boost Madame's morale."

"Well, let me get up and dress" Julia said. "She may be less embarrassed if I've got a frock on."

"Oh, it's to be a frock today, is it?"

"Yes. Darling, do clear off; I've got to fit in a feed before she comes, too."

"Greedy monster, young Philip Bernard!" the man said, as he went out.

At first Julia thought it was going to be rather difficult to boost Mme. Bonnecourt's morale. Luzia brought her in and introduced her easily and delightfully; sat her down in the solitary arm-chair, and suggested that she ask for coffee. Then she left. But even after the coffee was brought the hunter's wife sat on the edge of her chair, looking shy and frightened; she kept a steady gaze on Julia's dress, and the first remark she volunteered was—"*C'est de Dior, n'est-ce pas?*"

"*Non, de Hardy Amies*" Julia replied, amused.

"Ah, I have never seen an example of the *haute couture anglaise. C'est formidable!*" . .

Julia began to feel that the frock had perhaps been a false move; however, they talked clothes for a few minutes. How *little* she was, and how timid, Julia thought, at once compassionate and alarmed; how on earth would she get on with the rather dour and silent Highlanders? Edina was far too busy to spend much time in succouring her. She switched the conversation from clothes to cows, and spoke of the pedigree Ayrshire milking herd at Glentoran. This aroused a more hopeful sign of interest.

"Three *hundred* cows! But what do they do with the milk? Make cheese?"

"No; what is not required on the place goes by lorry to Glasgow, twice a day. But Mrs. Reeder always needs more help than she can easily get for cleaning out the churns and the coolers, and for feeding the calves. Of course the milking is done by electricity."

"*Tiens!* I have heard of this; I should like to see it. These tubes and so on, also, must need great attention."

"Indeed they do; and of course they make their own butter" Julia added, encouraged.

"Ah, this I can do! But I believe the English use salt; we, we make sweet butter."

"Putting the salt in is quite easy; Mrs. Reeder could show you that" Julia said. She got up and opened her despatch case; she had made time the evening before to hunt through her suit-cases, packed at Larège by Luzia, and found a folder with some snap-shots taken at Glentoran. "This is Mrs. Reeder" she said, holding out a photograph.

"She is *so* like Monsieur Monro" the Frenchwoman said. "Have you any pictures of the cows?"

Alas no, Julia had not—but she showed pictures of the big house, the garden with the rhododendrons in flower, the azalea glen. Mme. Bonnecourt was impressed.

"But this is a Paradise!"

"Yes it is, really, in spring and summer. In the winter it's a bit cold, and it gets dark early—and it rains a great deal all the year round. But of course there is electricity in all the cottages, and any amount of wood for fires."

"*We* cut this?"

"No, the foresters do that, and a tractor brings loads from the saw-mill to each house."

Now they really got down to brass tacks. Julia described the cottage at Ach-an-Draine, and its garden and byre—"If you wanted to keep pigs too, there is a stye." Mme. Bonnecourt was startled, as well she might be, at the degree of comfort in which employees on big British estates live. "But we pay for our milk?"

"No, that's thrown in."

"And the wood?—and the electricity?"

"Certainly not for the wood; I'm not sure about the electricity." She had an idea that since Glentoran stopped making its own supply and went onto the national grid Philip Reeder, shocked by old Mrs. Monro's fecklessness (which had practically reduced the place to bankruptcy) had insisted that his workers should pay for their own electric light, as in the past they had always bought the paraffin for their lamps. "Anyhow, that's about all you do pay for."

"But the rent of the house is how much?"

"Usually there is no rent. Estate people get their cottages free, or at a tiny rent; something like 5/6 a week—say 8 francs." Julia tried to explain to the astonished French-woman the English system of "tied cottages", which the Socialists now use as a dirty word; to Mme. Bonnecourt it did not appear dirty at all.

"It seems impossible! A house with five rooms and a bath-room, *eau courante*, and a garden and a *maison des cochons*, at such a price! How can the *propriétaires* afford it?"

It was the custom, Julia told her.

"*Eh bien*, I should wish to do all I can for Madame Reeder, since she is so liberal. How far is our house from the dairy?" She became very practical; Julia felt much more hope-ful. After several further questions—"And is there Mass in the village? Or how far off?" Mme. Bonnecourt asked.

"Well actually 25 miles. But don't worry" Julia said hast-ily, seeing the horrified look on the little face. "The Church of England church is in the same town as the Catholic one; Mr. Reeder drives his wife and any other Anglicans down every Sunday morning, early, in the Estate van; and they pick up one Catholic family on the way. He calls it 'the ecumenical bus' " she added, smiling.

When Luzia arrived to take Mme. Bonnecourt out to luncheon she found the little woman very cheerful; Colonel Jamieson drove them to the small restaurant he had chosen, and over their *déjeuner* the hunter's wife expatiated on the wonders of life at Glentoran as described by Julia. "Écosse must be a marvellous place—*all* provided!" She had found Mme. Jamieson wonderful too: "So practical, so full of un-derstanding." Presently Luzia took her in a taxi to get her hair-do; no, Mme. Bonnecourt said, she had no desire to do any shopping, except for a pair of shoes, and these could be bought practically next door to the coiffeur. But she would dearly like to go to the cinema; there was a splendid film, beginning at a quarter to four. It would be over by 5.30; would that be too late for Monsieur Nicolas to drive her home? "I adore the films, and I so seldom see them" the little woman said wistfully. "But of course, not if it is inconvenient."

Luzia realised that this would make Nick terribly late for dinner; he could not get back till well after nine. However she took upon herself to say that it would be all right, and that she would tell him. The cinema was quite near the big tree-shaded *Place* in which the Hotel de France stands, and she settled that Mme. Bonnecourt should go straight to a seat near the hotel entrance; it would be easier for Nick to pick her up there than among a crowd of people swarming out into a narrow street, where he could not park. They parted with warm farewells.

Luzia walked back. She wanted time to do some thinking, and she had very little time left in Pau. When Lady Heriot had told her that she could stay to move Julia from the clinic to the Victoire she had written to her Father, telling him that she would be starting home on the twenty-seventh, and asking him to book her a sleeper from Bordeaux to Lisbon —the voucher had come that very morning. But today was Friday; tomorrow she would be first packing, then unpacking for Julia, and seeing that she was comfortable. She had slipped round to the Victoire that morning during Mme. Bonnecourt's interview and inspected Julia's room; she demanded another arm-chair and two more small tables. "But for books and papers, and for *les boissons,*" she replied firmly to the *patron*'s protests. "Does Monsieur not desire that Madame should be in comfort?" She had switched on the bed-side light; as usual in France it was a 25-watt bulb; she pulled it out. "This must be replaced with one of 60 watts; Madame will read much in bed. *Monsieur le Patron* cannot wish to put out her eyes!" With a reluctant laugh the *patron* had agreed—"But there must be a slight surcharge." Luzia told him to discuss that with *M. le Colonel.* The Jamiesons could afford "surcharges", outrageous as they were. Anyhow the move would occupy tomorrow—and Monday was the twenty-seventh! Oh goodness, and she had forgotten to get any flowers when she was up in the town; down here in the suburbs there didn't seem to be any flower-shops. (Luzia had grown up with the idea that any move to a new place must be greeted with flowers in the room.)

She walked on; the pretty, light-filled streets were getting hot; suddenly she felt tired and discouraged. She hailed a passing taxi, and drove to the Heriot mansion; she dismissed the cab at the gate, and turned into the shrubberies. If she went up to the house she was sure to be caught by someone, and she must think—especially about if, and when, she should carry out Miss Probyn's injunction to "be fair to Nick," and tell him that she had broken with his brother. The girl felt uncertain about this, much as she trusted her ex-governess's judgment. If she did, Nick might feel obliged to propose to her, even if he didn't want to; and if he *did* want to, he would propose, and he didn't feel equal to deciding about that either, yet. Everything was happening much too fast; she wanted time, and quiet; and there was almost no time left.

At such moments important and unimportant matters jostle one another in the agitated mind. Catching a glimpse of the rose-garden, glowing brilliant through the dusky shrubs, Luzia thought again of some flowers for Julia. She always carried nail-scissors in her hand-bag; she could cut a bunch of roses. Lady Heriot would not mind, there were thousands; the second blooming was in full flood. She emerged from the shrubbery into the rosery; there she was fairly caught—Lady Heriot, seated on a camp-stool, wearing a shady hat and armed with a vast basket, was snipping off dead flowers. Luzia tried to retreat, but her hostess caught sight of her too soon. "Come and tell me how it all went" she called.

Reluctantly, Luzia walked down one of the grassy paths which intersected the rose-beds.

"I think it went well" she said. "Mme. Bonnecourt seemed quite enthusiastic about going to Scotland."

The old lady glanced up at her.

"You look tired" she said. "Come and sit." There were wooden seats at the end of all the intersecting paths; Lady Heriot chose one in the shade, and again studied the face of the girl beside her as they sat down.

"It's rather hot today" she said. "I expect you've done too much, with that second early start, and all. I hope you'll be able to have a quiet day tomorrow."

"Tomorrow I pack for Mrs. Jamieson, and take her to the Victoire" Luzia said.

"Oh Lawks!—so you do. I wish I could help you in any way, my dear child."

"Could you perhaps give me some roses for Mrs. Jamieson's room? I was *distraite* in the town, and forget to buy any flowers for her."

"Yes of course—I'll cut you some. There's never any need to *buy* flowers, in this house! Now I think you should go in and rest; tell Jeanne to bring you tea in your room."

"Lady Heriot, I have done one thing which perhaps I ought not—only I am so sorry for Mme. Bonnecourt." She mentioned the arrangement about the cinema. "This will mean that Nick is terribly late for dinner; I hope that Lord Heriot will not mind?"

"My husband is sorry for Madame Bonnecourt too; I feel sure he won't mind" Lady Heriot said comfortably. "Anyhow I don't think you *can* do wrong, in his eyes!" she added smiling.

"Oh, he is kind!—and you also. But where is Nick? I must tell him how to meet Madame—just after 5.30, outside the Hotel de France."

"I will see to that. In the *Place*, about half-past five? Right; leave it to me. Now you go and rest."

There was something else that Lady Heriot considered saying, but she decided against it; clearly the girl had had all she could manage for the moment. As far as Dick was concerned, she had carried out the "soundings" enjoined on her by her husband, and learned that Luzia had refused him the night before. The boy had made no bones about telling his Mother. "Yes, she turned me down flat. She's been saying No all along" he said ingenuously, "but this was absolutely final. I don't know why, except that I made a fool of myself at the Gave the other morning." After a moment of hesitation—"And she's seen a bit more of Nick, now" he added.

"Does Nick know?"

"Yes, I told him. I thought I'd better." He hesitated again. "But *Maman*, she *hasn't* been playing about with me—don't ever think that! She's never said anything but No. It was just I that kept on and on."

"I don't wonder, dearest. She's a most dearly-beloved person." Lady Heriot used the charming Scottish phrase for someone completely lovable. But she had left it at that with Dick, and now she left it at that with Luzia.

Her considerateness was in vain, as far as sparing Luzia any more emotion just then went. When the girl emerged from the lift Nick popped out of the twins' sitting-room—he had heard that give-away click when it reached the landing.

"Oh, there you are" he said.

"Yes—I go to rest."

He studied her face.

"I expect you'd better; you look a bit tired." He hesitated. "I did want to see you for a moment" he said, doubtfully. "Everyone's out, so it seems a good chance. Could you spare just a few minutes?" He opened the drawing-room door as he spoke.

"Very well" Luzia said. Whatever it was, better to get it over: there was so little time left. She went in and sat down. "*Alors?*" she asked, still with Julia's injunction in mind.

What Nick had to say let her out on that. Rather nervously, he repeated what his brother had told him the night before.

"This was good of Dick" she said.

"Yes—he *is* good. All the same, I'm pretty sure you were right. But what I wanted to say"—he checked, troubled by the difficulty of saying what he did want to say.

"Yes?" She leaned towards him, her vivid face now full of sympathy and attention. "*Dites,* Nick."

"Well, I don't feel that we can go ahead too fast, just now. He's frightfully in love with you, and he's taken this knock. It's so wretched that it should have to be *him,* of all people!" the boy said sadly, and not very lucidly. "I mean, I don't know how you feel about me, though I know how I feel about you. But I'd really rather let it all spin, for the moment—and later on you might let me come to Gralheira, and meet your Father, and see how it all looks then. What do you say?"

"Oh *dear* Nick! This is exactly how I have been feeling. You understand everything!" Luzia exclaimed, greatly relieved.

Nick too was enormously relieved, as well as startled, by the implications of this—they answered all the questons that he had so carefully refrained from putting. He wanted very much at least to take Luzia's hand, but managed not to. After a pause—"Well, don't ever forget that I love you" he said. "Let's leave it at that." (The Heriots were all great ones for leaving things at that.)

"Yes, let us do this." Suddenly she gave a little broken laugh.

"You must pick up Madame Bonnecourt outside the Hotel de France at half-past five, to take her home; she goes to the cinema after the coiffeur. I have told your Mother that I arranged this, though it will make you so late."

"Of course I'll do that. But why do you laugh?"

"Because this matters so little, and we so much; and yet it must be arranged. Your Mother promised to tell you, but now I do." She went quickly away to her room.

Luzia was rather thankful that organising Julia's move to the Victoire kept her out of the house for practically the whole of the next day. Lady Heriot, with her usual wise kindness, arranged that old Pierre should drive her there early in the morning, instead of either twin; there was a big basket of roses in the car, and another with assorted vases. "They never have any vases that it's *possible* to arrange flowers in in these small hotels" she said to Luzia, as she saw her off. " Tell Mrs. Jamieson that they're mine, and she'll see that they come back." "Oh yes, of course you'll want to lunch there" she pursued, in reply to a remark of Luzia's. "No point in running to and fro all the time! I'm sure the Colonel will bring you back. Don't get too tired, my dear."

At the Victoire the all-time *valet-de-chambre* carried the

baskets up to Mrs. Jamieson's room; at Luzia's request he
brought her a jug of water to fill the vases, and looked on
with pleasure while the girl arranged Lady Heriot's roses.
The room was large, with two French windows giving onto
a wide shady verandah; as a result of Luzia's urgency with
the *patron* it now contained a reasonable number of chairs
and small tables—when the roses were disposed about it the
general effect was very pleasant. Satisfied, Luzia walked
round to the clinic, and set to on Julia's packing. Philip
Jamieson was there.

"Ah, good. Julia wouldn't let me touch a thing till you
came! Now, is there anything I can take along in advance?"
Luzia said he could take the sherry and the *vin du pays* out
of the cupboard, and most of the suit-cases which she and
Dick had, so happily, brought down together from Larège.
Oh, *poor* Dick, the girl thought sadly, as she folded night-
dresses and stowed slippers and toilet accessories. There was
really not much to do; Julia had brought very little in her
hurried flight to the clinic, when Bonnecourt had packed for
her.

"I could really have done that myself" Julia said, when
Luzia had finished. "However, I'm most grateful to you.
Now sit down and rest for a minute, till Philip comes back."
She thought the girl's face looked rather drawn, and was
anxious to learn how she had got on, if at all, with the awkward task of dismissing one young man and accepting the
other; she wished she had thought of some errand to dispose
of her Philip for longer. Luzia, for her part, was equally
anxious to tell her most trusted friend the new develop-
ments. There would be much more unpacking to do at the
Victoire than the packing here, since Julia would want all
her things out, now that she was up and about—and probably Colonel Jamieson would be hanging round the whole
time. But she felt nervous about embarking on a difficult
explanation which might be interrupted at any moment; she
felt unwontedly nervous, anyhow. In fact a moment later
Philip Jamieson walked in.

"All set?" he asked. "You've made the room lovely with all
those flowers" he said to Luzia.

The words "the room" gave Luzia the cue that Julia had sought in vain.

"Colonel Jamieson, just one thing. Did you try the light by the bed? It had only a very weak bulb in it; I told the *patron* to put in one of 60 watts, so that Mrs. Jamieson could read in bed, but I stupidly forgot to look at it just now. I am not sure that he would keep his promise."

"No, I didn't. But we can see to that this afternoon. Come on, now."

"*No*, Philip" his wife said, in her slowest tones. "This afternoon I shall want to be quiet, when this kindest child has done my unpacking—I shan't want any fusses over lamps! Do please go and check on it at once; if it isn't a 60-watt bulb, go and buy one. A 75 would really be better—you know what my eyes are like." (In fact Julia's immense and beautiful eyes were both myopic and weak.) "There's heaps of time before *déjeuner*" she added.

The Colonel, obediently, went off. But Julia had picked up her cue, too.

"That was clever of you" she said. "Now, dear child, do tell me how you are getting on—if you would like to, of course."

"I *wish* to" Luzia said, with her usual direct simplicity. She recounted how she had made the excuse of telephoning to give poor Dick his *congé* two days before. "Because really, Miss Probyn, I found all this so troubling that I wanted to *en finir* as soon as possible."

"Naturally; I quite understand. And what have you done about Nick?"

"I had no need to do anything! This good Dick told his brother himself, the same evening."

"Oh, well done Dick. You're right about all the Heriots being nice! Well, and then?"

"Then yesterday I had a most *dismal* drive up to Larège with Nick to bring Madame Bonnecourt down to see you" the girl said, with a half-rueful, half-comic little grimace. "I had looked forward to it! But of course I did not know that Dick had told him, and he could not know whether I knew or not, so it was merely embarrassing and empty!"

"How wretched for you both!" Julia exclaimed; she could

so well envisage that abortive drive, and was full of sympathy. But Luzia must have had some further reason for knowing that Dick had reported his dismissal to his twin. "So then?" she asked.

"Yesterday morning I remained at the Victoire, seeing about your room, till Madame B. and I went out to luncheon. But when I came back—I was so *énervée*, trying to think what to do, that I forgot to get any flowers in the town—I went to the rose-garden to pick some, and Lady Heriot was there, and said that she would do it. Oh, if something really happens she will be the kindest of *belles-mères!*" the girl exclaimed. "She thinks of everything to make all easy for me."

"But is anything likely to happen?" Julia asked—she was tantalised by all this round-about story, sorry as she was about Luzia's predicament, and longed to get to the point.

"I think perhaps yes; presently. When I went indoors— Lady Heriot insisted that I should go and rest—Nick intercepted me; he said it was a good opportunity, as everyone was out." She hesitated for a moment, and then went on: "He told me, then, that Dick had let him know that I would never marry *him;* but he felt it was too soon to settle anything between us two. I feel the same; it would be *inconvenable*, at this moment. But later on he wishes to come to Gralheira, and meet Papa; and I think that then, things may arrange themselves."

"And would you like to marry Nick, apart from his helping your Father?" Julia was still acutely conscious that she was responsible for leading Luzia into this imbroglio, and that she would be going back to Portugal, completely out of reach, in forty-eight hours; she felt that she *must* know where the girl herself stood.

"*Yes*" Luzia said, this time without the smallest hesitation. "I am quite decided. He is *tão bom*"—she fell into her native tongue to express her sense of Nick's goodness. "Miss Probyn, how often does one find a man who even when he is in love puts the feelings of others before himself, is honourable, has delicacy? I have not met any such yet, except Nick!" She paused. "And you say 'apart from' his helping Papa, but

I cannot put these things apart!" she stated roundly—"they belong together."

Julia fastened on one phrase in Luzia's words: "even when he is in love"; she dealt with it.

"Has he said that he is in love with you?"

"Yes. He said I should remember that, till we meet again." The girl's sudden expression of happy confidence made any question about her own feelings unnecessary.

"Dearest, I *am* so glad" Julia said. She would make a point of seeing Nick, and forming her own opinion, while she was at the Victoire; there would be plenty of time before young Philip Bernard would be *à terme,* and strong enough to undertake the flight home to England. Meanwhile her husband's judgment was wholly in favour of Nick.

"I wonder how much the old Heriots know" Julia speculated—"I mean, about you and Nick."

"I think *she* has some idea" Luzia was beginning, when Philip walked in.

"It was only a 40-watt bulb!" he exclaimed. "Really, French hoteliers! I bought a 75 one and put it in myself; and I told that wretched old *patron* that I wasn't paying any damned surcharge either! Now, shall we go?"

Julia looked at her watch.

"If I could fit in one more feed before lunch, I shouldn't have to come dashing back the moment after" she said. "Luzia, do go and see the old *sage-femme,* and ask her, would you? It's not far off the time, anyhow."

The *sage-femme* agreed to the baby's being fed fifteen minutes early, and herself suggested that he should be given a bottle for the next meal—"Then Madame can get some rest after her *démenagement,* and need only return at 4.30. Since the child does so well, one feed of le Glaxo will do him no harm." So the Philipino, as Julia had begun to call him, was nursed, and then the little party went off to the Victoire.

Julia was delighted with her room, the profusion of flowers, and the cool shady balcony. "*Perfect!*" she said.

"The food's pretty poor" Philip warned her.

"Never mind; I have a splendid appetite." After lunch they had coffee brought up to the verandah; then Julia lay on her

bed while Luzia unpacked and stowed everything in accord-
ance with her wishes, Philip parking the suit-cases on an
inner corner of the balcony, where no rain could reach
them.

"Dear child, how *good* you are to me!" Julia said, when all
was done.

"You have been good to me in the past, for a long time" the
girl replied. She had no wish to leave, and was glad when
Julia caused Philip to have tea brought up; afterwards Mrs.
Jamieson went off on the first of many sunny strolls from the
hotel to feed the Philipino—down the drive under the
acacias, along the Route de Toulouse, and in at the gate of
the clinic, where a room was provided for nursing. Luzia
stayed and talked with Philip, who spoke with gratitude of
all she had done for his wife. "She'd have been sunk without
you. I hadn't realised what the position is now at Larège
about—er—domestic help and so on; I never dreamt of your
having to do what you did."

"I enjoyed everything" Luzia said, pleasantly.

"Well, I hope your Father won't be furious when he hears
about it" Philip said, a little anxiously. He knew, far better
than the British press ever encourages its public to realise,
the immense importance of good relations between England
and Portugal from the strategic angle, with the Azores com-
manding the Western Approaches. He also knew precisely
how important a figure the Duke of Ericeira was in the
counsels of his country, for all his retired life on his estates
for so much of the year. And his daughter had scrubbed
Julia's floors!—as well as doing much of her cooking, and all
her washing-up.

"I tell Papa what I think fit, in my own way" Luzia said,
coolly. "In any case it was not Julia's fault; she had no idea of
the circumstances at Larège when she invited me" she
added, with a faint glint of malice. Like Lord Heriot, the girl
thought Philip Jamieson had been extraordinarily reckless
over the whole plan; she could not resist, at last, this slight
dig at him. "After all, *she* had never been there," she observed dispassionately. As the man stared at her, actually
blushing a little—the implication of blame in her words was

so clear, for all their restraint—"Let us be thankful to *le bon Dieu* for the Heriots with their car, and all their help; and also for this good Bonnecourt" Luzia pursued, looking him straight in the face. "Without them, we should *all* have been what you call 'sunk', Colonel."

Perhaps it was just as well that at that moment Julia walked in.

"Greedy pig, the Philipino" she announced, sitting down. "Nearly the whole of *both* sides, this time! He prefers Mother to 'le Glaxo', it seems. Philip, is it too early for a spot of sherry before Luzia goes back? I believe stout is the thing to nurse on, but one can't get it out here, and one must have *some* restorative." She had noticed her husband's face, and a certain rather complacent expression on Luzia's; when he went in from the balcony to fetch the sherry—"What have you two been talking about?" she asked, in a lowered voice.

"Life at Larège!" Luzia said, with a mischievous little smile.

Chapter 15

There was quite a party at the station on Monday to see Luzia off: all four Heriots, and Julia as well as Philip Jamieson. "Of course I must come" Julia said firmly to her husband. "The creature can have a bottle, like he did on Saturday."

All railway farewells are apt to be mildly awkward occasions; there is too much time to fill in, and generally nothing to say that has not been said already, or cannot be said in public. Both the twins were rather tongue-tied; they set out Luzia's suit-cases, and stood at the ready at the edge of the platform; the elders talked. Lady Heriot embraced the girl warmly. "It has been the greatest possible pleasure to have you with us." The only surprise was afforded by old Lord Heriot, who said, grasping Luzia's hand and shaking it up and down—"Haste ye back! You can't come too soon." The twins avoided one another's eyes, and looked at the luggage; as the train drew in Dick leapt aboard, found a seat, and opened a window; Nick passed the cases up to him. Luzia gave Julia a last fond hug, and climbed into the train; Dick beckoned her along the corridor to her place.

"There you are—not such a crowd today."

"Thank you so *very* much, Dick" the girl said. "You have been so good."

"Nothing to thank me for" the boy said awkwardly. "Goodbye, Luzia." "Best of luck" he mumbled, as he went out and down the corridor; Luzia dabbed sudden tears from her eyes before she went to the window, and waved to the little group on the platform as the train pulled out.

Driving back to the Victoire—"Well, it looks as though the old boy wouldn't mind her as a daughter-in-law, even if she is an R.C." Philip said to his wife. "What a *démarche*, from him of all people!"

"Yes, I daresay she has subjugated him" Julia said. "She does do that to lots of people." She glanced with a certain amused interest at her husband; she was still wondering what Luzia had said to him about "life at Larège", but had refrained from asking. "Not you, though, I fancy" she said now, in an oblique enquiry. She did so hope that Philip and her precious Luzia had not, and never would, "get across" one another.

"She's a cool little cuss" Philip said, with a non-committal expression.

"Oh Philip, she's much more than that!" his wife protested. What *could* Luzia have been saying?

"Yes, she is" he agreed, as he swung the car into the drive of the Victoire. "She's dead honest, and I'm sure she's completely trustworthy; one can't say that of everyone." But he didn't explain—few men care to admit to their wives that they have been ticked off by a young girl. Julia was left guessing. "Honest" gave her a faint clue; "trustworthy" none. She had never given a thought to the dear old Duque's importance from the diplomatic angle, and did not guess at her husband's professional anxiety about his daughter having scrubbed her floors. She changed the subject.

"I should so like to see Lady Heriot" she said, as she got out of the car, "and hear what she thinks about it all. I wonder if you could get her to come round."

"I'll ring her up", Philip said. The Victoire did not run to telephones in the bedrooms, but as they went into the hall the *patron* met them with an important expression; there had been an urgent call from Paris for *M. le Colonel;* he should ring back the moment he came in. He handed Philip a small, rather crumpled piece of paper, on which had been scrawled, in purple pencil, a familiar number.

"Thank you; I will see to it." Upstairs he said to Julia— "That's the Office. I think I'll ring them from the Heriots; then I can ask Lady H. at the same time if she could come round and see you."

The call proved to be a message from Major Hartley in London, passed on by the Paris Office, announcing the safe arrival of Colin and Bonnecourt at Glentoran; Philip, as so

often before, received it in Lord Heriot's study, and jotted it
down on the block which always lay by the telephone, a
pencil fastened to it by a length of string. Of course no
names were mentioned. "Your wife's cousin and his companion have arrived at where you might expect; they got a
plane a day early." Then followed a typical Hartley-ism; the
Major was the most humane of men, and loved it when
things turned out right, and he could give pleasure. "Young
C. says his chum is thrilled with the place, and the house,
and his job; and his wealthy employer seems very pleased
with him. They're ready for Madame at any time; and the
chum particularly wanted her to be told that the house is
fully furnished; she need not bring anything." Then a sort of
post-script—"I've ordered the camels." Major Monteith, who
read the message verbatim over the telephone to Philip,
said—"I'm not sure about that last word. Can it really be
'camels'?"

"Yes, that's quite correct" Philip said.

"But I thought from what London said that these blokes
were going to Scotland. Can camels live in Scotland?"

"No; and they're not wanted to. Thanks, M." He rang off.

Lady Heriot gladly agreed to come and see Julia after tea.
"I should have suggested it sooner, only I didn't want to
burden her. But I thought she was looking *blooming* at the
station. Very well—5 o'clock."

Lady Heriot's and Julia's conversation was really highly
satisfactory to them both, each filling out gaps in the other's
knowledge. Julia could be satisfied at last, completely, that
the Heriots would warmly welcome a match between Nick
and Luzia; even more important, that they had no feeling
that the girl had played with one twin, and then jilted him
for the other.

"Dick is always so impetuous" Lady Heriot said at one
point; "he dashes at every pretty girl he sees, with loud cries,
and runs them to death! Whereas Nick has very little self-
confidence; he's altogether more serious, and rather slow to
make up his mind about people. I don't believe he has ever
been seriously in love before. But do you think this lovely
creature might marry him, in the end? We think her almost

perfect—she is so sensible, and *honest;* not the most common characteristics of great beauties!"

Julia was determined not to betray any confidences, but she did allow herself to say that she thought Luzia probably might marry Nick, if he pursued the matter. "It was all a little difficult for her, happening as it did; I think they both purposely left it rather in the air, partly out of consideration for Dick, and because of the hurry—and—and everything. But she had already quite made up her mind not to marry Dick."

"Yes; he told me so himself. And she was right; even his Father recognised that. I think she has behaved perfectly, in really a most trying situation" Lady Heriot said. Then she pursued her main question. "But you think she might marry Nick? We feel she would be absolutely the right person for him."

Julia thought for a moment; she spoke carefully.

"Lady Heriot, Luzia has continental ideas about marriage, which personally I think so much wiser than our English ones! She does not hold with dashing to the altar merely to satisfy her own emotions; she looks on it as a family affair. If Nick still wants to marry her three or four months hence, he should write and ask himself to Gralheira, so that he can meet her Father, and see the whole set-up. If he and the old Duque get on—and I feel sure they would; he's an absolute darling, is the Duke, and knows a good man when he sees one!—I think it might well come off. I gather Nick has various ideas for improving the estate, and of course presently that will belong to Luzia; she is the heiress, and she feels her responsibility in that respect acutely. But Nick would have to decide whether he wanted to spend most of his life in Portugal; that would be inevitable. They don't believe, there, in absentee landlords."

Lady Heriot was slightly taken aback by this pronouncement; she was silent for a little while.

"It sounds rather cold-blooded" she said at last. "Do you mean that she would only marry someone her Father approved of?"

"Not *quite* that. I think she would rather wrestle with the estate alone, unmarried, than marry someone she couldn't love. But she would never marry anyone who didn't care tuppence about the well-being of their *hundreds* of tenants!" Julia exclaimed energetically. "And who couldn't *show* decent filial affection to her old Father. Would *you* like to have a daughter-in-law who didn't give a blow for you and Lord Heriot?" She was quite upset by Lady Heriot's use of the word "cold-blooded."

"No, we should hate that" Lady Heriot said, pacifically. "I see your point. In fact I think I rather agree with you that our English idea of marriage isn't necessarily the best—only it is so ingrained. Of course people at home gird at parents abroad for making *mariages de convenance* for their children, but look at the *mariages d'inconvenance* that our young people make for themselves!"

Julia laughed, relieved; they parted on excellent terms. Lady Heriot asked when Colonel Jamieson would be leaving? "Of course then you'll have no car. But do please let me know if you want to shop or anything; Pau is rather a good place to get *layettes*. Pierre or one of the twins will always be delighted to drive you. Well, of course not the twins after term begins; but that's not till October."

The old *sage-femme*'s suggestion of giving Philip Bernard a bottle when Julia moved to the Victoire had put an idea into Jamieson's head, especially after this was followed by a further day-time one to allow Julia to see Luzia off.

"Look here" he said a few days before he was due to leave—"Couldn't that creature be given two successive bottles in one day? Wouldn't do him any harm, would it?"

"I don't suppose so—why?"

"I thought we might take a picnic lunch up to Larège. We've never been there together; I should like to look at it again with you. Would it fit in?"

Julia worked it out. The Philipino was now a fortnight old, and was thriving so well that the intervals between his feeds had been extended to two-and-a-half hours.

"Yes" she said, after a pause. "If I nursed him at nine we could get off before half-past; then if he had a bottle at

11.30, and again at two, I shouldn't need to be back before 4.30. That would give us three hours up there—how lovely! I'd better just have a word with the old trout, but I'm sure she'll agree." Julia had as usual established excellent relations with the old *sage-femme*, who agreed heartily. "Pau is still hot; the air of *la montagne* will do Madame good."

They went two days later. Philip had a sense of occasion, and was determined that this should be a *good* picnic; he did not rely on the almost certainly dim sandwiches of the Victoire's providing, but went into the town and bought *pâtés en croutes*, butter, cream cheeses, tomatoes, salad, and a supply of Melba toast from the Hotel de France, which he coerced the kitchen staff at the Victoire into reviving in the oven while Julia was nursing the baby; he put this in a biscuit-tin borrowed from Lady Heriot. "Is there any wine up there?" he asked his wife, before she went round to the clinic, "Or shall we take some?"

"Oh no, there's masses; sherry and all. I made a list for the Stansteds of what extra I bought, and left for them."

"I hope we shall need to alter the list" the man said cheerfully. "All right—hurry along and feed greedy-pig."

It was a perfect autumn day, warm and still. In the lower valleys all the woods were russet; higher up, on the slopes, there were silvery patches left from the first early snowfall —dead leaves dotted them like golden and copper coins. Julia exclaimed at their beauty.

"Yes, it's a nice place" Philip said, pleased. Presently the circle of limestone peaks, the curved silver saw of the frontier ridge, opened up in front of them, more silver than ever with the light dusting of snow.

"But that is *quite* magical" Julia said. "Oh, I am glad we came today."

They called at Barraterre's to get the key of the house; Mme. Barraterre greeted Philip with an enthusiasm which amused and rather touched Julia. "And now Monsieur the Colonel has a son—the one thing that was lacking! Madame Bonnecourt told me that you were in Pau, but I had not hoped for the pleasure of seeing you. And Madame so much *en beauté!*" Mme. Barraterre went on, turning to Julia. "After all these adventures. How is *le petit?*"

Julia said that the little one was doing splendidly.

"This good Monsieur Bonnecourt!—what a providence that he was at hand in this emergency" Mme. Barraterre exclaimed. "But where is he now?" she asked, with a sudden keen glance at Jamieson. "He has not been seen here since he drove Madame down to Pau in the middle of the night. His wife is evasive; she will only say that he has gone abroad, and that she expects to follow him soon."

Philip was a little disconcerted by this, though of course it was Larège all over.

"Yes, he was offered a good appointment abroad, and accepted it, so I hear" he replied casually. "But now, Madame, if we might have the key? We have not too much time; my wife must return to Pau to feed the child at a certain hour."

"Ah, Madame nourishes it herself? That is good." Mme. Barraterre could take a hint as well as anyone; she brought the key, realising that further questions would be useless— M. le Colonel could be as silent as the tomb if he chose.

"Now you wrote something about a car-turn, quite near the house" Philip said to Julia as he started the engine. "How do we get there? It's since my time; we used to park here in the Place. Do we go the way one used to walk?"

"Yes." As her husband twisted the car round the several narrow and sharp right-angled turns which ultimately led out onto the broadened track to the car-turn, narrowly missing one of the maisons des sarrazins at a corner, Julia was struck afresh by the utter impracticality of her Philip's original plan for the later months of her first pregnancy. Without the car-turn, let alone the Heriot twins, how could she have managed? But she was not going to let that spoil their first day at Larège together; she pushed the thought out of her mind.

"That's very handy" Philip said, turning the car when they reached the spot. "Can't think why it wasn't done years ago." He carried the picnic-basket (also borrowed from Lady Heriot) along to the house; Julia preceded him, and unlocked the door. The big room was flooded with sunlight; thanks to Luzia and the sturdy Emma everything was spotlessly clean; the glasses, cups, and plates which Julia set out on a tray glistened in the brilliant light. They found the garden-table and chairs which had been parked by Dick in the down-stairs bathroom, formerly the *maison des cochons;* Philip carried these out to the spring, while Julia switched on the water and the electricity, unearthed the corkscrew, and col-lected a bottle of sherry and another of the old farmer's red wine from the familiar place under the great walnut table. When Philip came back for the tray she said slowly, looking round her—"I do *love* this place."

He was overjoyed. "Darling, do you really?"

"Yes. I think it's perfect. Absolute simplicity, complete beauty; and yet everything one needs. Where else does one find that? And what a place to bring a child up in!"

"Children!" he said, putting his arms round her.

"Dearest, let's go and eat" Julia said after a moment or two. "I have to live by the clock, now! That old chatterbox Madame Barraterre wasted a lot of time." But at that mo-ment there came a knock on the half-door—there stood little Mme. Bonnecourt.

"I see you as you leave the inn" she said, "so I came to speak with you. It is not inconvenient?"

"Not in the least, Madame," Julia said kindly. "Come and sit down in the garden. Philip, could you get a chair and another glass?" She led her unexpected, and unwanted, guest along the narrow path under the house to the little lawn, where Philip had set out the table and chairs in the shade of the small trees, with their pale trunks, by the spring; he followed, opened the sherry, and suggested that they should drink Bonnecourt's health.

"We hear that he is safely arrived in Scotland" he said.

"Yes. I have received a letter—so quickly. He is charmed with the place and the house, and the occupation—already he has killed a stag! So what I wished to tell Madame is that I have already completed my arrangements to leave."

"How excellent" Julia said, although rather taken aback by this promptness. "What have you done about the cows?"

"Ma voisine will take them over, and stall them with hers, and milk them, provided that she can have some of our pas-

turage, which of course I have agreed to. It is on a profitable basis" Mme. Bonnecourt said; "she will pay a certain sum monthly, since she gets the milk."

"To whom will she pay it?" Julia asked, most reasonably mistrusting most of the Larègeois, and confident that the neighbour would be quite incapable of remitting money to Scotland.

"To Madame Barraterre. I went to consult her about the house—to arrange that it should be aired from time to time, and fires made, so that all does not deteriorate, in the winter especially. And imagine, she has an old relation who wishes to come and live in Larège this winter, perhaps longer, in order to be near her! Is this not wonderful? Now the house will be occupied, and kept dry and warm. And when she takes the rent of the house, Madame Barraterre will also collect the money for the milk."

Julia was relieved by this. Mme. Barraterre was one of the few fairly trustworthy people in Larège, really forced to a certain degree of honesty by prolonged contact with her foreign—largely English—clientèle. But she pursued her enquiries. What rent would the ancient relation of the inn-keeper's wife pay?

"*Voyons,* Madame, if the house had been left empty, *I* should have had to pay for the lighting of fires, or suffer damage to my effects! So I ask only a little above the rent that Madame told me I should pay for the house in Écosse; Madame said 8 francs a week, so I ask 12. Mme. Barraterre is delighted; she agreed at once."

Julia could well believe in this delight; she wondered privately how much Mme. Barraterre would get as a rake-off on the deal? Twelve francs a week was a ridiculous rent for a furnished house; in fact she almost began to doubt the existence of the aged relation, except that few people would wish to live in Larège in winter. But she was not going to discourage the hunter's wife, now so happy over her plans; she merely said how glad she was that everything had worked out so well, and that Mme. Barraterre was so helpful.

"Yes—so now I can be ready to leave at any time! I

thought perhaps I might travel with Madame, when she returns to Écosse? I have never been outside France."

Philip had listened to this conversation with a certain astonishment, especially at Julia's evident understanding of the set-up at Larège, which he had known all his life, after only a few weeks' stay. But at this point he intervened. Julia would have her hands full bringing the baby home; he was not going to have her saddled with the care of Mme. Bonnecourt on the journey as well.

"We will communicate with Madame about this. But rest assured that all arrangements will be made" he said, pleasantly but firmly, "and that we shall let you know in good time." He got up. He was longing to be rid of the nice little woman; all this had not been in the least his idea of a picnic with Julia at his adored Larège.

But Mme. Bonnecourt stood her ground; actually she achieved this by remaining firmly seated in her chair.

"One little moment. Madame, when you and I were speaking of our new house there, I forgot to ask if it was furnished? Shall I need to take anything?—sheets, blankets, *de la vaisselle* at least?"

In fact Julia had forgotten this too; when she was telling Mme. Bonnecourt about Glentoran she didn't herself know whether Ach-an-Draine was furnished or not. Usually estate houses are not furnished. But thanks to Major Hartley's considerate message, which Philip had read out to her after he had jotted it down at Lord Heriot's desk, she was able to reassure the hunter's wife now. (Edina must have been combing out the attics, full of unused furniture, the linen-room, and the china-cupboards at Glentoran.)

"No, *chère Madame*. All is provided. I apologise that I did not mention this sooner."

Philip was relieved by his wife's last words; when she began to reply he was disturbed lest she should mention the telephone call, and Bonnecourt's own message. But of course with Julia he need not have worried. At length satisfied, Madame Bonnecourt took herself off—Philip saw her up to the path.

"Well, thank God *that*'s over" he said when he came back. Julia had been unpacking the lunch-basket and setting out its contents on the table—"Darling, what *extravagant* deliciousnesses" she said.

"I thought we might eat well, as it's our first meal here together," the man said, opening the country wine and filling their glasses. He sniffed his own, and then drank. "This is very good—where did you get it?"

"The twins took us to a farm where old Lord H. gets his. Oh look, Philip, I think we ought to alert the Heriots about all poor little Madame's arrangements, so that they can keep Mother Barraterre up to the mark, and see that she really does pay what's due for the milk and the rent. She's better than most of them here, but an eye ought to be kept. I bet Lady Heriot can put the fear of God into her."

"I agree. In fact I think the best plan would be to arrange for the money to be handed over each month to the Heriots by Madame Barraterre; I don't suppose *she'd* have much of a clue about remitting to Scotland."

"Excellent. I'll fix that; I'm sure Lady Heriot will play— they dote on Bonnecourt. Thank you for saving me from taking little Madame to England" Julia pursued. "But who *is* to take her?"

"I think she'd better come with me, next week. I'll ring the Office tonight from the Heriots, and tell them to get Colin down to London to take her straight up to Glentoran. I can write a note here before we leave, telling her when to be at Pau, and drop it in on her. But now, dearest, do let's forget about the Bonnecourts, and have some food, and think about the Jamiesons!"

Julia laughed. She was more than ready to think about the Jamiesons. They ate their delicious meal to the sweet accompaniment of the sound of water dropping into the pool below the spring behind them, and the deeper music of cowbells coming up from the meadows below, where the cows had been put out to get a last feed of fresh grass before the winter, now that the aftermath had been cut. She spoke of these things, and of the happiness that such homely sights and sounds had brought her throughout her stay.

"You *do* like it, I see. You don't think I was mad to suggest your coming here?" Philip asked, looking anxiously at her.

"Well yes, in a way I do" Julia said frankly. "Luzia coming

was Mrs. Hathaway's idea, and you didn't even know about the Heriots, or the car-turn! How you expected a pregnant woman to hump all her supplies from the *Place* herself I can't imagine—besides fetching the water, *and* the milk, and emptying *la poubelle!* It was a dotty idea, darling, really. But I don't hold it against you" she added quickly, seeing his face. "In fact I'm glad you *were* so dotty, since it's worked out all right, because I have loved it so."

He caught her hand.

"Dearest, you must forgive me. I hadn't in the least realised what you would be up against—it all seemed so easy the last time I stayed here." He paused. "Luzia thought mud of me about it, too" he added, with belated honesty.

So *that* was what Luzia had been up to when she talked to him about "life at Larège", Julia thought, amused. Poor Philip! She put her other hand on his.

"All men are clots about practical things" she said cheerfully. "Very well; you were a clot!—that's agreed. But that's all over now, so let's forget it, as well as the Bonnecourts, and think about us. Could you persuade your miserable Office to let you have August and September off next year? —then we could come together, and have some walks. I've seen nothing but what is visible from this house, and the path."

They talked on. Philip said one never could be sure when the Service would want one; Julia stated roundly that she refused to be pregnant again next summer, because she wanted to explore the surroundings of Larège, and that through Luzia she should lay on a Portuguese girl to help in the house, and wheel the Philipino about in his pram. "Nannie MacKenzie would *hate* it here; we'll send her off for her holiday." She added that the year after Master Philip Bernard would be walking—"So you'll have to put some wire, or railings, along the path and the lawn here, to stop him from falling over. It wouldn't matter so much if I were preg then, because I shall be rather tied anyhow."

Julia's happy plans for the future at Larège enchanted Philip. Plainly the place was already beginning to mean to her something of what it had meant to him, since his boy-

hood—the ideal refuge from modern life—in pastoral surroundings, in simplicity, and peace, and beauty. And now, in
his mind, really the place where his first son was born; labour had begun here; the clinic didn't count. But he looked
further ahead than the years of toddling childhood.

"Of course in twenty years time Bernard will *have* to come
back" he said presently. "He'll be eligible then for his *service
militaire.*"

"What *can* you mean?" Julia asked.

"But naturally. Born in France, birth registered in France;
he is due for conscription, like all the other young men."

Julia was aghast.

"But *we're* English. So he's English too, surely?"

"No—he has dual nationality. If he'd even been born on a
French ship at sea, he would still be liable for conscription."

"*La loi de France* again!" Julia exclaimed, bitterly.

"No, I believe it operates in all countries which have
conscription" Philip said temperately. "By the way, have you
done anything about having him registered as a British subject with the Consulate-General at Bordeaux?"

Of course Julia hadn't; no one had told her that she ought
to do so.

"Oh well, I'll see to it on my way through. Their time-limit
isn't so strict as the French—I believe it's four or five
months."

Julia was still thoroughly upset at the idea of her Philipino having to serve as a conscript in the French Army.

"What happens if he just doesn't?" she asked.

"He will be liable to arrest as a deserter the moment he
sets foot on French soil, if he fails to present himself" Philip
told her.

"But that means that he can't ever come to Larège!" Julia
exclaimed wretchedly. "Oh dear!—I wish he hadn't been
born here. Why did I have to fall down those bloody steps?"

Philip had never heard about the fall—they had really had
so little time to talk, what with the child's perpetual feeds,
and one interruption or another.

"Yes, I stumbled when I was bringing back the *poubelle*

after emptying it; Luzia had gone down to the ball. But in fact I wasn't feeling too well before that" Julia said, in reply to his question. Suddenly she looked very alert.

"What about the twins? Why aren't they doing their military service?"

Philip didn't know. "Were they born in France?"

Julia didn't know that, either. In fact, as she learned later, Lord Heriot had wisely taken his wife to Scotland for her confinement, precisely in order to avoid this complication.

"But look, dearest, being a French conscript isn't all that bad" Philip said. "It seemed to do Hilaire Belloc all the good in the world! Anyhow, I believe one can pay someone else to take one's place—didn't the Curé d'Ars do that?"

Julia knew nothing about the Curé d'Ars; she was surprised that Philip should, when she learned that he was a relatively modern French Saint. "Oh well, we must find out nearer the time" she said. "Twenty years is a long way off. But the others had better be born at home!"

"They may all be girls" he said, smiling fondly at her.

"Oh I hope not—three of each is what I should like! I think we ought just to be able to fit that in in the time."

"Even if you take every other summer off to walk?" he asked, with affectionate mockery.

"Well, I might not. Anyhow a great-aunt of mine had her last child when she was fifty!"

Presently Julia looked at her watch.

"Oh dear, time's getting on! Let's take all this in and get it washed up and stowed; then we might have a few more minutes out here. I do love sitting by the spring."

The water was hot by now, and there was anyhow very little to wash up; Philip looked on with pleasure at his wife's swift bestowal of plates and knives, as he wiped them, in their appropriate places, and then switched off the water and electricity. She had so much made this house of his her own!—was so fully and happily the mistress of it, in spite of all the preliminary difficulties. His heart, his normally unexpressive Scottish heart, fairly sang with happiness, confidence in the future, and grateful love.

"Now your note to Mme. B." Julia reminded him, remembering what he had forgotten.

"Oh God, yes! What a bore she is, poor little soul—taking up all that time." Julia found him paper, and gave him the Biro from her hand-bag; while he was writing his instructions she fetched the table and the extra chair in from the lawn and put them in the *maison des cochons*.

"Got a stamp?" he asked, when she came back.

Julia had stamps in her hand-bag too. "But my pen, please," as he made to put it in his pocket.

"Oh, sorry. Well we'll post that; she'll get it in oceans of time. Let's go out again—how long have we got?"

"Eight minutes."

"Philipinus Tyrannus!" Philip said, as they walked back to the spring and sat down. "Why did you say you love sitting here?" he asked; he couldn't hear enough about Julia's reactions to Larège.

"Oh, the shade, and that dropping water, and the view"— she stretched out a hand towards the section of the silver saw of peaks, with their pine-clad slopes below them; drooped it to indicate the meadows with their grazing cows, just under the house. "And I sat here so much, while angelic Luzia was doing all the work. Do you believe in pre-natal influence?" she asked suddenly.

"Yes, I do. Why?"

"Only I should like it if some of this could have seeped through into Philip Bernard; then he might love it, presently, as much as we do. I want him to."

Philip got up, knelt beside her chair, and enfolded his wife in a long embrace. This was completely satisfying; everything he had hoped to achieve by his ill-thought-out plan *had* been achieved, child and all. When he released her Julia looked at her watch again.

"Time to go. We've got to post that letter, and drop the key at the inn. Bring in the chairs, darling." She got up.

Philip folded the canvas chairs; then he put his arm round her.

"Till next summer" he said. "*Au revoir*, Larège."

About the Author

The wife of a British diplomat, Ann Bridge has travelled around the world and has lived in China, Switzerland, Portugal, Italy, Hungary, France, and Germany. Drawing upon her unique international background and upon her formidable amount of knowledge about a vast variety of things, from botany to mountain climbing, she writes with the spellbinding detail and precision of a widely travelled, sensitive, and observant author. Her dramatic stories of the diplomatic world and of international intrigue and her brilliant discussions of everything from menus to rare wild flowers have made such books as *The Lighthearted Quest, The Portuguese Escape, The Numbered Account,* and *The Dangerous Islands* great favorites among her enthusiastic public here and abroad.